In the River's Mist

Dean Ream

PublishAmerica
Baltimore

ISBN: 1-4137-3730-7
PUBLISHED BY PUBLISHAMERICA, LLLP
www.publishamerica.com
Baltimore

Printed in the United States of America

For Janna, and her unselfish dedication.

Chapter One

Claude Ghetter rocked as he glanced at the idle bulldozers and waiting flatbeds. Only one was still running, its churning engine breaking the stillness as it leveled huge mounds of dirt near Claude. The dam was finished and tomorrow he'd be leaving. The old chair creaked when he rocked back and he'd meant to fix it, but it didn't matter now, he wasn't taking it with him. The Three-Stop Café, whose porch he was sitting on, was no longer open for business—hadn't been for years, but he still came up every evening and watched the day end.

It was dusk and Claude could just make out the end of the road where it met the river. The dust and wavering heat blurred his vision, but as always he could see his friends standing on the bank around a small fire. Mother Mabel was bent down over a frying pan cooking fresh-caught catfish, while Elmer dozed with his head against a log. Preacher and Jack were laughing, and Kristen, Claude's wife, waved at him. Tubbs was there too, standing in the water with a sack slung over his shoulder. They were all there, waiting for him.

Claude saw the young man standing by the dozer. He'd just climbed down and was wiping the sweat from his forehead. He cupped his hands around his last match and pulled it to the cigarette hanging at his lips. He raised his head as if something caught his attention, and when he looked back his match was out, the smoke filtering up in the still air.

"What the...?" He looked at Claude. "Got a light, old-timer?"

Claude reached into his shirt pocket and pulled out a kitchen match and held it up. "Sure, here you go."

The young man stepped to the porch and took it. "Thanks." He struck it against the railing and lit his cigarette. "You live around here?"

"Not anymore," Claude said.

"I guess not. There's not much left is there? Don't look like there ever was much." He sat on the porch of the Three-Stop and looked out over the road.

Claude adjusted his eyes back to the river. He could see its slow roll as it passed by the fire. At some point close to dawn the haze would start its rise from the cool water and his friends would disappear in the mist. He'd sat at the river many nights and visited with them and made his trek back to the cabin at first light.

"How old are you, son?"

"Twenty-two," the young man said. He took his cap off and set it on his knee and swiped his hair back. "Sure is hot, even this late in the day." He took a deep drag on his cigarette and let out the smoke with a tired blow. "How long have you lived here?"

"A long time."

Claude had lived longer than his friends and wife. In some ways he wished he were with them now, so he wouldn't have to witness the loss of the town. As the years went by and the families left, he'd stayed, refusing to leave. He walked from the cabin to the Three-Stop every morning, just like back then, only now there was no coffee waiting, and no friends either. He'd sit on the porch and look out over the road, which was more overgrown path than anything.

The young man spit out a piece of tobacco. "Why would you live in a place like this?"

"You're a city boy," Claude said. "Might not understand."

The young man huffed. "Well, I don't live out here in the sticks. Couldn't make a living."

No, Claude thought, not now. Back then it was enough. They'd lived here for the solitude. It was odd that those that reached out for isolation would be placed in such close proximity—choose to stay together—and stranger still that their search for seclusion would tether them like no bond of blood could.

"How'd you make ends meet?"

"You're talking about money," Claude said. "Didn't have much in the way of legal tender. We had a fairly tough go of it, in that regard."

"Spare me, Pops. You old guys think you had it worse than anyone else."

"I wouldn't say that at all. Except for money, we had it real sweet." Claude looked from the young man back to the river. "Real sweet indeed…"

"Oh, yeah?" The young man swatted the dust from his hat and put it back on. He wiped off the knees of his jeans and stood.

"They're loading up the other dozers," Claude said. "How come you're not?"

"They're through, but I've got a little more to do. Won't take long."

Claude kept rocking as the young man flipped his cigarette on a pile of dirt and walked down the steps. The dust was settling from the work and the sun was hitting the top of the mountains. Claude closed his eyes and wandered back to those days when he and his friends would meet on these same steps in early evening. Taking their fishing poles and a tin of nightcrawlers they'd make their way to the river. They'd throw their lines in and sit back on the bank. Mother Mabel would ready the fire for the frying, Elmer would rest his head on a fat stick of wood, and Preacher and Jack would begin their storytelling. As darkness fell, a quiet set in, and they'd listen to the wind in the mountains and the flow of the river.

Claude heard the footsteps returning, but didn't open his eyes. On this last evening he wanted no distractions.

"Life in this God-forsaken place was good, huh?" The young man shook his head in disbelief. "The world's a pile of crap, and this place looks like the top of it. I gotta ask you, what made you stay?"

Claude opened his eyes and saw the young man standing by the steps. He was looking out over the road and down to the river, much the same as Claude had done for most of his life.

Claude leaned forward. "You see the river down there?"

"Yeah, I see it. It's probably nothing but sewage. So…?"

"Just to the left about twenty yards was an old tree lying in the water. Two young kids were sitting on it kicking their feet in the river when the limbs gave way. The trunk rolled, carrying them with it and trapping their legs against the riverbed, their faces in the water. I was holding their heads up, but it wasn't enough. Sean was six and Holly was five—they were drowning.

"'Hold on, just hold on,' I told them. They were panicking, getting weaker, and so was I. Then I saw Jack and Preacher running toward me.

"'WE'RE COMING, CLAUDE!' When they reached us they tried to pull the kids free but couldn't.

"'YOU'VE GOT TO LIFT IT!' I yelled. They tried but it didn't move and I couldn't let the kids go long enough to help, or I thought I couldn't anyway. I've always wondered about that.

"'We'll dig under it,' Preacher said. 'Dig under the limbs, Jack, there's more leverage.'

"They filled their lungs and went down, digging at the gravel, trying to make room to crawl under and lift it with their backs. I saw the blood from their hands swirling in the water.

"When they came up for air, I said, 'There's not much time, they're dying.'"

"'One more time,' Preacher said."

"They went back under and I could see their feet pushing on the riverbed, forcing 'em through the clearance. Then the tree moved and fell back again.

"'COME ON!' I yelled.

"Then it rose again, inches, just inches. The kids weren't struggling anymore. Then the tree rose higher and I pulled on their bodies."

Claude stared at the river, still tilted forward in his rocker. The young man was looking back and forth between him and the water, waiting, but Claude didn't say any more.

"What happened?"

"What's your name, son?"

"Pete Connor. So what happened?"

"If I told you it wouldn't matter," Claude said, settling back in his chair. "You didn't know those kids and you didn't know those men either."

Pete Connor chuckled scornfully. "Almost had me there, Pops. I've heard about you old goats back in these hills. Got nothing better to do than spin tall tales."

Claude nodded. "Always was a fair amount of that. Especially with Dan…"

"He the one that dreamed up the kids and the log story?"

Claude glared at Pete. "You've gotten to be tiresome, boy. Some things ain't for joking about."

Pete blushed, embarrassed. He looked behind Claude at the old store. "That shack been here as long as you have?"

Claude nodded. "Even longer."

"I'm dozing it down tomorrow. It's the last thing to go."

"I know," Claude said.

"I'll make short work of it in the morning."

Pete Connor headed back to his pickup. Claude pulled himself up, grabbed his fishing pole and can of worms, a sack containing a frying pan, a tin of bacon grease, a cup of cornmeal, and a coffee pot with grounds already in it, and started his nightly walk to the river. He picked up a few short limbs for the fire as he walked. They'd always built a fire at night at the river, no matter the weather. They saw their fishing lines with it and the whistling embers helped Elmer sleep. At the bank he readjusted the stones around his old fire and threw some leaves into the old stone firepit. Then he put in some twigs and set the limbs he'd gathered on top.

Claude was startled as a couple of more sticks were dropped into the pit. He looked over to see Pete. "I'd like to hear what happened with those kids. I mean if you're willing to…"

"You got nothin' better to do, son?"

"Not really."

"Nobody to go home to?"

Pete shook his head, sadly it seemed. "Just a motel room."

Claude knelt down and lit the fire. He wondered what good it would do to tell the story, especially to this young upstart. But then it might be the last time he told anyone about his life here. He pulled up his sitting log and waited for the fire to catch.

"It's not just about those kids. It's a long story."

"Okay by me. Has to be better than watching Sid Caesar on television."

"Who?"

Pete could see it didn't matter.

The moon was already coming up, a white nickel in the south, and the cicadas were calling and the crickets were sounding and upstream an old bullfrog grumped. It would be a clear night and the catfish would bite. Claude stared out over the river and listened as it lapped against the bank. The only reason he was here now was to wait until the Three-Stop was gone. It was the one place that meant more than anything; without it he and his friends may never have stayed together. Besides, where the state wanted him to go, to live in a small bedroom in a big city, no one would care.

"It was the late summer of 1900," Claude said. "And by the summer again I knew I'd never leave these mountains. Each one of us had chosen to live here, even though some had kin in other places, and we became a family of our own. What we went through in that year made us all one, closer than our own blood. When I think back on it I never shared so much good and bad. I believe it only happens once, that a person would find such friends. Most folks drift through. They care less what's left behind; mostly there's nothing at all."

Chapter Two

Pete looked at his watch, then pulled up a log and sat, while Claude stacked a few more limbs on the fire. He watched the flames licking up and seemed lost in thought, but shortly he began again.

The fire's what brought us together. Up until then we all seemed to go our own way, only stopping by the Three-Stop for a few supplies and nodding at each other in passing. It was late August, just like now, hot and dry, only hotter and drier; the brush was kindling and so were the trees, the pastures were brown, the springs dried up, and the river was down. Heat lightning's what caused it.

It started northwest of us and spread so fast most folks could only grab their kids and run. Elmer was staying with me and he was so old there was no running left in him. He had trouble breathing and the smoke was killing him. I put him on my mule and tried to walk us out but the fire was at our heals and the mule was scared. He bucked Elmer off and left us stranded. I knew I couldn't carry him and so we headed to the river.

Mother Mabel, Jack, and Preacher saw us standing in the water as they were leaving and came to help. By that time the fire was on both sides of the river and there was no place to hide and no way out, so we worked our way upstream. We found a deep hole in front of a bluff and held there for that day and through the night, clinging to the rock and taking turns holding Elmer. The next morning the fire was past us and we walked through the char to our homes, but there was nothing left, only the Three-Stop Café.

The road in front and the clearings around it had saved the building, but our cabins were burnt. Jack let us stay at the Three-Stop that night and we discussed our fate.

"It'll take years to build back up," Preacher said.

"Not all the trees are burnt," Elmer said. "A good burn-off does good."

Mother scoffed. "It ain't done us no good—we got no place to live."

"I'm staying," Jack said. "Anybody feels the same can stay here till we build 'em a cabin."

"You'll see," Elmer said. "The woods'll be back next spring, even better."

Elmer was trying to be uplifting, but we all knew the same thing: none of us had any place to go to.

"I like it here," I said. "I'm staying."

"If we all work together it'll take half the time to build the cabins," Preacher said. "I'll stick."

Mother looked at each one of us in turn, and I believe she saw in our faces that we wanted her to stay. Somehow fighting for our lives under that bluff, neck deep in water, had tied us together, and from then on we needed each other.

"I don't guess the fire reached my root cellar," Mother said. "Let's go see what I can fix for dinner."

"Years before the fire my father worked on the childer crews on the Black River, that is until he broke his back, the result of a spooked mule team. After that he moved us here, to Dogleg."

"What's a childer crew?" Pete asked.

Claude had a surprised look on his face, but he cracked a smile and said, "You wouldn't think a man would forget how old he is."

Pete smiled, more smirk than anything, and threw stones in the river as he listened.

"When the growing railroads needed ties, these mountains provided 'em. The trees were cut and tie hackers scored the log. The juggles were popped out and the sides were trimmed. Then the ties were taken to the river to air-dry for a year so they'd float on the river drive. Men called river hogs worked the drive, some two hundred thousand ties, and sometimes it took three or four months.

"Once they made it to the crossing the ties were loaded onto boxcars. These were the men called childer crews, and they carried the two-hundred-pound ties on their shoulders and stacked 'em in the cars."

"Sounds like a hard way to make a living," Pete said. "Why didn't he move to a city where there was more jobs?"

"My father wasn't much on city life, but my mother had other ambitions. She was from St. Louis, a schoolteacher, and didn't take to the mountains as my father did, and so they parted ways. I was fifteen and stayed with my dad, and I never saw my mother again until her funeral, although we did write from time to time.

"When I was twenty my father moved to Kansas, but I had no inclination to live on the plains, and so I stayed in Dogleg. My father taught me the skill of masonry and I sold a few mules and hogs. It never amounted to much.

"My blond hair, sturdy build, and blue eyes made me a proper candidate for marriage, but I was in no hurry. I was in love once with a girl about the same time my father died. Her name was Judy and it was my intentions to have her, but her parents didn't have the same intent. Her father was a lawyer and her mother was a socialite. I'd never understood the bigotry of the social elite, but I was about to learn.

"Judy lived in Harrison, Arkansas, and I met her on one of my frequent trips for supplies. She was a redhead and fair-skinned, with beautiful green eyes, and we fell in love the first time we met. I courted her for two years but her parents took a hard line with me and wanted Judy to marry someone with more means.

"They refused to allow me in their home and forced us to hide our time together. Those were sweet times, though, and for a while I thought her love for me would overcome her loyalty to her parents, but I was wrong. My stubbornness was as much at fault as anything; I couldn't see myself living in the city when I could stay in the mountains. Judy wanted to remain close by her parents and that was the final cut."

"What about that old shack up there?" Pete asked. "You act like it means something."

"That's the Three-Stop Café; we always met there between five-thirty and six in the morning. It was standard procedure for us, even if Jack wasn't there. The sign read, 'Jack's Three-Stop Café and Dry Goods, Breakfast-Lunch-Dinner.'

"It was the only store in town, and all Jack had was a token choice of staples and canned goods on a five-foot shelf behind a three-foot counter.

"He didn't cook breakfast, lunch, or dinner at the store, but he didn't mind if you brought your own. Jack was short and round, like a rain barrel. His stubby fingers would barely run through what little hair he had, although he wasn't completely bald, but the sandy brown hair on the sides never seemed to grow. He rarely wore a hat and his head was as tanned as a beaver's pelt. The legs of his overalls had to be shortened 'cause he couldn't find any to fit.

"Jack didn't mind being short though. He said all things started on the ground or ended up there, and it was the good Lord's intention that he see under things while everyone else looked over the top. He always wore a smile and his brown eyes had a sparkle to 'em. His wife died of pneumonia before they had kids and Jack never remarried. He held a good mood and was always aggravating somebody."

Claude stopped talking and Pete stopped skipping stones. He could see the faraway look in Claude's eyes as he looked through the fire.

"Jack was always interesting," Claude said quietly. "And he held no grudges."

Claude picked up his fishing pole and took a worm from his can and threaded it on the hook, then stood and threw the line in the river. He rested the pole in the crook of a limb he'd stuck in the bank and sat back down.

Pete reached in his pocket and pulled out a knife, picked up a stick, and began to whittle, and looked at Claude from time to time. He too had lost in love, just recently, and had tried to put it out of his mind. He didn't like being reminded of it, but it came to him that even old men remember their first time.

Claude took a deep breath and coughed, grimaced, and scratched his chest.

He looked at the river and then at Pete, and turned his eyes up the hill toward the Three-Stop Café.

There was one road leading in here and the same road out, and that suited us just fine. It was a logging road and it seemed to come out of the mountains at a starting point that no one could see. I'd venture a guess that back then the population of Dogleg was ninety-six. At the time I hadn't counted in a while, but I don't remember anyone dying or birthing either.

Livestock was the main means of trade but there was a few that dabbled in moonshine. Preacher Dan Deveneaux had a particular bent in that direction, and he made good shine, but it was more for his own use than anything.

Preacher Dan was passionate about the good Book but also about his potation. That's what he called it—Passionate Potation, and it was the most famous blend of libation in six counties.

He came to Dogleg one morning riding a horse, his legs so long they dangled below the stirrups. Preacher was a walking stick, tall and thin. He had no cheeks on his behind whatsoever, having to set on a pillow when he was riding, otherwise his bony butt would be so sore he'd have to stand for hours. He had a head full of thick, black hair, long and wavy, hanging down to the collar of his white shirt, and his black pants and boots set off the notion he was different.

His intentions were to spread the good word and move on, but the joy he was spreading was helped along by the joy he was drinking and by late afternoon he couldn't stay mounted, and the only thing spread was him, so he took up permanent residence.

We never knew if he was a real preacher or not, but his long bony fingers could whip through a deck of cards the same as a Bible. We always knew when Preacher finished another batch of Potation, 'cause the hills shook with so many amen's that it made us all feel uplifted. His good nature was contagious, but he liked having the last word. The good Book said "Vengeance is mine," but Dan just mumbled "sayeth the Lord."

Jack put orange food coloring in Preacher's washbasin one night when Dan was so oiled he couldn't light a lantern. He dipped in as usual and washed his face and went to bed. The next morning he looked like a tangerine. He blamed it on his consumption of Potation, and so quit drinking, until he stumbled across the bottle of coloring behind Jack's cabin. He wasn't so mad about being orange, but he was upset about missing all that drinking.

Jack was no stranger to drinking either, and one night when he'd went to bed drunk, Preacher and a friend, I won't say who, snuck into Jack's cabin where he lay naked, fast asleep. They carried him, mattress and all, down to the river and laid him on a raft. Preacher spread two buckets of mule manure on it and a quart jar of honey on Jack and pushed him off the bank. The next morning Jack woke up three miles downriver and had so many skeeter bites he could hardly carry his mattress home.

Preacher, Mother Mabel, Elmer, and I were sitting on the porch of the Three-Stop Café when Jack came stumbling up the road. He'd tied the mattress on his back with a grapevine so he could free up both hands to scratch with. He was covered with welts from head to toe, and he had a nasty rash starting at his ankles and disappearing under the mattress. He walked up the road, head held as high as the mattress would allow. He'd grabbed a patch of leaves when he hit the road to cover his privates and when he passed by Mother her eyes widened just a tad.

"Just like Jack to garb up poison oak," she said.

Mother Mabel Morrison was fifty-five, big boned and big in girth. Both her twins were stillborn and the delivery almost killed her too. There would be no more children, she said. She bred mules, and she handled the job quite well.

Mother was just as strong as she was large and just as round as she was tall, and she took no sass. We called her Mother because she took care of everyone she saw. She had a gentle nature behind her fiery, hazel eyes, and she always wore a bonnet and a dark dress that reached down to the ground and up to her neck, and I never saw her in anything that didn't have sleeves to the wrist.

Her round face would light up in laughter as fast as it would scowl, but either way you knew what to expect. She had dark brown hair turning gray, and her double chin jiggled when she laughed. She was straightforward and we all admired her.

Elmer Sneed was the oldest person living here. He'd worked on the childer crews and was bent over like a dogleg. He was in his late sixties, a small man with a slender build. He had white, thin hair combed straight back, and he always had stubble on his leathered face. He'd lived through the Civil War, fighting with the South, coming out with just a minié ball through his left calf. He claimed to have been at Appomattox when Lee surrendered to Grant, but his stories varied from day to day. He was a Southerner, born and raised in Richmond, but he never went back after the war.

He lived in a cabin so far back in the mountains it took half a day to get there. He was in poor health but stayed hid in the hills, so one of us checked on him once a fortnight. It was my turn one day and I'd packed my mule with some substantials that I thought Elmer might need: flour, corn meal, some canned goods, coffee, and a quart of Potation.

I started off after my morning coffee at the Three-Stop. I'd spend the night with Elmer, cut him some firewood and straighten up the place before I left.

When I reached his cabin I was taken aback by what I saw. Elmer was sitting with his back against a tree, a small fire in front of him, almost gone to ashes. It looked to me like he'd been staying out there, even sleeping there, as I saw his bed of leaves and an old quilt twisted on the ground. His arms were draped over his knees, his head drooped to his chest.

"Elmer," I said. He didn't move. I climbed off the mule and tied him to a tree. I walked tenderly toward him, thinking he'd fallen asleep. As I got closer I could see his chest moving and knew he was napping. I stopped and looked around, trying to understand what his notions were staying outside.

The cabin looked lonely against the hill. The sun setting behind the mountains put the shadows of evening an easy hour ahead of the clock. The screen door was open, beckoning for someone to come or go. A cool breeze came through, almost too cool I thought.

The place was a mess. Elmer wasn't the tidiest man in the world, but normally he wouldn't let the place trash out. I squatted next to him and picked up a stick and poked the embers in the fire.

"Elmer," I said again, nudging him with my elbow. "Can you wake up, old man?"

He huffed a snort and jerked his head against the tree, his eyes still closed. I stayed squatted, playing with the fire, trying not to startle him. Soon his eyelids began to flutter and his knees moved apart, and his arms began to slide down the inside of his legs. Then they dropped to the ground, and he woke up. He turned his head toward the cabin, as if expecting something, then turned forward again, looked in the fire and saw my stick stirring the ashes. He turned to me and gave a shriek, like he didn't know who I was.

"Don't," he yelled.

"Elmer, it's me." I reached out to touch his arm and he twisted away.

"Elmer, don't you know me?" My thinking was he'd had a stroke, and his mind wasn't in its proper place.

"Don't," he whispered.

I pulled my hand back and flattened it between our faces. "It's okay, Elmer, it's just me. I'm not gonna hurt you."

His left arm was raised in front of his face and then it began to drop. I gave him all the time he needed and in a few minutes he came to his senses.

"Oh, it's you."

"Hang on," I said.

I walked to the mule and grabbed the quart of Potation. Sitting next to him I picked up a metal cup by the fire and poured some in it, then put it in front of Elmer's face. He was still wide-eyed and staring and I couldn't tell what he was thinking. Little by little I inched the cup to his lips. I touched them with the cup, but his mouth wouldn't open.

"Take a drink, Elmer."

His lips parted and I tipped the cup. He dribbled some down his bearded chin and swallowed a small amount. I took the cup away and took a small sip myself and sat it between us.

"Claude?"

"Yeah, it's me, Elmer." I patted his knee.

"Claude," he said, his eyes fixed on the ground.

"What are you doing out here?" I asked. Elmer stared, rocking from side to side.

"I'm gonna put some wood on the fire, and then we can sit and talk."

"I'm glad you're here, Claude."

I scrounged around and got some limbs and a few chunks of wood and got the fire going. By then it was dusk and the flames warmed and colored us.

"How come you're not in the cabin, Elmer?"

"Somebody's in there."

"You don't care if I take a look, do you? If there's someone in there maybe we can talk to them and find out what they want."

"They don't want you in there, that's what they want."

"How long have you been out here?"

"What's today?"

"Friday."

"Jack come up last time?" he asked.

"Yeah."

"After he left someone made me get out. They throw stuff at me."

"I'm gonna take a look, Elmer. You stay here."

I walked toward the cabin and I could see inside the open door and the square shape of the window sharpened by the light of the fire, but the black inside seemed to go on forever. I knew Elmer had a kerosene lantern and that's what I wanted to find.

When I mounted the first step I saw Elmer's things scattered on the porch: cups, dishes, a chair, a frying pan, and one of his old boots. When I stepped onto the porch I reached in my pocket and came out with a match. I lit it, heard it sizzle, smelled the sulfur, and squinted to see with what little light it gave off. All was quiet in the cabin. I looked back at Elmer and he was watching me, sipping on the cup of Potation. I turned back around and thought I saw a shadow moving across the inside of the doorway, but I heard no footsteps. I inched my way closer, but my match burnt down and I shook it away. I pulled out several matches then and lit one. I stepped inside the door and looked for the lantern. The floor was filthy and scattered with Elmer's belongings. Then I thought I saw another shadow. I lit another match and spotted the lantern by the bed. I made a quick step in that direction and caught my foot on something and fell to the floor.

I could hear Elmer shouting, "Claude, get out of there."

I picked myself up and lit another match. In front of me lay bits and pieces of broken plates, Elmer's other boot, and the sheet from his bed. I stepped across the clutter and grabbed the lantern, pulled the glass off, turned the wick up and tried to light it. My match went out and I lit another and it went out too. I tried again, but the lamp was torn from my hand this time and thrown against the wall. I started for it, but something blocked my way, something cold and thick. I tried to step around it but it was moving with me.

It had to be fear working my imagination, so I stopped trying to go around and tried to walk through it. I was lifted and thrown across the room, landing on my back in the glow of the doorway. The stench was sickening and I retched for the first time. I turned my head to the floor and heaved. My guts cramped and then I felt the sheet on top on me, covering my head. Pushing myself up I stood in the room fighting it, but couldn't get it off. I felt a strike to my back, as if hit with a fist or a boot. I fought the blanket from my head and saw the outline of

17

the doorway. I lunged for it but tripped again. I couldn't tell what it was but it didn't matter. I flung myself through the doorway and down the steps, landing a few feet from the cabin. Looking back in I saw something crossing the doorway. I scrambled backwards toward the fire, my feet pushing, my hands pulling. My arms couldn't keep up with my feet and soon I was pushing my own dead weight, shoving myself on my shoulders. I stopped next to Elmer.

By then Elmer had finished the cup of Potation and filled it again. He held the cup with both hands in front of his mouth, staring at the cabin.

"It don't come outside," he said.

I grabbed the jug and took the biggest gulp of Passionate Potation I've ever had. It went down slick and I took another. Finally my head started to clear and my body stopped shaking.

"Why didn't you come off the mountain, Elmer?" I took another drink.

"Mule run off the first night they come. I couldn't make the trip without him."

"You sure they won't come out here?" I asked.

Elmer turned his head in my direction, cup still at his mouth, and said, "They ain't yet."

I took a deep breath and heard the mule snort. He could tell something wasn't right. I unloaded him, saddle and all, and led him fifty yards down the path. I hobbled him and tied him to a tree with fifty foot of rope to let him graze. When I got back to the fire Elmer was asleep. I didn't sleep all night and as soon as day broke I packed up Elmer, put him on the mule and walked us out.

When we got back to Dogleg I put him up at my place. After he cleaned up and I got him something to eat he slept for twenty hours.

It's hard for me to say if Elmer's cabin was haunted or not; I'm not much on superstition. Jack, the last person up there before me, hadn't seen or heard anything, and he'd stayed in the cabin with Elmer that night. I suppose I could have imagined the lantern being torn from my hand, or I could have just dropped it. And I guess I could have tripped and fallen rather than being thrown, but I never wanted to go back to that cabin and Elmer felt the same way.

Once he got settled into my place he was content to stay. He was no trouble and it was nice having someone to talk to on those long winter nights. It was time for him to come down anyway.

Elmer was much like all old men—he did what he wanted and said what he meant. The only good thing about getting old, he said, was acting crazy and getting away with it. He'd fart anytime he felt the need, something that irritated Mother, but he didn't care. He liked to communicate that way rather than waste his breath talking. He'd shake his walking stick at a tree or the empty air in front of him and talk about what was on his mind; it didn't matter to him what people thought—he wasn't running for office, he'd say.

We kept him close through those coming months, floating, fishing, and hunting. He was a humble man and never complained. His life had been hard and perhaps we saw in him the way our own lives might go. He lived longer than most, and for that we were grateful.

It was at that time that a man came into our lives, a man we considered to be our friend, but only I knew the truth. A friend he was, but there was more.

I'd sometimes spend the nights on the riverbank in that late summer. It never bothered me being alone—I liked it. I especially enjoyed the sunrise lifting over the hills. It was on one of those mornings that I met the man that knew us all.

I was sitting on the bank by a small fire. I remember the leaves turning to color. It was early morning and I'd spent most of the night fishing and was preparing to leave, gathering my things but in no hurry. The sun was barely making its way through the trees.

I was standing, reeling in my line, keeping an eye on the bend, when I heard the call of a great horned owl as he flew in front of me and landed on a tree across the river. Then I saw a man round the corner, down at the bend, up to his waist in water, walking toward me with a sack slung over his shoulder. He was a big man and the water didn't seem to slow his movements. When he got closer I could tell there was no threat, even though he looked as if he could throw a mule. His arms were the size of a railroad tie and his chest as big as a barrel. He had no shirt on, just overalls, his right hand dragging in the water.

I knelt by the fire and waited. He waded to the bank and came to the fire, threw his sack down and squatted across from me.

"Morning, Claude," he said.

It took me by surprise 'cause I'd never met the man, and I suppose he saw it on my face.

"Have we met?"

"No, we haven't," he said. "But I know who you are. Was the fishing good?"

For some unknown reason I felt no apprehension as a man might when confronted with a stranger; somehow I could tell he meant no harm. He had a pleasant look about him and his dark eyes had a caring in them that put me at ease.

"The fishing was fine," I said.

"My name's Tubbs Tucker. I've come to see you, but before we get started I sure would like to have a bite to eat."

He opened his sack and pulled out a small skillet and laid it across two rocks close to the fire. He dug in the sack, moved things around, peered inside, and pulled out a brown paper sack. He opened it and pulled off four strips of salt-cured bacon and placed 'em in the pan. I cleaned two catfish and waited for the bacon to fry and when they were done I placed the fish in the hot grease. He dug around in his sack and came up with two small snuff tins. He opened 'em and sprinkled some salt and pepper on the fish.

After the fish were cooked we both ate in silence, just eating with our hands, wiping the grease on our overalls. When we were done he stood and took the skillet to the river, washed it out with gravel and returned it to the sack along with the salt and pepper.

"How's your friends?" he asked.

"Fine," I said. "Have you been here before? I don't remember your face."

"I've been here many times. There's changes coming, Claude, and I'm here to help you through them."

"Where are you from?"

"Oh, I travel around, wherever I'm needed."

"Not much changes in these hills," I said. "The weather mostly."

"You like it here by the river don't you?" he said. "Watch it close; there's more to the river than water."

"What kind of changes?"

"Good ones and bad ones. I'll know before it happens and so will you if you listen and watch for the sign. You and your friends have stayed hidden in these hills for quite some time, but it's coming to an end. The country's growing and progress is headed your way. You won't be able to fight it, but you'll try, and it'll change your lives. There's more but I can't say much about it. I do know this— some will die and others will live, and for some there will be a choice."

I could only think about Elmer, but I had no choice in that matter. I wasn't superstitious and didn't believe in signs, although there were plenty of myths in the mountains. I was young and foolish and passed it off as the ramblings of a man who thought himself a seer. But I was wrong.

"I take it you'll be sticking around."

"No," he said. "There's others I've got to see; I'll be coming and going."

I know I had a questioning look on my face and we stared at each other for a moment, and then he said, "I'll be here when you need me."

Tubbs was special in a lot of ways. He took a particular affection to Elmer, helping him get around and taking care of his chores, but I can't say that he did more for him than he did anybody else; he was able to sniff out needs and help take care of 'em. Tubbs came and went as he pleased. Sometimes he'd be gone for weeks and then show back up and stay around for a few days and then be off somewhere else.

The day I met Tubbs, I took him up to the Three-Stop. Jack always had coffee on and there was always someone there to drink it. Tubbs was accepted without question, just like I'd done, like he'd been with us all along. Even Mother, who could be irascible at times, just looked him up and down and continued on her mission, which at the time was admonishing Jack for letting his mule run free and getting in with hers. Jack's mule was not of the same caliber as Mother's, or that was her opinion anyway. He was the horniest mule on the MO-ARK line and would try to mount anything with four legs, even though he was sterile. We always questioned whether four legs was a requirement with him and gave him a wide berth just to be sure. He treed Mother once for six hours and would've been up there longer if Elmer hadn't got lost and stumbled across her. She never did like that mule.

Chapter Three

Mother Mabel might seem cantankerous, but she cared about us all. She lost her husband when a mule kicked him in the head, but she never missed a step. Her husband brought her up from the bayou and she could make a meal out of anything that crossed her path. She made her own clothes and her Sears catalog stayed in the outhouse. She usually met us in the mornings and evenings to check on things, and most of the time she had something for us to eat, maybe a pot of beans and cornbread or a pie. She tended to her mules and her garden but she always knew what was going on and kept us informed if she thought we needed to know.

She never shed a tear after the fire and Mother had more to lose than any of us. We men didn't have much in the way of conveniences, furniture or otherwise, but Mother did and she set about saving what she could. We built her cabin first 'cause we knew it was difficult on her staying with the four of us in that small cabin of Jack's.

There was some three thousand acres burnt, so finding trees to cut turned out to be a time-consuming ordeal. Most of the fire was contained west of the river, so we went east some five miles and found plenty of forest we could use.

Most of our livestock found their way back home but there was plenty that didn't. No one had much money, Mother had the most, but Preacher's moonshine kept a steady draw coming in. As the families started returning, Jack's trade picked up, and once the rebuilding started I got enough work building and patching fireplaces and foundations that soon money wasn't that big of a problem.

Mother spent most of her time collecting and repairing furniture and taking care of her fall garden, which turned out better that we'd expected.

We made a lot of trips to Harrison for supplies during that time, but it wasn't all work. We found time to have fun too. Mother and Jack usually made the trip, and one time Jack came back with a dog.

Greyhound is what Jack called him, and he said he was the fastest rabbit dog in the States, or that's what the gentleman said that sold it to him. Jack said the dog ran for money and went around in a circle chasing a wooden rabbit, so it just made sense to Jack that he'd have a steady source of meat to eat. This particular dog looked as if it was a little tired and his white whiskers made me think it might be a little old. Six dollars was what he went for, and Jack was proud of him.

They hadn't been back fifteen minutes and Jack was holdin' Lightning, that's what he named him, and bragging like it was a newborn. We were standing around listening to him boast when Elmer spotted a hare a hundred yards down the road toward the river. The rabbit was sitting in the middle of the road looking like bait, and when Elmer pointed him out, nothing would do but what we had to see that dog work.

"Let him go, Jack," Preacher said.

"We'll have fried rabbit tonight," Jack said, laughing.

He let Lightning loose and that dog took off like a gunshot, a dust storm swelling up behind him.

We watched him run and couldn't believe it, that is until he passed the rabbit. It was still sitting in the road cleaning its paw. Lightning raced past him, jumped into the river, swam across, and we never saw him again.

"Just as well," Elmer said. "Wooden rabbits are likely to taste a bit gnarly."

Jack was entertaining, mostly because he was the unluckiest man walking. He could sit on a turd in a church pew. But he brought most of it on himself 'cause he couldn't turn down a good argument, or wait long enough to think things out.

It was early September when Jack and Mother got into an argument about who could catch the most fish. We were doing more fishing than usual 'cause the wild game hadn't made it back in good numbers yet, 'cause there wasn't nothing to eat. Mother claimed she could catch twenty catfish before midnight, starting at sundown, and Jack couldn't let that go by.

We met at the riverbank at sundown, and Preacher was the counter, I was the fry cook, and Elmer, he just slept. They were using nightcrawlers and crayfish and Mother was ahead by ten o'clock with eleven fish and Jack was trailing with nine.

He was getting testy when he remembered a large hole on the other side of the river. He just knew there was catfish in that hole and he set about to throw his bait in it. Mother saw what he was doing and it just so happened she had her line in and was ready to throw, so she tossed it in. Her line wasn't there long enough to hit bottom when she pulled out a three-pounder. Jack was mad and wasn't about to let Mother get away with stealing his hole. While she pulled in her fish, Jack threw his line in and pulled one out. Mother threw again and before the worm made it to the bottom she had another.

"That's my hole!" Jack shouted.

"You don't own no hole," Mother stated.

"I seen it first, so it's mine," Jack said.

Jack would argue about the time of day if he was standing in front of a clock. Mother preferred not to argue at all. She didn't talk that much, but when she said something, that was that.

"The whole hole is mine!" Jack shouted.

"I don't know what a whole hole is," Mother said.

Jack couldn't contain himself. He waded into the river and started across to claim the hole. The farther he got the deeper it got and by the time he reached it he was up to his neck. He couldn't fish like that so he started backing out. As he was walking, Mother was baiting and throwing and reeling in fish. Then Jack tried to grab Mother's line. She didn't like that 'cause she was real possessive when it came to fishing, so she started throwing rocks at him. Mother was a good rock chucker and Jack was afraid to come any closer.

"Stop, Mother, you can have the whole hole," Jack yelled.

"You've scared the fish," Mother said.

She threw again and we heard the thunk up on the bank. What we couldn't hear was Jack, nor could we see him. Elmer was sitting up now, the shouting having brought him out of his slumber.

"I think you got him, Mother," Elmer said.

"Might have killed him," Preacher said.

"I don't know whether he's dead or not and I don't care. That hole business is nonsense."

I waded into the water where I thought Jack went down and started kicking around. I finally kicked something soft and I went under and pulled him up. Sure enough, he'd been knocked out cold; he had a knot on his forehead as big as an egg. I pulled him to the bank and Preacher helped me drag him up by the fire.

Elmer walked over and poked Jack with his walking stick, and seeing that he moved, went back to napping.

"I guess the fool's lost his fishing pole," Mother said. "That means I win."

Preacher mulled it over and said, "Nope, not till it's midnight, he might get up and start fishing again."

"You find mites on a chicken's ass," Mother said. "He ain't got no pole, so he can't fish."

Preacher studied for two more swallows. "Okay, let's eat."

Jack and Mother never let things get between 'em, even though Jack agitated her into a frenzy most of the time. She liked Jack and looked after him a little more than the rest of us; he was more like a kid in his ways. He was more interested in having fun than working, but there was a little of that in all of us; he just took it as far as the branch would bend.

Pete Connor quit whittling when Claude stopped talking and was watching his fishing pole. They both could see the end of it from the light of the fire as it bent slowly and came back up.

"He's sucking on it," Claude said.

"What is it?" Pete asked.

"It's a cat," Claude said. "Anything else but a cat or a carp would run with it."

Claude tenderly reached over and picked up the pole and waited till he felt the pressure and then set the hook. He reeled in a bluecat and stepped on him to unhook it.

"Grab that cord," Claude said. "Run it through his gills and tie the ends around the limb on that log near the water. Be careful he don't stab you with that spur. We'll keep him alive till were ready to eat."

"Is that all you people did was fish?" Pete asked.

Claude threaded another worm on his hook and threw out again. "That wasn't all we did, but we did fish a lot; we had to, it fed us. We'd set trotlines across the river and run 'em two or three times a night. We got a lot of fish like that and one time we caught Jack."

Claude threw another limb on the fire and sat back down. He looked at the darkening sky and figured it to be eight-thirty or so. At first he'd thought the young man might get bored with the talk and decide to leave, but Pete seemed more attentive than ever and Claude wondered why. Well, he was glad to have someone to talk to, even if it was his last night; Pete would probably be leaving soon anyway.

Pete made sure the fish was in enough water and came back to the fire.

"You say you caught Jack?" Pete asked.

"That Jack," Claude said. "He could get in more trouble than a toad in a toilet."

The trotline we'd set that night had paid off well. It was our third run and had produced over a hundred pounds of fish, mostly catfish, some gar, and two large snapping turtles.

Jack was running the line and that's then we heard him shout, "He's forty pounds if he's anything." He was standing in the middle of the river, right around that bend to your left.

A forty-pound catfish is big, but there's bigger ones in this river. We had a rope tied around Jack's waist because the current was strong. Jack, with his proportional dysfunction, as I liked to call it, had a tendency to float and bob like a cork. He was walking the line 'cause it was a short run and the river was only up to his chest. He could feel if there was a fish on the next hook, and if it was a big one, like the forty-pounder, he'd go to the opposite bank, untie the line, tie it around his waist, and we'd pull him and the trotline over to us.

He was halfway across the river and I was standing on the bank. I was holding the rope keeping it tight—then the rope went limp.

"KEEP PULLING," Jack yelled.

By the time I knew the rope broke it was too late to warn him; he was already slipping and stumbling, yelling and gurgling downriver.

Jack was rolling with the current and with each turn he'd wrap another three-foot of line around his body, fish and all. Preacher grabbed our end of the trotline and started into the water, pulling himself toward Jack.

"Hold on, I'm on my way," Preacher shouted. "Don't let them fish get off, that's supper for a month."

By then Jack was out fifty feet, wrapped up in the line, with fish strapped all over his body. Unable to walk, tied up like he was, he was bouncing off the bottom using his toes and hands to push with. Preacher was halfway out to him when he ran on to a nice eight-pound flathead.

"Hold on, Jack," he said. "I've got a nice one here. Let's not forget why we came."

"You…bas…I'm…drow…" It was hard to understand what Jack was gurgling, but we were relieved he was talking at all. Every time his head popped up we could hear a few more gurgles and it made us feel good that we still had him on the line.

Preacher threw the fish on the bank and continued toward Jack. There was plenty of fish he could've unhooked, but Preacher said later he was afraid he couldn't make the throw to the bank, and besides, Jack's yelling was getting less frequent.

Dan finally reached him and grabbed him by the collar and pulled him to the bank.

"Whooeee," Preacher yelled. "I ain't ever seen such a mess of fish."

Elmer and I ran down to help and saw that Jack had twelve fish wrapped around him, all of them squirming and wiggling and tails slapping. The big forty-pounder was strapped under his chin competing with Jack for air. Jack looked a little dog-eared. We untangled him, helped him back up to the fire, gave him a sip of Potation, and with a little rest he seemed to be fine. We quit fishing 'cause we couldn't talk Jack back into the water, and we figured we had enough to put up anyway. Jack had a superstitious nature, and when something disagreeable happened to him he usually let it rest a day or two.

We spent most of our time together in those late summer days and I was to learn more about my friends than I'd ever thought possible.

My father had only been dead for a year and Preacher had only been in our midst for two winters, and I'd spent very little time with him up until that point. Jack's wife had died in the fall of the previous year, and so I only knew him as a friend that owned the Three-Stop Café. Elmer had always been safely hidden deep in the hills, and I'd seen him only when I made the trip to check on him. It seemed as if fate had somehow pulled us together, and even though our community was small enough to be called a family, very seldom would it have brought five folks like us together. Looking back though, I can see how our lives would have crossed.

Preacher had been a drifter, always moving from place to place. I didn't know much about his past, only the bits I could put together from his stories. There was no reason to believe that he was a true preacher, not from his inclination for moonshine, women, and good times, and I believe he used the vocation as a ruse to get from town to town and meal to meal. It made no difference to us whether he was real or not. He'd been to the cities and didn't like 'em; he'd traveled out West and didn't care for the scenery, and he'd been to the Indian Territory and it didn't suit him. Preacher wanted solitude, but more than that he was after trust. It could have been his own mistrust in mankind that finally made him stop, but whatever the reason, he found a place he could tolerate.

As for Jack, after his wife died he made no attempts to marry again. He loved his wife and during her long illness he stayed by her side night and day. I remember after her funeral Jack left without a word and we thought he was gone for good. He left the door to the Three-Stop open and didn't come back for ten days. Mother came down every morning and watched the store, but she had no idea where he'd gone or if he was coming back, and then he showed up one morning and took over where he'd left off. It took a long time before his good mood returned but he finally found it. I suppose he felt it was bad luck his wife passed, and I guess he resigned himself to it.

We just adopted Elmer. He'd lived here longer than any of us and had always been referred to as the old man up the hill. He'd seen more hate and death than all of us put together, and in the end I believed he was the best of us all. He talked very little about the war but we knew what he'd been through. We came to believe that he stayed deep in the mountains so all he could hear was the wind and the forest. He found a place where there were no cannon blasts or screams and when he looked out from his porch all he could see was the best nature had to offer.

We were all single, some by choice and some by circumstance, and we'd been brought together by chance. We enjoyed each other; we tolerated each other, and above all we believed there was good in each of us.

Mother had taken on the responsibility of looking after us like the sons she never had, even though Elmer was older than she was. She was more than a friend and more than a guardian; she filled that void, that emptiness all men have and refuse to acknowledge. Without her disapproving glances we would have lost our way many times—she held us together.

We liked going to Harrison with her 'cause she did all the shopping and we did all the playing, but when we did go something always happened to make her proclaim she wasn't going back with us.

One morning Mother showed up and said, "I need to go to Harrison for supplies. From the looks of things it wouldn't hurt you any, Jack."

"I could use some," he said. "But I don't want to be gone long. A man with a trade can't be shut down."

"If you don't have anything to sell then you're already shut down," Mother said.

She had a hard time with the way Jack rationalized his situations and it was a constant irritation to her. She held no room for slackers and Jack walked a sharp edge in her mind. He only sold enough to get by and sometimes would put up his closed sign in mid-morning if he thought he was on track for the week, no matter that he was the only store in town and sometimes folks might ride for an hour to get to him. The closed sign didn't mean anything anyway because he had the door key hanging in plain sight. Most of us just unlocked the door and wrote down what we got, or for those that couldn't write they'd tell him the next time they saw him. He had the notion that a stranger wouldn't use the key to get in and would wait until he showed up, another thought process that irked Mother.

We started out on a Monday morning at sunup and figured we'd hit town that evening, if we didn't have any problems. It was raining hard that morning, so we covered the wagon with a tarp, and Tubbs, Elmer, and I slid underneath. Jack said he knew better than to camp under a tarp with Elmer and he was right that time. It didn't take long before Tubbs and I ended up walking.

The rain quit at mid-morning and the sun came out. It started getting hot and the air was thick.

"Mother," Tubbs yelled. "We've got to stop."

"Not stopping," she said.

"Tubbs is right," I said. "We're boiling, besides, we've got to check on Elmer. He's been under that tarp all morning and I haven't heard him sound off lately."

"Oh, all right, we'll stop," she said. "But I won't wait long; I'll be moving on with or without you."

Mother pulled the team under a hickory tree and parked in the shade. We caught up and Preacher had already pulled the tarp back and exposed Elmer. He was asleep, but wet with sweat. I woke him and he sat on the tail of the wagon and I gave him some cool water to drink.

We noticed two men on horseback coming toward us. One was taller than the other and both men looked hard. One had a rifle in a scabbard and the other carried his across the saddle. When they got to us they looked things over before they spoke.

"Where you headed?" the short one said.

"We're going to Harrison," Preacher spoke up.

The short one spit out a stream of tobacco, which landed too close to Mother for her liking. Tubbs walked up and stood next to Mother. When he moved both men stopped talking and took notice.

"What's in the wagon?" the short one said.

"That's none of your business," Mother said.

The tall one kicked his horse and reined him closer to the tail of the wagon, pulled his rifle from the scabbard and lifted the tarp so he could see inside. Tubbs moved to the end of the wagon and grabbed the tarp and held it down. The rifleman froze, the end of the barrel still under the tarp.

"Back off," the gunman said.

Everyone was quiet, waiting for a reply, everybody except Elmer, who seemed to be unaware of what was taking place. He moved sideways and let out a low rattle and hopped off the wagon and sauntered around the side. The short one's horse moved back a step and he raised his rifle up on his thigh.

"You're kind of noisy, old man?" the short one said. Tubbs and the other man were still fixed on each other.

Jack stood up and moved to his left a couple of steps, putting him within a quick jump of the short one's horse. The tall one pulled his barrel slowly from under the tarp. Tubbs let the tarp down and stepped closer to the horse.

"We're just passing through and not looking for trouble," Preacher said.

The tall one took his gaze from Tubbs and stared at Preacher. "These roads can be dangerous and it don't look to me like you're prepared."

"Looks can be deceiving," Preacher came back. "The Lord makes up for weapons with numbers."

"I didn't come here to get preached at," the tall one said. "I'll know what's in that wagon." He smiled at his partner and lowered his rifle, and Tubbs stepped to his horse and grabbed the halter with one hand, the pommel with the other.

"You've said enough," Tubbs said.

"Shoot him, Delbert," the man said, but then we heard the click of a hammer being set back.

It was Elmer, standing behind the wagon with my rifle perched across the seat pointing at the tall one.

"You're noisier than I am," Elmer said. "So you might as well be first."

Both men were surprised and so were we, but the look on Elmer's face showed he wasn't bluffing. They backed up their horses, Tubbs walking beside the one, and turned their heads to the road.

"You've not heard the last of us," the tall one said.

"Hearing ain't nothing," Mother said. "Seeing is."

"Your sass can get you shot, woman," the tall one spat out. "Come on, let's go," he said to his partner.

The two men trotted their horses down the road at a steady pace for fifty yards and then slowed to a walk, looking back at us.

If it hadn't been for Elmer things might have turned out different—we weren't much of a threat without the rifle, and it made us consider Elmer in a different light.

"We should be moving along," Tubbs said.

We packed ourselves back into the wagon and headed down the road at a good pace, hoping the closer to town we got the more people there might be. I took the rifle and laid it under the tarp behind me. We were off to a bad start.

It was slow going because of the mud and we were making poor time. We wouldn't make Harrison that night, and started looking for a place to camp.

Tubbs spotted a place near a small creek with a bluff behind it; if we were gonna have trouble, it'd have to meet us head on.

Jack unhooked the team, hobbled and tied them to a tree near his bed. We all made our own sleeping arrangements while Mother started a fire and cooked biscuits and beans. Tubbs scouted the surrounding area and Elmer fell asleep on the back of the wagon.

There was no moon that night and when the sun went down we could see nothing past our fire. We were quiet, trying to hear the unusual out of what had always been second nature to us. We decided to sleep in shifts; I'd stay up till midnight, Tubbs from then to three, and Jack taking us to daybreak; Preacher would fill in where need be.

Going to town meant we had things to sell or trade, and it also meant that we had some money on us. Those men would be back. No one but Elmer would sleep well that night.

I couldn't decide whether to keep the fire going or put it out. I don't like sleeping without one, but I didn't want to make a target out of us either. Of course, without the fire I couldn't see any better than the bandits. I decided to keep the fire going and Tubbs agreed with me; if there was gunfire we didn't want to shoot our own people.

I kept watch until midnight, trying to pick through the sounds, wanting to hear the noises that a person might make sneaking through the woods, but the only sound I could guarantee was the snoring. Sometime during my watch, Elmer started adding his own noises. For some reason they were almost comforting. I was sitting on a log ten feet from the fire, which was probably good because about midnight I caught myself falling off my seat. I was dozing in and out when I felt myself floating and knew I wasn't flying but I was too tired to care. That's when I felt a hand on my shoulder and I woke with a start. It was Tubbs and I doubt he'd even been to sleep. I passed the rifle to him and found my bedroll.

Next thing I knew the sun was up and I could smell bacon and coffee. Tubbs was cooking over the fire and the two horsemen were sitting across from him, tied up like kindling. Mother was picking up her bed, Elmer was sitting on the back of the wagon drinking coffee, Jack was hooking up the team, and Preacher was at the creek washing up. I relieved myself behind a tree and walked to the fire and squatted beside Tubbs.

"Smells good," I said.

Tubbs handed me a cup and I poured some hot coffee, topping off his cup too.

"What happened?"

"Nothing much," Tubbs said. "They weren't much trouble."

"Hang 'em," Elmer said.

"Can't hang 'em, Elmer," Preacher said, wiping his face with a rag. "The laws don't allow hanging anymore. The quickest way to end this thing is to shoot 'em."

"How'd you catch 'em?" I asked.

"They weren't real smart," Tubbs started. "They were sneaking up the road like they owned it. I'd crossed to the other side to see if I could spot anything and when I turned around to come back, there they were, standing in front of me in the middle of the road, looking straight at the fire and whispering to each other. I wasn't but three feet behind 'em. They were having trouble figuring out what those strange noises were mixed in with the snoring. They thought it was a buck, snorting like that, but of course it was Elmer. Their faces were so close together all I had to do was smack their heads and tie 'em up."

We ate breakfast in the morning sun and laughed about how things turned out, what with Elmer saving us twice. We loaded the wagon and put out the fire, tied the two horses to the tail end of the wagon and then tried to decide what to do with the varmints.

"Tie 'em to the mules," Mother said. "That way we can keep an eye on 'em."

That's what we did. When we got to Harrison we turned 'em over to the sheriff, along with their horses, and set about to find a place to sleep.

It was always interesting going to Harrison, even though it wasn't a very big town. Still yet, it was a growing place and there were always new things to see and do. The first place we stopped was the Dew Drop Inn saloon. Preacher had brought two cases of quart jars with him and the Dew Drop Inn usually took 'em off his hands.

The rest of us waited at the wagon. Elmer could hardly hide his glee and we let him wander around a little. He hadn't been out of Dogleg for as long as I could remember, and the main reason we brought him was because we thought he might not get a chance to go on many more.

Preacher came out of the saloon with a grin and a handful of greenbacks. "Praise be to the Dew Drop Inn," he yelled.

We agreed with that, as it was mostly his money we were using to make the trip. The next stop was a hostel and Mother went in, figuring she'd make a better appearance than the rest of us. She got four cots in the back for Preacher, Elmer, Jack, and I and a small room for herself. Tubbs would spend the night with the wagon.

One of the best parts of going to Harrison was getting a good hot bath. That was the next stop. There was a bathhouse down the street from where we were staying and we made a line for it, all of us except Elmer. He claimed he didn't have to bathe, seeing as how all the dirt had worn off while he was getting old. We left him and Tubbs with the wagon and the three of us walked to the bathhouse.

We went in and paid our money and stripped down and hung our clothes on a peg and sat in the tubs. Two men came in and started dumping hot water and we started soaping down. Jack had bought a handful of cigars and we all lit one up and leaned back and soaked. A man who called himself Fiddlin' Phil occupied a tub beside us and Jack offered him a cigar and he was happy to take one. He said he had four wagons at the end of town offering amusement, and it didn't take us long to figure out what kind of entertainment he was talking about.

"What kind of fiddling is it?" Preacher asked.

"Why, my gals can play any tune you want to hear," Phil said.

"Gals! You mean you got gals playing the fiddle?" Jack asked.

"Sure," Phil said with a wink, blowing smoke rings at the same time.

"They must be talented," Jack said.

"Can they sing, too?" I asked.

"Sing? I guess they can if you want 'em to."

"Damn," Jack said. "What time does the show start?"

"It never stops," Phil said.

"Those girls must be tired," Preacher said. "How much does it cost?"

"Two dollars per show."

"Do they dance?" Preacher asked. "I love to dance to good music."

"They don't do much dancing," Phil said, with a sideways glance.

Phil said he had an arrangement with the sheriff that let him stay at the end of town as long as there wasn't any trouble, and as long as there was something in it for him. Phil was a businessman and it was easy to see. He was having his slacks, shirt, and jacket cleaned and pressed while we were taking a bath. A boy brought in his boots polished to a bright luster and Phil flipped him a one-dollar gold piece like it was routine.

He said he'd been in the traveling show business for several years and things had paid off well enough that he'd decided to stay put for a while. Harrison was a growing town and more and more people were starting to head south as things built up after the war.

Phil wore his hair short and combed straight back and he said he was heading to the barber for a shave as soon as he was through bathing. Jack asked him if he bathed in the middle of the day all the time and Phil said he always did, and he always shaved at that time too. His workday was just getting started, and the type of entertainment he was into demanded a professional look. He was a fine gentleman as far as we could tell, and we were anxious to see the show.

When we got back to the wagon Elmer was leaning against the side and Tubbs was sitting on the back swinging his feet.

"You heard from Mother?" I asked.

"She came out an hour ago and said we should eat at the inn close to six."

"Come on, Elmer, let's go," I said. "You coming, Tubbs?"

"I'll stay with the wagon and eat later."

We walked inside the boarding house and washed up for supper. Mother met us at the dinner table, where there were twelve people arranging themselves in chairs, and Miss Wanda, the owner, was bringing out the food. She had quite a meal set up for us: fried chicken, mashed potatoes and gravy, corn on the cob, black-eyed peas, cold milk, and hot apple pie.

Preacher Dan was asked to say grace: "Thank you, Lord, for the grub we're gonna eat, Amen."

Everyone eyed each other, heads still bowed, probably questioning Preacher's vocation. I assumed he'd slipped a couple of snorts of Potation before he got back. Elmer was having trouble keeping his face out of his plate 'cause he was still snoozing. Preacher was sitting next to him and was holding his face up by the back of his shirt. Miss Wanda was sitting at the head of the table passing plates and Mother was sitting next to her. They'd hit it off from the beginning and were chattering like two crickets after sundown. All plates filled, we started eating and talking about the local politics, of which none of us knew anything except Miss Wanda, who was having a difficult time talking and stuffing her mouth at the same time. She was a good eater and her physical arrangement was a testament to her overindulgence.

Preacher woke Elmer up long enough to eat something and leaned him back against the chair to snore some more. Jack was shoving it in so fast he was losing track. He had a clump of mashed potatoes and gravy on his fork and somehow he fumbled it. When he tried to catch the fork it spun and slung. The tators and gravy made a circle around the table, hitting everyone but him.

Dinner was over, for most of us anyway. Jack stayed, being the only clean one left. Mother said she'd never come back with Jack.

Since it was early we decided to head to the edge of town, and Mother wanted to get some shopping done and took Elmer with her. Tubbs wasn't interested in our appointment with the traveling female minstrels and bunked down at the wagon.

"Let's go see the musicians," Jack said.

While we walked, Preacher told us about the time he was held in a Missouri jail.

"I learned how to puke on command while on sabbatical at the Florence County Safe House. They made us clean out the privies every morning and the first thing I did was puke. After three weeks of spewing it became second nature. I can vomit right now if I want to."

"What were you doing in jail?" I asked.

"It was an event which I had no control over," he said. "I was in the Boot heel of Missouri practicing my seminary skills on a group of small gypsies, or at least I thought they were gypsies; come to find out they were midgets. They were a sideshow for a traveling carnival and had been jailed for impersonating children. Seems they'd pick out farsighted folks and offer themselves for adoption, just long enough to steal their belongings of course. They only had one problem: being midgets got 'em in the houses, but they were so small they had to drag what they stole, leaving a rut behind them big enough to fall in. I was misidentified as their leader because I was the tallest, and the sheriff stuffed me in the pokey with 'em. Justice shows no favor where midgets are concerned. Let that be a lesson to you, never travel with people three feet shorter than you are.

"I was incarcerated for four weeks, but I masterminded a release program that set me free. One night I instructed my comrades to sew their clothes together, two shirts and two pants. The next day when we got to the privies, my friends donned their new outfits, jumped on each other's shoulders and walked away from the jail like free men. I was the only one left behind, and when the sheriff couldn't find his other guests, he questioned me about their whereabouts. I folded like a pocketknife and told all. He let me go for my outstanding display of citizenship, and to my knowledge my small friends were never seen or heard from again, at least not in that town. I did hear that a group of midgets were jailed in Illinois for impersonating tall people. I guess the ruse worked so well they decided to carry it one step further. They began following the carnival again, and when it hit town they'd put on their outfits and while the people were at the show they'd rob their houses. They thought anyone seeing 'em would think they were normal adults and any suspicion would be directed away from them. Unfortunately, they made the same mistake twice. They didn't take into consideration that one midget on another's shoulders does not make twice the carrying capacity. They still had to drag their merchandise, and a blind donkey could have followed the trail they left."

Mother, having heard enough, said she was crossing the street to shop for dry goods. She took Elmer's elbow and headed that way.

"Now Elmer, I don't want no trouble out of you tonight," Mother said. "You stay right in front of me so I can keep an eye on you."

She helped him off the dirt street and on to the walkway in front of Greerdon's, the dry goods store.

The store was shaped in a long rectangle with one aisle down the middle and all sides and ends filled with everything from canned goods to linens. People kept moving in a circle until they thought they'd seen it all, or got too dizzy. Elmer was moving slow and that suited Mother fine, 'cause she wanted to get everything she needed so she wouldn't have to go back. Elmer was ten feet in front of her and there was a woman and a small child about the same distance behind her. Mother thought she smelled something unfamiliar, and when she took note of what it could be, she realized her mistake. Sure enough, as Elmer rounded the end of the aisle, she heard a familiar sound. She knew she had to get him out of the store, but as she quickened her pace her eyes started watering and she knew it was too late.

Mother turned the end of the aisle and saw Elmer, still excited, still expressing his contentment. She quickened her pace and when she caught up to him she grabbed him by the scruff of the shirt and shoved him out the front door. When she turned to set her things on the counter and get the money from her purse, the woman and boy rounded the other end of the aisle. Mother hurriedly dug through her bag, knowing there was bound to be repercussions from the disaster.

"There she is, Ma! That's her!" the boy shouted.

Mother looked up, startled at the shouting. That's when she realized the woman and boy hadn't seen Elmer.

"No, no, not me," Mother said, pointing at herself and shaking her head. The woman was holding her hand over her face, staring at Mother, shocked. The boy was still pointing at her, somewhat paler than before, and still shouting, "That's her, Mama."

The owner, just then beginning to get the drift, looked at the boy and then at Mother.

The store was emptying fast, everybody looking at Mother. She closed her purse and walked out the door. Elmer was standing on the walkway looking out over the street. Mother grabbed him by the shirt and pulled him along, carrying him with his feet barely touching the ground.

"There she goes, Ma!"

Mother looked back over her shoulder and saw the people standing, pointing in her direction, and could see the closed sign swinging on the door. She took Elmer back to the wagon and left him with Tubbs.

"I've never been so humiliated in my life as I was tonight," she said, speaking to both men. "First there was dinner and that awful mess Jack created, and now this, Elmer disrupted the whole store and closed it down. Now everybody in Harrison thinks I've got a problem and will avoid me like the plague. You men aren't worth the trouble to keep around. Now Tubbs, you keep Elmer in sight and put him to bed, and if you can't keep him in sight, keep your nose in the wind, I'm sure you'll smell him. I'm going to bed and hope and pray that I don't have to worry with you sorry men tomorrow."

Tubbs looked at Elmer with a questioning slant. "What went on, Elmer?"

"Not sure," Elmer said. "Mother must have had some trouble, 'cause I ended up on the walkway as a lookout."

"You didn't have anything to do with it?" Tubbs asked.

"I don't see how, she was behind me."

"She was, was she?"

"Yup, directly behind me. I'd hate to think she did something embarrassing."

"I know what you mean," Tubbs said. "Why don't you get some sleep."

"I'll stay with you if you want. Hell, I've been on guard duty half the night anyway."

Jack, Preacher, and I were hustling to the edge of town. We were excited about the all-female band we were about to see. It had to be the only one in the country and we felt lucky to be in the same town. Jack stopped in the barbershop and put some lilac water on his scalp just in case one of the women took a liking to him, and Preacher smoothed back his wavy, black hair with some water, and I spit on the toes of my boots and cleaned them on the back of my pant legs. Women always like a man that wears shiny shoes.

We got to the edge of town and were looking for the wagons and listening for the sweet sounds of music. But we could hear no notes, only the sounds of laughter coming from a small stand of trees. We stopped to listen and came to the conclusion that the band hadn't started yet. We saw some men coming toward us, out of the grove of trees, and figured we'd missed the first set.

"We're looking for a traveling band of female minstrels," Preacher said. "Have you seen anything like that?"

"Haven't seen no band," they said, "but we have seen some women."

"They weren't playing music?" Jack asked.

"I guess you could say they were," one of the men said. "The sweetest music there is."

"Well, what kind of instruments were they playing?" I asked.

"The same ones you play with at home," they said, laughing.

We looked at each other and decided they were drunk; how would they now what kind of instruments we played with. We let 'em pass and then headed to the trees. When we got closer we heard soft voices and knew we were in the right place. We could make out the wagons and could see shadows inside, coming from the light off the kerosene lanterns.

"This'll be the talk of Dogleg when we get back," Jack said.

"Quiet now," Preacher said. "They may be warming up."

"Hey, you men, over here," a woman said in a quiet voice. She was standing between two large oak trees about twenty feet from the wagons, parked on the other side of the grove. We walked over and saw she was wearing a short skirt and low-neck blouse, and her hair was long and golden, hanging down around her shoulders.

"My name's Gloria. You here for the show?"

"You bet we are," Jack said.

"There's four ahead of you and three girls are resting."

"Don't you all play together?" I asked.

Gloria had a surprised look on her face, and I knew then that she probably hadn't run into such knowledgeable men as the three of us.

"You want all eight of us?"

"You bet we do," Preacher said.

"You three men want to play with eight girls at the same time?"

"We just want to watch." Jack said.

Then Phil came out of the dark, from behind the wagons.

"Hello, boys," he said. "Who's gonna be first?"

"These fellas want all of us to play together," Gloria said.

Phil got a serious look on his face, but after a moment, dollar signs showed through the lenses in his eyes.

"That'll be forty-eight dollars."

"They just want to watch, Phil," Gloria said.

When Phil heard that it almost brought him to tears. "Pay up front, boys. This ain't no charity."

"Now hold on," Preacher broke in. "A while a go you said it was two dollars a piece, now you want forty-eight."

"It's two dollars for one show," Phil said. "You want eight shows, that's forty-eight dollars."

"You mean it's two dollars to see one girl play," Jack said. "That don't sound like a band to me."

"Now don't get upset," Phil said. "Maybe you should take a look at the players."

Phil was rubbing his chin, thinking things through. He wanted that forty-eight dollars and he knew he had to conjure up some showmanship to keep his audience.

"Let's give these boys a peek, Gloria. Just think of it, eight naked women and you men with a front-row seat."

"Naked!" Jack shouted.

"We better think about this," I said.

"We're ready over here," Gloria said.

"Let's go," Phil said.

We walked toward the wagons, following Phil, Dan trying to figure his money, and Jack dancing like a child waiting in line.

The girls were in two wagons, four in one, three in the other, and Gloria standing on the ground. The girls were dressed in nightgowns, most of them open in the front.

"Mighty tempting, ain't it?" Phil asked.

By then our worldly knowledge had kicked in, at least mine did.

"This is a fine-looking group of ladies," I said. "But I don't believe this is the right time for me to be spending money on musical entertainment. How about you, Preacher?"

"Well," he said, "I do believe there's sinners about, and it's difficult to turn my back on those in need."

"You don't know what you're missing," Phil said, not quite as amiable as before.

"I think we should go," I said, but before I could say any more Jack took two large steps and jumped right in the middle of the wagon with the four girls in it. He was three-quarters in and somehow had latched on to all four of 'em in one fashion or another. Gloria jumped to the end of the wagon and was able to grab both of Jack's feet before he totally immersed himself. The women were screaming and hollering and slapping at Jack. Gloria was pulling as hard as she could, trying to back him out of the wagon. Jack had a death grip on all four of 'em, and I could tell it was gonna take more than her to pull him off.

"That's eight dollars right there," Phil yelled. "Don't you hurt my girls." Phil didn't seem too upset about the commotion, paying most of his attention to Preacher, who was holding his money in his hand.

I jumped to the wagon and grabbed Gloria by the waist and pulled on her in an effort to help get Jack dumped on the ground.

"There's two dollars more," Phil yelled. "That's ten."

"There ain't nothing going on here worth ten dollars," Dan said.

"You touch, you pay," Phil said.

"I'll not pay—" Preacher started, but that's where it ended. Phil connected with an uppercut that straightened Dan out like a board. He hung in the air like he was weightless before he landed on his back, the money still gripped in his hand. Phil took Dan's money and then turned to help Gloria and me. He grabbed me by the waist and just then I felt something give. Me, Gloria, Phil, and Jack's boots and pants fell backwards on top of each other. Jack didn't wear underwear in the summer and I was sure that would cause more commotion.

Jack had squiggled his way a little farther into the wagon then, there being no resistance on his forward progress, and was forcing his face into every fold of flesh he could touch, see, or breathe on. The three girls from the other wagon decided to help and were at the end of the wagon pulling and clawing at Jack. By the time we picked ourselves off the ground the seven women had overcome Jack's obsession. They extracted him from the scuffle and dumped him on the ground, his legs still in the air, heels resting on the tailboards of the wagon. His arms were stretched straight back over his head and what was left of his shirt flopped over his face.

"Pick up your friends there," Phil said. "It's time we parted ways."

I grabbed Jack by his outstretched arms and pulled him backwards till he lay next to Preacher.

"Put your clothes on, Jack," I said.

"What happened to Dan?" Jack asked.

"He took a hit," I said. "And I'd say he's gonna blame you."

Jack got dressed and I borrowed some water and poured it on Preacher's face and walked back to our room. The next day we ended our business, Mother pushing us as fast as she could, and headed back home.

Chapter Four

Claude reeled in another catfish and unhooked him and tied it to the stringer. Pete walked to the edge of the water to watch. He'd never fished much—never had the time, or so he claimed. The truth was no one had ever shown him how, what line to use or pole to buy, or what bait worked the best. He'd half expected Claude to have a cane pole with a safety pin on a string, but could see the old man knew what he was doing. He thought that he could be driving back to Harrison listening to the radio instead of hearing the crickets and the river and the soothing sounds of the crackling flames. He looked up at the star-filled sky and then followed Claude back to the fire.

"How come Mother Mabel never remarried?"

"That's a good question," Claude said. "One I can't rightly answer. She was a good woman, a hard worker, and the finest cook I believe I've ever met. Oh, she had her suitors. Many a man would've been proud to have her, but she had no use for a man, she said. Once she found out she could get along well enough without one I guess she decided to enjoy the solace. Besides, she had us, and we were enough trouble. She had a cat named Crisis and a dog called Worthless— both of 'em males, if that gives you a clue to her thoughts."

"What about Preacher?"

"Preacher never did marry, but he liked the women sure enough. He spent a lot of time tracking 'em. He had a daughter named Bonnie that lived in Texarkana and she came through one time on her way to St. Louis. Preacher didn't even know he had a daughter. He would've made a good husband, I believe, once he got settled down, and I'm sure he would've been a decent father. I know that after he found out about Bonnie he was."

Claude picked up a stick and stared at the ground and was silent for a while.

Pete felt he must have been thinking about his friends.

"Where do you live, Pete?"

"Kansas City. The company I work for contracted the clean-up after the dam was built. I'm staying in Harrison, but tomorrow's my last day."

"You have a lot of friends there I guess," Claude said.

"Some, but I don't get to see them very much. I'm on the road a lot."

"Do you miss 'em?"

Pete thought about the question. He'd never thought about missing his friends.

Everybody had jobs and Kansas City was a big place and it took some effort to organize the time to meet.

"I guess I do," Pete said. "It never crossed my mind."

"They're hard to replace," Claude said. He held a silence for another few moments and then got back to the story.

I was beginning to feel a closer connection to my friends. The ordeal with the two gunmen had proven that we worked well together and were willing to stand up for each other. I'd always been independent, feeling that I could handle my own problems, but I was learning different. There was safety in numbers and they better be your friends.

I'd had little use for numbers; Dogleg being as small as it was I knew everybody there. But Tubbs was right, the country was on the move. I was seeing more and more strangers coming down the river, floating to the White, and from there they'd ride to the Mississippi, the highway that took 'em north or south.

Most of the time I avoided others, not because I didn't like 'em, I just liked the quiet better. But after Jack lost his wife I started meeting at the Three-Stop every morning for a cup of coffee, listening to what was new and laughing a little before the day's work started. That's when I found we had something in common.

The river was getting busier, and I was about to learn how dangerous it could be.

It was October and we were preparing to make a four-day float, the last one before winter. The burdensome heat was over and fall was quickening its pace toward winter.

We built a raft out of old logs so they'd float, and tied 'em together with rope. A few days before we'd took two mules and a wagon down to our take-out point.

Our supplies were plentiful but necessary: one rifle and a shotgun, fishing poles, an axe, matches, two large frying pans and one large pot, rain gear, a tarp, flour, cornmeal, coffee and pot, beans, two pounds of bacon and a tub of grease, salt and pepper, a kerosene lantern, trotline, three pounds of corn bread provided by Mother, bedding, fifty feet of rope, a grappling hook, shovel, four jugs of Potation, and a Sears catalog. All the small supplies were put in wooden boxes, which we used as seats. We also tied a small flat-bottomed boat to the tail end of the raft; we'd use it to set and run our trotlines.

We shoved off at daybreak on Saturday, Tubbs and Preacher handling the long poles that would push us along. I was in the back with a paddle, using it for a rudder. Elmer was sitting on a box up front in the middle. His job was to look for rocks and limbs that could stop us or capsize the raft. He was nodding off most of the time though, so the job was kind of honorary.

It was a clear morning, still cool in the early light, a mist hanging over the water. We drifted with the current for several hours, sipping on coffee. Every now and then a fish would make a splash, turtles would slide off their sunning perches, and the birds would give warning cries of intruders. The slapping water against the front of the raft lulled us in a half-sleep.

We floated under trees hanging out over the water at such angles that it was hard to believe their roots would hold 'em. We stopped at mid-morning to stretch our legs and relieve ourselves of Mother's strong coffee. It was time to sip some Potation and let Jack and Preacher rig up their fishing poles. Jack had some other business to take care of first, and he started up the bank to find a place, taking several pages of the catalog with him. The gravel bar we'd parked on was small, and the bank behind it rose up at a steep angle, lending to a difficult climb for him. He was grabbing at weeds and roots, trying to find something that would sustain his weight long enough to get a foothold for the next lurch upward.

The rest of us were sitting side by side, passing the jug, when we heard a shout. Jack had made it to the top, but whatever he had a hold of gave way. We didn't have time to move, he was flipping so fast, but fortunately on his second flip, he landed right beside me, legs sticking out in front of him like he'd been there all along.

"You sure you don't want to wait?" I asked.

"Nope," he said. "Coffee kicked in. Someone push me up the bank."

"Knowing what you're mission is," Preacher said, "I doubt you'll find anyone willing to get behind you to push, pull, or kick."

"Tubbs, you'll help, won't you?" Jack asked.

Tubbs sighed, and we knew Jack's begging had fallen on the right ears. Tubbs couldn't seem to turn anybody down that needed help, especially someone squeezing and squirming like Jack was.

"You stand here," Tubbs said, pointing to a spot behind us. "I'll grab you by the seat of the pants and the collar of your shirt and when I say go, you start up the bank and I'll give you a throw that'll get you over the top."

Jack got up, legs so tight together he was taking baby steps, his arms stretched out trying to keep his balance.

"Okay, Tubbs, I'm ready if you are," Jack said.

"On the count of three, make your move," Tubbs shouted. "One—two—three!"

Jack pitched forward all he could muster and Tubbs gave him a throw that had Jack flying up and over the top of the bank.

"Yeeehaaw," Jack yelled.

He'd barely got the joyous yell out of his mouth when the next thing we heard was, "Ohhhh, nooo…"

Expecting to see Jack land on top of the bank, we were surprised to see him disappear from sight. We scrambled up to see what happened.

The ledge Jack was aiming for was only a foot wide; from there it dropped into an undercut that fell ten feet into a nasty quagmire. The only reason we hadn't smelled the putrid odor was because we were sitting on the high side of the breeze. Jack lay splayed out, belly down, all four limbs pointing in different directions, face buried deep in the dark gumbo. The mire was at least thirty feet wide, and Jack had landed six feet from the bank. Even if we could've stood on it to reach him, the undercut was too steep, and it was just as bad as the bog Jack was laying in.

"Get the grappling hook," I said.

Dan jumped down the bank and grabbed the hook from the raft.

"Who's going in?" Tubbs said.

"Nobody," I said. "We'll hook him and pull him up like a turtle."

Tubbs got as close to standing as the slope would allow and swung the hook a couple of times and let go. The hook hit Jack on the back of the head and stayed on his shoulders. I pulled on the rope and snagged his overalls.

"Okay, let's pull him in," I said.

We grabbed the rope, one behind the other, and walked our way down the bank, pulling Jack with us. Everything was fine until we got to the bottom and there was still no Jack.

"Jerk him over the lip," Preacher said.

We pulled hard and Jack flopped over the ridge like a dead hog. He rolled into us and all four of us went tumbling, ending up beside Elmer. Elmer never looked up but he did sniff the air.

"There's a dead beast about," he said. Elmer stood and walked to the raft and sat on his box.

Jack had to bathe in the river before we could go on. Tubbs rigged up a clothesline on the raft to dry his clothes and we made Jack sit in the back and steer because he still smelled suspicious.

It was noon and the sun was bearing down. Even though it was October it could still get hot, so we decided to float for two more hours and hunt some shade and get some lunch. Jack was feeling better, with the help of a few sips of shine, but his steering was getting erratic. Preacher spelled him and Jack took up his fishing pole.

"Got one!" Jack yelled. "He's a fighter, too."

"What is it?" Elmer asked.

"Don't know yet," Jack said, struggling with the line. "He won't show his face."

"You ain't got him hooked good," Tubbs broke in.

"Set the hook, Jack," Preacher yelled.

Jack bent forward and jerked back hard enough to pull the whole river in on us. He set the hook all right, and he pulled his catch clean out of the water, the only problem being it was the biggest water moccasin we'd ever seen. The thing headed for Jack's head. He screamed and dropped flat, his pole dropping in the water, the snake passing over his head and landing in Preacher's lap. As soon as he landed Dan shot up and the snake fell to the raft in front of Elmer. The snake was everywhere at once, and it seemed he was heading for everyone at the same time. All five of us bailed off the raft and watched silently, standing chest deep in the river, as the raft continued downstream, the snake now the sole owner of all our possibles.

"Get the pole! We'll pull him off the raft," I yelled.

We started diving and Preacher came up with it, but before I could holler he jerked the snake off the raft and into the water. My thinking was to wait until we got to the bank before we shared our space with him.

The snake was heading for us, but unlike him we couldn't make very good time.

"Get rid of the pole," I yelled.

"Make up your mind," Preacher yelled.

Considering his age, Elmer was actually making faster tracks than the rest of us, bubbles popping up behind him like popcorn on a skillet.

What happened next surprised us all; all those warm bubbles Elmer was leaving must have distorted the snake's sense of detection, 'cause he stopped dead in the water, nothing doing but his head peering out over the waves.

Luckily the raft was hung on a submerged limb not far downriver. No one was interested in getting the fishing pole back, not even Jack. He thought the whole business with the snake was bad luck. I viewed the quagmire as an ill wind, but Jack was convinced that getting bitten by a pit viper was top on his list of misfortunes, and no one could argue the point. We walked along the bank, picking our way through the brush until we came to the raft. Tubbs retrieved it, and we loaded back up.

We planned to find a shady gravel bar to fix our lunch on, but we were still leery about what we'd left upstream, so we decided to put another mile between it and us, even though it figured he'd have a difficult time unhooking himself.

"You ever seen a snake that big before?" Tubbs asked Preacher.

"I've never seen a water snake that big before," Preacher said, "but I have seen some rather large diamondbacks. One time I stumbled across a group of religious fanatics that used snakes in their ceremonies. I was traveling through northern Arkansas and ran into some problems with the daughter of one of the so-called ministers of the viperous legion. Seems she was enamored with my illuminating dissertation on the rewards of abstinence, and somehow got the impression that in order to abstain, one must first engage in the act of which one must abstain from. I was fully aware of my duties at that point and convinced the young lady that perhaps a private lecture in my quarters would be appropriate. I felt it my obligation to clear her mind of all sinful thoughts in order to see the way to complete and total self-restraint. Her father got wind of the session and misunderstanding my intentions, threw ten large rattlers into the room. I was forced to throw myself out of my own window, and had to run naked for several miles through the brush, the band of heathens following me with clubs, guns, and a frightening array of poisonous pit vipers. It was only with a large amount of luck and my long legs that I was able to outpace 'em, otherwise I might not be here today telling you this story."

"What were you doing naked?" Tubbs asked.

"Well, uh…I was changing into my preaching clothes, of course."

"What were you doing out of 'em?" Jack asked.

"I, uh…stopped into a saloon on the way to my meeting with the young lady, to see how many sinners were quaffing their downtrodden souls towards the abyss of Hades, when a drunken rogue threw up on me. I was changing into cleaner garments when the woman appeared at my door. I told her to wait but she was so anxious to hear my sermon, she let herself in. It was only moments later her father appeared, and with a vengeance I might add."

"Where'd you learn to be a preacher, anyway?" Jack asked.

"I went to seminary school after I was accused of bilking newlyweds out of ten dollars by selling them family Bibles. Unbeknownst to me only the first five pages had any scripture in it, the rest of the pages were scribbled with an unknown print. The judge gave me the choice of two years in jail or two years of Christian service. I chose the latter, hating small spaces like I do."

"Look ahead," Tubbs said.

There was a sharp bend in the river turning to the left and on the right there appeared a large gravel bar with a fifty-foot bluff behind it.

"Let's make camp and cook supper," I said.

Tubbs poled us in while the rest of us got our things. When we hit the bank it woke up Elmer, who'd fallen asleep somewhere between rattlers and heathens. We threw out our bedrolls and grabbed the frying pan and Potation; camp was set.

Jack and I started fishing while Tubbs gathered wood for a fire. Preacher took the shotgun and headed into the woods.

"Storm moving in," Tubbs said, looking to the northwest.

Jack and I saw the same thing, hills of clouds turning from light gray to charcoal.

"How long?" I asked no one in particular.

"About sundown, not much longer," Tubbs said.

"I'll get the axe and tarp," I said, "Jack, you find some trees we can make poles with."

The bluff would give us some protection from the wind and rain if things got temperamental. Tubbs was moving the wood up the bank.

Every now and then we could hear shots downriver, and that gave us hope that Dan had killed dinner. Jack found some small trees and we cut 'em down and trimmed them. Tubbs retrieved the shovel from the raft and was digging holes for the poles while Elmer started the fire. Then Preacher came rambling into camp, carrying four rabbits.

"Storm's coming," he said.

We set the four corner poles and tied the tarp to them, standing the fifth pole in the middle to give us some height. Jack and I laid out the bedrolls, while Preacher cleaned the rabbits, and Tubbs and Elmer carried a few flat rocks to the fire to make a cooking stand. The clouds were moving over faster then but the wind hadn't picked up yet. Jack went to the edge of the bank and checked our fishing lines and I started tying down loose items on the raft in case the wind did get out of hand.

Elmer scraped some hot coals from the inside of the fire to the flat cooking stones and laid out two frying pans, forking in the bacon grease and watching it melt.

"Think we should set the trotline tonight?" Jack asked. "A fella can catch some big catfish when it's thundering and lightning."

"Probably a good idea," I said. "We can use the rabbit guts for bait, if we can keep Elmer from frying all of it."

Elmer loved fried liver and heart and would eat it before any other part of the animal, but his favorite meal was fried squirrel brains, a delicacy that only he and a few others I've known shared. Jack went to the raft to get the trotline and I spotted a tree to tie our side of the line to. The bend we'd just come around was shallow, so I headed downstream thirty feet where it looked like a deeper hole. Jack and Preacher hopped in the flat-bottomed boat and paddled to my side of the river. I gave them the line and they tied it on the other side and made their way back across, Jack tying on the hooks and Preacher baiting them as they pulled themselves along.

I made my way back to camp, sniffing the fragrance of fried rabbit. Tubbs was standing in front of the fire looking up at the sky.

"It's raining behind us," Tubbs said. "I can smell it."

Then we heard the rumblings of thunder. The wind went from breeze to blow, leaves loosened from their limbs, twisting and turning in the air, some landing on the ground and tumbling on, some lifting up again, circling and flipping. The river was vibrating, and the wind was picking up drops of water and spraying 'em.

Jack and Preacher were having trouble keeping their boat straight in the water, the line pulled tight in a curve, them holding on trying to finish hooking and baiting. I watched as they finally reached our side of the bank, and as they let go of the line, the wind caught 'em and pushed 'em downriver a lot faster than the current would have. They began struggling with their paddles, trying to make their way upriver, but weren't making any headway. They were in the middle of the river, paddling as hard as they could, the water rolling under 'em, the boat remaining in the same position. They finally gave up and turned sideways and made it to the bank. They pulled the boat behind them and made their way back to camp.

"Getting blustery, ain't it," Preacher said.

"We'll catch big ones tonight," Jack said.

"Better get that boat up on the bank," I said.

"'Upper's ready," Elmer hollered, his mouth full of fried rabbit and cornbread.

Tubbs tied the raft to a big maple tree and met the rest of us at the fire. We sat down to eat just as the rain started.

We shoveled the fire under the tarp to keep it going. The rain was coming down so hard, sometimes blowing sideways, it was almost impossible to keep it lit. We needed the warmth more than anything, the temperature having dropped by ten degrees in the last hour, our clothes damp from the blowing rain. The thunder was deafening and lightning was cracking all around us, brightening the view from our shelter only to show sheets of rain so thick it was difficult to see the river thirty feet in front of us.

We sat under the tarp in back of the fire, passing Potation and time. Elmer had already fallen asleep while the rest of us stayed up watching the storm and telling stories. We were on flat ground in front of the bluff, but our things were still wet, so we had our beds stretched out as close to the fire as possible. It had been raining hard for several hours and I could see the worried look on Tubbs's face. I knew what he was thinking, but I'd already been out once to check the river level and it had barely raised a foot, the front of the raft still within stepping distance from the bank.

It was late evening then and the talk was slowing down. I made sure the lantern was fueled and working and turned it off. We were ready to lie down on wet beds using our rain gear as sheets, all of us except Tubbs. He was going to sit up for a while longer. I knew he was worried and I hoped he was wrong.

I'd just fallen asleep when I felt my shoulder being shaken.

"Claude," Tubbs whispered. "We better wake the others; I got a bad feeling about this rain."

I looked about me and could see the rain hadn't let up. We woke Preacher and Jack and said we were moving to higher ground. Waking up Elmer would be more difficult, so I decided to help pack and wake him when we were ready to leave. He'd fallen asleep with his clothes on anyway, like the rest of us.

We got everything ready to go except for the tarp, and I shook Elmer to wake him; that's when we heard it. We could hear it over the rain and the wind and in between thunderclaps. It sounded like a twister. It was a flash flood and it was on top of us. Our only chance was the raft; there was no way out on land. The bluff behind us, which we'd sought for protection, was blocking our path to higher ground.

Tubbs dropped the things he was carrying and picked up Elmer in his arms and ran toward the river, the rest of us on his heels, carrying what we could, most of it scattering to the ground. I was the last in line and felt for the tie line and followed it to the tree. I took out my pocketknife and cut it as close to the tree as I could and ran back to the raft. I pushed us off and jumped on and Preacher and Tubbs turned us downstream, Jack trying to steer us from the rear.

The water was pushing us then and we could tell the river was coming up—fast! We knew up ahead there was a right angle in the river just around the edge of the bluff, and that was higher ground.

The roar of the river filled our ears and it was so dark I could hardly make out the outlines of my friends. Our raft was rising upward, so quick our bodies could feel the movement. The river was falling over the raft on all sides throwing limbs and debris at us.

"Elmer!" I screamed. I couldn't see him and I knew he'd have no chance without our help.

"Elmer!" I yelled again, falling to my knees and searching for him. I touched something that felt like clothing and jerked on it and it felt like a leg. It had to be Elmer. I made my way up his body and grabbed him under his arms and clasped my hands together around his chest. I was kneeling on the raft with Elmer sitting in front of me and we were both just a few feet in front of Jack. I could feel the water pouring over the rear of the raft in waves and knew the flood had caught us.

"Right—right—hard right!" I could just make out Tubbs's screams. I had no idea where he was going but it didn't matter. I yelled as loud as I could over my shoulder, "Turn right, Jack, hard to the right!" I didn't know if he even heard me, I just kept hanging onto Elmer, somehow comforting myself by the action.

I could feel the tail end of the raft swinging around to the left and now the water was pouring over the side and I thought for a moment Elmer and I were going over.

"Shove—shove!" I heard Tubbs shout.

I felt the raft lift into the air, the mass of the river finally catching us. We were riding its crest. Then the left side of the raft collided with something and threw all of us into its wall and we slammed back down on the logs. Then we shot forward and hit again, this time shooting Jack, Elmer, and I to the front. Tubbs and Preacher had been thrown off, but I could tell they were lying on land and not in the water. They picked themselves up and came toward the raft.

"Come on, let's go," Tubbs shouted. He reached out his hand and I shoved Elmer to him. Tubbs picked him up and started running, Jack and I scrambling as fast as we could behind him.

"Water's coming up fast," Preacher said. I jumped off the raft, Jack behind me, and landed right beside him, both of us at a full run.

We followed as close to Tubbs as we could, him knocking down brush as he went, staying well ahead of us, even carrying Elmer. In what seemed like hours we slowed down to a walk. The roar of the flood diminished and the ground was firm under our feet. We knew we'd made it, but we kept walking.

We came to a small clearing and plopped ourselves on the soggy ground. We laid back and let the rain fall on our faces, knowing we'd just used up an ace.

After we had a chance to catch our breath we took stock of our wounds. All we could do was feel around, it was too dark to see anything. If we were bleeding, it would have to wait till morning. We weren't grumbling though, we were happy to be alive.

By then the rain had slowed and the black sky was graying over us. We could start to make out each other's faces.

"Here," Preacher said, poking me on the shoulder.

I looked over and be damned if he didn't have a pouch filled with Potation.

"How'd you manage that?" I asked.

"First thing I grabbed," he said. "If I'm gonna drown, I want to pick the source."

We passed around the pouch and quietly waited till morning, nodding off from time to time, but glad we were all still together.

It was luck that saved our lives, that and Tubbs. We'd shot around the bend at the edge of the bluff but the current had been too strong to pull us in. With Jack unable to see the river in front of him and not being able to hear Tubbs, he had no idea where to steer us. It was only chance that the lightning had flashed and Tubbs had seen the cut on the right with a high bank on its left. He yelled at Dan to pull to the right, the rest of us having no idea where they were heading.

Tubbs thought that if he could point the raft toward the inlet, the river might shove us on in and we could try to scramble up the bank. Things worked out just about that way. The left side of the trough was about twelve feet high and Tubbs and Dan positioned us on the right side of the river. We were riding the swell and as we approached the mouth of the cut, the front of the raft hit the bank, and the river shoved our tail around, then moved us sideways and slammed us into the embankment. If it hadn't been so high it would have thrown us off the raft, but as it was, the river sped on by the opening, flooding the inlet and throwing us to the end.

The river was going down as fast as it came up, and by daylight things were almost back to normal, except for the mess. The raft was damaged but not bad enough we couldn't repair it. Tubbs had tied down the boxes of small supplies and we still had the axe, which was stuck into the logs of the raft. Dan had shouldered his shotgun when we left camp, putting a box of shells in his pocket.

We lost the rifle, tarp, the fishing poles, hatchet, lantern, most of our bedding, and the shovel.

We weren't far from our camp and we decided to backtrack and see what we could find. Elmer and Preacher stayed at the raft and cleaned it up, while the rest of us walked back to the bluff. The river and its banks were cluttered with trees and brush. The tall grass and weeds were lying flat, still rooted in the water.

The first thing we saw was the flat-bottomed boat, broken in half around a tree; there was no way to salvage it. When we reached the bluff, the gravel bar was gone. We were looking for the tarp but couldn't find it. We saw nothing else, the place washed clean of our first visit.

"Look," Jack said, pointing to the opposite side of the river. "The trotline's still tied to the tree."

We looked on our side to see if it was still tied, but it wasn't. Tubbs waded across to get it because we still had good use for it. Tubbs was pulling in the line and coiling it up when we saw him struggling.

"Probably hooked on some brush," I said.

"It's hooked on something," he yelled back.

Tubbs kept pulling and little by little he was getting a foot or so at a time. We saw something coming to the top of the water but it didn't look like wood. Jack recognized it first and then I figured it out myself; it was a snapping turtle, and a big one.

"Keep him on the line," Jack yelled. "It's a snapper; the best eating there is."

Jack and I hurried across the river to help Tubbs pull him in. The turtle was thirty pounds or better. I got in front of Tubbs and Jack got in front of me, and we all started pulling. He was dead weight and he was trying to back himself into the river again. He had a hold of a small catfish that had hooked himself sometime during the night, and he wasn't letting go.

"A couple of feet and he's ours," Jack yelled. "Give a good pull and let's get him on the bank."

All three of us reached forward and got a good grip and pulled with all our weight and dragged the snapper up on the bank, right in front of Jack's feet. As soon as the turtle hit the gravel he spit out the fish, lunged forward and snatched onto Jack's foot.

Jack was kicking as hard as he could but it wasn't making any difference to the turtle. He'd found himself something he liked better than catfish and he wasn't letting go. Jack was down on his back kicking the turtle's head with his other foot, trying to back his way as far from the water as possible. The turtle was holding tight just staying put, while Tubbs ran up and grabbed his neck and tried to strangle him, but the snapper seemed content to hold on, no doubt thinking he had supper for a month. I pulled out my pocketknife and kneeled down beside Tubbs.

"Cut him, Claude, cut him," Jack yelled.

"Let go and stand back, Tubbs," I said.

I cut through his neck and Jack scrambled backwards, the turtle's head still clamped to his foot. Tubbs and I tried to pry the jaws apart but couldn't. We decided to go back to the raft and get something a little stouter to pry with.

"How's the foot?" I asked.

"Numb," Jack said.

"Can you walk?" Tubbs asked.

"With a turtle on my foot?"

Tubbs finished pulling in the trotline, untied the hooks, and we started back to the raft, Jack carrying the trotline, Tubbs and I sharing the load of the turtle. We weren't making good time trying to climb over the mess the flood had left, and Jack stopping every few feet to wiggle his boot.

When we arrived at the raft Preacher and Elmer had straightened things up and were frying some bacon and gravy for breakfast. We got the turtle's head off and then ate, sopping up the gravy with Mother's cornbread.

We cleaned the turtle, and Tubbs tied the meat in his shirt and put the bag in the river to keep cool.

It was closing in on mid-day and the river had reached yesterday's banks again, so we loaded back onto the raft and started off. It was rough going at times, having to stop and dislodge trees and brush to make room for the raft to pass.

Elmer was worn out and sleeping; I was steering, and Jack, Tubbs, and Dan were poling and clearing a path through the river. The sun was bright and the sky was clear, and the water was slapping a little louder than the day before, and there was a nice, cool breeze blowing out of the south.

Up ahead was a long bend in the river and a set of shoals at the end. The noise it was making made it more difficult to hear, so when I saw Tubbs put his finger to his mouth showing all of us to be quiet, I didn't quite understand. Tubbs motioned for Dan to head to the right bank and we settled into it with a small bump.

Tubbs had his arm in the air and his fist closed signaling for us to remain quiet. We sat there for a few minutes straining to hear what Tubbs could hear. Then I thought I heard voices. They weren't happy either, and I could hear crying too, and it sounded like a woman. Tubbs pointed up in the woods in front of us and as I struggled to see through the brush I could just make out people standing. I came up to the front of the raft and huddled with Tubbs.

"There's folks up there," Tubbs whispered, "and something ain't right."

"Can you tell what's going on?" Preacher asked.

"Can't tell exactly," he said. "But I hear a woman crying."

"Let's find out what's troubling 'em," Jack said.

"Not so fast," Tubbs said. "I saw a flash of steel coming in and I'm betting it's a gun. Claude, wake up Elmer and tell him there's trouble. Preacher, you load your scatter gun and come with me. Jack, you and Claude sneak your way up the front here, but don't get too close. We'll circle back upstream and come in from the rear."

Tubbs and Dan hit the bank and started upriver fifty feet and turned into the brush. Jack and I did the best we could not to make a sound and closed in on the voices step by step. We made it thirty feet up the hill and could hear the voices clearer and see the people.

There were two women with a small boy and two grown men standing with their guns pointed at them. One woman was lying on the ground on her clothes. The other woman was standing to the side, the boy clinging to her legs, scared to death, tears rolling down his face. She was hiding his eyes so he couldn't see what was happening.

"We'll have our way," one of the men said. "It's best you get used to it."

Both men were wearing overalls with no shirts, one of them with the straps hanging down around his legs. One was tall and lean and the other short, but just as thin. The place smelled stagnate and from the looks of the men, they were filthy and mean. They no doubt were living in the woods and probably had a still in the cave to the right of them.

"Boy," one of the men said, pointing his rifle at the child, "you get away from her and come over here. Woman, you get them clothes off."

"I'll go first," the short one said.

"Why?" the tall one asked.

"I seen 'em first."

I touched Jack's arm and pointed up the hill. Tubbs and Preacher were standing in the brush, not twenty feet from the back of the men.

The shorter man stepped up to the woman lying on the ground and kicked her in the back. "You shut up." He turned to his partner. "Keep an eye on the other one and don't let her run off. If she tries to bolt, shoot her legs; don't spoil her."

The short man laid his rifle to the ground and dropped to his knees.

I looked at Tubbs and he saw me and nodded.

"You there," I yelled. Jack and I both stood so they could see us over the brush.

Both men turned their heads to look our way, the one standing turned his rifle at the same time. He took a shot and Jack and I hit the ground in different directions. He had a lever action, and by the time he'd shoved another shell in the chamber Tubbs had him by the throat with one hand and the rifle jerked free with the other. The short one was still kneeled behind the woman but Preacher had his shotgun shoved to the back of his head, his foot standing on the man's gun.

"Don't move," Preacher said.

By then Jack and I were there helping the women. The young boy, still scared and crying, was clinging to his mother.

"You men lay belly down on the ground," Tubbs said.

Jack went into the cave and searched for some rope.

"These is our women," the short man said.

"I think not," Preacher said.

"I weren't part of it," the tall one said.

"We heard it all," Tubbs said."

"Did we get here in time?" I asked the women.

"Yes."

"You men cain't charge my camp," the short man shouted.

Jack came out of the cave with some rope and tied the men's hands and feet.

"There's a still all right," he said. "And there's lots of stuff in there too. I suspect these two have been robbing and killing folks on the river for quite a while."

"Gag 'em, Jack," I said.

"How'd you women get in this fix?" I asked.

"We're headed south to meet up with Frank's—my husband's family, at the White River. Our mule came up lame and Frank decided to take the river. He traded the mule and wagon for a boat and we've been on the river for three days. We tried to outrun the flood but couldn't make it. It was so dark we couldn't see and Frank brought us up to higher ground and went back to the river to pull the boat up, and we've not heard from him since. When daylight came we saw the cave and sat in it until Frank could come and get us. Instead, these men showed up."

We looked at each other and all thought the same thing. If her husband hadn't showed up yet, then he probably wasn't going to. It was my guess we'd find him downriver, dead.

"I'm Carmen Morgan and this is my son, Frank Jr. She's my sister, Annie Eldridge."

Carmen looked to be in her early twenties, a small woman with petite features, short-cropped brown hair, and fair complexion. Her sister was slightly larger with darker hair and darker skin, a year or two younger. They were both wearing coveralls and plaid wool shirts, and their rain slickers were still in the cave. The boy looked to be six or eight.

"We should be looking for your husband, ma'am," Tubbs said.

"Is there anything in the cave we can use?" I asked Jack.

"I'll take another look, I'm sure there's something."

"Don't you think we should stay here and wait for Frank?" Carmen asked. "He might be back anytime."

"Ma'am, I do believe it would be best if you came with us," Tubbs said. "We'll get you to a town where you'll be safe and maybe we'll find your husband between here and there."

Carmen looked at the ground with tears in her eyes, her hands on Frank Jr.'s shoulders. "You don't think he'll come looking for us?"

Tubbs and I looked at each other and Preacher scuffed the ground with his boot.

"I believe we'll find your husband," Tubbs said.

"See, Junior," Carmen said to the boy, holding him tight.

"He'll have to come upstream to find you though," Tubbs said. "He didn't have any choice last night but to go downstream. There's no roads in these hills, so I think it'd be best if you came with us and maybe we'll run into him on the river."

Carmen nodded and Preacher started them down the hill toward the raft.

Jack found a good-sized pot in the cave, along with two fishing poles and a shovel. There was some bedding too, but we decided not to take it; if those vermin had been laying in it, we didn't want it. I found a rag and wrote on it with some charred wood from their fire: *rapist thieves and most likely killers*. I tied it to the mouthy short man and we dragged 'em into the cave.

"We'll tell the sheriff," I said. We picked up their guns and never looked back.

Elmer was introduced to the ladies and the boy, and he and Junior took a liking to each other right away. We took to calling him Junior because we had a good feeling Frank Sr. had met with disaster, no matter what hopes anybody had.

Tubbs and Preacher pushed us off the bank and we were on our way; this time like a floating hotel.

"If I'm not prying," I asked, "where did you start from, going so far into Arkansas?"

Carmen was looking downstream and hadn't heard the question; no matter, we knew what was going through her mind.

"Council Bluffs, Iowa," Annie spoke up. "On the Nebraska-Iowa border, not far from the Missouri line. We're going to Baton Rouge, where Frank has family. His brothers were to meet us at the mouth of the White River in Arkansas. From there we were going down the Mississippi and catch a ride to Louisiana."

"What made you leave Iowa?" Jack asked.

"We were farming, corn mostly, but Frank's horse spooked one day and threw him and broke his hip. He was never right after that and always walked with a limp. His brothers own a supply store in Baton Rouge and offered to give him a job. The trip's been cursed from the beginning. We lost all our things in St. Joseph, everything we had except the clothes on our back. We parked our wagon at a livery stable, thinking it'd be safe, and got a room. During the night the stable burned to the ground. The mule was saved but our wagon and belongings were gone. Frank bought another wagon, but that took most of his money. We've been struggling ever since, and now this."

"When was the last time you folks had a good meal?" Preacher asked.

"We've been eating jerky mostly," Annie said. "Two days ago Frank caught a catfish and we cooked him, but now we don't even have a pan."

"Tonight we'll eat good," Jack piped up. "Turtle stew with cornbread."

The sun was beginning to fall in the west and the river light was starting to fade with the shadows. We looked for a place to camp. The long, slow curve of the river in front of us allowed a good look at what was ahead; on the left a large gravel bar appeared and a huge bluff faced it. It'd be a good place to spend the night, but Carmen didn't want to give up the hunt for Frank.

"Can't we go a little farther? Frank might be needing help."

"Ma'am, we won't be able to see much in another hour," Tubbs said. "It's best if we find a place to camp. If he's out there, then we'll find him tomorrow."

You could tell she was hurting, but the boy was hungry and so were we. We pulled into the bank and set up camp.

We laid out what bedding we had, which wasn't much, but enough for the women and the boy. Elmer and Jack started a fire and Tubbs wandered down around the curve to check things out. Preacher pulled the turtle meat out of the water. I grabbed the big pot we took from the cave and washed it out. Elmer had found enough flat rock to make a decent cradle over the fire and I sat the pot on it. We cut the turtle meat in chunks and fried 'em in the grease.

"I'd like to help," Annie said.

"Be my guest," I said. "I can't say that I'm much of a cook."

Annie used the bacon grease and flour to make a dark roux. All we had to make stew with was river water, and Preacher filled up the coffee pot and was boiling it. Annie threw a pound of bacon on the frying pan and cooked it. Three coffee pots of water and a pound of bacon, Annie's roux, six pounds of turtle meat, salt and pepper, and we had a meal. The only problem was we didn't have eating spoons or bowls, having lost our utensils in the flood. We did have a few coffee cups left—three to be exact. Preacher cut twigs and shaved the bark off and we held 'em together and shoveled the stew into our mouths, passing around the cups and sharing cornbread. Carmen didn't eat much, only nibbled on the cornbread, always looking downriver.

It was late evening then, the stars as bright and clear as I'd ever seen 'em. It was a good night to sleep. The next day we'd have to make good time if we wanted to get Carmen, Annie, and Frank Jr. someplace safe. We could hear the frogs grumping and the water rippling and the fire was popping and we heard a lone whippoorwill high on the bluff across the river. I didn't believe we would ever sleep so well.

We didn't either. That damn whippoorwill sounded off every two minutes for twelve hours straight. Early on, around midnight, Preacher loaded his shotgun and fired two rounds into the bluff, of course not hitting anything, only aiming at the noise. Tubbs exchanged the gun with Potation and quieted him down, but you could still hear him grumbling all night. Jack got up once and started throwing rocks across the river, barely hitting the bottom of the bluff. He ran down to the raft to get a closer throwing point and got to going so fast he ran right off the edge into the river. Carmen didn't sleep at all; I could hear her walking the bank until it got too dark to see and then walking back to the fire.

The next morning we warmed up some cornbread and made coffee and started off again. We'd gone about three hundred yards and made the bend when Tubbs pulled us to the bank. We could see the boat on the opposite side of the river, and the rope around a foot sticking out of the water. We hoped against hope but it did no good. Annie held Carmen and the boy, while Tubbs, Preacher, and I untied the rope and pulled Frank's body free. Somehow he'd got tangled up in the line and the river took the boat and him with it. He was snagged on a tree trunk, the rope having gone under a limb and Frank straddling it, the river unforgiving with its force. I'm sure he was gone long before that. We wrapped him in our rain gear and bedding and buried him high on a hill, not having a way to keep the body. Preacher said a prayer as we lowered him down and dust-to-dust we covered him up. Tubbs made a marker out of limbs and shoved it in at the head of the grave.

"Can we go now?" Carmen asked, staring at the dirt.

She seemed to hold herself up well after it was over. Having Frank Jr. there must have given her hope. The waiting was over and Carmen knew it. The tears stopped at sunset and she was ready to move on. We never heard another word about it and she never showed any self-pity.

That night we camped at a calm stretch of water and Preacher made a fire and we ate beans cooked with bacon and finished off Mother's cornbread. We would hit the take-out point about sundown the next day.

The next morning after coffee and bacon and fried catfish that Jack had caught, we started the last leg of the trip. Carmen and Elmer entertained Junior while Annie straightened up the raft. Jack was trying his luck at fishing while Preacher was steering, and Tubbs and I were pushing the poles.

With the weight of Frank's death behind us things were not as tense as the day before, and we were easing in to a more relaxed conversation. Preacher asked Carmen what her future plans were.

"I'm not sure exactly. It wasn't my idea to leave Iowa and move to Louisiana, it was Frank's. I believe we could have made it in Council Bluffs, but Frank had it in his head to get back down south. I've never even met his family, so I have my doubts about whether they'd be willing to take in three more mouths to feed. Our parents are in Iowa but they can barely feed themselves, and Annie and I swore we wouldn't be a burden on them. Annie's beau ran off with a butcher's daughter, so I know she has no reason to go back to Iowa."

"Carmen," Annie spoke up. "You've got no right telling my problems. If I want to tell, I'll tell."

"Nothing to be ashamed of," Carmen said. "That boy didn't have nothing to offer you anyway, all he wanted to do was diddle. You're better off without him."

The girls were arguing then, as sisters will I guess, and I turned my attention to Jack's fishing. Preacher was still interested in the girls' talk, or that's what he claimed; my thoughts were he was just as interested in Annie as he was anything.

We floated for four hours and it was time to hit the bank and take care of some personal matters. We guided the raft to a shady spot and everyone got off to stretch their legs.

"If you ladies need to take care of business now's the time," I said.

"Thanks," Carmen said, and her and Annie took off to the right through the brush.

"Those women have a long haul ahead of 'em," Preacher said.

"They're probably right about going south," Tubbs said. "Frank's brothers won't be too interested in feeding three more mouths."

"Maybe they'd want to stay in Dogleg," Preacher said. I saw the gleam in his eye but it was wishful thinking. There wasn't a one of us that had the money or the inclination to take on a family. We'd have to take them to a town and try to get 'em situated the best we could. We might be able to pool our money and get 'em a ride to Baton Rouge, but that would be the end of it.

When the women got back we started the last leg of our trip. We'd left our mules and wagon at Jake's Landing, a small concern that afforded river rats a place to put in or take out, restock supplies, or just sleep for a night on a cot under Jake's porch.

Jake was famous for his fried catfish dipped in buttermilk and cornmeal, if one was lucky enough to catch him in the mood. This particular day Jake was uncommonly ecstatic. Seems his wife had run off with a horse trader the day before and brought to a conclusion something he'd been trying to accomplish for years.

Jake's wife Jasmine was a three-hundred-pounder and ruled the marriage with an oak broomstick that history has it was unbreakable. When something displeased her, which was quite often, she was inclined to pummel Jake, regardless if he had anything to do with the problem or not.

It's important to know that Jake was only five foot tall and weighed under a hundred pounds. His wife was almost petite when they first married, but proceeded to balloon like a grain-fed Holstein the day after the nuptials.

It was not uncommon to see Jasmine pulling Jake around with his head tucked in the crook of her arm, smacking him with that oak stick. She had a devious slant to her, too. She kept the end of her stick sharpened to a point and would follow Jake and poke him whenever she felt the need. Because of her threatening disposition, Jake was especially nervous about bending over in front of her, and was forever looking over his shoulder. It got to be a habit with him and it was difficult talking to him 'cause his head was constantly swiveling trying to keep track of that stick.

We all understood Jake's euphoric behavior as we unloaded our gear and stored 'em in the wagon. We'd spend the night at the landing and head out early the next morning. Carmen was still in a quandary about what her intentions were and needed more time to make a decision.

Jake always kept a trotline set and him and Tubbs jumped in a boat to run it. They came back with enough catfish to feed us all, and Jake got his recipe ready while we cleaned the fish. Jake's cellar was full of canned goods, so we picked out some green beans and Annie made the cornbread with molasses on the side. Over dinner we related our run-in with the two snakes at the cave.

"I know those two," Jake said. "No meaner villains walk the earth. Jasmine run 'em off two weeks ago with a scattergun; caught 'em trying to steal a boat in the middle of the night. The sheriff knows who they are too. He'll be glad they're tied up somewhere."

"What about you ladies?" Jake asked. "Have you decided which way you're going?"

"I don't believe we have much choice but to keep going south," Carmen said. "There's nothing left for us up north, and Frank Jr.'s got to get settled in somewhere. Maybe Frank's brothers can help."

"It's a hard trip," Jake said. "I've got an aunt in Batesville, not too far from here. She owns a boarding house and always needs help. It'd be a place for you to eat and sleep and make a little money. You could contact your in-laws from there and make sure you were making the right decision before you head out."

Carmen and Annie looked at each other and I could tell they were neither happy nor sad. I hated to see such good people be so destitute. All they had was the clothes on their backs and each other. Being so young and not having much experience in the ways of traveling, they had a difficult journey in front of them, if they could make it at all.

"That makes sense to me, Carmen," Annie said. "We can't do anything without some money. Are you sure your aunt will take us in?"

"I'm sure. Why, I just got a letter from her last week asking Jasmine and me to come help. My aunt don't take to the river like I do, and ever since my folks died she thinks she's supposed to watch over me. Hell, I'm thirty-five; I don't need no guardian. I'm a river rat and this is where I'm staying. If you want, I'll take you over there myself. We can leave in the morning. Don't be saying nothing about Jasmine though. If she thinks I'm batching she'll try to make me stay."

"Yes, all right," Carmen said. "It would be a place to start. We can't thank you enough—all of you."

"My pleasure," Jake said.

"Well, it's settled then," I said. "You folks'll have a fresh start if you want, and Junior here can sleep in a soft bed at night."

"Those men would have killed us, we both know that," Carmen said. "How can we repay you?"

"Take Jack with you," Elmer said.

The next morning we loaded up the wagons and hitched up the teams.

"Jake, you tell the sheriff about those men and this woman's husband," I said. "If he needs to talk to us, you know where to send him."

"I'll do it."

We said our goodbyes and watched as they pulled away.

"They forgot Jack," Elmer said.

Chapter Five

When we got back to Dogleg Mother was still rocking on the porch of the Three-Stop Café, right where she was when we left. She'd been watching the store while we were gone.

"You're late," she said.

"We're never late," Jack said. "We're just not here when we thought we'd be."

"You don't make sense, Jack. I don't see no blood, so I'm guessing things went well."

"Well as could be expected," I said.

"Take in any money while I was gone?" Jack asked.

"One dollar. A pan salesman gave it to me to burn the place down."

"I'd better take over then," Jack said. "No one can make cash flow like I can."

"The only thing you produce belongs in a privy," Mother said, standing up from her rocker. "I better be going, I've wasted a week sitting here waiting for no one. This place don't bring in enough money to keep a chicken alive."

"My chickens are alive," Jack said.

"Not anymore. Fox got 'em last night. I made chicken and dumplings; it's sitting on your stove."

Jack's eyes widened and he made a quick run through the store and out the back. Sure enough, he'd been wiped out. He did have a fine fox pelt hanging on the fence though, thanks to Mother's straight shooting. Chickens were easy to come by in Dogleg, but Jack had a peculiar way of getting attached to his hens. The dumplings cheered him up some, as it did us all, not having taken the time to eat that day.

It was late afternoon and we were all tired from the trip. A couple of snorts of Potation and we were ready for bed. The next day was wood-cutting time, storing up enough firewood for the winter. We always cut the wood for Mother too, 'cause she did a lot of cooking in the winter that kept our bellies full.

That was something else I was coming to respect—helping each other out on the day-to-day drudgeries that came with living without conveniences. We could cut and stack enough wood for all of us for the winter in seven days, but if I had to do it alone I'd be cutting all fall.

Elmer and I were the last ones to arrive at the Three-Stop that morning; Jack, Tubbs, and Preacher already had their axes and saws sharpened. We drank coffee and ate some biscuits and bacon and loaded up the wagon and headed to the woods. We were a mile or so from our cabins on an old logging road on the side of a hill. We turned the team around so they'd be pointing up the grade.

Tubbs could cut faster than any two of us, so he felled the trees while Jack and Elmer trimmed them, and Preacher and I cut 'em into suitable lengths. By noon we had enough to fill the wagon.

Tubbs and I held the mules while Jack and Preacher threw in the saws and axes and hopped on top of the logs. Elmer sat up front with us. I didn't see the snake and I don't guess Tubbs did either, but the mules sure did. They reared up and stomped and wrestled so much we could hardly hang on. It didn't do much good to hang on anyway, the tongue breaking from the wagon like it did.

Jack and Preacher had been facing backwards when the tongue broke, so by the time they figured out what was going on they were headed downhill at a good roll. The road had a straight cut for a hundred feet before it veered to the right, and both of 'em were standing up looking for a place to jump. But a wheel hit a rock just as they were ready to leap and jerked left, smacking into a tree.

Jack didn't fly so high through the trees as Preacher did. Jack straddled a six-inch limb and fell to the ground, holding his crotch with white knuckles. But Preacher ended up with a different problem; his flight landed him on a giant hornet's nest. It broke free, Preacher riding it like a saddle, and when they hit all we could hear was buzzing.

Preacher started downhill as fast as he could heading for the river. He was swatting and slapping and yelling, dodging to the left and then to the right. In a short time we heard the splash. We knew it was a rough run, but with Preacher's long legs we felt he'd outdistanced most of his attackers. Come to find out he only had twenty or thirty stings. The bulbous bump between his eyes had come from a rock he'd hit when he dove into the water.

The wagon had a busted wheel so we had to walk back to Dogleg leading the mules. Jack was lying on his back on top one of 'em, the swelling between his thighs constricting his ability to walk.

As soon as we got back Mother mud packed Preachers welts, but she wouldn't get near Jack. He had to suffice with a basin of spring water, from time to time squatting down and settling his fist sized gonads in the deep pan. Mother, affectionately or not, nicknamed him Peaches, and much to Jack's dismay had taken to calling him by that moniker, especially when strangers were around.

Tubbs left a few days after the woodcutting and I wouldn't see him again until the snow fell, but that was just the way he was, coming and going when he felt like it. When he did come back he would have a message for me, one I wished he'd kept to himself. But for the time at hand we began the process of busying ourselves for the winter.

The process of busying ourselves for the winter always involved putting enough shine in storage so we wouldn't have to light the fires in the naked hills. Prohibition and the ratification of the eighteenth amendment was still a long ways off, but the winds of change were already blowing through the country.

The making of spirits was quickly becoming regarded as a detriment to society, more likely than not by the same politicians that were guzzling the grog by the gallons at the end of their business day, of course hiding it so their wives wouldn't see their unscrupulous behavior. Knowing the truth was one thing, seeing it was another.

We were, on the whole, unfettered in our production of enlightening elixir at that time, but we'd heard the rumblings of the hypocrites and wanted no part of their delusion. We tossed the cause around as easily as the jug but could come to no understanding about how the law could control the consumption of a liquid that could be produced in a hole in the side of a hill. We came to the conclusion that in order to make a law, you first had to consider yourself above it, so you could look down on it and pass judgment. But we contented ourselves with the work at hand, letting the trappings of the growing bureaucracy fend for itself.

We were making good progress on Mother's cabin and the weather was holding up for us. The days were cool enough that we could work without wearing down and we'd put in fourteen hours most of the time. By the end of the month she'd have a roof over her head and a good fireplace, and Mother was ready for it too. It was more than a little difficult living with Jack and the rest of us in his small cabin and she was itching to get some privacy. It didn't bother us men much 'cause Mother did most of the cooking and we had more decent meals than we were used to.

All the work didn't stop us from having some fun though. Seems like every day there was something happening to take our minds from the monotony of building, and of course we still had to eat, and the game was slowly making its way back into the area.

One morning we were sitting on the porch waiting for dawn to break when we were startled by the appearance of a coon boldly walking across the road. Coons don't usually have much to do with people, but they do have some to do with chickens and eggs. This one stopped beside the porch and sniffed at us and walked toward the back. It took no time to understand what his intentions were as soon as we heard the racket in Jack's chicken coop. This was particularly upsetting to Jack, as he had just re-established his brood of laying hens due to the unfortunate dispute with the fox. Jack went through the cabin and picked up his shotgun, loading it as he ran. The coon headed for the woods.

"We're going coon hunting tonight," Jack said, coming around the corner of the porch.

We rounded up two redbones and a bluetick and readied ourselves for what is usually an eventful evening of drinking, sitting, running, and listening to the hounds howling. The first thing we did was build a fire, so we could sit around it and tell past stories of heroic coon hunts. We'd set the dogs loose about midnight, for no other reason than because someone, somewhere, had decided that coon hunting had to be done late, otherwise there wouldn't be enough time to get all the stories told.

The dogs knew what their jobs were and were anxious to be let loose. Preacher had been annoying 'em with a coonskin hat he threw in front of them, pulling it back to him with a string attached to the tail. He always wore that hat on a hunt for luck, saying that if the dogs couldn't tree the coon, his hat would attract the varmint like a love potion.

We let the dogs go and followed 'em with our lanterns held high. After a while we could tell they were on the chase because there's no sweeter sound for a coon hunter than to hear his dog howling on the scent. When we caught up to 'em they had the coon treed in front of a sixty-foot bluff; no way for him to get out but through the dogs and us.

Jack wanted to catch the coon alive because he didn't want the dogs tearing up the pelt, so he headed up the tree with a snare and a potato sack. Preacher and I were standing below him with our lanterns so he could see. About the time Jack got close enough, the coon decided there was only one way out. He flung himself off the limb and landed on top of Preacher's cap.

The first mistake Preacher made was dropping the lantern and grabbing the

66

coon, but the coon wasn't leaving and dug his claws in tighter. The lantern broke, covering Dan's boots with fuel, which caught on fire. The dogs were so wound up that they didn't care if it was man or beast they were after and started circling Preacher, nipping at him to get closer to the coon. Dan couldn't see 'cause the coon was riding him backwards and his tail was flopping in his face, but he could make out the fire on his feet and could feel the heat rising at a steady pace.

Preacher started running downhill as fast as his scrawny legs would carry him, his hands pulling and jerking at the dug-in coon, his feet on fire and his pant legs ready to ignite.

We were having a time catching up with him, but we were able to locate him by the glow around his feet and the excited howls of the hounds. The next thing we saw were two balls of fire flying through the air, a good twenty feet off the ground. The slope he was on was too steep, and he could only see a few feet in front of him, with the help of his flaming pants, but he did see a large boulder and jumped as high and far as he could muster.

He landed where he hoped he would, in the limbs of a large tree. But it was the largest Osage orange we'd ever been honored to see. By the time we caught up to him he was howling louder than the redbones. He'd forgot about the coon; it was already down the tree and gone, but the hounds stuck with Dan at the base of the tree while he was flogging his feet and legs. All we could see was smoke rising up through the limbs and could hear the faint sounds of what we thought was a small pup whining.

The thorns of that tree are so long and hard we use 'em to sew up the soles of our shoes. The older the tree the longer the thorn, and sadly, in Preacher's case, the tree he was in looked older than earth.

"You all right, Preacher?" I asked.

"I'm near dead," he whined. "Don't move me. Find my Bible, I'm close to the Lord."

"You're close to the Lord 'cause you're as high in a tree as you've ever been," Jack said. "Now don't move till we figure out how to get you down."

"Move," Preacher grunted. "I can feel my life draining from a halo of thorns."

"That's blood from them coon scratches," I said.

"I'll get as close as I can," Jack said, "and hook him by the boot with this snare and we'll jerk him down."

"We could wait till dawn," Elmer said. "If he's still alive, he can see how to climb down."

"Can you move at all?" I asked.

"I'm stuck like a button," Preacher said.

"Well, at least throw down the hat," Elmer said. "These dogs need some entertainment."

Preacher tossed the hat to the ground, but the hounds didn't pay any attention to it. Then we heard a low growl and figured Preacher was running out of steam.

"Elmer, hold the light up so I can see to climb," I said. "I'll go up and ease him down."

I started up the tree, tenderly touching each handhold not wanting to grab a thorn, when I heard another growl. That one didn't sound human, no matter how hurt Preacher was, but it was so dark I couldn't make out anything but a few wisps of smoke.

"Hand me the lantern," I said

I was on the first limb and Jack hooked the light with his snare and poked it up to me. I took it and raised it above my head, noticing Dan was an arm's length away. I made one more grab upwards and was almost even with him. I held the light on the limb next to him and was taking note of the damage when I heard another growl, this time accompanied by a snort.

The dogs were still on a rampage, jumping and barking and running in circles. I shoved the light above my head and stretched my neck and come face to face with a black bear. Apparently he'd run up the tree when he heard the dogs and it was just bad luck that Dan would land under him.

I let out a yell and fell backwards, dropping the lantern but grabbing Preacher by the boot. I jerked him free and we fell to the ground, landing side by side on our backs. The fall knocked the breath out of me and all I could do was point.

The bear was headed down, either ready to fight or just as confused as the rest of us, but we knew it was time to go.

I got my breath back and pulled Dan up and threw him over my shoulder and headed downhill as quick as I could, Jack and Elmer passing me as I went. The dogs held the bear at bay and we made it back to our fire. I more tossed than laid Preacher down, being so tired I could hardly stand myself. He was a sorry sight. Elmer refused to look at him till Jack cleaned him up.

Preacher's face was streaked with lines of blood from the coon's claws and his boots were mostly charcoal. His pant legs were burned up to his knees hanging in strips, the hair on his legs burnt to a curl. We took his coat and shirt off to inspect the wounds, and he had so many thorn holes in him Jack swears they spelled stupid. We cleaned him up with Potation, Preacher complaining that the healing needed to take place on the inside. He had some bruised ribs and his legs were pink and tender, but he was back to new in a few weeks.

The wild game was as resilient as we were. Those that made it through the fire went on the same as we did, rebuilding their homes and preparing for the coming winter. As the seasons rolled around we had to take advantage of it, and there was no better time to do some squirrel hunting than in October. We always used what we killed, from the meat to the skin, but sometimes the critters made it difficult on us.

It was cool on that particular October morning and we had our fall coats on, sitting on the ground by a tree. Elmer popped a shot at a red in a large hickory and the squirrel upped and jumped in his nest like he'd never been hit. Preacher was best at climbing, his long legs and arms giving him the reach necessary to make decent headway.

Dan was making excellent time, considering the nest was about thirty feet in the air, while the rest of us were sitting on the ground entertained by his more-than-agile tree-scaling skills.

When he finally reached the nest he held fast, caught his breath, and carefully elongated his scrawny neck up and over the edge of the squirrel's house. There's no telling what that poor squirrel thought when he saw Dan's thin face, but whatever he sensed confused the hell out of him 'cause he shot down into the front of Preacher's coat.

Dan started dancing and grabbing and reaching, all the while trying to keep his balance on the limb. We couldn't make out if he was screaming or laughing.

He was doing a jig on the limb, moving east and then west, his arms traveling in and out of his coat, now down the back of his collar and then inside the front. He finally straddled the limb below him and with his legs crossed around it, swung himself upside down, swinging in the air like a possum, but he still couldn't catch old red. He took hold of the limb below him and let his feet go and dropped down the length of his outstretched body, now hanging on with his hands, kicking and yelling and squirming.

The squirrel made an exit out the back of Dan's collar, and be damned if he didn't go right ahead and enter the front of the coat again, Preacher unable to swat him away, his hands holding on to his perch. There was nothing left to do but drop down to the next limb and jitterbug around on it for a while. This time he dropped to his stomach and swung around under the branch, hanging on with both feet and one hand, beating himself with the other.

The squirrel must have gotten tired of the flogging 'cause he hopped out of the front of Dan's coat onto the limb, ran down a few feet and squiggled his way up Preacher's pant leg. We could see from the ground, by the bulge in Dan's pants, that the little varmint was making good time moving up his leg, and Dan needed to stop his forward progress one way or the other.

In all his shuffling and dropping, Dan had come down fifteen feet in the tree. He half swung himself up and let go and smacked face first into the next limb. He laid there, legs hanging below him, butt to head bone flat against the limb, just like his little buddy would have been if he'd had his way.

He'd caught the squirrel with both hands right at mid-thigh, but he was wrapped around the limb in such a fashion that he couldn't get unhinged. We knew the squirrel was gnawing up his thigh pretty good by then, 'cause we could hear Dan's primitive screams.

I jumped up and pulled myself onto the limb, opened my pocketknife and cut off his pant leg just above his hands. I tore it down the backside and Dan was able to throw the creature, wrapped in his pant leg, as far away as his tired body would let him.

Preacher was worn down, what with all the cavorting, balancing, slapping, and fighting. He was hanging on the limb like moss, his legs dangling on one end, one of them bare from his crotch to his foot, blood dripping from his knee to his boot with a splat, so as one could set time by it. His arms were hanging down on the other end and one side of Preacher's face was pressed against the tree branch, pushing his mouth and nose over to the side in a strange and contorted manner. The squirrel had untangled himself from the pant leg and ran back up to his nest, having never been shot in the first place.

We let Dan rest for some time while we sipped on Potation, re-thinking the circumstances. Elmer was disgusted with the whole thing, not able to come to grips with the thought of a full-grown man having had so much punishment inflicted on him by a red squirrel. Preacher, he hadn't moved at all, blood still dripping, with a little saliva stringing down from his crooked-up mouth.

"You gonna be able to walk?" I asked.

"Is he gone yet?"

"Is who gone?" I asked.

"Beelzebub."

"Climb on down from there," I said, helping him off the limb.

We helped him back to Dogleg, Preacher still in a delusional state, muttering the whole way about fallen angels and demonic goblins. We passed Mother in front of the Three-Stop and she just shook her head.

"What got a hold of him?" she asked.

"Red squirrel," Jack said.

"Say no more," Mother said. She went into Jack's cabin to boil some water and gather some bandages.

Brisk, cool mornings and warm afternoons marked the month of October. Some mornings the fog was so thick on the river it'd last till noon before the sun burnt it off.

Daylight came later and sundown came earlier, the shorter days and longer nights reminding us of the changing season. It's a pleasant time in the mountains, though. Mother spent her time making curtains and putting up her fall garden. There didn't seem to be enough hours in the day to finish what we needed, and it was our hope to get my cabin in shape by December. I had two walls left that we could tie to so it wouldn't take as long as Mother's. It was at that time that Elmer got lost and we ran into something that scared us so bad that none of us wanted to go back into the forest at night.

It was on a Sunday morning and we were taking our time getting started. We were entertaining ourselves by looking out across the road.

For no reason at all Elmer grabbed his walking stick, trudged through the brush and walked out of sight. Not a word was spoken on the porch, the three of us still sipping coffee and looking in bewilderment at the brush and trees, and no sign of Elmer. We decided that he'd make his way back soon. After thirty minutes though, there was still no Elmer. He had a inclination to take short walks without telling anybody where he was off to, and sometimes it was necessary to have to hunt him down; he could get lost going to bed.

"Whose turn?" Jack asked.

"I did it yesterday," Preacher said.

"I did it this morning," I said. "Elmer headed out back to the outhouse, walked past it and sat on a rock. I asked him what he thought he was doing."

"'I'm consulting with injuns,' was his sassy answer.

"'Do you see any walls, Elmer?' I asked.

"He looked around and mumbled something about thieves and finally found the privy."

"All right, I'll go," Jack said. "It ain't like I'm gonna miss anything around here."

Jack walked across the road and into the brush and disappeared just like Elmer. Preacher and I continued our enlightening daydreaming and waited for Jack to bring Elmer back. Thirty minutes passed and there was no sign of either one of 'em.

"What'd you think?" Preacher asked.

"Don't know."

"Should we go looking for 'em?"

"Let's wait, there's plenty of daylight left. They couldn't have wandered off too far."

Then Jack came running back. "Can't find him," he yelled. "Can't find a trace; it's like he disappeared."

"A turtle could outpace him," Preacher said.

"Jack, you go back the way you came," I gestured, "and Preacher, you go to the right and I'll go left. We'll make a circle and meet a hundred yards out."

We started off yelling Elmer's name and tramping through the woods. It wasn't surprising that Elmer could get lost or misdirected, as he was just as prone to his feet wandering as his mind was. Half an hour later we met up on the other end, but there was still no Elmer. We were starting to get worried, 'cause we could usually find him in a few minutes.

"Let's make a circle for another hundred yards," I said. "He's got to be around here somewhere."

We started off again in a westerly direction, moving faster than we had before. It was getting on toward noon and the sky was clouding up. Elmer didn't need to be out in the rain. Once before we had to bring him down from his cabin in the middle of January, Mother looking after him for two months, him with the croup and a bad case of pneumonia. We thought we were close to losing him then, but Mother nursed him back to health.

We met again after an hour and came up empty-handed. By then the thunderheads were rolling in and we knew we had to find him fast.

"Let's go back to the Three-Stop and get some gear and supplies," I said. "We might have to spend the night out here."

We doubled back and grabbed our slickers and some matches. Jack picked up his rifle and a coil of rope, while Preacher gathered some leftover cornbread and a lantern, and I stored some dry clothes for Elmer in his own rain jacket. We weren't looking forward to the afternoon; the temperature had already dropped ten degrees since noon, hanging around the mid-forties. It would be a cold, wet night, and even worse was the thought of Elmer, alone and lost, with not even a match to start a fire.

We started out the way he left and hadn't traveled far when the thunder started rumbling. Not far behind it came the rain. It was mid-afternoon and almost as dark as night. Lightning was crashing and the boomers were pounding.

We made poor time, the rain stinging our faces and the ground slippery with wet leaves and mud. We decided to stick together instead of spreading out, not wanting to lose each other. The wind was blowing so hard you could hear the limbs of the trees cracking. Elmer was probably already holed up somewhere. Yelling for him was doing no good 'cause the storm was drowning out everything but itself. All we could do was keep struggling through the woods and hope we'd stumble across him.

Jack was trying to whistle, as he did sometimes when he was nervous, but the rain was falling so steady on his face he could hardly get a note out. Preacher was worried too, I could tell, with his black hair hanging in strings across his face. We had no business out in this storm, but neither did Elmer.

We tramped through the woods until we couldn't see our hands in front of our faces and then gathered ourselves under a small rock overhang, just barely wide enough for all three of us to get out of the wind and the rain. It was a dreary situation and we were all afraid for Elmer. The rain was slowing down by then, but the clouds were still thick; there would be no moonlight that night. The overhang where we stood wasn't big enough to spend the night under, so we decided to move on and try to find something more suitable.

Jack led the way, with me behind him and Preacher in the rear. The slant of the hill was steep and we were holding onto the brush while we walked. Jack had the rifle slung over his shoulder and was holding the lantern in one hand and grabbing whatever he could find with the other.

The lantern was giving off just enough light to see a few feet in front of Jack, but it was not any help to me, his body hiding most of the glare. Preacher was holding on to my rain slicker trying to keep himself in my tracks, and I was holding on to Jack. We finally made it to a semi-level grade and Jack spied an overhang on a small bluff, big enough that all of us could sit down out of the rain.

"Lord, I just don't know," Preacher said. "It don't make any sense, Elmer being lost like this. It's never taken us this long to hunt him down. He's got to be holed up somewhere around here."

"Hell, he's probably asleep in the cabin by now," I said. "He don't usually get off track so much that he has to sleep out in the woods."

"He's probably thinking we're the ones lost," Jack said.

"I don't believe it'll do any good to keep looking tonight," I said. "We can't see five feet in front of us with that light, and this wet weather isn't helping either. If I know Elmer he's got enough wits about him to find shelter."

"I'll drag up some wood and build a fire," Preacher said.

Jack and I pulled some rocks under the ledge to make a ring for the fire and a decent-size limb to sit on. The rain was a drizzle then and the wind was just enough to feel. We were cold and wet, but the fire Preacher had started was warming us up. We tried to set close to it in hopes of drying our clothes, but the wet wood was smoking so much it kept us back. We ate the cornbread and silently wondered about the condition of Elmer.

"I see no benefit in staying out here all night," Jack said.

"I agree with Jack," Preacher said. "We might as well sit here for a spell and if he don't show up, let's head back and get an early start in the morning."

"You're right," I said. "It won't do any good to make ourselves sick and not be able to carry on tomorrow."

Then we heard a noise above and behind us on the hill. It sounded like something moving around, something big.

"Elmer, is that you?" Jack said.

It was quiet and still, just the sound of the crackling fire and the rain falling through the trees. Then we heard it again, just the rustling of wet leaves. We knew it was bigger than a possum or a coon; we could tell that from the noise.

Preacher took the lantern and stepped out from the overhang and tried to look in back of us, but couldn't make out anything. As he stepped back into the shelter a small rock rolled down the hill and passed over where he'd been standing.

"Come on now," Dan yelled. "Who's up there?"

The rustling came again, this time moving across from one side to the other. Jack shoved a shell into the rifle.

"Might be a bobcat," Preacher whispered.

"No," I said. "A bobcat wouldn't come this close to humans or a fire. Neither would any animal that I know of."

Then we heard limbs cracking and breaking, not small limbs or sticks lying on the ground, like something or somebody was walking on them, but good-sized branches, like someone was tearing them off the trees.

"Must be a bear," Jack said.

"That's no bear," I said. "You ever heard of a bear breaking trees down except when he's hiding in one of 'em?"

"Well, it ain't Elmer either," Preacher, said. "He can barely tear the page off a catalog."

The breaking of limbs stopped and all was silent again. I was listening hard for more noises, but it seemed all I could hear was the thumping of my heart. Whatever was out there wasn't interested in us being where we were. It would make no sense to try and run for it, it was too dark and the hillside we had just come from was too steep to travel in a hurry. Besides, whatever it was was stronger than us, and we couldn't shoot something we couldn't see. I noticed Jack was shivering and I was sure it wasn't because he was cold. Dan had hunkered down beside Jack and I behind the fire.

"Let's meet it head on," Jack said, holding his rifle in his lap. "I can't sit here all night listening to this."

"You can't shoot something you can't see," I said. "Besides, this is the safest place there is, at least it can't come in from behind us."

"I'm gonna fire into the air," Jack said. "Just to let him know we've got a gun."

"How many bullets you got?" I asked.

"Eight or ten."

"It's worth a try," Preacher said.

Jack stepped out in front of the fire and pointed the rifle into the air and pulled the trigger.

"Whoever you are," he shouted, "we've got firepower and we're not afraid to use it."

Not a sound was heard, only the hissing and popping of the fire. I wished the fire wasn't even there so I could listen better, but then again I didn't want to be sitting in the dark with only a lantern for light.

Then we heard the rustling of steps again, if you could call them steps, more like dragging through the leaves and brush, and it was closing in, just above us on the ledge, and then it stopped. We were dead still, not even breathing that I could tell. Then a low guttural sound came from above us; so soft we couldn't be sure it was even a sound we knew; it was a long, slow, moaning, and heavy with dread. It kept coming, more intense, the pitch getting higher, yet still muffled with deep hollowness. It didn't stop coming. We pressed ourselves against the bank with our backs and could do nothing but listen to the sound overcome everything around us.

Then it got harsher, more extreme, yet still rough and throaty, and we could tell it was turning into a grating wail. On and on it came with no relief. Then the braying was lifting higher, turning into a screeching, ear-splitting scream. We covered our ears with our hands but we couldn't muffle the shrill cry. Louder and louder it blared until it became a deafening shriek, going on and on, controlling the forest and us and never stopping. We were bent double trying to find escape from the high-pitched wailing, stumbling over each other, unable to open our eyes for fear of what we might see.

Then we heard a loud thud and opened our eyes—it was in front of us, in front of the fire, still screeching, its back to us, running down the hill, still howling—and then it was gone. Once again all we could hear was the hissing of the fire and an occasional pop of an ember. We stared in disbelief at the darkness in front of us, not moving, afraid to move; afraid the piercing scream might return.

It had landed several feet in front of our small dying fire, and we were so frightened and so intent on covering our ears that it was impossible to register in our minds what exactly had taken place.

Not one of us could describe the apparition; only that it was upright and large. We were so tormented by the howling that the ability to focus on anything else was lost. We stood in back of the dim firelight, shoulder to shoulder, looking into the darkness, not even able to make out the trees a few feet in front of us.

We listened to the silence. The rain had stopped, and the soft breeze that a few minutes ago toyed with our fire's low flames had now slowed to an unnerving calmness.

"Somebody say something," Jack whispered.

"Shhh, be quiet," Preacher murmured.

Then all three of us let out the air we'd caught and held in our lungs.

"I think it's time to leave," I said.

"I agree," Preacher said. "Let's get the hell as far away from here as we can."

We lit the lantern and began backtracking, Jack carrying his rifle instead of shouldering it. We didn't talk as we walked, still listening for any unnatural sounds. I was the last in line and couldn't help myself from looking over my shoulder, even though I couldn't see in the darkness, making sure no one was following, always feeling someone there.

We'd gone deeper into the woods than we'd realized and it took several hours to reach the Three-Stop. By then it was midnight and all was quiet in Dogleg, the only surprising thing being the light in Jack's cabin, as he hadn't lit one before leaving. We trudged up to the porch and entered the front of the store.

There sat Mother, rocking gently to and fro, while Elmer sat peacefully sleeping in a chair beside her, his chin on his chest, hands folded across his belly, the fire in the stove sending a quiet amber glow across the two of 'em.

Mother seemed shocked at our appearance and quit rocking.

"You men look like you've seen a ghost," she said. "There's coffee on the stove; looks like you might need some." She pushed herself out of the rocker and poured us all a cup.

"Just where have you men been, anyway? Elmer and I been waiting all night."

"We been looking for Elmer," Jack said.

"I figured as much," she said. "I found him wandering among my mules. I went to round 'em up before the storm hit and there he was, pointing his stick at 'em and talking like they was listening. You look shook up—tell me what happened."

As we told our story Mother rocked and sipped on her coffee; we mixed ours with Potation. She didn't seem surprised at our adventure. When we finished, she filled her cup once more and took a small sip of Potation herself.

"There's a story behind what you've been through tonight," Mother said. "I've never seen or heard the same thing you have, but I have been told the essentials. It's been a part of the mountains since the Civil War, and no one that I know of can tell me the truth of it, if there is any to be told. You've come as close to it as anyone I guess, and you can make up your own minds and get out of it what you will.

"His name was John Lee Dunrite, and he was a farmer in these mountains, exactly where I'm not sure, but he was also a Union sympathizer. It's been said he helped runaway slaves get up North. Some say it was William Quantrill himself, and others say it was Bloody Bill Anderson, and others just say it was Confederate renegades, but I guess it don't matter one way or the other. It was late eighteen sixty-three or early sixty-four when it all took place.

"Seems John Dunrite was caught unaware one day and the renegades tied him to a tree and burned his house and barn and killed all his livestock. But that wasn't the worst of it. They raped his wife and two daughters in front of him, while he was tied to the tree, and then killed 'em. His one young son, not yet old enough to join the fighting, was hung by the neck and burned from a limb of the very tree Dunrite was strapped to. They didn't kill John Lee Dunrite; they left him like he was, screaming to be shot himself, them laughing as they rode off.

"Some say they could hear his screams for miles and others say he's still screaming. When neighbors saw the smoke from the burning house they came to help, but there was no sign of John Dunrite; the ropes still hanging around the base of the tree.

"No one ever knew what became of him, but they say he's still out there, walking the mountains, screaming for the lives of his family. There's been tales of him as far east as Illinois and as far west as Oklahoma. He walks the wide berth of these mountains searching for his wife and kids, and the pain he witnessed is found in the agony of his screams. He's called the Ozark Mountain Howler, and some say he'll never die, and others say if he is dead, his soul will never leave this earth, and his screams will go on forever.

"I don't know what you men ran into out there, but I'd say it's better left alone, and you might find yourselves lucky if you never run across it again.

"I'm tired now, waiting half the night for you rogues. Preacher, you walk me home; I've half scared myself with my own story."

Chapter Six

"You getting hungry?" Claude asked Pete. By then he'd caught two more cats and didn't need any more.

"I could eat something," Pete said.

"Drag them hot coals between those two flat rocks," Claude said. "I'll clean these fish."

"I still don't understand how you got by without any money," Pete said.

"It wasn't like it is today," Claude said. "We owned the land we were sitting on and there weren't any taxes—all we had to do was feed ourselves and buy a few necessities. It wasn't like we didn't have any money—Jack was making some with the store and Mother was selling mules, and I had more work than I wanted, building foundations and fireplaces. Preacher made a little with his shine and we all raised and sold livestock. We didn't live like folks today; it was a lot simpler. There were no utilities to pay, no televisions to buy, and no gas stations to stop at, nor any of the other amenities that people think they have to have now."

Pete knew it was true. He was rarely home and had little time to himself, or for his friends. It was one of the reasons he'd lost his girlfriend. Even though he was seldom home, the mailbox was full of bills. He spent his time working so he could pay money to people he didn't know, had never met, had never even spoken to. Pete made sure Claude wasn't looking, and slipped off his watch and put it in his pocket.

Claude put some grease in the pan, and while it melted he sprinkled the cleaned fish with cornmeal. When the grease was hot he laid the slabs in the pan.

"The mountains provided just about everything we needed. We had more game than we could eat and of course we raised hogs and chickens and cattle. We worked hard at our gardens and put up the produce in root cellars. We lacked for very little."

"Didn't you ever want more?" Pete asked.

Claude took his eyes from the frying pan and looked at Pete. "More what?" Then he laughed. "We didn't know what we didn't have. It mattered very little; the mountains gave us what we needed."

"So you fished and hunted for food," Pete said.

"We did do that, but sometimes it was difficult with Jack and Preacher. They were always thinking up new ways to do things and most of the time it just got 'em in trouble."

That November Preacher came up with an idea that was supposed to have the deer eating out of his pocket, but it didn't turn out that way.

We started out an hour before daylight. The morning was cold; a hard freeze had taking its hold leaving a thin white glaze on the grass and low-lying brush. It would give the final blow to what life was left in the plants. We could hear the heavy crunch of our steps as we walked through the woods toward our destination, Jack in front so the swinging brush wouldn't hit him in the face, his height making it a disadvantage to follow from the rear. As we were getting close to the area where Jack and Preacher would plant themselves, daylight was stretching through the naked trees, the woods still gray with the early morning light.

Preacher had brought along the parts of his somewhat peculiar outfit and we began tying it to him. He'd been working on this idea for the past month in secret, telling us that when he was done a deer wouldn't be able to tell him from a tree. He'd cut limbs from an oak, the dead leaves still stuck to 'em. By the time we'd tied all the limbs to him he looked more like a walking brush pile than a tree, but there was no way to convince him of that. The biggest limbs were tied to his legs starting at the ankles and reaching up over his head, his arms poking through the dead limbs. Then we tied small limbs and leaves to his chest and back; on his hat he had a round halo made of twigs.

The branches tied to his legs were making him walk stiff-legged and he'd mistakenly believed that he'd be able to sit down and wait on an unsuspecting deer to nibble at his bark. No doubt he'd been under the influence of some vile concoction, his thoughts muddled by the throes of grog-heightened enlightenment. Unable to sit, he had to make do by standing upright against a tree, and he was having trouble sneezing 'cause the leaves around his face were tickling his nose.

Jack headed east about a hundred yards while I took off down the hillside and up the other, giving me a good vantage spot to keep an eye on both partners.

The sun was just starting up over the hill, hitting the frozen ground and shining through the ice-covered weeds and brush. It was time to be quiet and wait and listen. The deer would be stirring for their morning meal after being curled up in the cold weather.

I could make out Jack from where I sat, and Preacher was blending in with the surroundings quite well. After a while the forest came back to life, the sounds of our tramping and noise-making gone, and it wasn't but a short time later that I spotted a buck heading in Preacher's direction, fifty yards to his right.

I glanced over to Jack's side to see if he was watching, but not surprising to me, he was fast asleep, sitting on a low limb. Then I heard a commotion coming from Dan's direction.

I saw a six-foot-tall brush pile clambering down the side of the mountain out of control. Now that I had my bearings, I could keep a good eye on what was happening, but at that point I couldn't comprehend what was making Preacher scatter like he was. The buck took off heading east toward Jack. I kept my eyes on the stumbling brush pile, it jerking one limb in front of the other, wavering from side to side, picking up momentum as it headed toward a steeper incline. Then I noticed the reason for Dan's excited departure; a skunk was on his heels, like he was following his mother.

The skunk had taken Dan for a good hiding spot and plopped down in between his legs. Dan tried to keep as calm as he could, but the pressure got to him, forcing him to try a daring getaway. But the skunk wasn't giving up and kept nose to heel on Dan's boots, not that Dan was paying any attention to what was going on behind him, 'cause he was picking up speed at an alarming rate.

I made another quick glance toward Jack and saw the buck standing under his tree, watching the brush pile pitching downhill. Jack, of course, was still asleep, his chin resting on his chest. By now Preacher was totally out of control and the skunk wasn't giving up either. A couple of more jerky strides and Dan would be at a small ledge, one that I had crossed earlier, having to set my rifle down and lower myself the five feet to solid ground. Dan had to be entertaining some means of escape from his ill-fated route, but I'm sure whatever he was thinking was merely wishful.

The speed at which his getaway and downhill plunge had propelled him was a huge disadvantage at that point, something I'm sure he was wide-eyed aware of. He hit the top of the ledge and it flipped him up and over, flopping like a card in the wind. When he hit bottom he had so much momentum built up he just kept tumbling, like a stick on a staircase; he was flopping on his front and then on his back, his shrieks muffled only on the face flop.

The screams of terror coming from the flying brush pile woke up Jack long enough for him to accidentally pull the trigger on his rifle and hit the buck square on top of the head, dropping him dead in his tracks. But the shot jerked Jack backwards so that he lost his balance and fell off his perch, landing on top of the dead deer.

I headed toward Preacher to see if he was hurt, but when I got close enough I saw that the skunk was digging into his limbs and leaves trying to identify what he'd been chasing. As bad luck would have it he was digging in between Dan's legs and when he hit the money jar Dan let out a yell and squeezed his legs together, trying to stop the skunk's claws from making any further withdrawals. Not much more needs to be said about that. Since Preacher had yelled, I knew he was still alive and my nose told me I should check on Jack.

By the time Jack and I got the deer dressed out Preacher had untied his trappings and was headed back to Dogleg. We let him get quite a distance in front of us, Jack and I having to go to a lot of trouble just keeping downwind of him. When we reached the Three-Stop we could see the smoke coming from out back of the cabin; it was Preacher burning his clothes.

November comes with signs of winter riding its tail. Cold mornings mark the dawn, and the frost and freezing air in the early light remind us of the gray days ahead. As the sun lifts above the mountains you can see the fog lifting off the river, hovering like a blanket, the water moving beneath it lapping at the banks, an occasional fish, invisible, arching out of the cold water and slapping back to his wandering home. The sight of the heavy, white air makes me believe there is a heaven on earth, and if there are angels they must live in that beckoning mist.

We'd finished Mother's cabin and she was staying in it and we'd started on mine. It was good working weather and we were making good progress. My fireplace was still intact and I'd been staying there as we worked, but I still walked to the Three-Stop for coffee in the mornings. If we weren't at the river we'd build a bonfire at Jack's and sit around and tell stories.

One night we cooked the haunch of Jack's deer, the story of his daring hunt to be told later that evening after the jug loosened his tongue.

The bonfire, some thirty feet around and piled as high as Jack's cabin, would burn all night, and those that stayed would sit in the warmth of its light until all was silent except the cracks and whistles of the dying coals.

The best time was late at night after we'd finished eating and the fire was burnt down to glowing embers, just listening to tall tales and sometimes listening to nothing but the fire.

Elmer was usually dozing, but on that night, in between naps, he was telling stories about the war and I knew those memories didn't come easy.

"I seen those men at Andersonville," he said. "They wasn't men at all, they was just walking bones. We didn't have anything to eat ourselves so we couldn't feed 'em, but it was a sorry sight. A man's eyes ought not to have to vision such meanness, much less have to live in it. I was sorry for those men, but weren't nothin' I could do, by that time the war was all but over. We had nothing left to fight with, no food, no clothes, and no shoes. I seen men marching barefooted through mud and stones and briars, with maybe a rag tied around their foot just to keep the blood from spilling."

"How you'd happen to make it here, Elmer?" Preacher asked.

"Wasn't nothing left of Georgia—not after Sherman. My ma, she had a sister in Arkansas and I moved here with her. I lost my pa and two brothers in that war, all for naught. What good we had was taken from us and my ma never could get it out of her head. She died not more than half a year after we moved."

Elmer stared at the fire, no doubt remembering those times and his losses. Everyone had lost in the war, North and South, some just not close enough to it to feel the pain that Elmer felt. He leaned back down on his blanket, eyes still fixed on the fire, and before long was asleep again.

The jug made another pass, Mother taking a sip that time. Jack was stoking the fire and Preacher was pulling in his outstretched legs, the heat too close to his feet.

"You boys are about as entertaining as boiled chicken," Mother said. "I think I'll go to bed."

"Speaking of boiled chicken," Preacher said. "Did I ever tell you about the time I was almost tarred and feathered?"

Jack snorted, "How'd they miss?"

"I was passing through Lawrence, Kansas, minding my own business (another snort from Jack), when I was accosted by a group of hooligans. I had been misidentified as the tall, thin, traveling salesman pandering the latest Paris fashions—women's silk undergarments. The gentleman in question had rented a ground-floor room at a local hostelry, hanging a sign out front explaining his wares. By chance I was staying at the same inn, only two doors down.

"I was making my way back to my room one evening, coming down the alley after having dinner with a small congregation of Christian Chinese launderers. As might be expected, with my overly vibrant senses, I noticed a small hole in the back of the building with a light shining through it. Unbeknownst to me, the hole belonged to the gentleman salesman. My curiosity was aroused and as any inquisitive person might do, I took a peek. Well, much to my horror, I saw several young ladies in different stages of undress, trying on the silky undergarments, pulling them over their smooth, milky white— "

Mother smacked him on the side of the head with a quick slap, snapping Preacher's glazed eyes back to normal.

"Pardon me," he said, shaking his head. "As I was saying, the ladies were trying on the silky undergarments, and I at once diverted my eye and was taken aback by what I'd just witnessed. Of course, never one to shy from adversity and knowing full well that I might have to confess to the town's constabulary about the villainous actions of the panderer, I quickly took another look with my other eye, only on the pretense that I might have to verify what I'd already seen. I made my way around the building and was walking up to the front door when I noticed a disagreeable gang of mischief-makers. Come to find out they were all husbands and they'd set a trap for the unsuspecting peddler.

"'That's him,' one of 'em shouted, taking me by surprise.

"'Gentlemen,' I said. "'May I be of service?'

"'You certainly may, you scoundrel,' the answer came back.

"'You men have made a mistake,' I said. 'I'm a man of the cloth.'

"'We know what you are,' one of them shouted. 'We see them coon eyes.'

"Well, the trap had been sprung. The louts had put charcoal around the hole in the wall, and unable to see in the dark, I'd come around the corner looking like a six-foot raccoon. I backpedaled as fast as my long legs would accommodate me. The original huckster, having heard the commotion, escaped through the back entrance, leaving me in a most precarious circumstance. I could see by the look in my assailants' eyes that a quick prayer meeting was out of the question, and when I heard the words tar and feather, I knew that running like a rabbit was my only future. Fortunately for me, my choice of routes would verify my innocence.

"I turned and ran back around the corner of the building and at once stumbled over the escaping vendor, who, confused by the turmoil, had chosen the wrong avenue to freedom. Knowing who he was by previous meetings in the hostel, I immediately identified him as the villain. My attackers, not yet convinced, needed more evidence, which the poor wretch beside me unknowingly provided.

"As we were taken back into the light of the inn, it was easily perceived whom the real offender was. Unable to pass by his peephole, the miscreant had stopped to take another look, thereby blacking the outer perimeter of his right eye. I was able, quickly I might add, to explain my own condition by testifying that I was an agent of the sheriffs' office, sent to gather evidence against the lawbreaker. By that time several of the lovely young women had come forth and identified the young man as the culprit. As the crowd was mulling over the situation, I snuck back to my room, gathered my things, and caught the first ride I could procure out of town."

It was midnight by then and Mother had had enough. She said her goodbyes and wandered off to bed, shaking her head until out of sight. The rest of us did the same.

The next morning we were sitting inside the Three-Stop Café, drinking coffee as usual, looking through the front windows at the light gray dawn. Elmer was still asleep, having more and more trouble getting up in the morning, so it was just Jack, Preacher and I. We were nibbling on some leftover deer from the night before and taking our time about it too, not wanting to get in any hurry, the day coming as quick as we anticipated anyway.

Jack was sweeping up the floor as he usually did every other day, whether it needed it or not, most of the time looking like he never hit it with a broom half the time anyway. Preacher was kicked back in a chair, the front feet clearing the floor by six inches, trying to balance himself on the back legs, a coffee cup in one hand and a piece of haunch in the other. I was keeping preoccupied with wondering whether Dan was gonna fall over backwards or not, and Jack had decided the floor couldn't get any cleaner, so he pitched the broom toward the far corner, the dirt he'd swept up still laying by the back door. It didn't matter all that much, most of the dirt fell through the cracks in the floor anyway.

All of us heard the footsteps at the same time; none of us thinking it was Elmer because they were heavier than his. It was unusual that anyone would be coming up those steps this early in the morning, not unless there was trouble. Then came the knock on the door, and without waiting to be answered the door opened, and in walked the shortest, roundest trapper we'd ever seen. He looked about four foot six. He had on tanned buckskins from head to toe—if he'd had antlers we'd a shot him.

The only thing that wasn't deerskin was his coonskin hat, and of course it had a tail on it. His face was round and tan with a little dirt mixed in, and his clear brown eyes showed bright as he stood in the doorway and scanned the room. He had a dark brown beard with lines of gray hanging down to the top of his rounded belly. His arms hung down at his sides with small hands and stubby fingers extending from the dirty sleeves. I couldn't help believing I'd run into him somewhere.

"I'm lookin' for Jack Stepp," he said.

Jack was still hanging in the back corner where the light was dim, and made no move to come out.

"Who's asking?" Preacher spoke up.

The man just looked around. He took off his coonskin hat and showed a dark-tanned bald head with some long grayish-brown hair hanging around the back of his head from ear to ear. He was the spitting image of Jack. Dan and I turned our heads and looked at each other in astonishment and then did a double-take on the gent. Sure enough, it was Jack Stepp, just in another outfit.

"Is that you, Cliff?" Jack asked.

"It's me, Jack."

"Cliff!"

"Jack!"

And then them two run together right in front of Preacher and I, hugging the best they could, not being able to grab all the way around on account of their bulging bellies, and jumped up and down like kids.

After they calmed down and the introductions were over, Cliff and Jack pulled up chairs by the stove and with a cup of coffee in hand began catching up on old times.

"How long's it been?" Jack asked.

"Ten year or more," Cliff said.

"Where you been?"

"Up North on the Black."

"What brings you down here?"

"Too many people. It don't matter no how, place was trapped out. It's that damned railroad that's ruinin' it all, takin' people where they ought not to go."

"So what are you gonna do now?" Jack asked.

"Don't know yet. Thought I'd sit with you a spell and trudge back up North, maybe Canada. I'm not worth a damn around a town, you know that. I always wondered what become of you and I see you haven't wandered far. What kept you here?"

"Had no reason to move on. After the wife died I saw no reason to take another, and I had no bent to live in the city, much like you, so I pulled down and stuck."

"How's the trappin'?"

"There's trapping but it's slim. It's hard to make a living at it. The trade ain't what it used to be."

"There's not much use for it anymore, is there? My kind of life is dwindlin', but it's all I know. I s'pose I'll stick with it; a man's got to do what he knows and

I'm too old to change."

"How about some breakfast, Cliff? I've got bacon and eggs."

"Had some jerky at daybreak, but it's been a while since I've eat fresh hog."

Jack stoked the cook stove and divvied out the remaining coffee and started another pot.

"I best be gettin' my horse and possibles," Cliff said. "I left 'em up the hill, not knowing who I'd run into."

"Need any help?" I asked.

"Nope," he said. Cliff opened the front door and stood on the steps and put two fingers in his mouth and let out a whistle. In less than a minute here came his horse with a pack mule keeping up a few paces behind, tied to the saddle horn. They trotted up to the front of the Three-Stop and stood quiet like they'd been there all night. Cliff had a Remington repeater in his scabbard, a bedroll behind his saddle, and his saddlebags were stuffed full to busting. The mule was packed with two large bags on both sides, stuffed full of supplies I guessed, and a gutted doe lying across its back. Cliff came back inside and sat back down at the stove.

"You got somewhere that I can graze my horse and mule, Jack? I been pushing 'em hard. I need to skin that doe too. She walked up on me early this mornin'. They ain't as skittish as they are up North; must be the people."

"Out back," Jack said, not lifting his eyes from the frying bacon.

"I won't be long." Cliff stepped out the door and led the animals around the cabin.

"I didn't know you had a brother," Preacher said.

"He's two years older than me. We were living in western Kansas when we were kids, up around Dodge City. We moved to Missouri when I was ten, but Cliff, he always took a different path. He was always different, at times being gone for days, even back then when we were young. The morning we left, Cliff was nowhere to be found. What clothes he had were gone, along with his rifle, and my pa knew right then he wasn't coming with us, so we left without him. He knew where we were headed and Pa said if he wanted to find us he would. Three or four years later he caught up to us over in the Boot heel and stayed long enough to see our mother die of consumption, and then was gone again up North somewhere. That was the last time I saw him until today."

"I wonder how he located you?" I asked.

"No telling. Cliff can track a fish in water."

It wasn't long before Cliff came back inside and Jack spooned him out some bacon and eggs. He ate 'em in silence, wiping his mouth on his sleeve when he was done, and then, leaning back in his chair, patted his belly and let out a boisterous belch.

"Mighty fine, mighty fine indeed," he said. "I ain't had a bath in a fortnight, Jack. I seen that tub out back and was thinking I might not be blendin' all that well."

"I'll heat some water. There's soap on the step. I'll lay out some clothes; it won't do no good to put them greasy buckskins back on."

"I could use a haircut and a shave, too," Cliff said.

"I know just the person. Claude, run up to Mother's and tell her what we've got; looks to me like it'll take all her skills."

It took till noon to get Cliff cleaned up and when it was over, them two standing side by side, you could hardly tell which was which. Cliff's face had a few more hard lines in it than Jack's, but otherwise they were cut from the same cloth. There was one difference though—Cliff had a scar running from his left earlobe along the curve of his jaw to his chin, and then it went north, straight up to the corner of his mouth. It was healed, but just recently, and was still pink with color.

"You didn't have that scar the last time I saw you," Jack said.

"I was up on the Muddy, running with a another trapper named Big Jim Coltrain. I was havin' better luck than he and come spring we was headed to Saint Louie to sell our skins. One night he decides to take my pelts for his own and it didn't set with me. He caught me in my sleep ready to cut my throat, but I jerked awake just as he made the slice."

"That can't be the end of the story," Preacher said.

"I s'pose it is," he said. "He's dead and I ain't."

We were sitting in the sunlight now on the steps of the Three-Stop, Cliff and Jack on the bottom step and Preacher and I on the top. Mother had already gone back home, wanting to take the buckskins with her, but Cliff not letting her, saying that when he left he wanted to smell like the rest of the mountains.

Preacher and I wandered away to let the two brothers have some time by themselves.

"Boys, there's something that bothers me about Cliff," Mother said.

We were sitting at her table in the kitchen eating a slice of rhubarb pie. She'd invited us over after she'd finished cutting Cliff's hair, having taken me aside whispering her wishes.

"The bell don't ring true," she went on. "True as truth he looks close enough to be Jack's twin, and I'm not doubting he's his brother, but brothers can be different, and something tells me the sun ain't setting on Cliff's head at the same time it's going down on Jack's. Now, this business about him killing that man up on the Muddy, could be it happened and could be it didn't, and could be it didn't happen the way he says. I say he's a varmint and he's here for no good."

"But, Mother," I said, "he didn't bring any harm with him that I can tell. He seemed as happy as a kid at Christmas to me, him and Jack dancing all around when they first seen each other."

"I've got to agree with Claude," Preacher said, chewing on his last bite of pie. "I've seen nothing in Jack that would lead me to believe he's not glad to see his brother."

"That may be what you see, but I see different," Mother said. "Next time you see Jack take a close look and make note of his somber attitude; he ain't as chipper as yesterday's Jack."

Preacher and I didn't quite know what to think, but one thing was certain. Mother very seldom missed her mark, and she was one hell of a judge of character and when she felt something was wrong, it usually turned out that way.

"What do you want to do about it?" I asked.

"We'll let it lay a day or two, but keep your eyes open. That Cliff, he'll cross over the line one way or the other."

"You think he's after something then," Preacher said.

"It don't make sense to me," Mother said. "He shows up out of nowhere after ten years carrying pelts that should have been sold along the way. There's plenty of places between here and up North to get rid of hides, both of you know that, so why's he still holding 'em? That's what I want to know. That scar's he's totin's not so old and them pelts ain't either. Something tells me he comes by 'em dishonest and he's looking for a safe place to drop 'em. More pie?"

"One more piece and then I'll take one home," Preacher said. "I don't want to spoil my dinner."

That night we were sitting at Jack's place pulling on the jug listening to tall tales of Cliff's travels. Jack appeared to be somewhat distracted, not joining in the conversation as much as the rest of us, making me wonder if Mother's bucket of suspicions might be holding water. At one point Preacher got up and headed towards the back door.

"Where you off to?" Cliff asked.

"My cup runneth over," Dan said.

"Fairly small cup if you ask me," Cliff came back with a snicker.

"You take a good-sized interest in other people's activities, don't you, Cliff?" Jack said, without a smile.

"Just havin' fun, brother."

Things were getting tense from where I was sitting and it was making me uncomfortable. It was getting late anyway so I decided to head out. I said my goodbyes and took my leave out the front of the Three-Stop. I barely made it past the corner of the cabin when I heard a noise in the bush.

"Psst, over here." It was Preacher.

"What's going on?" I asked.

"Shhh. Keep quiet."

"What's all the fuss?" I whispered back.

"I took a look inside them mule packs when I was out back," he said. "There's knives, pistols, gold chains, gold coins, a wad of greenbacks, watches, women's rings, and necklaces. You name it, he's got it."

"What'd you make of it?"

"Well, his name ain't Sears or Roebuck, so he must be a thief."

"God a mighty," I said. "What'll we tell Jack?"

"Why, we'll tell him Cliff's a thief, that's what. You saw Jack in there tonight; he's not acting himself, so he must know something he ain't told."

"I took note all right," I said. "But you just can't walk up to him and say you're brother's a thief."

"Why not? It's the best thing for him."

"I don't know," I said.

"I'll tell you what I think," Preacher whispered. "I think Mother's right; he come down here to find Jack for some reason, but it wasn't out of brotherly love. He's looking for something, or he's running from something. My guess is he's running from the law and he's been looking for Jack because he needs a hiding place."

"We've got to figure out a way to make Jack see the truth," I said. "Just telling him won't do. Jack'll just confront him and Cliff'll just lie, and that won't do any good."

"You got any tender?" Preacher asked.

"I got ten greenbacks, why?"

"Give it to me; I've got ten. I'll go back inside and sit down beside Cliff, making sure he sees it hanging out of my pocket. He'll think I'm just drunk and being careless. I'll get up to leave and drop it on the floor. You sneak back up on the porch and peek through the window; I guarantee ol' Cliff will pick it up and put it in his pocket."

"That won't prove nothing," I said. "Soon as we confront him he'll just say he was waiting until you were sober to give it back."

Preacher pondered on that for a second, as did I, both of us trying to think of a way to snag Cliff.

"Okay," Dan said. "I'll drop it on the floor beside Cliff and then say goodnight and walk out the front door. When he picks it up and pockets it, you wave to me out front here and I'll go back inside and ask if anyone has seen my money. You take note of where he hides it so we can go right to the spot."

"It's worth a try. I sure do hate it for Jack, though."

"You'll hate it worse if he robs all of us, including his own brother, which in my mind he won't have a problem with."

"Go on then. I'll keep watch."

Preacher sidestepped me and headed for the front door.

"Hey," I said in a loud whisper. "You went out the back; you better not go in the front."

"Oh, yeah. All this detective work has turned my head. I was just now thinking I might have chosen the wrong vocation."

"What you chose was the wrong door."

Dan walked around to the back and I snuck up on the porch and squatted down in front of the window, my eyes just over the sill. Jack and Cliff were still sitting by the fire; Jack on one side of the stove and Cliff on the other. Cliff was doing most of the talking, Jack just leaning back in his chair, listening.

Then in came Preacher, acting like he was drunk, which he wasn't, the greenbacks sticking out of his right pocket. This got me to thinking that if he went out sober and came back soused it might get Cliff to wondering. I made a quick note to let Preacher know he needed more work on his investigating skills. Jack noticed right off that Dan was acting strange. I could tell because he wasn't taking his eye off of him. He knew Preacher well enough to know he wasn't drunk, but Jack never said a word.

Preacher walked right in front of Cliff, but it was his left side he was showing and not his right. He must have realized Cliff couldn't have seen the flopping bills, so he turned around in front of him, his hip directly in line with Cliff's eyes. Then he took two steps backwards and sat down, missing the chair and landing on the floor.

Cliff popped out of his chair and bent down to help Preacher up, swiping the greenbacks out of his pocket as slick as a snail's trail. He shoved them up his left sleeve with his right hand, all the time pretending to help Dan. It happened so fast I barely saw it myself, and Dan didn't see or feel anything. He was sitting in his chair squirming, feeling his right side for the bills, a worried look on his face, not knowing where he'd lost the money since it wasn't lying on the floor. I guess he figured it must have dropped out of his pocket on the way in, 'cause then he stood up and said he had to go back outside again. This brought a frown to Cliff's face but a smile to Jack's.

"You don't have to go back outside, Preacher," Jack said. "I know what you're doing."

"What'd you mean?" Preacher asked.

"I saw those greenbacks in your pocket and I saw Cliff steal 'em."

"What?" Cliff said. "I didn't steal nothin'."

"Cliff, you're the biggest thief this side of the East Coast and you know it. I haven't looked because I already knew; if those saddle bags ain't full of stolen goods then my name ain't Jack Stepp."

"I'm nothin' of the kind," Cliff said, trying to act indignant.

"Them bills are up your left sleeve, Cliff."

Cliff stood up and made a threatening move toward Jack.

"Hold on," Preacher said, stepping in between them. "Jack's right and you know it and so do I."

I walked through the front door just then. "I saw it all from the front window."

"You men are poor trackers," he said. "I've done nothin' wrong."

"You might as well fess up, Cliff. We know what you've done," Jack said. "I'm not a big enough fool to let you slide like I've done in the past. Them days are over. Lay that money down and gather your things and light out wherever you're off to—you're not welcome here."

"A fine day it is when your own kin don't trust you," Cliff spit out. "I'll find better company on the banks of the Black." Cliff headed for the back door like he was leaving.

"Cliff," Jack said. "Leave those bills here."

Cliff turned and scowled at the three of us, pulling the money out of his sleeve and throwing it on the floor. He went out back and the three of us followed him, watching as he packed his mule and saddled his horse. He threw off his borrowed clothes and dressed back in them filthy buckskins, mounted his horse and headed out to the road.

"I'll piss on your graves before it's done," he said, trotting up the lane.

"Sorry this had to happen," Jack said. "He always was sour."

"You can't pick your kin," Preacher said.

"Truth be known," Jack said, "I was surprised to see him again. I always figured he'd be killed by his own kind. He was on a troubled road, even when we were kids. That's why my pa didn't take much time looking for him when we left Kansas. I guess he knew the truth as well as the rest of us. Trouble finds you quick enough without packing it with you."

"Let's go back in and have a pull on the jug," I said. "He's the kind that might circle back. I think I'll stay up just to make certain he's gone."

Cliff never did make his way back to Dogleg and we were better off for it. Jack didn't seem to mind either. It came to my attention that he had given up on Cliff and his misguided ways long before and wanted no more than to be rid of him.

Claude flipped the catfish over and scraped a few more hot coals under the pan.

Pete was now sitting on the ground leaning against the log but still wide awake, which surprised Claude. It was ten o'clock and the moon was high, glancing on top of the water and making it shine white. He was glad now Pete Connor had stayed with him. It made it more like old times and he knew his friends wouldn't appear until the mist formed early in the morning hours.

The stars were bright and a whippoorwill was crying across the river and Claude heard the great horned owl mourn his call. He wondered if it was some relation to the owl that had been around when Tubbs was there. Maybe it was and he was saying goodbye. They say people who are close to dying feel relieved at times. Folks aren't supposed to live forever—they get tired close to the end, and Claude was feeling tired himself. He'd never thought about not being close to the river, but now it was on him. There would be no river where he was going, leastways not this river, and it was the only one that made a difference to him. His friends and wife still lived in these waters and he wondered if he died in some other place if he could get back here. Of course the river would be gone, passing quietly under a lake, and the thought struck him that maybe his friends couldn't make it to the top and the mist on the lake was different; it was heavier and it spread too far, and a lake wasn't a river at all. The river lived, but a lake, it didn't move like the river and nothing was the same anymore.

"You okay, Claude?"

Claude jerked at the sound of Pete's voice and looked to the river as he passed his forearm across his cheek.

"Got smoke in my eyes," Claude said. "This fish'll be done soon but I've just got the one tin plate."

"That's all right," Pete said. "We'll just eat them with our hands like you and Tubbs did. Are you too tired to go on?"

"No, I'm not tired if you're not."

As the November days passed we watched the season pass with 'em. Temperatures were as varied as the winds that brought 'em. One morning it might be cold and the next it'd be like a spring day. But it was late fall and you could see the signs of the coming winter. By then most of the trees stood naked, their limbs reaching out like crooked arms and fingers, searching for cover. The brush had all but died and lay slumped on the ground. Thanksgiving was close and it was time for turkey hunting.

Now those gobblers, with a brain about the size of your thumb, are one of the smartest creatures walking the earth. The surest way to hunt 'em is to become a turkey yourself, but in Jack's case nothing came easy.

We went out early one morning, leaving Elmer behind, his ability to stay awake a drawback to the hunt. If he wasn't snoring, he was farting, neither one of which sounded like a turkey. We spaced ourselves a hundred yards apart, me in the middle of the two. Each of us planted ourselves at the base of tree, and quietly waited for dawn to break, Jack starting to make the sounds of a gobbler with his call, me thinking the whole time it sounded like a wounded owl.

By and by, I spotted one high on the ridge opposite our hill, just moseying along. He was in no hurry; walking back and forth along the ridge making his way down to the bottom and slowly meandering his way up again toward Jack.

All three of us had seen the bird and it was a simple thing at that point to sit and wait for him to close in and hope the wind stayed in our favor. It was Jack's bird, being too far away from Dan or me, and all we could do was sit and watch. Pretty soon he got close enough for Jack to make a shot. My hopes were that if Jack got rattled, like a hunter will with a twenty-pound gobbler staring him in the face, the bird would run in my direction and cross in front, giving me the opportunity to make the kill. But, as luck would have it, things didn't turn out that way.

All of a sudden Jack got to twitching and squirming. I was watching from my seat against a tree and could see him jerking like he had spasms. It didn't take the turkey long to figure out that what was happening wasn't normal, something Mother had been saying for years. Old Tom took off like he was the special on the twenty-fourth and flew right past me and directly into the path of Preacher Dan, who surprisingly had enough wits about him to fire a well-placed shot and bring the main course to the ground. I took note of his shot, while at the same time trying to keep an eye on Jack, who was now up on his feet dancing a turkey trot. While Preacher headed downhill to fetch his kill, I made my way toward Jack.

By now he was rolling on the ground, tearing at his clothes, arms and legs flinging outward and inward, yelling like he'd been hit by buckshot. When I reached him he was nearly stripped. His coat was flung in one direction, his shirt in another, his pants pulled down to his ankles, and he had his hat in his hand beating himself like he was swatting hornets. The only thing he had left to discard was his red flannel underwear and he was tearing at them with a vengeance. He was having considerable trouble getting around, his pants down at his ankles like they were, keeping his movements to short hops.

I still didn't understand what was tormenting him so much until I picked up his shirt and found it full of red ants. He must have sat down on the largest colony of the vicious insects in four states. Once I looked around I could see the ground was covered with 'em. Jack had fought his way some fifty feet from his starting point, leaving his outer garments strung along the way.

Now he was struggling with his boots trying to tear them off, not having much luck with the venture, seeing as how his pants were all wadded up around 'em, and he didn't have much time to fool with it, the ants biting him so often it was keeping his hands busy just slapping. There was only one way to rid himself of the problem and that was either find some water to jump in or get naked so he could see where to slap. Since there was no water around, he only had the one choice.

I propped my gun up against a tree and tried to catch him, which was a tricky proposition at best, since he was making such good time hopping and rolling downhill. Once I caught up to him I grabbed him by the armpits and pulled him up on his feet, and taking hold of the neck of his underwear, jerked them down as hard as I could. Turned out it was a good clean jerk, having peeled his flannels down to his ankles like skinning a rabbit.

He was covered with the little red insects, and they weren't difficult to find, Jack's skin being as white as a fish's belly. What was difficult was discerning what was an insect and what was a welt. A person has more nooks and crannies than he thinks when he's chasing red ants, and Jack wasn't missing any corners or crevices that I could tell, but he still couldn't reach his back, which is where they were starting to accumulate.

I found the closest limb that still had some leaves on it and started swatting on his backside, leaving some unsightly welts and scratches of my own. Finally, having removed most of the ants from his upper body, Jack started concentrating from the waist on down, myself having decided that it was indeed his best option, but wanting no part of the procedure. He took enough time to sit down and get his boots off, his pants and flannels coming with them, and flung them as far as he could.

Having rid himself of the infested clothing it took no time at all to swipe off the rest of his attackers. By now Preacher had joined us. He laid the turkey down and squatted beside it looking up at me with a questioning eye.

"Red ants," I said.

Preacher nodded. He pulled off his leather pouch and took a gulp of Potation and handed it to me. I in turn took a decent swallow and handed it back. We were staring at a peculiar sight.

Jack had worn himself to a frazzle. He was on the ground on his stomach, arms and legs spread out to the four winds and breathing fairly heavy to my accounting. His naked body was covered with welts, except of course for the bleeding abrasions I'd inflicted with the branch. He was huffing and puffing, eyes wide open, probably wondering when the next wave was hitting him.

Dan and I started gathering up his clothes, which were scattered all over the hill. Jack was in no mood to dress himself again, fearing his attackers might be hiding somewhere in his garments, and it took some time before we could talk him into at least wearing his red flannels and boots. We carried the rest of his clothes back home on the end of our guns.

Two days later we had the biggest Thanksgiving feast Mother could cook.

Mother Mabel's cabin set back against a hill, her front door facing south, the back yard not thirty feet from a steep incline upwards. A freshwater spring rolled down on the east side, small but plentiful, especially in the spring, but dwindling down to a trickle in the summer months and fall. Sometimes when we had a downpour her little spring bubbled out of the mountain so fast you couldn't hold a bucket to it. She called it the Trickle Down, because most of the time that's what it was doing. But it was enough to keep her in fresh water and kept her from making the daily trip to the river that most of us had to make.

It was a rough-hewed log home chinked with mud with a cobblestone chimney, much the same as all the cabins. She had a thirty-by-forty that was bigger than most cabins, but of course Mother was a big woman. Out back was covered with moss, being on the north side, but she had a green thumb and kept what little space she had filled with plants and ferns.

Her garden was out front on the southwest side of the house, and she always had a big one. Potatoes, carrots, peas, corn, and green beans were part of it, along with squash, spinach, cabbage, lettuce, turnips, onions, broccoli, and tomatoes. She prized her cukes, some saying she made the best pickles in the Midwest. Her pumpkins would get so big it would take two of us to haul them out of the patch.

She had a small section of rhubarb and another of asparagus, and she made the most mouth-watering asparagus and cream soup you'd ever want to taste. The blackberry patch was stretched from one tree to another, a wire tied between 'em holding up the heavy branches. Out front, just off the steps to the right was a strawberry patch, and when that season came along there was nothing better. She'd let the kids come by and pick the sweet red fruit, but not until she made her jams and jellies, the same with the blackberries, raspberries, and blueberries.

Mother's front yard was filled with white dogwoods and redbuds, and when they bloomed in the spring they would set your mind to dreaming of late summer sunsets. The small walking path, some fifty feet long, ended in the forest before hitting the road and was lined with flat river rock on both sides, filled with flowers.

She had a small orchard holding apple and peach trees on the southeast side, and Mother's pies and cobblers could make your mouth water.

The cabin had a front porch some ten feet wide, the length going from corner to corner of the cabin. The roof of the house covered the porch to supply the shade, and right in the middle was the porch swing made of hedge and pine, planed down by hand.

The inside of the cabin was open, no walls or doorways to hinder her wide girth. Mother always said that if she wanted to be in a small room she could go out to the privy.

The kitchen was on the west side, her countertop made of pine, curtains around the bottom hiding the shelves. She had a porcelain sink, which she'd ordered from Sears, one of the few I'd seen, most of us just using a bucket to wash in. Hers drained out the side of the wall under the window, which looked out over the garden.

The cook stove sat against the wall next to the counter, the back door just to the north. Her nightstand sat next to her bed, an oak post situated in the corner with a window on the east side so she could wake up to the morning sun. She had a changing room in the corner where her large six-drawer dresser stood, a tall mirror in the middle and washbasin sitting in front. She had curtains hanging for privacy, with a chair beside the bed.

The fireplace stood just east of the cook stove on the back wall. Her pine floors were swept daily and not a cobweb could be found in any corner. The kitchen table could be extended to accommodate ten chairs, but normally had only four around it. She had a cedar chest at the foot of the bed and a secretary by the front door.

Mother Mabel's cabin was everyone's home away from home, and when you were there you felt as if you were back with your own family, mothers and fathers and grandparents, a young child again, safe and warm.

There would be fifteen or so for Thanksgiving dinner that year. We always combined what we had, Mother making up the most.

The ham was cooking on the spit in the fireplace and the turkey was in the cook stove packed with stuffing. There were mashed potatoes with turkey gravy and giblets; canned green beans cooked with pieces of bacon had been simmering for hours; Mother's bread had been baked early in the morning, before dawn. Canned peas and carrots, squash, creamed corn with real butter, and homemade apple butter on the side completed the fare.

For dessert there were three pumpkin pies, two apple pies, two peach cobblers with cool cream, and biscuits with blackberry and strawberry jam. A large pot of coffee was kept hot on the stove.

After dinner the women cleaned and divided up the leftovers, the men sitting around sipping shine and washing it down with coffee. Those that had fiddles played some tunes and we all danced and sang some songs, Preacher throwing in a hymn every now and then.

As evening came the wind picked up and the air turned cold; clouds rolled in from the northwest.

"There's snow in them clouds," Elmer reported.

"It very seldom snows in November," Preacher said.

"I've seen it before," Mother said.

Not long after that we stood on the porch and saw the stirrings of the first winter storm. The kids were bundled up and everybody got ready to go to their own homes, some on horses and some with wagons and some just walking. Elmer and I had walked to Mother's that morning, because it was such a fine day at the beginning, but it was a mile or more from our cabin to hers and Elmer wasn't as perky as he had been, his breathing seeming to get more labored as the day went on. We'd got the roof on a few days before and Elmer and I were staying there.

Mother loaned us a mule, and we helped Elmer on him and I walked him back to the cabin. By the time we reached home the air was thick with snow, the wind carrying it sideways; a wet sticky snow covering the north side of everything it hit. We were walking away from it, and by the time we made it to the cabin our backs were covered and the mule was wet and cold.

I helped Elmer down and got him into the house and put him to bed before stoking the fire. He was quiet that night, not saying a word on the trip, his shoulders and head hunched forward, his coat collar pulled up covering his neck, hands in his pockets, with me leading the mule by his reins. I unsaddled the mule and put him out back with my team, throwing some hay into the lean-to they had for shelter.

When I came back inside I threw another log on the fire for comfort's sake and checked on Elmer one more time. The only light in the room was the dim orange glow from the fire.

"I'm cold," he said.

"It'll warm up soon. I'll get another blanket."

I pulled another blanket from the shelf and laid it over the small, curled-up old man, him shivering slightly, his eyes still open.

"When will winter be over?" he asked.

"It just started, Elmer."

"I hope I don't die in the winter. I don't want to lay in frozen ground."

"You don't feel like dying, do you?"

"I'm not sure if I feel like living. I'm tired."

"You're just having a spell, Elmer. You'll be fine in the morning. Close your eyes and get some sleep."

"Claude, when will winter be over?" he whispered, his eyes closed now.

I pulled the covers up to his neck and tucked them close around his head.

"Soon, Elmer. It'll be over soon."

I pulled up a chair and sat it next to Elmer's bed and sat down beside him. I could hear the wind blowing outside, howling at times, then other times whistling through some vacant cracks in the logs, but I couldn't see the snow passing by the windows, but of course, I knew it was there.

The fire cracked and popped and the light changed from bright orange to a shaded yellow and back to orange again…and again…and again. I could hear his labored breathing mixing with the cold north wind, and as the shadows from the firelight blended in and out over his bed, I fell asleep in the chair beside him.

"Get up," Elmer said, kicking my feet.

I'd fallen asleep with my legs outstretched, my fingers intertwined, resting on my stomach. It was close to sunup, but there would be no sun that day. The room was dim, the fire just now beginning to flame from the chunk of wood Elmer had thrown on, the lantern in the kitchen on low glow. I rose from the chair and stretched my arms above my head, bringing 'em down in clenched fists to my shoulders, then to my stiff lower back.

Elmer had already started the cook stove, a skillet filled with bacon on one side and a big pot of coffee behind it. The dark, gray light of dawn was now inching through the mountains. I walked to the window and saw the white blanket covering the forest floor. The tree trunks were covered with sticky snow, the north side the heaviest, and the heavy limbs were bending toward the ground.

I made my way out the front door and stood on the porch and watched and listened to the quiet. The silence was calming, not a breeze was stirring, not a creature to be seen or heard. It was cold but not freezing, and every now and then a clump of snow fell to the ground from the burdened limbs. It looked to be a foot of snow, a hell of a storm for November. Everything and everyone would be slow in getting around on that day. I went inside, the smell of bacon frying and coffee perking drawing me back. I leaned over the washbasin and cupped the water in my hands and washed my face and neck. Then, putting on my coat, I trudged out the back to the privy, stepping high, placing my boots in Elmer's footsteps. When I got back to the house Elmer was frying eggs, and we sat down at the small pine table and ate breakfast.

"You're feeling better this morning, I take it?"

"Never felt better. The cold air makes me breathe easier; don't know why but it does."

"Near fourteen hours of sleep don't hurt either," I said.

"Fourteen for you maybe. I've been up since four."

"Why didn't you wake me? That chair liked to broke my back."

"What were you doing in that chair anyway? Hell, your bed ain't but ten feet away."

"I didn't want you dying on me in the middle of the night, for fear I'd have to drag you out and freeze you."

"It was your snoring woke me up," Elmer said.

I was glad he was in good health that morning, knowing somehow that from now on his time would go from good to worse as the days passed.

"We better get around," Elmer said. "Jack'll wonder where we are."

"Jesus, Elmer, there's a foot of snow out there. We can't walk through that."

"We'll take Mother's mule then, by God. I'm not gonna be stuck inside this cabin all day. There'll be plenty of time for that when winter does hit."

I knew he was right and I also knew what he knew; you had to get up and go when you felt like getting up and going. I saddled Mother's mule and one of mine, knowing we'd take hers back, while Elmer put up the plates and utensils. He met me out front, and I helped him up and crawled on the other one. I gave the mule a kick and we made our way to the Three-Stop.

Jack was up of course, standing on the porch drinking coffee, the steam floating up around his face.

"Well, I never would have thought you two would be out so early," he said.

"We come to wake you up," Elmer said.

I hopped off my mule and tied him to the porch railing and took the reins of Elmer's. He slowly lifted his leg, swung it over the mule's rump, letting out a long, melodious toot, waking up the morning silence and perking up the mule's ears.

"He's in high form this morning, ain't he?" Jack said.

"He sure is. Been that way since daybreak. Must have something to do with the snow."

"Well, pure driven snow don't have a chance around him."

Preacher Dan was coming down the hill riding his mule Heathen, named that because he didn't like Preacher and would take every opportunity he could to kick the living crap out of him. Heathen had a particular dislike to being ridden and would go to great lengths to dismount any rider that wasn't paying attention, and in Dan's case, with his predisposition for jug gulping, it happened quite often.

"Good morning, my fine friends," Preacher said. "Ain't it a day to revel in? Nothing like a good snow to purify the soul and cleanse the heart."

"This snow's gonna pack down like sun-baked mud," Jack said. "I believe we should take advantage of it and put our sledding skills to use."

"Who's got a sled?" I asked.

"Why, Mother does," Preacher said. "I've seen it hanging in her barn. She uses it to haul wood in the snow. It's rigged up to tie to a mule. I think Jack's on to something; no sense in just sitting around."

"Go up and get it then, Preacher," Jack said. "I'm ready to sled and slide."

Dan took off to Mother's, leading her mule with him. We went in the cabin, Jack to get some gloves, Elmer and I to get some coffee.

An hour later Preacher showed up towing the sled. It was three foot wide, but five foot long, enough for three men to sit in, a loose two in our case, Jack taking up more room than ordinary. It had sides on it, three foot high so the wood wouldn't fall off on the rough trails. There was no way to steer it, the ropes being used to hitch to the mule, which Preacher had already done, tying them to either side of the saddle.

"Who's first?" Jack asked.

"You and Claude get on," Dan said. "I'll ride the mule and steer him."

Jack sat at the front of the sled and I piled on behind him, grabbing him by the sides of his coat to hang on. Preacher turned Heathen up the hill and we began the trek. But the snow wasn't packed down hard enough and the sled just sank like a steel ball in a sponge. The wet snow was piling up in front and eventually it became too much for Heathen to pull.

"We'll have to wait till nightfall," Jack said. "This snow ain't packed down yet. What we need is for it to freeze, then we can scoot along the top like a snake on water."

We adjourned to the porch and mixed our conversation with Potation and coffee.

By mid-afternoon there was a soft breeze blowing out of the northwest, getting colder by the hour, as we were getting warmer by the minute. By five o'clock, the hooch having lifted our spirits to a point of bravery, we were hoping for another storm, just to insure a hard surface on the road; the faster the better we were saying. It was spitting snow by sundown and the clouds were just hanging, not drifting that we could tell, making us believe the weather was on our side. We'd moved into the cabin and were standing around the stove, making our plans for the ride.

"How're we gonna see?" Jack asked.

"We'll put a lantern at each end of the road and build a fire close to the cabin," Preacher said. "As long as we're heading for a light, we'll be all right."

"We better get the sled sliding before this party comes to an end," I said.

Elmer and I piled up some wood close to the road and started a fire, while Preacher and Jack ran the lanterns to the ends.

"Let's go, Claude," Jack shouted.

Jack climbed in the sled and I got in behind him. Jack's legs were short enough to stretch out in front, mine on either side of his wide hips. Preacher headed Heathen up the hill, and the frozen crust offered just the right surface for our intentions. It was a slow pull uphill, Heathen not exactly in the same mood as his guests, but in between swills of Potation, Dan gave him a few kicks of encouragement. Once at the top we made a wide swing and pointed the mule downhill.

"Weddy," Preacher slurred.

True enough, he started off slow, ol' Heathen finding the downhill jaunt much more pleasant.

"Speed him up a bit," Jack yelled. "I can walk faster than this."

"Otay," Preacher said.

We were right in front of the fire, Jack and I both yelling and waving at Elmer, him just standing there warming his hands over the flames.

Preacher took a long pull on the jug, and with a big rodeo yell gave Heathen a kick with both boots. Heathen snorted, surprised at the violent blows, and decided to rid himself of his obnoxious passenger. He reared up on his back legs and rolled Dan over his rump in a perfect flip, Dan landing on top of Jack and I, jug still in his hand. Heathen took off at a dead run, the sled careening from side to side behind him. He was scared, running in the dark with all three of us screaming for him to stop. The light at the end of the road must not have made any connection with him, 'cause he made a quick left and headed out through the woods, tossing Dan in the air and smashing Jack and I to the bottom of the box. Dan had tossed the jug and was holding onto the sides of the sled, his feet hanging out over the edges, his body bouncing up and down on our heads.

"Get off me," Jack yelled. He was trying to push Preacher out and over the side, but Dan was hanging on for life.

"No! No! No!" Dan yelled. "I ain't weaving!"

There was nothing I could do but wait out the ride, not being able to lift both of 'em off me, but I was sure feeling the weight of those bouncing bodies. I could hear Heathen crashing through the woods but had no idea where we were headed until the sled stopped bouncing and once again I felt the smooth slide of the road.

We'd made a full circle around the Three-Stop and were now headed back up the road, Heathen still running as fast as he could. The smooth ride gave us an opportunity to adjust ourselves enough for Dan to pull himself up and drop inside the container. That made three drunks in a box, our heads poking out just above the sides, pulled by a scared mule with no one in charge.

Heathen was headed for the lantern at the top of the hill and was struggling with all the dead weight he was pulling. He must have remembered the same turn a few minutes ago, 'cause the next thing we knew Heathen had made another swing, this time short and quick, and was now headed back down the road in front of Elmer and the fire.

"Stop him, Elmer," Jack shouted. "Stop him!"

We had our heads turned toward Elmer, eyes popped wide, hands gripping the sides, screaming in his direction. All we could see was Elmer's smile and his arm raised above his head waving at us.

"Cut him loose, Preacher," Jack yelled. "It's our only chance."

Jack pulled out his pocketknife and handed it to Dan. Dan opened it and Jack pushed him forward so he could reach out front and cut the ropes. Just as he cut the right rope we hit a bump and knocked Dan back down in the box again. Now the sled was swinging from side to side, tugging at Heathen, him overcompensating and running in the other direction, us trailing him out of control. The next lantern was coming up, and we all knew what was below that—the river. Jack pushed Preacher up again and he struggled to cut the other rope. Heathen was snorting and bellowing as we passed the last light, Dan hanging over the front of the sled, butt to face against Jack.

Heathen must have had a good idea where the river was even in the dark. Just as we passed the light our sled made a wide swing to the right and Heathen made a sharp left turn that slung us out in a blur. In mid-sling Preacher got the rope cut, but it was too late. Free from the mule and now on our own, we were moving sideways down the hill, but with no forward pull on us the sled didn't want to go sideways. As soon as the rope was cut the right rail dug into the snow and flipped us over like a pancake. All three of us went flying, the sled tumbling behind us, and into the river we went.

By the time we made the walk back up the hill our hair was frozen and so was our clothes. Elmer was still standing by the fire, smiling, and Heathen was standing beside him as calm as could be. We stripped down on the porch and stood by the stove in the Three-Stop until we stopped shaking.

The river had snapped the slurring out of Dan, but Jack had lost his voice, only repeating in a husky whisper, "Dumb ass." Elmer said he must be a smart ass 'cause he was the only one not wet. Preacher stopped the bickering by stating that the world was a tricky place, and you never knew when you might get hooked up with either one.

Chapter Seven

The fish were done cooking and Claude sat the frying pan off the fire. He transferred the slabs to the tin plate to let them cool. He was thinking about winter and cold nights and setting in his cabin with Elmer. They'd watched the flames in the fireplace night after night. It seemed to Claude that fire was embedded in his mind so deep it would never leave. He'd always liked listening to it, and when electricity and gas had finally come to Dogleg he'd declined to have it. The heat from a good blaze was better, and there were stories in the flames.

Claude remembered Elmer sleeping in his bed, and he'd be rocking in front of the fire late in the evening while the cold winds whistled outside. After everyone was gone that life had come back to him. Many years had passed and he'd spent the winters rocking in front of the fire, thinking about the past, never the future. He knew what the next day would bring—more of the same, and that's what he wanted. He still had his chores, feeding what few chickens he had and taking care of his mule. No one used mules anymore, but Claude kept his. Now everyone had a horse that they never rode. He had his garden, and it kept him busy and he still put up his vegetables for the winter; everyone else went to the store. He felt out of place.

Many thought he was crazy—he'd heard the stories. That old man that still lived in a cabin without a furnace or running water. He'd eventually had to take the electricity, though, so he could get a well. Too many people were what caused it. They'd polluted the water and it had to be boiled before he could drink it, but the biggest reason was his age. There were plenty of pure springs left in the hills, but Claude couldn't make the haul.

Water and fire. His whole life had revolved around those two things, and they meant more to him than anything. Those two elements had taken many things from him, but they'd also given back in abundance.

There were a few that looked in on him, much the same as he'd done with Elmer. It was hard for him to believe that he'd lived long enough to be standing in Elmer's boots.

"Are you okay?" Pete asked. He could see what he felt was sadness in Claude's stare, and he knew that he'd never had such times with his own friends. Now he was beginning to wish that he had been with Claude back then. He wished that he had these same memories, and that time had not brought Claude with it.

"Sure, I'm all right. Here, take some of this fish; watch out for the bones."

"Winters must have been tough out here," Pete said. "Seems to me you'd just be penned up in your cabins most of the time."

"When it got too cold to sit at the river we'd sit at the Three-Stop till dark and after, and then go home. There was always something to do in the daytime; the chores never stopped, and of course we had to eat, so we spent a lot of time hunting."

December in the mountains is much the same as November. Winter doesn't usually hit hard until the first of the year, except for those tricky snaps nature hands out. The air is cold, but there are many bright sunny days, unlike January and February when it seems so many weeks go by, dark, windy, and labored. The full grip of winter would be on us in those months, but not then, not December. In that month only the freezing nights convinced us of the coming solitude, when staying inside became more important than being outdoors.

It's the best time of the year to hunt rabbits. Jack always felt a kinship with the furry little varmints, being almost as close to the ground as they were. Shotguns and beagles were the tools of the trade, and Preacher's beagle Boots was one of the best, or so he claimed.

"He's a rabbit magnet," Preacher said, patting Boots on the head. "He can smell a hare a mile away."

"Any dog worth his biscuits can smell a rabbit," Jack said. "The question is, can he flush 'em?"

"He can flush 'em. He can outrun 'em too."

"Ol' Boots has enough trouble making it to his lunch bucket, much less catching up to a scooter," Elmer said.

"Boots don't know he's old," Preacher said.

"Them white whiskers on his chin might say something," Elmer said.

"Don't talk so loud, his feelings get hurt easy."

"Them ain't his feelings hurting," Jack said. "It's his body."

With our shotguns ready, we headed to the fields and fencerows where our prey lay in wait. Boots was pulling up the rear, not as excited about the journey as the rest of us.

"Come on, Boots," Preacher yelled.

"I bet he wishes you were the dog today," Elmer said.

"Looks like his time's up to me," Jack said, looking back at Boots. "If he don't pick up his pace we'll be the one's flushing them hares."

"He's pacing himself," Preacher said. "A good rabbit dog knows when he'll peak."

"Peak," Elmer said. "He's already lying down; I calculate he's pooped."

Sure enough, Boots had stopped and was lying down, his tongue hanging out of his mouth, panting in quick huffs.

"What'd I tell you," Preacher said. "He's resting; he knows his stuff."

"He's figuring right now the farther he stays back, the less chance he'll have of running into a rabbit," Jack said.

"When the time comes, Boots'll make his move."

"I'll bet it's a slow one," Elmer said.

We made it to a flat field bordering a small, wet-weather creek lined with brush and trees, perfect ground for rabbits. We spread out, thirty feet apart, Elmer and Jack on one side of the creek bed, Preacher and I on the other. Boots was lying in the tall brown grass behind us. As we walked we stomped on brush piles and thick tufts of grass. I scared one up in just a few feet, the hare scrambling out of the brush with lightning speed. I shot and missed, but it turned the rabbit in front of Preacher and his shot hit, the hare tumbling in a somersault. Boots ran up to the kill, smelled it, and lay down beside it.

I skinned and gutted the rabbit, cut off his head and feet and put him in my pouch. I wasn't finished with the project when Elmer shot another one, and then Jack got one, running out of the same brush.

"It's a good day for a hunt," Preacher said. "And a good rabbit dog makes all the difference. Did I ever tell you about the time I was in Kansas City, Missouri, courting a lively young redhead? It was my intention to present her a gift of a rabbit fur coat. I hunted for many weeks to supply the tailor with enough furs for the project and finally accomplished the mission. Much to my dismay the tailor in question was half-blind and deaf to boot.

"When I sent the young lady to his shop to pick up the coat, the monstrosity was three sizes to big and had one arm longer than the other. Due to a severe sinus congestion, the agent hadn't tanned the hides and couldn't smell the hideous odor coming from the pelts.

"I was on my way to meet her, having stopped long enough in a pub to warn its clientele of the dangers of inebriation. As I crossed the street I saw her coming out of the tailor's door. The poor sweet thing, believing that my intentions were honorable, but my taste in clothing atrocious, was wearing the hideous ensemble of untanned hides. No sooner had we met in the middle of the street than every dog in the city sped to our vicinity.

"Turning on my heels I tried to make an escape, hoping the innocent girl would follow suit. Follow she did, leaping on my back and clutching my body in a death grip, her screams and cursing deafening my hearing. I ran as fast as I could, high-stepping all the way, back and forth across the street, trying to enter one establishment after another and finding the doors completely barricaded from the inside, the owners watching in horror as I pleaded for help. I'm aware that it must have been a startling sight, a man running down the street with what might appear to be a rather large rabbit clinging to his neck, and more than twenty howling dogs nipping at his heels.

"I was tiring fast, the smell overcoming my senses, my head swimming in fear and my legs failing from the weight of the young lass wearing thirty pounds of hare hides. At last I saw my avenue to safety; a wagon with the back gate closed sat not more than half a block down the street. I gave one last push and leaped into the rear of the wagon. The only thing I failed to note was the condition of the shelter, the pungent odor surrounding my head confusing my senses. Although we were safe from the hoard of mongrels, by an unfortunate bit of luck we'd landed in a street cleaner's manure wagon.

"I stripped the foul fur from her body, her cursing unabated, and threw it as far as my tired arms could muster, the dogs following it through the air, and as it hit the ground, tearing it to pieces in a fit of frothing madness. I crawled through the manure to the front of the wagon, the somewhat disheveled minx throwing clumps of dung at my back, and slapped the reins on the horse's rump and drove us to safety."

By the time Preacher finished his tale we had three more rabbits killed and cleaned, one on our side and two on Jack's; more than enough for a fried rabbit dinner and one of Mother's delicious stews.

We sat in the afternoon sun and sipped on Potation, enjoying the mild December day before making the walk back home.

On the way back Boots went into a sneezing fit and stumbled onto a covey of quail. The noise they made bursting from their hiding spot sent him into a seizure and Preacher had to carry him.

"He's tuckered out, boys," Preacher said.

Boots was simpering lying in Dan's arms, his seizure all but over, his head hanging over his arm, drool dripping off his extended tongue.

"He's not acting himself," Preacher said.

"Looks to me like he is," Elmer said.

"A good warm bath will fix him right up," Dan said. "I've never seen him so worn down. Next time we'll have to cut our hunt short so as not to tire him."

"Next time I'll bring my dead turtle," Elmer said. "He won't weigh you down near as much and he'll out-hunt ol' Boots."

"Boots," Dan said. "Boots, are you there?"

We gathered around Dan and the dog to see what the problem might be, which became evident as soon as we saw his lifeless form.

"How old was ol' Boots, anyway?" I asked.

"I'm not sure," Dan said. "Somewhere between twelve and twenty, I think."

"He looks dead to me," Jack said.

"He don't look that much different than when we started," Elmer said.

"I believe he's passed on," Preacher said.

"Maybe we should bury him right here," I said. "It only seems fitting that he should be put to rest in the rabbit fields he loved so much."

"Buzzard bait," Elmer said. "If one'll take him."

"No, I'll take him back to the cabin and put him down beside the porch where he liked to lay so much."

"Look close," Jack said. "He may already have a hole wallered out."

That next morning a steady rain was falling. I walked out to the porch and listened to the rain as it fell through the trees and dripped to the ground. I was waiting for Elmer to ready himself for the walk to Jack's.

I saw Mother through the trees, coming up the path leading to our cabin. It was unusual that she'd be out that early, coming up my lane, her umbrella hitting the heavy low limbs that I never thought to cut.

"Annie Clover's missing," she said, before reaching my steps. "Her mother came early this morning. Her dad's been out most of the night looking, but came back without her."

The Clovers were the poorest of the poor, if there is a standard for the downtrodden. The childer crews had beaten down Ben Clover many years before, his shoulders slumped and back bowed from carrying the heavy ties. Charlene Clover, a slim and worn woman, the mother of five, was old before her time. They lived farther back in the hills than most of us that surrounded the

Three-Stop, rarely coming out of their hidden homestead to visit, keeping to themselves, as those with less will sometimes do.

"Preacher and Jack are at the Three-Stop getting ready for the search," Mother said. "The others are there, too."

"Come in while I get my things," I said. "Elmer's almost ready to go. Tell me what you know."

I gave her a cup of coffee while I gathered my coat, hat, and gloves.

"Annie's been sparking with a boy from Cedar County, one Charlene's not happy with, and neither is Ben. But you know how that can be. Trying to keep the young un's apart when they figure out why they're changing is no easy chore, especially when the pickings is so slim. Charlie Combs is the boy's name, maybe you know him."

"No, I don't know him," I said. "But I do know of his father. I can't say that I'd want anything to do with him. I've heard he's been in trouble for stealing, and some say he beats his kids. His wife died, two, maybe three years ago. Some say he beat her to death, but the cabin burned to the ground with her and one daughter in it. No one ever knew the truth."

"I've heard the stories," Mother said. "Charlene says the mother killed the daughter and then set the place on fire, dying with her, to stop the old man from getting at the girl. It's a bad mix, Claude."

"Let's go, Elmer," I said.

I saddled two mules, one for Elmer and the other for Mother, and grabbed my shotgun and shells and handed Elmer the rifle.

We talked as we hurried along, Mother filling us in on what she knew. Annie had been seen about sundown the day before, finishing her chores. Earlier that day the Combs' boy had been to the house and Ben had run him off, saying that Annie was too young to be courted; she was thirteen and just starting her path to womanhood. Charlie Combs was mad and told Ben he'd be back. Annie was upset too, not knowing bad blood when it was standing in front of her. Ben thought the boy probably stayed hidden until Annie started her chores and then made off with her.

All the men and women of Dogleg were gathered at the Three-Stop, some with mules and horses, others on foot. The women were inside fixing sandwiches and coffee. The rain was still steady and the gun barrels were pointing out the bottom of the slickers. Ben Clover was sitting on the steps of the porch, his face in his hands, his clothes soaking wet, and his boots heavy with mud.

"Cedar County's north of here," Preacher said. "But that don't mean much.

I count forty-seven men. We'll start at Ben's place and split up in equal amounts and head in all four directions. Two shots in quick order tell if you've found something."

The women handed out the food and coffee and in an hour we were at Ben's. We broke up in equal shares and started the search. It was nine o'clock in the morning, thirty-eight degrees, and still raining. It was the twenty-third of December.

By noon we'd covered less than two miles, scouring under every dead log, in every cave, and along the banks of every creek we came across. No shots had been fired. Jack, Preacher, five other men, and myself were headed north toward Cedar County. Elmer stayed back at the cabin with Charlene and the four young boys. Four men and Ben Clover had ridden horses to the Combs place; it would take 'em two hours.

We'd seen no sign of Annie, not a piece of clothing, not a cold fire, not a broken twig. We ate our sandwiches as we searched. A quiet determination was setting in and desperation was taking hold. By mid-afternoon the rain had stopped, but the temperature was dropping. It would be freezing by nightfall and the search would have to wait.

"Only a few hours of daylight left," I said. "We'll have to decide to go on or head back."

"It won't do no good to stay out all night," Preacher said. "We'll just be worn down."

"Maybe we can find a cave and get out of the weather," Jack said.

"I hate to give up knowing she might still be out here."

"We won't be able to hear gunshots the farther out everyone gets," Preacher said. "We'll have to meet up and take note of everybody. Maybe someone found something."

By the time we made it back to Ben's place it was dark and freezing. Some of the men were there and others were straggling in. Ben hadn't shown up yet. Mother and the other women were cooking beans and stew, with several pots of coffee brewing.

As each of the men came in Charlene met them at the porch and searched their eyes for hope, but there was not a one that could give her what she needed.

Ben and the men he'd been riding with were the last to arrive.

"The place was empty," he said. "Not a soul in sight; not the boy or the old man. Hogs weren't slopped, nor the chickens fed. Looks like they lit out in a hurry."

The men had built a fire outside the cabin, warming themselves, waiting for word to stay or leave. No one wanted to go home, not without finishing the search, not without finding Annie. Each man knew that if it was his own child it couldn't end until she was found.

"Those of you that want to stay can bed down wherever," Ben said. "The cabin ain't big, but it'll hold some. The barn's got hay to sleep on. We could build a fire."

His look was tired and worried. He'd been up for two days with no sleep and would get none that night, staying awake on nothing but hope. His daughter was in the mountains freezing, and there was nothing more he could do until first light.

No one left; we all stayed. The fires got bigger as the men prepared for the rest they needed. The women brought out the food and coffee, and Charlene rounded up all the bedding she could, just blankets, but not enough to go around. It was no matter—there wouldn't be much sleep anyway.

As the night wore on and the talk slowed to whispers the men's heads began dropping to their chests, just sitting by the fire, some stretching on their gear or a blanket, some on hay to keep the wet ground from seeping in. The women stayed up all night feeding the fire and keeping the coffee going. Around four in the morning the lights in the cabin got brighter and we could hear the noises of fires being stoked, pans clanging together and the small, quiet talk that women have when they don't want to wake the children. They were cooking breakfast and making sandwiches for that day's search.

The men began to stir and ready themselves for another day of searching. Ben Clover had not slept at all, the same for Charlene. Before daylight we were on our way, split-up and returning to our areas of the day before.

"Odd, don't you think," Preacher said, "that there was no one at the Combs place yesterday. Seems a man can't just up and walk away from his livestock, leaving no one to tend 'em."

"It is strange," I said.

"Let's start at the Combs cabin and work our way north," Preacher said. "We made it better than halfway there yesterday, without a sign of Annie or the boy. My guess is if they were headed in that direction, they probably made it. Let's see if anyone showed up last night."

We talked to Ben and told him of our intentions, and he decided to come with us. After two hours we were close enough to the cabin to tie up our mounts and look the place over from a distance. It was still freezing and the frozen leaves made walking difficult, trying to pull ourselves in and out of the hollows.

"Seems quiet enough," Ben said.

"Too quiet," Jack said. "It ain't right. I say we surround the place and move in slow and easy."

Walking from the backside of the cabin through the barnyard, the jersey started calling, her bag full of milk, stretching her skin in pain. She hadn't been milked for two days from the looks of her and she needed relief soon. Two mules stood in the corner of the corral by their usual feeding spot, but there was no hay for 'em. They stared and turned their heads as I made my way past them, hoping they wouldn't bray with hunger pangs. The chickens were scattered, pecking at the frozen ground, and the hogs were restless in their pens, grunting for food. There was no smoke coming from the chimney. The place seemed deserted except for the stock.

I was at the back corner of the cabin and I could see Jack to my left and Preacher coming up the front, and Ben was on my right. I peered in the window of the back door, but could see nothing, the pane of glass filthy with smoke and dirt. Walking around to the side of the house I ran into Jack looking through the window.

"See anything?" I whispered.

"No," he said. "Damn thing's too dingy to see through."

We could hear no noise coming from the inside of the cabin. We walked around to the front corner and saw Preacher crouched behind a wagon.

I pounded on the side of the cabin with the butt of my shotgun. "If anybody's in there, call out your name and come out with hands high," I shouted.

Everything was quiet.

"Come out with your hands in the air," I shouted again. Still no answer.

"There's no one here, Jack," I said.

"Peers so," he said. "Let's go in."

"We're going in," I yelled to Preacher and Ben.

I motioned for Ben to meet me in the back.

"We'll come through the back, you and Dan go through the front."

Ben and I opened the back door and looked inside before stepping in. It was colder in the cabin than it was outside and our warm breath hung white in the air. We were in the kitchen, and the table was covered with scraps of food and dirty plates. A mouse was standing on his hind legs in the middle of it, sniffing the air and staring at Ben and me.

"In here," we heard Jack say.

We walked around the wall separating the kitchen from the main room, and there, lying dead on the floor, was old man Combs. A shotgun blast to the chest had done him in.

"No need to see if he's breathing," Jack said.

"Nope," Ben said. "And good riddance."

Preacher knelt down to the body and felt the hand. "He's been dead quite a while. He's froze near solid and most of his blood's run out."

We searched the cabin but could find no sign of a gun.

"Whoever did this still has the shotgun," Jack said.

"Did you come in the house yesterday, Ben?" I asked.

"Sure we did, but there was no one here, just as empty as it is now, 'cept for him, that is."

All of us heard the footsteps on the front porch at the same time. We scattered in four different directions, guns pointed to the front door.

"Who's in there?" someone shouted.

"Who goes there?" Preacher yelled.

"It's Charlie Combs," came the answer. "I've got Annie Clover with me. Don't be a shootin'."

"You got the gun, boy?" Jack yelled.

"I've got the gun," he said. "But I don't want it—you can have it."

"I'm going out the back," I whispered to Ben as I walked past him. I made my way out the back door and around the side just in time to hear Preacher's words.

"Drop the gun on the porch so's I can hear it hit," he said.

I was standing at the corner of the cabin and saw Charlie Combs holding Annie's hand in his and the shotgun in the other. He threw the gun down and they both stood there, still as a post.

"Hold your place," I shouted, pointing my gun at the boy. "Come on out, men, I've got him covered."

Ben was first out the door and straight to Annie. He picked her up in his arms and held her close.

"You've scared us terrible, Annie," he said.

"I'm sorry," she said, tears coming down her face. "I didn't know it would be like this."

"Charlie Combs," Preacher said, "you've got some explaining to do."

"I know," Charlie said. "I had to. Annie'll tell ya, I had to."

"Jack, let's get something to cover up the body and get a fire started," I said. "These kids are freezing. Preacher, shoot off two rounds, maybe the others will hear."

Preacher helped Charlie to his feet and waited until Jack and I covered up his father before bringing him inside to the kitchen stove, where he couldn't see him lying on the floor. Ben brought Annie in behind 'em. Jack started a fire and pulled the two chairs up close to the stove and let Annie and Charlie sit. I found some coffee and took the pot off the stove and filled it from the cistern out back.

"You hungry?" I asked both of them. All of us pulled out our sandwiches and offered them to the kids. They each took one but didn't begin to eat.

"Tell us what happened," Preacher said.

"I just wanted to see Annie, that's all it was," Charlie began, wiping his dripping nose on his sleeve. "When Mr. Clover run me off, I couldn't stand it. I knew she'd be doing her chores and I went into the woods and waited. When she come out I told her to come with me. She didn't want to, but then she did. I just wanted to see her and talk a bit."

"He didn't make me go, Dad," Annie broke in. "I went on my own. I was coming back home, I promise."

"We was both on the mule," Charlie said. "We were ridin' and talkin' and the next thing it was dark. We was more close to my place than hers, but I was gonna bring her back, for certain I was, but Pa come up on us right then. He'd been out lookin' for me. He said it was too late to head back and that he'd come back with us in the morning and sort things out.

"But I should a know'd. My pa's got bad things in his head. He does bad things. My sister, he did things to her; I could hear her cryin' in the night, my ma fightin' with him, him hittin' her so hard she couldn't walk. Then back at my sis, he was. Night after night he did it. He told Ma he'd kill her if she tried to run, he'd shoot her in the back, he'd say. My sis and me, we were in the same room. He'd come in and run me off. I'd sit in the kitchen with Ma, listenin' to sis cry. Ma, she cried too. She'd go in, and Pa, he'd beat her down to her knees and kick her till she crawled back to me. Then back at sis, again and again, Ma holdin' on to me, blood dripping out of her ear sometimes, he'd kick her so hard.

"I just wanted to get away. I wanted Annie and me to get away, but when you run me off I had to come back, I had to see Annie. I was telling her I was leavin', but I'd come back for her.

"That night Pa was at Annie. He wouldn't leave her alone. I fought with him but he beat me with the shotgun. He went in the kitchen to get more whiskey and I grabbed Annie and lit out for the woods. We spent the night in a cave not far from here. Pa was too drunk to follow us, but by daybreak he'd found us and took us back."

"It's true, Dad," Annie said. "Charlie tried to keep him off me; he tried, but he got beat every time."

"Did he get at you, Annie?" Ben asked.

"No, he never got to me. Charlie made sure."

I found some cups and cleaned 'em up the best I could and poured us all some hot coffee. Annie had taken a few small bites of her sandwich, but not Charlie. He held the warm cup in his hands and went on with his story.

"When we got back I knew he wasn't gonna take Annie home; I could see it in his eyes. Then we seen you comin' up the road, you and the others, and Pa, he made us get in the hidin' spot."

"The hiding spot?" Jack asked.

"In the barn, in the back corner. Pa built it special for hidin'. He dug a hole and put boards on top covered with straw. Cain't tell it if'n you ain't lookin' special for it. He put me and sis in it when we was beat bad, so's folks that come by couldn't see us. He'd make Ma get in it, too, when she was beat. Sometimes he'd make me and Ma get in it and he'd roll the wagon on the boards so we couldn't get out till he was done with sis."

"Take a drink of coffee, boy," Preacher said, his hand resting on Charlie's shoulder.

I handed him my handkerchief so he could blow his nose, and he went on.

"Pa put out the fire so's there wouldn't be no smoke and took us to the hidin' spot and all three of us went in, Pa holding the gun to us. One scream, he said, and he'd shoot. After you was gone, he took Annie back inside and made me stay in the hole, but the wagon was out front so he couldn't roll it on the boards. He pulled the old rain barrel on top of it and left. It weren't enough to hold me in, and after a while I pushed the barrel off and snuck inside. He was after Annie and she was fightin' him. The shotgun was standin' in the corner by the back door, right there by the stove. I couldn't let him do to Annie what he'd done to sis, I just couldn't. I picked up the gun and cocked it and yelled at Pa to quit. He turned on me and came at me. I shot both barrels."

Charlie's hands were trembling so bad he couldn't hold the coffee cup, and Preacher took it from him. Annie's head was bent down, her eyes fixed on the floor. Ben was standing behind her with his hands on her shoulders.

"Were you in the hiding spot when we showed up?" I asked.

Charlie nodded, his hands covering his face.

"Why?" I asked.

"Scared," Charlie said. "Scared Mister Clover would kill me for takin' Annie. We went to the barn after...after...Pa, and then we seen you men walkin' toward the cabin, and you, mister," pointing at me, "we seen you comin' from the back. We was just scared. We waited for a spell, but Annie said nobody would hurt us 'cause we didn't do nothin' we couldn't help. Was she right, mister, what other could we a done?"

Charlie Combs was fourteen years old. He'd lost every member of his family. His mother had killed his sister and then herself, and Charlie had killed his own father. They'd all been too scared to run and not strong enough to fight. Now he was alone.

"You got any family that you know of, Charlie?" Ben asked.

"Pa's got brothers in Texas, but I ain't never seen 'em. Ma, if she had family, never told of it. Most people just stayed away, and Pa, he wouldn't hardly let us go nowhere."

"We'll be back," Ben said, giving Annie a squeeze with his hands. He looked at each of us men and pointed to the back door.

"I say burn the place to the ground," Ben said. "Cabin, barn, outhouse, everything."

"What are you saying?" Preacher asked. "What about old man Combs?"

"All I see is a mean, old, drunk bastard, who's gone and burnt himself up in his own cabin."

"What about the boy?" I asked.

"He can come and live with us," Ben said, "till we figure out the best road for him to take."

All four of us looked at each other, standing there, arms crossed, as men will do when a problem rears its head.

"All I see is a drunk that burnt himself up in his own cabin," I said.

"Damn fool couldn't hold his hooch, if you ask me," Jack said.

"It's fitting," Preacher said. "That he should be on fire when he walks through the gates of hell."

"Ben," I said, "tell Charlie what you're up to and have him get his things. I'll milk this cow, and Jack, you and Preacher feed these animals. Looks like Ben just inherited a couple of mules, some hogs, and some chickens."

"There's a rooster over there I wish I had," Jack said. "I wonder if Charlie would mind if I bought him."

"Last time I looked, Ben had a rooster," Preacher said.

We packed up what things Charlie had, took the mules and cow with us, and burnt the cabin to the ground, along with everything in it. It was Christmas Eve. On Christmas Day we went back for the chickens and hogs; most of 'em were divided up among the folks of Dogleg.

Charlie Combs never left the Clovers' home, that is until him and Annie got married and moved to St. Louis. Years later I heard they had three sons and

Charlie was a carpenter and Annie was a nurse.

Jack's rooster was big, red, and strutting. But he and Jack didn't see eye to eye, even though they weren't that far from the same height. Reddy, is what Jack named him, as the rooster's stamina was gaining him quite a reputation.

Controlling a henhouse was a full-time job, and Reddy took control like Sherman's march to the sea. No hen was left untouched or unguarded. Jack could hardly get his eggs in the morning without having to go through Reddy, who paraded in front of the henhouse from dawn to dusk, that is when he wasn't chasing off intruders.

Reddy would lie in wait for Jack to come out of the cabin for his morning chores, which included a trip to the outhouse, feeding the hogs, checking on his mule, and then swinging back through the chicken coop for his eggs. Reddy was sneaky too, never hiding in the same place, sometimes on the roof of the cabin or henhouse, other times in a tree, and one time he even popped up out of a bucket, scaring Jack so much he dropped his eggs and had to scramble what was left.

We started getting to the Three-Stop earlier than usual just to see the show, even moving our chairs out back so we could sit and drink coffee while the entertainment continued.

When Reddy was on full attack he'd drop down from the roof and snatch a grip on Jack's bald head, flapping his wings and crowing like the rebel yell. Jack would run like a wild man, trying to pull ol' Red off, wings flapping around his face and the rooster pecking at his forehead. Blood was drawn more than once, and after a while Jack's head took on the look of a speckled egg, something that must have pleased Reddy.

It was only Jack that he was after, not bothering the rest of us. Any one of us could enter the chicken coop undisturbed except Jack. Jack took to disguising himself in the mornings, dressing in different outfits trying to fool the rooster, but it did no good. Reddy was much smarter than that and he'd let Jack get a step or two away from the nesting hens before he attacked with full vengeance. Jack started going out the front door of the Three-Stop and circling the cabin, sneaking toward the back, looking in all directions, mostly up, the ambush from above causing most of the pain. But it didn't help; Reddy couldn't be fooled.

One time Jack dressed up like Mother Mabel, black dress and shawl, one of her bonnets draped over his head. That time ol' Red came in with a full-front-face attack, scratching him up so bad he had to be doctored.

It riled Jack up so much that he spent many an hour scheming on how to fool the old cock. He finally came up with an idea that seemed to all of us a stroke of genius.

Early one morning, just at daybreak, Jack put on a pair of red flannels. He tied an old fox fur over his back, the head of the fox still intact, lying over his head and face, obstructing his vision to a certain degree, but Jack felt sure it would do no harm.

His plan was to come around the side of the cabin, crawling on his hands and knees, scaring the daylights out of Reddy, and gaining easy access to the henhouse. All went according to plan for a while. As Jack slowly made his way to the chicken coop Reddy spied him, and seeing the largest fox he'd ever set eyes on, clucked and crowed, running in circles, jumping up and down, all the while Jack giggling under the fox fur. Jack had forgotten only one small item— the back flap of his flannels. By the time he noticed the cool air hitting his bare rear end it was too late, he was already face to face with Reddy.

One last fling through the chicken yard and Reddy had had enough. He flew straight up in the air and over the fence and Jack's head. In the few seconds that Reddy was in the air Jack was trying to see where he took off to, but not being able to see all that well, he just naturally assumed the bird had flown off, but it didn't happen that way.

Reddy flew over the fence all right, but as soon as saw those white cheeks blazing in the morning sun, he knew he'd been fooled and redirected his flight. He made a dive that would have stunned a chickenhawk and latched on to Jack's buttocks like a snapping turtle, pecking at the tenderest spots one could imagine. Jack was so startled at the surprise attack, all he could do was slap at his butt, but since he couldn't see his attacker, there was nothing to do but get up and run.

He was twisting, turning, and slapping at the rooster, contorting his head trying to get a fix on him, the fox head flopping in his face. Reddy was hanging on for life, flapping and striking with his beak so hard that every time he hit pay dirt Jack would let out a yell. Not being able to see, Jack was just running here and there, bumping into things as they got in his way. Then he hit the side of the cabin. It was a solid hit, and Jack just kind of hung there for a second before he fell straight over backwards. But that didn't deter Reddy. He hung on, still pecking away.

The only thing running into the wall did was make things worse. When Jack fell on his back there was no place for Reddy to go, and not wanting to get smashed, he entered the only place available; he wiggled his way into the back flap. This woke up Jack quick. He was back on his feet again, but he didn't have a rooster hanging from his butt anymore, he had one thrashing in his drawers. The trouble was, the part that was half in was the one that was capable of doing the most damage.

Jack didn't know which way to grab. He had one hand clutching his crotch and the other twisted around the back, hanging onto the rooster, trying to pull him out, hopping and jumping with every stab from Reddy's pencil-sharp pecker. The only thing that saved Jack was ol' Red ran out of air. Reddy fell limp and Jack pulled him out, both of 'em lying on the ground side by side, too exhausted to move.

They had more respect for each other after that and became fast friends. Reddy was letting Jack get his eggs anytime he wanted, and Jack gave him the run of the place.

Chapter Eight

"Eat another piece of fish, Pete," Claude said, handing him the plate.

Pete took the plate and set it in front of him, then wiped his hands on his jeans.

"You must have known everyone that lived here," Pete said. "Doesn't sound like there were too many strangers that came around."

"Oh, we had lots of visitors," Claude said. He picked up his fishing pole and hung the hook on an eye and tightened the line and set it beside him.

"The river was a getting-off point for lots of people because of the road, but we had folks just passing through too. There were a lot of characters wandering the country back then, and one of 'em had their sights set on Jack."

"Mind if I tie my horse up?" she said. "I don't want him wandering around. Not that he'd run off, 'cause he's the best-trained horse in the nation."

Elmer, Preacher, and I were sitting on the porch of the Three-Stop that morning when she showed up, a tall, broad-shouldered gal, dressed in buckskins from head to foot. Jack was out back collecting eggs, Reddy on his heels.

Her flaming red hair was falling out from under a hat made of muskrat fur, long and thick, spilling over her shoulders like a blanket. She looked to be close to two hundred pounds, but didn't appear to be fat. She was as stout a woman as we'd ever seen, with many characteristics of a man. Her hands were big and strong, the knuckles large, the fingers long with nails bit down to the skin.

I'd put her at six foot, but we never had a chance to measure her. Her buckskins were dark and greasy with a fringe across the back of her shoulders. Her face was full of freckles, kind of cute in a way, but her features were bold, the jawline square, eyes close together, gray like a wolf's, and hard. Her full lips were pulled to a thin line, her teeth yellow with one front tooth broke in half—the better to whistle with, she said. She had a fat chaw of tobacco stuck in her jaw and every minute or two she'd spit out a stream and wipe her mouth on her sleeve. Her broken, crooked nose lay flat on her face and wheezed when she breathed.

She was a woman like no other and she made no bones about being able to handle a man's job. Her large breasts pushed out the front of her shirt, showing no doubt there was a female underneath those deerskins.

"What's a matter, cat got your tongues?" she asked. "Never seen a woman in buckskins afore?"

"No, ma'am—I mean, yes, ma'am," I stuttered.

"Who's in charge?"

"In charge of what?" Preacher asked, shocked as I was at her appearance.

"Why, this here eatin' place, if that's what it is."

"You're a big woman," Elmer said.

"I can handle the likes of you, old timer. You ain't nothin' but bones—brittle bones, I'd guess."

Elmer was taken aback by her straight talk, but the smile on his face showed he liked her attitude.

"I like big women," Elmer said. "A big woman can pull a big load."

"Well don't be lookin' for me to pull yours. Now, who's cookin' up the grub?"

"That'd be Jack Stepp," Preacher said with a smile. "He's the owner."

"Well, round him up, I'm hungry. Ain't had nothin' but possum since yesterday, and he was still kickin' when I ate him."

As luck would have it Jack came through the front door with Reddy strutting behind him.

It was love at first sight the way her jaw dropped, showing a snaggled smile, and her eyes opened wide with a dreamy look.

"Is that him, the one with the dinner chasin' him?"

"That's Jack," Preacher said.

"Jack," Preacher started. "Meet...uh...I don't believe I caught your name."

"Bull, is what I go by," she said, staring at Jack. "But you can call me Pearl."

"Well, Pearl—" Elmer started.

"Not you, limb line, you call me Bull." She looked at Preacher and me in turn, her lips pulled tight and eyes narrowed. We understood the message.

We could tell Jack was nervous, being no way he could misunderstand her mooning expression. He had no intentions of mixing it up with her and was backing his way toward the door.

"Hold on there, stubby. You don't mind if I call you Stubby, do you. Who's your pal, there? Sure is an ugly dog."

"That ain't no dog," Elmer said. "It's a rooster."

Pearl's eyes shifted to Elmer. "I'm just making small talk." She turned her attention back to Jack.

"I hear tell you're the cook around here, honey. I sure could use some grub, and while you're cookin' I might just freshen up a bit." She took off her hat, ran her hands through the matted hair to loosen it up, then dug out the chaw and threw it behind her.

"I don't really cook," Jack said.

"Sure you do. You'll cook up something for Pearl, won't you?" She winked at Jack as she started up the steps. "One of you men take care of my horse." She put her arm around Jack's shoulder and turned him toward the door.

"Now, sweetheart, you caught my eye, and when something as good-looking as you comes along, why, ol' Pearl's just got to latch on to it. I caught your eye, too, didn't I? It's okay to give Pearl a hug, she won't mind." She squeezed Jack's body next to hers, the top of his head barely coming up to her large, hanging breasts.

Jack was in stunned silence. He was wary of the woman, as we all were, and was unsure about what her reaction might be if her feelings were rejected. Preacher took the horse out back and put him with the mule while Elmer and I followed the two lovers inside.

"How'd you happen to find your way to Dogleg, Bull?" I asked.

"Lost mostly," she said, letting go of Jack's shoulder.

"Been up on the Platte, carryin' supplies for the Army. I got into it with the post commander and he told me to get out. I sold 'em my mule team and wagon, bought a horse and headed south. Figured I'd ride the Muddy down to New Orleans and see what was doing. It's rough going through these hills and somewhere I got off the main track. I spotted this road and remembered I'd been here before. Lucky for me it dead-ended at Stubby's. Ain't that what you say, Stubby?"

"My name ain't Stubby, it's Jack."

"I know that, but Jack just ain't fittin' somehow. This place needs a woman's touch, now don't it?" Pearl was looking over the cabin with hands on her broad hips.

"And who might you be?" she asked, without turning to face me.

"I'd be Claude and this is Elmer. We live down the road."

"Well, bust my britches," she said. "You think I'm stupid. Of course you live around here."

"It'll take a big swing to bust them britches," Elmer said.

"Now you listen here, string bean. I don't have no reserves 'bout pounding down old codgers like you, so don't irritate me."

"I like big women," Elmer said.

"You done said that," Pearl said.

"I know, but I meant it like a compliment."

"Well, don't go a courtin' me, not in front of Stubby. He's liable to take a dislikin' to it."

Jack was looking irritated on the one hand and confused on the other. Reddy was circling his feet, pecking at the floor.

"I guess you'll be moving along then," Jack said.

"Honey, my days are filled with time. If you want me to stay on, just give the call."

"No," Jack said. "I wouldn't want to stop you from your obligations."

"No obligations, none at all. I'm thinking I might like it here. I hope you got a tub. I ain't had a bath in a month."

"You can tell it too," Elmer said.

"Is that pencil your pa?" Pearl asked, looking at me.

"No, he's just Elmer. He don't belong to nobody."

"Then you won't mind if I kick him. Just kiddin'—I like a man with spunk. What about you, Stubby, you got spunk?"

"Quit calling me Stubby."

"Now, don't get in a huff, sweetie," Pearl said. "You and me got things to talk about."

"Like what?" Jack said, his voice rising.

"You need a wife."

"I had a wife once. She passed away."

"You need another one. What about Slim, where'd he go?"

"You mean Preacher Dan," I said. "He's putting your horse up."

"A preacher, huh," Pearl said, her hand scratching her butt. "This place's got everything."

"You take on airs when you come to a place, don't you?" Elmer asked.

"I take what I need and leave the rest. You can bet I won't be totin' you very far."

"I like a woman what says things straight," Elmer said. "You want to bunk with me tonight?"

"I told you not to be talkin' that way in front of my soon-to-be."

"Soon to be what?" Jack asked.

"We'll talk later, sugar buns," Pearl said. "Now where's that tub? Boil me some water, honey pie. I want to wash off some mountain mud before we get down to business."

"I'll tell you what kind of business I'd like to get down to," Elmer said.

"Stubby, you tell that old man to stop love-talking."

Jack just stood there. I didn't know what took hold of Elmer. Either he'd lost his eyesight or his nose had plugged up. The rest of us weren't seeing or smelling the same thing he was. Preacher came in through the back door carrying Bull's rifle and bedroll.

"Thought you might want these," Dan said, standing the gun in the corner and handing the bedroll to Bull.

"Mighty kind of you," she said. "By the way, are you a marryin' preacher?"

"Who's getting hitched?" Preacher asked.

"Just stay close," Pearl said. "There may be work for you. Is that coffee? Get me a cup, would you, sugar pie?"

"I will," Elmer said, getting up from his seat.

"Stay put, shoestring. My man'll fetch it."

No one moved, especially Jack.

"I gotta go," Jack said, walking toward the front door, grabbing my arm as he passed.

"Don't be long, sweet cheeks," Pearl yelled. "I can't stand lettin' you out of my sight. You there, bean pole, boil me some water."

"What's with her?" Jack said.

We were on the porch and he was nervous, peeking through the window at Pearl.

"I think she intends to mate with you."

Jack's eyes got big. "She can't mate with me. I'll not have it."

"She don't act like she'll take no for an answer," I said. "Her bedroll's in your cabin and her horse is in your pen. Looks to me like she's settling in."

"God a mighty," Jack whispered. "What'll I do?"

"Elmer seems taken with her. Maybe you could talk her into considering him. Of course, they'd have to live with you. I don't need her at my place."

"Live with me! Why would I do that?"

"It's what you call a love triangle," I said. "The way I see it, she's in love with you, Elmer's in love with her, and you, well, you're just stuck in the middle. Elmer's too old to do her justice, you'll have to pitch in to keep her satisfied."

"What? Satisfied. What's that supposed to mean?"

"You know…satisfied. A woman like her has needs. There's no telling where her tastes run, so you'll have to keep her happy, just to keep Elmer safe."

"It is a love trisickle," Jack said.

"Triangle, love triangle."

"Honey lips, where are you?" Pearl yelled from inside. "Will that tub fit the two of us? I need my back scrubbed."

Jack's mouth dropped as he peeked through the window.

"This is bad, Claude. Real bad."

Preacher was backing his way out of the front door.

"There's a foul wind in there, boys," Dan said. "She's taking her clothes off."

"Where's Elmer?" I asked.

"He's watching."

"Maybe one of us should do something," I said.

"It's up to Jack," Preacher said.

"Me! Why is it up to me?"

"She's your woman," Preacher said.

"She ain't my woman!"

"That's the way she sees it, and I'm not arguing with her."

"Damn love tricycles," Jack said.

"Triangle," I said again.

"I've heard of that," Preacher said. "Lord save us, it's a house of sin. Jack, pray with me."

"Don't pray *with* me—pray *for* me."

"Go stop her, Jack," I said. "The sight of that's gonna curdle milk. Elmer'll have a stroke."

Jack made his way into the cabin, stopping just inside the front door.

"Uh…Bull, don't you want some privacy?"

"What? You afraid the old man's fancy might get tickled?"

"I'm already tickled," Elmer said.

"This kind of excitement might stop your heart," Jack said.

"Good," Elmer said. "I need a heart-stopper. Now, move out of the way."

"Dumplings," Pearl said to Jack, "would you pull down on my trousers? They seem to be stuck."

"I'll help," Elmer said.

"You stay where you're at, tent pole," Pearl said. "Is that water hot? Get it in the tub. Stubby, grab my knife, I'll need you to cut my toenails."

"I ain't cutting nothing."

"Sure you are, sweet lips. Pearl wants to be nice and clean for her man. You can rub the dead skin off the bottom of my feet, too. Them ol' boots make my feet sweat so the skin just peels off like paper."

"You ever thought of hitching up with an older gentleman?" Elmer broke in.

"You look to me like you got one foot slipping on the ditch. Now, get me another pot boiling while sugarplum cleans my ears. I got a bug in one three days ago and he ain't never come out."

"I ain't never met a woman like you before," Elmer said.

"I'm spoke for, old man. Stubby, you got any lice killer? My scalp's itching."

"You got things all wrong," Jack said. "I ain't looking for no woman."

"Now, pumpkin, don't go getting wet feet before you jump in the river. There's plenty of time to plan for things to come."

"I ain't making no plans," Jack said.

"I got a plan," Elmer said with a smile. "I could use a woman to care for me."

"You don't need a woman, you need pallbearers," Pearl said.

Preacher and I were still on the porch looking through the window when we heard someone in back of us.

"What's going on?" It was Mother Mabel.

"There's a woman in there that wants to make Jack her man," Preacher said.

Mother looked through the window and huffed.

"That's ol' Pearl," she said. "I wondered when she'd show up again. What's her story this time?"

"You know her?" I asked.

"Sure I do. Pearl's been looking for a husband since she was thirteen. Last I heard she was working for the Army. I sold her two mules six years ago when she came through headed west. What's Elmer doing in there?"

"He's taking a liking to her, but she won't have nothing to do with him," Preacher said.

"What's Jack's thinking?"

"He's scrambling," I said.

"How long's he been sweating?"

"Quite a while. She stuck to him as soon as she saw him."

"More than likely soon as she found out he owned the store," Mother said. "Well, come on."

Preacher and I followed Mother into the cabin and stood back to watch the show.

"Cover up, Pearl," Mother said. "This ain't a whorehouse."

"Mabel!" Pearl said. "Long time no see. You're just in time to help with the wedding. Stubby's done asked me to marry him."

"I have not," Jack yelled.

"I'll take her," Elmer said. "I like big women."

"You can have Elmer," Mother said. "But you can't have Jack. He's mine."

"Yours!" Pearl said. "Sweetcakes, say it ain't so."

Jack was slow in catching on, his eyes bouncing back and forth between Mother and Pearl.

"Jack, tell her you're mine," Mother said. "I ought to thump your head for playing around."

"She's right," Preacher said, trying to help.

Mother went over to Jack and put her arm around his shoulders.

"He's not much, but I'm partial to him," she said.

"Shall I perform the ceremony tonight?" Preacher asked.

"Be quiet," Mother said.

"I guess I don't need that bath now," Pearl said.

"What about me?" Elmer shouted.

"Is that toothpick still walking?" Pearl said. She was putting her buckskins back on.

"You got any mules for sale, Mabel? I hate to leave empty-handed."

"Sure I do. Why don't you sleep in my cabin tonight and I'll fix something to eat and we'll look at those mules in the morning."

"It's your last chance, apple dumplings," Pearl said, looking at Jack and scratching her butt again.

Jack stayed silent. Mother slapped him on the back of the head.

"No—no," Jack said.

"You always got to slap him like that?" Pearl asked.

"He ain't the smartest pea in the pod," Mother said.

"Figures," Pearl said, as they walked out the door.

"What about me?" Elmer said, with a sad look on his face.

"Take a hot bath, fish pole," Pearl said. "Watch him, boys, he looks like a floater."

Chapter Nine

"That's the best fried fish I believe I've ever eaten," Pete said.

"You don't eat much fish I guess," Claude said.

"No, I can't say that I do. Meat, I eat a lot of meat, but I think I'll try more fish now."

"Well, eating it on the riverbank makes it tastes better," Claude said. "Do you do much fishing?"

"I don't do any fishing, not since I was a kid. My father used to take me to a lake a few times, but we caught perch, mostly. I've never sat on a bank at night and fished. It's peaceful out here."

Claude picked up his fishing pole and hooked on a nightcrawler and handed it to Pete.

"Why don't you try your luck; you might catch a nice one."

Pete took the pole and stepped to the edge of the water and tossed the line in.

"Just let it sink, I guess?"

"Yeah," Claude said. "Just let it lay there, they'll find it. We'll keep an eye on it."

"You know," Pete said, "it's nice out here sitting by the river, but it's summer too. I bet it got cold in the winter. The ice and snow must have made it difficult to get around. I just get in my four-wheel drive and go anywhere I want."

"A mule can just about get you anywhere you want," Claude said. "But you're right, winters could be hard this far back in the woods. The biggest problem with it was staying shut in, but we found lots of things to do. We'd meet at Jack's every morning for coffee, just like normal, and sometimes we'd stay there all day. If Mother didn't bring us a deer stew or a pot of beans, then we'd cook our own on a wood stove. It could get boring though, but Preacher and Jack kept things interesting."

Claude thought about how cold the nights were in those winters and how tough it was sometimes to get the stock fed and watered. As hard as it was, it was something he would miss. He reached in the sack and took the coffee pot out and walked to the river and filled it with river water and set it in the hot coals of the fire.

January takes the brunt of the cold and spreads it over the mountains. Everything seems lifeless with the freezing winds. Most of the time is spent taking care of the animals, breaking the ice in the ponds and tearing apart the frozen hay.

The river's edges are iced and at some points frozen over from bank to bank, the cold water running underneath. The mountains can't hold back the northern winds, and temperatures drop to freezing every night and day. The cold controls our movements and the gray days dampen our spirits. It's best to stay inside during those months, but it can lead to cabin fever, and that's not just a myth.

We spent our days at the Three-Stop Café, playing checkers and poker, stoking the fire, and sipping on Potation. Elmer slept, and Jack worried, the lack of trade dipping into his savings like the rest of us. Preacher, he walked the floor while I spent my time looking out the window, wishing for spring.

Jack kept something simmering on the cook stove all the time, with cornbread or biscuits to dip with. We'd lose track of the days if Jack hadn't crossed out the dates on his calendar. It was one of the few routines that raised our spirits, knowing we were one day closer to spring breezes.

I stared out the window on one cold January morning and I could see the dark clouds folding on top of each other; a storm was coming in fast.

"Looks like a boomer," I said.

Jack and Preacher came to the window to see.

"It is," Preacher said. "Those clouds got rain in 'em. They'll not pass over tonight; they'll hang and let loose."

"It's too cold to rain," Jack said. "It'll be ice."

"Best be prepared," Preacher said, grabbing his coat.

We went our separate ways to take care of the livestock and stack more wood in the cabins. I left Elmer asleep at Jack's.

An ice storm is the worst—it stops everything. The animals have to be brought in from the fields or they'll freeze; the chickens must be moved to the barn and a wood stove stoked to keep 'em warm. Dogs are brought inside and water troughs filled, even though they'll freeze; sledges and axes have to be laid out to break the ice.

By noon that day the weather had turned. A light mist was falling and the sky was dark and the thunder was rumbling. I finished my chores and headed back to Jack's to get Elmer.

"Leave him here," Jack said. "He won't be any trouble."

I left him and trudged back to the cabin. The mist was turning to sleet. I picked up another armful of wood and carried it inside. The fire was low in the fireplace, so I stirred it and threw in two more logs. I fired the cook stove and put on a pot of beans and coffee and sat by the fireplace and listened to the hiss of the burning logs and ticking of the sleet against the windows. It would be a long night.

By mid-afternoon the sleet had turned to giant raindrops, falling so fast and hard it was difficult to see the trees. I settled in and waited. At dusk the rain was freezing as soon as it hit. The ground, trees, and brush were covered with ice, the rain still coming down. By late evening the rain had turned to sleet again, so thick it was all I could see. I made some biscuits and ate some beans and sat down by the fire and dozed. Around midnight something woke me, but I was so groggy I didn't know what. Then I heard it, a loud knock. I lit the lantern and went to the door.

"Who's there?"

"It's me, Tubbs," came the answer.

"Tubbs!" I yelled and opened the door.

Sure enough, he was standing on the porch, near frozen, ice covering him from head to foot.

"Thought I'd make it before the storm hit, but she came in too fast."

"Get in here, Tubbs, and get out of the cold." I grabbed his coat and pulled him inside. "Stand by the fire." I poured him some hot coffee and handed it to him. He could hardly hold it.

"Where you been?" I asked. He'd been gone ever since my cabin was finished.

"I had other places to be."

"How'd you know?"

"I felt it. I knew I had to go, soon as possible."

I took the blanket off Elmer's bed and handed it to him.

"Get out of them clothes and wrap this around you."

He did and laid his wet clothes on the floor in front of the fire and stood with the blanket wrapped over him.

"What brings you back here in the dead of winter?"

"You," he said.

"Me?"

"There's a sign of things to come. You must know—you must have felt it."

I looked at him, confused.

"You'll understand," he said. "Is them beans I smell?"

"Sure is. I'll get you a bowl."

We sat in silence while Tubbs ate beans and biscuits and drank coffee, warming himself by the fire.

"Where's Elmer?" Tubbs asked, setting his finished bowl aside.

"He's at Jack's. He was asleep when I went to get him. We didn't think it'd do him any good getting out in this weather."

"No, no it wouldn't," Tubbs said. "Preacher, Jack, and Mother, how are they?"

"Good, they're good."

Tubbs turned his clothes over and moved 'em closer to the fire. He pulled the blanket up around his neck.

"There's death coming your way," he said.

I held my silence. The fire cracked and popped while the wind howled.

"It won't be you. It'll be others, but you'll be touched."

"Who will it be?"

"It's not for me to say, I only know it'll come. Watch for the sign."

"What sign, what do I look for?"

"You'll know when it comes."

"Why would I see the sign?"

"Remember when we first met at the river? The sign was there, you saw it."

"All I saw was you."

"You saw the sign. You'll remember when you see it again."

I didn't like the way the conversation was going and was getting upset.

"Can't you tell me more than that, Tubbs?"

"I don't know more than what I've told. All I can say is you're the one I'm supposed to tell."

I looked long and hard at the man sitting by the fire. He was a good man and I trusted him, but now I was confused by his talk, and his presence seemed unreal, arriving at my door after being gone so long and in the middle of an ice storm, talking about signs.

"Who are you, Tubbs?"

He looked at me with a knowing smile for just a moment and then looked into the fire.

"I'm your friend."

"I know that, but who are you? I don't know nothing about you. You come walking up the river like you could walk on water and fit in with the rest of us like you been here forever. Then you leave without a word and come back in the middle of the night in the worst storm in ten years. It's not making sense."

"Does it have too? Some things have to be held close without knowing why. Have you ever heard of a person dying of a broken heart?"

"I've heard of it."

"It don't make sense does it, that a strong body can die, just lay down and die from a broken heart? But it happens, and you have to hold that close, without knowing how it can be."

"What's that got to do with anything?"

"Everything. Just 'cause you never walked that road don't mean the road ain't there. You got to believe in some things, even if you don't know why."

He was right, of course, and as difficult as it was for me, I could understand that I didn't have all the answers. We talked through the night, through the storm, and I fell asleep sometime before dawn. When I woke up the storm was over and Tubbs was gone.

The gray light of morning spread over a world of glaze. Ice covered everything in sight. The heavy load bore down on the trees and I could hear limbs breaking, falling on top of each other, the sound of shattering ice sprinkling to the ground. It was all I could do to check on the stock and break the ice on their water.

I fed the fires and cooked some breakfast and waited for the temperature to rise. It was two days before the ice melted and I could walk to the Three-Stop and see my friends.

The talk with Tubbs haunted me, and the loneliness of the cabin drained me. To this day I'm not sure he was ever there; perhaps it was a dream, but the words were there and I carried 'em with me.

"He'll be dinner tonight," were the first shouts I heard as I opened the door of the Three-Stop.

"Take him, Claude, I've had enough," Jack yelled.

Elmer was running around in his greasy longjohns, Reddy the Rooster chasing him, pecking at his heels.

"These two been driving me crazy," Jack snorted. "Elmer's been sneaking up on Reddy during the night trying to wring his neck. There ain't been no sleep around here for days."

"Nobody has a rooster for a pet," Elmer said. "Roosters is farm animals and they belong outside. I'll ring his scrawny neck, I will, if I can catch him." Elmer did an about face and lunged for Reddy, knocking over a chair but grabbing some tail feathers. He was on his feet in seconds chasing the cock around the cabin.

"It's been this way ever since you left, Claude," Jack said with a tired voice.

"Them beans was a bad idea. I've had to air out the cabin three times and I'm sure that's what's got Reddy's feathers ruffled. Every time Elmer cuts loose Reddy attacks him. He's a sensitive rooster and Elmer don't understand that."

It did smell a bit stale, but what could a man expect with Elmer and a rooster living there.

Elmer was closing in on Reddy, and they were both headed my way. I opened the door, and they both ran through it and I shut the door behind 'em.

"How's the coffee?" I asked.

"It's hot. Pour me a cup too."

Elmer came busting back through the door, with Reddy flapping right behind him. And behind him were Mother and Preacher.

"Two mules are down," Mother said. "I need your help."

"What happened?" Jack asked.

"Pond's still froze over. Them mules walked out on it like they knew what they were doing. Both of 'em are spraddled belly down to the ice. We'll have to noose 'em and pull 'em to the bank. They can't get up the way they are."

We grabbed our coats and followed Mother to the pond. The mules thought they could get a drink of water somewhere on that shiny glaze and once they had all four feet on the ice they went down quick.

"The farthest one out looks like his leg's broke," Preacher said.

"Just my luck," Mother snarled.

She made a noose with a rope and threw it around the closest mule. All of us grabbed a hold and pulled him to the bank. He was hurt but not bad. Mother could mend his torn muscles, but the other one, he looked in bad shape.

"I can't fix a broke leg," she said. "We'll have to shoot him. Question is, should we shoot him on the ice or try to get him to the bank?"

"He'll just fight if we try to pull him in," Jack said.

"I'll go back to the cabin and get my rifle," Mother said, turning to leave.

The mule was struggling, still trying to get to his feet, bellowing in pain.

"Let's try and pull him closer to the bank," Preacher said. "He might just slide over."

We tried several throws with the rope but none of us could get it around the mule's head.

Mother showed up with the rifle, loaded it and handed it to Jack.

"I can't kill ol' Jackson," she said. "He's been with me too long. Would you mind, Jack? He didn't like you anyway."

Jack took the rifle and the rope, tiptoed out on the ice, put the noose around ol' Jackson's head, raised the rifle and took aim. Just as he fired, the ice broke, and him and the mule went under. Jack came back up like a bobber, and soon as his head hit air the mule popped up right underneath him, Jack sitting on him backwards.

"Hell," Elmer shouted. "He missed him."

The pond wasn't very deep and ol' Jackson's feet were touching the bottom. He was scared to death and freezing too, and the combination put him in frenzy. He started bucking and screaming, pumping his front legs up on the ice in front of him, busting it up as he dug in, Jack holding his tail so he wouldn't get thrown back in the water under the mule. It was hard telling who was screaming louder, Jack or Jackson.

"That mule's leg ain't broke," Mother said.

"Seemed broke to me," Preacher said, looking sheepish.

Jackson made it to the bank, and with all four feet hitting solid ground he was ready to get what was holding on to his tail off of him. I'd never seen a mule buck that high. Jack's body was flying up in the air and slamming back down on the mule's rump, with both hands gripping Jackson's tail.

"*He's gonna hurt my mule!*" Mother yelled.

"He won't hurt him," Elmer said. "He can't even shoot him."

Jackson was making a circle around the pond, bucking like a bronc, Jack bouncing on him like a ball.

"*Grab the rope*," I yelled. "*We'll pull him in.*"

The rope was getting away from us, trailing ol' Jackson, and as it passed by Elmer he made a lunge for the rope. He got it, but Elmer didn't have enough weight on him to do much good. Jackson hardly noticed, so he was dragging Elmer behind him as he bucked around the pond. We could hear Elmer's talent slipping into high gear as he sped away from us.

Jackson's bowels loosened up about the same time he took on his second load. He was dragging Elmer through manure with Jack flopping on his butt, and Preacher and I trying to catch up to the whole bunch.

We caught up to Elmer and the rope just as Jackson wore down and came to a full stop. Jack was lying on his stomach, arms and legs dangling down the mule's sides, his head resting on Jackson's rump. Elmer picked himself up, grabbed a stick and scraped off the mud and manure as best he could.

"If that don't beat all," Mother said, with an air of disgust. "Preacher, you and Claude get a grappling hook and get my rifle out of that pond. Elmer, you stink, go take a bath. Jack…" Mother just looked at him and shook her head.

She took the rope and led Jackson home, Jack still splayed out on his back, the other mule following 'em.

That night we were sitting by the fire watching the snow fall and listening to one of Preacher's stories. Whenever things got dull Preacher had a tendency to reminisce about his younger years and all the traveling he'd done. His tales were always entertaining, regardless if they were true or not, but I'm sure there was some fact in 'em, no matter the embellishments.

"I remember the time I was stuck in a dust storm in San Antonio, Texas," he was saying. "I was giving a series of lectures to a group of nuns, also trapped in the storm. They were headed west, I was going east, and it was by the grace of God that our paths crossed.

"They were the ugliest six missionaries I'd ever laid eyes on, but far be it for me to pass judgment on the physical frailties of the good Lord's devotees. I was expounding the virtues of the Ten Commandments and much to my dismay I was having trouble communicating. I could barely make out their faces, their heads and bodies completely covered by their habits. Only from time to time could I see their distorted features, as they whispered to one another, no doubt praising my dissertation. I could see their shoes though, which weren't shoes at all, but boots, some complete with spurs. I thought this quite odd, but with the ruthless storm raging outside, I decided they were well equipped for their trip.

"They were obviously well-rounded travelers, speaking in Spanish part of the time, and I could only conclude that they had recently performed their missionary duties in the wastelands of Mexico. Their tanned foreheads and grimy muscular hands also giving away their unselfish undertakings.

"As I was closing my lecture, spending more time than was necessary on coveting thy neighbor's wife, the giggles and whispering interrupting my speech, the sheriff burst into the room.

"'Hold on there, Preacher,'" he shouted. "'I'm looking for six Mexican banditos. Have you seen 'em?'

"'My good man, does this assemblage look as if it contains the worst of mankind. We are all peasants, workers of the Lord.'

"'I'm just asking, Preacher. They've terrorized the town for three days. They've robbed, killed, and raped—even stole the tithes from the church on Sunday.'

"'Not this group,' I said, waving my arm past the sisters.

"'Let me have a look at these nuns,' the sheriff said, 'just to be sure.'

"'I should say not,' I said adamantly. 'I'll vouch for their authenticity.'

"'They look a little rough around the edges if you ask me,' the sheriff said.

"'That's only because they've worked their whole lives trying to spread the good word to the lowest sinners of the land. You'll not disturb these ladies if I have my way.'

"'That one on the end looks like she's got a mustache.'

"'Oh, the shame of it all, Sheriff,' I said. 'Physical beauty is not a prerequisite of the Lord.'

"'Are you in charge of 'em?'

"'You might say that as a minister I hold certain responsibilities that I'm sure they look up to, but we have only just met this very day, our wanderings taking us in different directions. Am I right, ladies?'

"All six nodded agreement and with a rousing affirmation said, 'Sí, Señor!' They all looked at each other in surprise, knowing the mistake they'd made. The sheriff's eyes bulged, his hand went to his holster, and the sisters' habits flung off their bodies over their heads, hands holding their pistols—Mexican banditos, all of 'em.

"Of course I was as shocked as the sheriff, and as the gunfire commenced, I bolted through the closet door behind me. It was pitch dark in the small room and I immediately tripped on something and landed, much to my surprise, on the six nuns. All I could hear was their grunts and groans. Their mouths were gagged and their hands and feet tied. I could hear the fight continuing outside the closet and took a second to catch my breath. The ladies were squirming and wiggling beneath me, but it was so dark all I could do was feel my way around. I quickly understood the situation and knew my first efforts must be to untie the luckless females.

"It was a difficult predicament at best. As I ran my hands over their bodies in search of their bindings I could hear the turmoil outside quieting down. The sheriff's deputies had been right behind him and quickly took control of the situation. Meanwhile, in my efforts to release the unfortunate women, their groans had changed to moans. I can't remember how much time had elapsed until the sheriff opened the closet door.

"'*Here they are, men!* he shouted. 'What are you doing in there?'

"'Trying to release these poor sisters' bindings,' I said.

"The sheriff grabbed me by the back of my shirt and pulled me from the squirming group of bodies.

"'You been in there for fifteen minutes and ain't got none of them women untied?'

"The sheriff's deputies released the ladies.

"'It's very dark in there. In all the excitement it was difficult to locate their ropes.'

"'Bring 'em out here,' the sheriff ordered.

"I could tell he had a suspicious nature, but not knowing all the facts he was jumping to conclusions.

"'Are you sisters okay?'

"They all said they were, just scared.

"'Those Mexican banditos were trying to get out of town, but this storm had 'em shut in. You sisters just happened to be in the wrong place at the wrong time.'

"'We're so grateful, Sheriff,' one of 'em said.

"The deputies gave their habits back and the nuns were busy getting dressed, embarrassed as they were.

"'Now,' the sheriff said, looking at me. 'How'd you happen to be in a prayer meeting with six Mexican banditos?'

"'It was happenchance. I was merely practicing my trade. It's not the duty of a minister to bodily search missionaries. I took 'em at face value.'

"'*Face value!*' the sheriff shouted. 'They're *men.*'

"'Sheriff, believe me, in my line of work, one embraces the hideous as well as the handsome. It was merely an oversight on my part.'

"'Uh-huh, an oversight you say. What about you spraddled across those women in that closet for so long, without even untying or ungagging one of 'em?'

"'Sheriff,' said one of the nuns, 'if I may be so bold, it was dark in the room, and I can't say that the preacher didn't try to release us.'

"She had a small smile on her face, as did the others, most of their faces blushing. All I could think was that my efforts at groping for their ropes had somehow touched a sympathetic nerve.

"'We believe,' she continued, 'that his efforts at freeing our bindings, a failure though they may have been, were…well, satisfying to all concerned.'

"'I see,' the sheriff said. 'Well, I hope you're better at preaching than you are at untying knots.'

"So, as you may have gathered, I was actually the hero of the day. By holding the attention of the banditos with my spellbinding sermon I gave the sheriff time to apprehend the vicious criminals. And, while not being directly responsible for locating the missing nuns, my presence in their midst was, shall we say, comforting."

Jack had fallen asleep by then and Elmer was snoring. I was the only one awake to hear the story.

"How does it feel to be a hero?" I asked.

"Never felt better," Preacher said, smiling at the memory.

The winter days were long and boring. It was all we could do to keep ourselves occupied on those cold, dreary days. Anything that provided entertainment was welcome, and most of the time was spent inventing something to do. Jack was especially adept at coming up with simple, time-occupying notions, and one day he'd thought long and hard and finally put his finger on something.

"Barrel racing," he said.

"What's barrel racing?" I asked.

"Don't you know? You get in a barrel and roll down the hill and the first one past the finish line wins."

"Never heard of it," Preacher snorted.

"Sounds stupid," Elmer said.

"It ain't stupid. You're inside the barrel; it protects you. If you hit something, you just bounce off."

"Never heard of it," Preacher said again.

"You won't be no good at it anyway," Jack sneered. "Takes a man what knows how to roll in a barrel to be good at it. Now you take me, for instance. I've got the proper build to keep a barrel on an even keel. You, on the other hand, Preacher, are too tall and skinny. Your barrel'll just twist around and get off course. Some men ain't meant to barrel race."

Preacher just eyed Jack. "All right," Preacher said. "I'm in."

"We'll start at the top of the road," Jack said.

"Hold on, what's gonna stop us?"

"We'll tie ropes together and make a net," Jack said. "We'll stretch it across the road and tie it from tree to tree, right in front of the Three-Stop."

"Sounds feasible," Preacher said, rubbing his chin. "What's gonna keep us in the barrel?"

"We'll use rain barrels and Claude can nail the tops on."

Jack had thought of everything, even if he had just made it up. It took the rest of the day to tie the ropes together, but they looked like they might hold.

The excitement was growing in Dogleg as the rumor spread about the race.

Preacher even did some exercising to get in shape, doing sit-ups that night, in between sips of Potation.

We waited till noon, just to let the road get a nice glaze on it, then we tied the net from the Three-Stop's porch railing across the road to a tree trunk. The net would be the finish line and the first barrel in the net would be the winner. Elmer built a big bonfire across from the cabin so the crowd could keep warm and the race was ready to start.

We carried the barrels up the road a hundred yards, and Preacher and Jack crawled inside. I nailed the lids on and turned 'em on their sides.

"*Ready in there?*" I hollered.

"*Ready,*" Jack yelled.

"*Ready,*" Preacher shouted.

I raised my hand in the air and waved at Elmer to let him know it was time to watch the finish line, and he waved back.

"Here we go," I yelled.

I pushed 'em off and watched as they picked up speed, both of the barrels staying fairly straight in the road, Preacher on the right and Jack on the left.

It didn't take long before the barrels got to moving so swift it became worrisome. About the fifty-yard mark they were spinning so fast you couldn't tell where the slats fit together.

Just as they passed the fifty-yard mark I looked down the road to where Elmer stood by the fire and noticed something peculiar. Everybody was standing in front of the fire watching the race, but nobody was watching the fire. I could see the smoke drifting across the road, but it didn't look like wood smoke to me. On closer inspection, I could tell the rope was on fire. Elmer had made his bonfire too close to it, and the tree and the rope were flaming like gunpowder. It was too late to do anything and the crowd was yelling too loud anyway, so all I could do was stand and watch.

The two barrels were in a dead heat, side by side, gaining speed like a diving hawk. I could barely hear Jack and Preacher's screams above the roar of the crowd. Both barrels struck the net at the same time and when they hit, the rope snapped and the barrels sped on by.

I could tell by their screams that Jack and Dan knew something was wrong. The road was so slick there was no stopping 'em, and so they continued picking up speed racing toward the river.

I started running after 'em but there was no catching up. The whole crowd was in the middle of the road watching as the two barrels headed for the river. Both barrels hit the water at the same time. They were floating on the river like corks, headed downstream. No one was interested in jumping in the water, and so just lined the banks, watching as they drifted away.

"Told you it was stupid," Elmer said.

The evenings were particularly difficult to handle. Although sipping on Potation helped to make our moods more upbeat, it was still boring as hell. Dark came early in the mountains and stayed late, so entertaining ourselves by looking out over the countryside only lasted eight or ten hours a day, and that was plenty monotonous. A person can only sleep so much, with the exception of Elmer, who could put in a full fourteen hours on any given day.

Sometimes things got so boring we'd take bets among ourselves on how long Elmer would nap, staying up late at night just to see who'd win. It was treacherous territory though, trying to stay awake yourself, the temptation to give Elmer a kick when your time slot came in too great to pass up. Elmer didn't like the game, saying it bothered his nocturnal habits by worrying him, knowing we were putting a mirror to his face just to see if he was breathing.

Mouse racing was another game that occupied our time in those long, cold months. Field mice were abundant in the cabins, coming in to get warm, and it was a constant effort keeping 'em out. Every now and again we might find one that looked especially energetic and would match him to the current champion. People would come from miles to the Three-Stop Café to show off their hero and nothing would do except to qualify the new challenger. This was done by turning him loose in Jack's bedroom with a cat and shutting the door. After fifteen minutes, if the mouse survived he was worthy of competition, if he didn't, the cat had a good meal.

Jack had the master-mouse-maze, one he'd spent countless hours perfecting, just the right amount of twists and turns, he said, to make it interesting but not tiring. Everyone had their own rituals of training: Preacher liked to mix a drop or two of moonshine in his mouse's water bowl, while Jack would put his mouse in a bucket of warm water and let him swim around to loosen up his limbs. Elmer, he fed his a couple of cooked beans, thinking that any added propellant would give him an edge and the ensuing aroma might confuse the competition.

It was on a Tuesday when we got a disturbing letter:

To Jack Stepp,

It is my knowing that you might be interested in a mouse race. I have heard that you think you know how to mouse race. I don't think so. My mouse, Swifty, is the fastest mouse in three counties. I will be at your place on the twelfth of January. I will bring two chickens to wager and I spect to leave with enough chicken dinners to last a month.

Joe Bob Henry

It was unheard of, a challenge from another county, and Jack was fuming. "Who is this Joe Bob Henry, anyway?" Jack said.

"Is there three of 'em?" Elmer asked.

"That's his name, Elmer," Jack said. "Joe Bob Henry."

"What's today?" Jack asked.

"This is the eighth," I said. "He'll be here on Saturday."

"I better get to training Shooting Star," Jack said.

Jack went to his bedroom dresser and opened the drawer. Inside lay Shooting Star in a nest of paper scraps, his beady eyes focused on Jack.

"Get me a bucket and some warm water," he said. "The training begins today."

Word spread quickly and by the end of the week there was no fewer than twenty-four mouse racers signed up for the event.

Jack had Shooting Star swimming four times a day. He got him up early, six-o'clock, and fed him a special breakfast consisting of tiny pieces of fried egg yolk and ham. He wouldn't feed him any cheese, saying that since that was the bait he wanted Shooting Star to be focused on his favorite food.

By six-thirty Jack had him in the bucket, swimming in circles for five minutes. By the time he pulled him out of the water the mouse was near drowned. Jack wrapped him up in a towel and placed him close to the fire in a basket to keep him warm. At noon, with a small lunch of crushed black walnuts, Shooting Star was back in the bucket. Then at five he was swimming again. Jack wouldn't feed him then because he didn't want him getting fat. By nine he was back in the bucket and Jack gave him a snack of deer jerky before putting him to bed.

Preacher was just as dedicated with his racer, Demon Chaser. He let him run in the maze three times a day, putting a small cap full of water mixed with a few drops of courage at the end. Dan was sure that Demon Chaser was gonna win, saying that he had a secret weapon. He wouldn't tell us what it was until race time, afraid that if word got out everyone would be using it.

Elmer was as excited as the rest, feeding his mouse, Wound Up, mashed beans by the spoonful.

I was the judge 'cause my mouse didn't make it out of the bedroom.

Joe Bob Henry showed up Saturday morning like he said. "Where's the other two?" Elmer asked.

The Three-Stop was full of men, women, and kids, all waiting for the big race. Mother had made two large pots of deer stew and there was cornbread and pies. It was the biggest event of the winter.

The races started at straight-up twelve and it took two hours for the first round to be completed. Elmer's mouse was defeated right off, his theory backfiring on him.

By late afternoon the competition boiled down to Jack, Preacher, and Joe Bob Henry.

"Which one are you?" Elmer kept asking.

Everybody was milling around the cabin, the excitement growing. All the mice had been put in a box on top of the counter to keep 'em together. The moonshine was flowing, and the deer stew was almost gone, and the cats were gathering outside due to the mouse convention inside. Jack wanted to take a few minutes to let Shooting Star rest, and this didn't bother Preacher, as he was fixing his secret weapon.

As we waited for the race to start, Mother and I were looking out the window.

"Must be twenty cats out there," she said.

"Okay, I'm ready," Jack said.

Preacher was holding Demon Chaser in his hand, feeding him something.

"Okay, let 'em go!" I said.

Jack and Preacher sat the two mice in their starting alleys and the race was on. Shooting Star made the first move and was out front in a hurry. Demon Chaser seemed somewhat confused, barely making any headway, just sitting there gulping air. Then, all of a sudden he jumped straight in the air, came back down and started going in circles.

"What's the matter with him?" I asked.

"I have no idea," Preacher said.

"What'd you feed him?" Jack asked.

"Crushed red pepper. Must have fed him too much, his eyes are watering."

"Well, it's come down to us," Jack said to Joe Bob.

"Just as I figured. Where's all them chickens, anyway?"

"They're on the back porch."

"They won't be there long." Joe Bob grinned.

It was time for the last race, and everybody was waiting with anticipation.

"Let's see 'em run," I yelled, and both men let their mice into the maze.

Preacher was so upset about Demon Chaser he felt he needed to get him some air, but he'd been so focused on the race he'd never had a chance to look outside. As soon as opened the door a mountain of cats rushed in. They bowled Preacher to the ground, one of 'em grabbing Demon Chaser as he passed.

Cats went everywhere. Their first aim was the box containing the main menu. They knocked it over with no problem, scattering mice everywhere, with the cats hot on their tails. There was mice shooting up women's dresses and up men's pant legs, the cats doing everything they could to follow 'em. One cat jumped up on the maze and snatched Shooting Star by the scruff of the neck just as he was about to reach the cheese.

"Good, Lord," Jack shouted. "Shooting Star's been eat!"

People were bumping into each other trying to escape. It didn't take long for some of the women to make their way to the back door, Preacher still blocking the path out the front.

As soon as that door opened a couple of cats smelled them chickens and jumped to the back porch, leaving the hens nowhere to go but inside.

Folks were falling all over each other, lots of them on Dan, who'd been unable to pick himself up before others fell on top of him trying to get out. Chicken feathers were flying through the air and somebody threw a chair through a window and people started climbing out of it.

Joe Bob Henry claimed victory, but I had to deny his position, seeing as how Jack's mouse was extracted from the race.

Joe Bob went back home with two slightly scarred chickens.

"*Next time bring Bob and Henry,*" Elmer called after him.

Chapter Ten

"I believe you've got a bite, Pete."

Claude didn't get up; he let Pete run to the pole.

"Now don't jerk it out of his mouth," Claude said. "Pick the pole up real slow and let him take it, then set the hook."

Pete lifted the pole tenderly and watched as the line got tighter and tighter.

"Now!" Claude said.

Pete jerked it back and started reeling in.

"Don't pull so hard; you'll tear the hook out. Looks like you've got a nice one."

Pete was excited and was pulling faster than he was reeling, but he got it in.

"That's a two-pound bluecat," Claude said. "I haven't caught one of them in months."

Pete was having so much fun he just let the cat flop on the bank.

"Step on him," Claude said. "That way he won't spur you. Then pull the hook out."

"What should I do with him?" Pete was still standing on the fish.

"Unless you want to eat it, I'd throw him back in the river."

"I don't think I'll eat him tonight. Man, this is the most fun I've had in years. And you got to do it every day."

Every day, Claude thought. Yes, he could fish almost anytime he wanted to. He hated to think about where he was going, because his fishing days were just about over. He'd learned how to drive but he didn't own a vehicle. He'd sold his old mule just a few days ago; he hated to let him go. It meant the end in a way, and Claude could feel it. It didn't matter much, there weren't any fishing holes close to where he was going, and he was sure no one would be to enthused to take him. The simple things were gone for him, and he couldn't see himself gaining any satisfaction out of watching one of them TV sets.

The moon was high now and it was close to midnight. The air was cooler and Claude could see traces of mist beginning to lift from the water.

"Can I try it again?" Pete asked.

Claude smiled. "Sure, put another worm on and throw it back in. You're doing fine."

Pete looked at him with a big grin but then he saw Claude staring at the river, so he set the pole down and found his seat again. He didn't want Claude to leave; he still didn't know about those kids.

"I think I'll give it a rest for a while," Pete said. "What about Elmer? That winter must have been hard on him."

"I'm sure it was," Claude said. "But Elmer didn't show it, other than we could tell he was getting weaker. He was a fine old man."

The cold set in with determination that January. If it hadn't of been for the chores and eating there wouldn't have been any reason to venture outdoors.

It was January though, and after one more month the spring breezes would start, even if March could be temperamental. So it always lifted my spirits when January was over, knowing that I only had a month left to squander.

But right then the winter storms weren't over, and for others, like Elmer, it wasn't possible to enjoy the outdoors as I did, and so kept him prisoner by the fire. The walk to and from the Three-Stop was the biggest part of his day and even that took its toll on his breathing.

We didn't know why his lungs were wasting away, and it seemed to concern us more than it did him. Elmer's constant gasping for air inside the smoky cabins drained his energy and dulled his senses. But he wasn't a complainer and would do his best to keep up appearances. We knew he wouldn't be with us much longer, and it was our intent that he be able to enjoy the mountains for as long as possible.

He wouldn't stay in our cabin through the day, and many times I had to help him on the mule and walk beside him in the cold mornings.

"I'm not dead yet," he'd proclaim.

There were days when he had to have my help just to get out of bed and dressed.

"Are you sure you want to go this morning?" I'd ask.

"You don't get it, do you?" he'd say. "If I don't go, I'm dying. It's when I do, I know that I'm alive."

Those last days spent with him would forever live in my memory and I only hoped that I could be as pleasant as he was until the end. But, he was still kicking then, and there'd be many more days of enjoyment.

"You best let Elmer come and live with me," Mother said one day. "You can't take care of him like I can."

"I don't mind," I said. "He's no bother."

"That ain't the point. He's getting on and one day he won't be pulling himself out of bed. He'll need nursing and you're not a nurse."

"You've got as many chores as I do, Mother. Besides, I don't think Elmer's interested in living with a woman, except that hankering he had for Pearl. And I think he was just short on oxygen that day. Besides, you don't go to the Three-Stop every day, and he likes that."

"I ain't that interested in having a man in my cabin either, but there's gonna come a day when he won't care about the Three-Stop, and there you'll be, staying at home day and night."

"Let's wait," I said. "I want what's best for Elmer, just like you."

That night sitting by the fire I brought up the subject.

"Elmer, have you ever thought about what might happen when you get so frail you can't get out of bed?"

"Sure I have. What of it?"

"Well, is there a place where you'd rather be staying than here?"

"I'd guess I'd be better off at Jack's. That way I could still see my friends every day."

"Jack'll have a hard time caring for you, Elmer. He's got the store to run and still keep up with his chores."

"Good, I owe him a few," Elmer said with a grin.

"How about Mother? She said she wouldn't mind having you around."

"She's sly, ain't she? Mother's a mite younger than I am but I might be up to it."

"I don't think that's what she's got in mind, Elmer. She's just trying to be helpful."

"That'd be a big help. I don't think a man ought to go to his grave without one last charge up the hill. Maybe Pearl'll come back and I could be in one of them love triangles like you was talking about. I could walk through them pearly gates with a smile on my face then, couldn't I."

"You're gonna want someone around that knows more about comforting you than Jack or I would."

"Well, that'd be comforting, don't you think?"

"Yes, I suppose it would."

We both fell silent for a few minutes, the firelight dancing at our feet. Elmer stirred the logs with a poker and we watched the red embers burn orange, the sparks lifting and disappearing like magic.

"I know what you're saying, Claude," Elmer said. "Maybe we'll get lucky and I'll be gone when you wake up some morning. Maybe we won't be so lucky and I'll be stuck dying slow, taking other people's time with me. When it does come I won't be no bother, I'll stay where you think best. You folks are all the family I got, and it won't make no difference to me whose cabin I die in. I'd just as soon stay with you till then, if that's all right."

"You can stay with me as long as you like, Elmer."

"You know, Claude, some mornings I don't feel old at all. Then there's mornings I don't feel nothing but tired and I know I shouldn't, 'cause I sleep most half a day around. I think it's the good Lord's way of easing a person into leaving, making him sleep more as the years pass. It gets to a place where it don't matter if you're alive or not, you done slept through what's going on anyway."

"It matters, Elmer; it matters to us."

"You know I was just joking about Mother."

"I know."

We listened to the fire and watched the logs give way to ashes. It was late by then and Elmer seemed to be napping in his chair. I got up from mine and put another log on the fire for the night and jiggled Elmer's knee.

"Might as well go to bed, old man."

Elmer slowly pushed himself out of the chair and stepped to his bed and got in, still in his clothes, pulling the covers up to his neck.

I undressed to my longjohns and did the same.

"I bet that Pearl puts out," Elmer said in a whisper.

January rolled into February, and as far as I'm concerned the first two months of the year could be combined into one. There seems to be no difference between the two. They blend like water and ice, and the second month brings no relief to the freezing, bitter cold. Only toward the end does it sometimes offer a hint of better things to come.

I still walked the hills in the daytime though, and wondered in amazement at the stillness of winter. The bare trees were frozen statues, the wind having little effect on their limbs. It seemed like death had overcame them, but I knew there was life inside their coats of bark. I often thought that it's much the same for people, our outward behavior not always the truth of the worth inside.

Winter gives the mountains the chance to rest, and spring brings the opportunity to begin again. People don't look at it that way; they hope to reinvent their selves through procreation. It's the possibility that intrigues us, but in no form is it an absolute. Sometimes it works for the better, though.

I was fixing the side of the lean-to one morning, the mules having kicked it out, the result of a lone coyote's visit. Elmer was standing beside me handing me nails and holding the boards in place.

We were both surprised by the unfamiliar female voice behind us, and our startled expressions didn't go unnoticed.

"I apologize for not making my presence known farther back," she said. "I realize men don't like to be surprised."

"No problem," I said. "We don't get many visitors, especially in late winter, that's the biggest surprise."

The woman was young, nineteen or twenty I guessed. She was wearing pants, and her muddy boots and pant legs showed she'd been traveling for quite some time. Her coat was long, below her knees, and her hat was that of a man's, with earflaps. The face was pretty, her red nose and cheeks setting off big blue eyes, her full lips smiling, her golden hair barely contained by the cap, falling around her face. She was not a tall woman, nor was she short, just the right size in my opinion, and I could tell Elmer felt the same way. As she pulled her glove off I saw that her skin was fair and smooth, not that of a mountain woman's. All in all she was something we hadn't seen the likes of in a long time.

"My name's Bonnie," she said, extending her hand. "Bonnie Caldwell."

"I'm Claude, and this is Elmer. I've not seen you around here before, so I gather you're either lost or looking for something."

"I am," she said. "Not lost, but I am looking for something. Actually, I'm looking for Dan Deveneaux."

"You mean Preacher Dan?"

"Yes. Do you know him?"

"Of course we do. I could show you the way if you like."

"That would be kind of you. I've traveled a long way and I'm so glad I've finally found him."

"Would you like to step inside and warm up first? I've got some coffee on."

"Thanks, but no. It's taken so long to get here that I would prefer to see Dan as quickly as possible."

"Elmer," I said. "Put these tools up and I'll take her over to Dan's. I'll be back shortly."

I put a harness on my mule and didn't bother to saddle him, knowing she was in hurry.

"Have you come a long way?" I asked.

"I lived in Texarkana."

"That is a ways off."

"It hasn't been easy, but I had to make the trip. Is Dan doing well?"

"Yeah, he's doing fine. His cabin burnt down a while back and he's living with another friend. We'll rebuild Dan's in the spring."

"I see there's been a fire," she said, looking around at the charred trees.

"There's not much of chance to stop a fire around here. How long have you known Dan?"

"I've never met him."

I didn't want to seem too nosey and so didn't ask any more questions, even though I was well greased with curiosity. She was a quiet woman, or so it seemed. Probably tired from the trip, I thought.

"You want to know why I'm here to see Dan, don't you?" she asked after a few minutes.

"It's none of my business."

"It's such a small place, I expect word travels fast."

"It does at that."

"By tomorrow everyone will know I'm here, won't they?"

"They'll know your hat size by morning."

"Are you a good friend of Dan's?"

"I believe I am. At least I consider him a good friend of mine."

In a few minutes our mounts were standing in front of the Three-Stop. Smoke was curling from the chimney, but there was no sign of Dan. Then the cabin door opened and Preacher stood in the doorway.

"Claude," he said. "I was just on my way to see you."

"Should I introduce you?" I asked quietly.

She looked at me and a small smile appeared on her face. "Thanks for your help," she said. "No, I'll introduce myself. It might be awkward if you introduced me to my own father."

I was stunned by the admission and could only set in silence as I watched Bonnie tie her mare to the porch railing and step up to meet Preacher Dan Deveneaux. I couldn't hear their words but I saw the shocked look on Preacher's face as he glanced from Bonnie to myself. He staggered backwards for a step and then righted himself, speechless for the moment, then motioned for the young woman to enter the cabin. The door closed behind 'em without another word.

I dismounted and led Bonnie's mare to the back. I unsaddled her and brushed her down, threw some hay close by, and made sure the water trough was full and the ice broken. I then made my way back to my own cabin, wondering all the way why Dan had never told of a daughter, but also knowing that sometimes a man doesn't know and gave him the benefit of the doubt for the time being, not that any of us should have been privy to another man's personal past.

Elmer had finished the chores and was sitting by the fire, a pot of beans boiling on the stove, a cup of coffee in his hand.

"Who is she?" he asked.

"His daughter."

"I thought something looked familiar," he said. "Right nice to look at too."

"Seems like a fine young woman," I said. "Surprising, to say the least."

"Preacher's a leaf in a storm," Elmer said. "Or he was when he was young anyway. A man's life has many turns, and I'd say this one was not that far off the main road."

The next morning we made our way to the Three-Stop, and Mother met us out front.

"Tell me what you know," she said.

I told her and then she said, "Well, good for him. He's circled the barn enough, one day he was bound to find something in it."

We went inside and saw Bonnie, Preacher, and Jack sitting by the stove.

"My good friends," Preacher said. "I would like for you to meet my daughter, Bonnie Caldwell. She's the best of me and I'd like her to be treated so."

We made much to do about her and welcomed her with opened arms, Elmer having to be pulled away from his hug, it lasting so long we were afraid one of 'em might faint.

"She's a musician," Dan said proudly. "My dormant interest in the arts has no doubt awakened in my offspring. It's a sign from the Lord and should be taken as such."

Bonnie was quiet as we talked but stayed close to Preacher. She had a smile on her face that showed she was happy to be with her father.

"Are you here to stay, Bonnie?" Mother asked.

"For a while."

"She's headed to St. Louis," Preacher stated, wrapping his arm around her and pulling her close. "She's going to study music. She'll stay with me for several weeks, and I'll take her to Harrison, where she can get a ride to Missouri."

Bonnie still had the same clothes on she had when she rode up the day before.

"Well, you come with me," Mother said. "Unless you brought a trunk my guess is you'll be needing some clothes."

"I shipped my belongings to the school when I left Texas," Bonnie said. "I have very few things with me."

"Just as I thought," Mother said, rising from her chair. "Let's go see what we can do."

Bonnie gave Dan a peck on the cheek, making him beam with pride, and she and Mother left.

"You take good care of her," Preacher said, as they walked off the porch.

"You go back to strutting, Preacher," Mother said. "Your paternal instincts may be kicking like a mule right now, but they hold no water with me."

You couldn't wipe the smile off Dan's face with turpentine. He was a proud father on that day and nothing could dampen his spirits.

"Are you gonna tell us the story?" Jack asked. "Or do we have to get it piece by piece from Bonnie."

"I met Bonnie's mother Christine in a small settlement in Texas called Paris. It was named after Paris, France, to which I've no doubt my forefathers had something to do with. I stayed with her for less than a month, my calling taking me back to the road. Christine and I wrote to each other over the years, but I had no idea there was a child involved, and Christine never mentioned it in her letters. The letters stopped about the time I settled in Dogleg, and I never heard from her again.

"She did marry, though, and moved to Texarkana and started a dry goods store. The union only lasted twelve years, but Christine had a good head on her shoulders and kept the store and made a good living from it. She passed away from pneumonia a year and a half ago, leaving Bonnie alone. Bonnie's heart is in her music, so she sold the store and made provisions to study in St. Louis.

"She said her mother never talked much about me, but after Christine's death, she found a box with all of my letters in it and decided to track me down, and what a blessing it is."

"We should celebrate then," Jack said, reaching for the Potation.

"Not for me," Preacher said. "Too much to do. I've got to clean up the cabin and I'll need another bed. Place has got to be respectable."

"Why don't you stay at my cabin," I said. "Elmer and I can stay with Jack."

We made our way to my cabin and set to work on cleaning it up. We hung a curtain in the corner to give Bonnie some privacy and by the time we were through, the place looked almost new inside, the floors scrubbed, the windows cleaned, cobwebs knocked down from the corners.

Bonnie had taken a hot bath while Mother had visited the neighbors to gather some clothes she could make into something that would fit the young woman's form. By evening, when Mother and Bonnie showed up at the cabin, the girl in pants had turned into a beautiful young woman in a dress. We left the two of 'em alone, and Elmer, Mother, and I headed back to the Three-Stop with Jack.

"He sure is acting funny," Jack said, pouring us a jigger of shine. "He won't even take a snort of Potation."

"I never expected him to be so taken with the prospect of fatherhood," Mother said.

Preacher and Bonnie would take long walks on the good days, and they always kept close, Preacher with his arm around her.

"Tell me about you and my mother," Bonnie said. "She talked very little of you, even when I asked."

"I met your mother when we were both young and I was very unsettled," Preacher said. "Not that I've grown much more mature with age, just slowed down a bit. She was working for the church, cleaning, when I ran into her. I'd gone to the church in search of nourishment—the eating kind. In those days I had very little in terms of money, and the church was a good place to grab a meal. Our eyes met and we were both in love instantly. I walked her home that night and every night after that. She was the only woman I've ever met that could see through the wall I held in front of myself, and it pleased me to know she could. She knew I used the Christian slant to make my way through the country, but it didn't matter to her."

"She said you were a wanderer and couldn't be tied down. Not even for her?"

"If there was one thing I knew then as I know now, I am not the kind to accept much responsibility, and I have very little patience for the daily routine. Even then I might be gone for days and she would ask of my whereabouts, and all I could say was my feet would not stay still. She must have understood, because we never talked of marriage, even though we were in love with each other. She often asked if I had intentions of staying put, but I couldn't give her an answer and soon she stopped the questions.

"I suppose she felt it in her heart, that good heart of hers, and knew it could never be. It is with sorrow that my vagabond ways never let me feel the safety and permanence of a family, but I have no regrets, other than I did miss her. She didn't tell me of your existence, and if she had I wouldn't be telling the truth if

I said I would have made my home with you and her. It wasn't the ministry that kept me on the road, but the immaturity of youth that stayed with me always."

"I would have liked to have had you there," Bonnie said. "My stepfather was a good man, but I always wondered about you and hoped that someday you might come back."

"Had I known that you were there, I quite possibly would have made the attempt, but then again I don't wish to mislead you. It's quite likely I would have been a burden to your home. I have no business sense and probably would have squandered the opportunity. I hope that you're not too disappointed in me. I'm only trying to be honest with you, as I was with Christine. It did no good to try and sidestep her. She saw through my maneuverings, as I know you would too."

"I hold no ill feelings toward you," Bonnie said. "How could I? I never knew you existed. I only knew that my real father had left before I was born."

"It must have been hard on Christine, having a child without a husband."

"I'm sure it was," Bonnie said. "Her parents were shamed and she was put out of the house, but she never told of any regrets."

"Not that she would, not her. She was a strong woman and she never let pride stand in her way."

"She said you were kind and always thought of her, bringing her flowers you picked from the fields."

"Don't let that out," Preacher grinned. "I have my reputation to uphold in Dogleg."

"Why here?" Bonnie asked. "Why settle down in the middle of nowhere."

"It's simple, there are no expectations here. Here you are what you are and you come and go as you please. There are ties that bind me here, but only the pleasure of friendship and the goodness of the heart. I've found a place where I don't have to pass judgment on my fellow man, and I found that tiresome as I traveled through the country. Here I don't have to look over my shoulder, because I know the one behind me is looking out for my back."

"Doesn't it get lonely, though?"

"Not in the least. For me, loneliness is not knowing who your friends are. The politics of stature is as obnoxious as a fly in pudding; you can't eat around it; you must swallow it or throw it all away."

The days slipped by much too fast for Preacher and Bonnie. I could see the wistful look in his eyes as the time grew closer for her to leave. His quiet mood told the story of his life of solitude and the decision he'd made long ago not to settle down and complete the cycle of life with a family.

Bonnie was full of questions, and I'm quite sure his normal embellishments were disregarded, even though we were not privy to those conversations.

"You could come to St. Louis and stay with me," Bonnie said.

"No, I couldn't. No more than I suspect you could stay here. Our lives have crossed at this point, but they're different lives. I couldn't live with the pomposity of city life any more than you could withstand the isolation of the mountains. But if you ever change your mind, know that I am here, and this will always be your home."

Preacher and Bonnie stayed close together in the passing days, Dan coming to the Three-Stop in the mornings for coffee, mostly just to give Bonnie time to get up and around, then going back to the cabin and spending the rest of the day there. Sometimes in the evening they would both come to Jack's and spend some time with us, but it was short and we could see that Preacher was enjoying her company. It was a happy time for both of 'em, and it was good to see that it could turn out that way.

The change in Preacher was understandable and we missed his company during that time, but it was worth it to see him so close to his daughter. It would be hard for him when she left, but he would always have her to write to, and that was more than most of us had.

He took her to Harrison two weeks later like he said, and Preacher was in the doldrums for a few days, but soon he came back to his old self.

Chapter Eleven

We tried not to leave Dogleg in the winter, the rigors of traveling being so difficult, but sometimes it was necessary. Others were much the same, depending on Jack's meager line of goods to sustain 'em until the roads were more accommodating. I was never one too interested in making the trip to town anyway, but Jack and Preacher seemed to enjoy it, and I usually tagged along if only because it was less boring than sitting in the cabin most of the day.

Going to town always provided some entertainment though and I never quite understood how two grown men could attract so much trouble—it just seemed to hunt 'em down.

The closest place was Horseshoe Bend, half a day's ride by wagon. Harrison had more to offer, but the distance and winter weather made the decision for us.

It was in late February when Jack got low on supplies and we loaded up in the wagon and started out on a Monday at noon. We left Elmer behind to keep the fires going. The going was slow and the roads were rough, but six hours later we entered Horseshoe Bend, in the dark, cold and hungry.

"Let's find a stable for the mules and then hunt up a place to sleep," Preacher said. "Then we'll go to the Fin & Feather, an eating establishment I know of that also has liquid libation to warm the soul."

After we'd taken care of the mules and our sleeping arrangements we made our way to the Fin & Feather. It was the last building on the edge of town, and how it was still standing was a mystery.

It was an old building, and looking at it from the front you could see that it was listing to one side, making a person lean to the left without thinking, just to get it straight up and down.

The front door nearly hit the bar when we walked in, and there were only five stools in a line at the counter and all were taken with a few men standing in between. Tables were scattered along the three other walls with a pool table in the center of the room. The walls were so close to the game table that the cues were sawed off and it still didn't give enough room to play.

We were the only ones eating, giving Jack and I the unsettling suspicion that the menu might be suspect. There were just a few lanterns lighting the place, one hanging from each wall, and two behind the bar.

"Welcome, welcome," said the barkeeper as we entered. Several of the men at the bar nodded as we passed by.

"Take any seat you want," the barkeep said, as he made his way around the end of the counter. He was a man of slim build with a heavy white beard falling down to his chest. His bald head was shining as he passed the light on the wall. The white apron he wore was splotched with the makings of his daily routine, or possibly a week's worth. He was wiping his hands on it as he made his way toward us.

"You're new in town, I can tell. I know everybody and you're not locals. My name's Pappy and this here's Pork Chop."

We looked around but couldn't see anyone else. The questioning look on our faces turned to awe as we gazed upon the biggest pig we'd ever seen come from behind the bar and waddle up next to Pappy. He had a rope tied around his neck with a loop on the other end.

"We go everywhere together," Pappy said. "He's my favorite friend. Snores though. What can I get for you fellas?"

"What's the rope for?" Jack asked.

"For walking. Pork Chop tends to wander, and I don't want to lose him."

"We've made a long trip and we're hungry and dry," Preacher said.

"You've come to the right place. Ain't that right, Pork Chop?" The pig raised his huge head and let out a bellowing grunt.

We sat down at one of the tables, Pork Chop plopping down beside us, Jack having to step over him to seat himself.

"He's just like family," Pappy said, beaming.

"We'd like three beers and a menu," Preacher said.

"Three beers coming up. As for the menus, I ain't got none."

"Well, what's on the spit then?" Jack asked.

Pork Chop squealed and grunted.

"Whoa there," Pappy said. "Don't say that word, it makes Pork Chop nervous. It's all right, Pork Chop, they don't know no better. Fin and feathers, fish and chicken, it all tastes the same. I just hated the thought of changing out that grease every day."

"What kind of fish you got?" Jack asked.

"Why, the kind that swims of course," Pappy said. "And the chicken's the kind that clucks. Say, you boys ain't from the city are you?"

"Not in the least," Preacher said. "But we are thirsty."

"I'll get them beers while you make up your minds about the vittles. Pork Chop, you keep 'em company while I'm gone."

Pork Chop rolled over on his side and fell promptly asleep, snoring like a sawmill. It was a deafening roar and made it difficult to talk. Jack kicked him, but it did no good.

Pappy came back with the beers and pulled up a chair next to Preacher.

"Made up your minds yet?" he asked. "No hurry, I'm not trying to rush you. I like visiting with strangers, and so does Pork Chop. Looky, he's napping. He's just like family."

"I'll try the fish," Jack said.

"No fish, just chicken. Ran out of fish a week ago."

"But you said—"

"I said it tastes the same, and it does—it's all chicken. Is that what you want, chicken?"

"Chicken sounds good," Preacher said. "What's on the side?"

"Well, ain't nothing to the west of us, which I wish there was, that back wall don't have many days left in it. I got a board holding it up out there and I was thinking I might put some nails in it some day, but I just ain't had time, taking care of Pork Chop and all. Now, to the east is the rest of the town. Which way'd you come in that you didn't see no town?"

"I meant is there any other food that comes with the chicken."

"Oh, I get it. Tators. Fried tators is what comes with it. Tastes like chicken. Well, if you boys have made up your minds I'll just go turn in the order. I hope Pork Chop don't talk your leg off. He does enjoy good conversation."

"You wouldn't mind if we played some pool, would you?" Jack asked.

"Course not, make yourself at home."

"Could we get three more beers?" I asked.

"Coming right up."

Jack got up, stretched across Pork Chop and started looking for the balls. Preacher grabbed a couple of cues off the wall and began chalking up.

Pappy came back with the draws and set 'em on the table, picking up the empties.

"Where do you keep the pool balls?" Jack asked.

"Oh, don't have any. Pork Chop ate 'em. I don't know why he took a hankering for them things, they don't digest at all."

"Don't he have trouble passing 'em?" Jack asked.

"I'm not sure, one grunt's about the same as another. He swallowed three at a time once—you could hear them things knocking around every time he took a step. I kept thinking somebody was at the door. He sure is something, just like family. Well, the chicken's frying, it won't be long now. Pappy's got 'em in the grease."

"I thought you were Pappy," Preacher said.

"I am, but my pappy's cooking."

"There's two Pappy's."

"Sure enough, he's eighty-two and still kicking, or cooking."

We stretched our necks toward the bar and saw that in the far corner at the cook stove was an old man peeling potatoes. He looked just like Pappy, the one standing next to us, but a lot older. He'd lost some height in his old age, but the bald head and long white beard made the two so similar it was hard to tell 'em apart in the poor light. The old man's back was hunched over a bit and he kept feeling around with his hands to locate things.

"This is a family business, I guess?" Preacher asked.

"It sure is. Me, Pappy, and Pork Chop. Been here thirty years. Pappy's the one does the fishing, that's why we ain't got no fin to cook. He don't like to fish when it's cold, says it makes his joints ache. I do all the waitering and such, carpentry work included. Had to sell all my tools though—Pork Chop took sick in the fall, and I spent all the money on doctoring bills. He's all right now though, God bless him."

I was watching Pappy, the cook, as he sliced up the potatoes, dropping most of 'em on the floor. He just kept on cutting until he was done and then bent down and picked up the ones he'd dropped, throwing all the pieces in the frying pan together, the same pan as the chicken was in.

"He looks a little frail," I said.

"He can't hardly see no more. He fried up two forks and a spoon the other day. Them things liked to never cooled down. If you see something on your plate that looks peculiar, my advice is to try and cut it first. It's a full-time job just keeping him standing up."

Pappy was headed our way with a plate in each hand. He was having trouble maneuvering around the corner of the bar, spilling fried potatoes as he ran into it. Once he'd made the corner we thought he was on a straight path, but he veered to the left and bumped into the pool table, and off plopped a chicken leg and a thigh.

"You think he needs some help?" I asked.

"Nope. It makes him mad when you try and help him. He's got his pride."

Pappy took several more steps and set the plates down on top of the pool table.

"Here you go, gents," he said, staring out at nothing. "I'll just get the other one."

"He's a corker ain't he?" Pappy said. "You men want to eat on the pool table? It don't make no mind to me."

"That's okay," Jack said. "We'll just eat at this table."

Jack got up, stepped over Pork Chop, and walked over to the plates and picked 'em up, grabbing the leg and thigh while he was at it. Pappy was right behind him with the other plate, and just as Jack reached the edge of the table Pappy ran into him. Jack stumbled, but couldn't catch his balance, trying not to spill the plates and not wanting to step on Pork Chop. He made a swirl around on his heels but it did no good.

The next thing we knew he was falling face forward, stumbling on Pork Chop's butt. He landed on top of him, still holding the plates, but it woke Pork Chop up and he let out a squeal, jumped up on his feet and started running at a thundering gallop. Pappy stood right behind him holding the other plate, trying to focus on the racket. He was standing on the rope that was tied to Pork Chop, and when the pig took off, the loop slipped around Pappy's foot and off he went with the pig and Jack.

"Holy Jesus!" yelled Pappy. "Pork Chop don't like being rode."

They were at the end of the pool table, making the turn, heading back toward the bar. Jack had ditched the plates and was holding on as best he could, not able to get his arms around the pig's big belly. The old man was trailing behind, yelling something about tornados, and they were all picking up speed. As they rounded the end of the table, Pappy moved to the runway.

"I'll stop him when he makes the turn," he yelled. "God bless him, he's just like family!"

Pappy crouched down with his arms outstretched waiting for Pork Chop. Jack was flopping on the pig's back, and the old man was twisting and turning on the floor as the pig made the turn, knocking over tables and chairs. When Pork Chop hit Pappy he just took him with him. Now Pappy was riding on the pig's head, holding on to Jack, covering the pig's eyes, confusing and scaring him all the more.

Preacher and I saw what was coming right away. Not being able to see, Pork

Chop didn't know when to make the turn, so he headed straight for the wall. As the old man passed us we could hear him yelling, "Tornady! Tornady!"

Pork Chop hit the wall at a full run. The wall shimmied a little and then collapsed in a pile of debris on top of all four of them.

Preacher and I stood still for a second waiting for the dust to clear when we heard something creaking.

"What's that?" I asked.

"I don't know," Preacher said.

The men at the bar had walked up behind us and we were looking over the mess. Then we heard another creak and groan and we all thought the same thing.

"*The roof's falling!*" someone yelled.

"*Under the table!*" Preacher yelled.

He and I slid under the pool table and were joined by as many men as could fit, all of us protecting our heads, our butts sticking up and out the sides. The roof collapsed with a crash, and the two walls on either side followed it to the ground. The lanterns broke of course, and the whole mess went up in flames. We dug ourselves out and helped Jack and the others.

Pappy was unhitching his pappy, and tugging on the rope trying to wake up Pork Chop. We helped him drag the pig out to the street and stood there watching the place burn.

"Biggest tornady I've ever seen," the old man said.

"Poor Pork Chop," Pappy said. "His nose is smashed."

"How can you tell?" Jack asked.

"I just can. You know when family don't look right."

The Fin and Feather was a burning pile of rubble.

"I suppose we should be going," Preacher said.

"I'm still hungry," Jack said. "That pig-riding got my appetite up."

"I believe the Duck and Dunk is just up the street," Preacher said. "I heard it was a good place."

"Who told you that?" Jack asked.

"Walter Weathers told me."

"I don't believe I know him," Jack said.

"Not likely," Preacher said, dusting off his clothes. "He passed away a few years ago of a large intestine infection. I was at his bedside when he passed and his last words confused me: Don't eat the duck, he said."

The next morning we got our supplies and made our way back to Dogleg, taking our hats off as we passed the smoldering ruins of the Fin and Feather.

We took the time in the remaining days of February to fix up our fishing equipment, sitting in the warmth of the Three-Stop Café. Mother visited us more often then, the stirrings of spring weather so near, lifting her spirits as it did ours. Even Elmer got more excited, staying awake longer as the days did the same.

I enjoyed those days with the anticipation of warm weather coming, and as I looked out over the cold landscape it reminded me of why I decided to stay in the mountains. The few months of winter when it was too burdensome to pass the time outdoors were of no consequence when looking forward to spring. The coming months made up for the trying days of freezing weather, and my thoughts always took me to the warm stirrings of spring.

I knew there were other changes coming too. Tubbs had told me so, and I believed him. I had no reason to doubt the man, nor any reason to want to know what changes they would be. Life was hard in the mountains, and I gave thanks that they let me live in them as long as I could. The dry beds of the small streams would soon fill with cold, clear water as the rains came and made 'em once again the mothers of nature. Their waters would raise the river, fill the soil, feed the forest, and in turn would give the living another chance at fulfillment. I couldn't stop the changes Tubbs spoke of, any more than I could alter the turn of the seasons.

"I can tell you what's gonna happen," Mother said. "That road won't bring nothing but trouble."

"It's not trouble it's bringing, it's prosperity."

The man was drinking coffee with the rest of us. He'd come from Harrison. A civil engineer, he called himself.

"We don't need prosperity," Mother said. "What we need is to be left alone."

"The state doesn't see it that way." His name was Harold Patterson and he'd come to look over our road.

"We're going to build a road and it's going to tee off this road. There's no doubt about it. We'll be getting a lot of our supplies from different areas and the river's going to be a big part of that supply chain. They'll be off-loaded right down there, where this patch of dirt hits the bank."

"What's all this about?" Jack asked.

"What's it about," Harold said, "it's about progress. It's about people getting where they want to go."

"Seems to me they been getting where they need to go just fine," Mother said.

"Before it's over there's going to be more roads crisscrossing this state than you ever thought about," Harold said. "You can't fight it."

We looked at each other with solemn faces. There had been more strangers pass through in the last year than we'd ever seen before.

"Things are changing," Harold said. "You people stay hid down in these hills and think progress won't touch you, but you're wrong."

"I don't like it one bit," Mother said with a pout.

"You said you bred mules," Harold said. "The state's going to need mules, and wagons and lumber and food for the workers. Not to leave out the jobs it'll provide for you and the others around here. This little café you got here, what's it bring you now? Not enough to sell it, from the looks of it. There's going to be people on this road bringing supplies up from the river. If you don't feed them someone else will."

"Why here?" Preacher asked.

"It's not the only spot, by far, but we can build east, west, and north from here, and the distance from the river to the crossing point is closest from right here for the time being. We can bring supplies upriver faster than we ever could over land. It's a matter of logistics."

"Log what?" Elmer asked.

"From point to point this is the easiest, fastest, and cheapest," Harold said.

"I still don't like it," Mother said.

"You don't have to like it," Harold said, standing up to go. "But you might as well learn to deal with it."

Harold took his last drink of coffee, put on his coat, and headed for the door.

"When's all this gonna take place?" I asked.

"It's already taking place," he said. "We're signing up workers as we speak. As soon as the weather breaks we'll start cutting the road in."

"Good day to you," he said, opening the door. He stopped for a moment, his hand still on the doorknob.

"The road crews will be out of here by summer," he said. "And there'll be no reason to come down this patch of dirt. Make the best of it, or someone else will."

He closed the door and we watched as he climbed into his buggy and headed back up the road.

We sat in silence for a while, looking at our feet, out the window, then at each other. This new event would disrupt our lives and change the way we liked to live, but like Harold said, the state didn't care. They'd be gone quick enough and what would be left was yet to be seen.

"I'll fight 'em till hell freezes over," Mother said.

"Me too," Jack said.

"I think," Preacher said, "I'll fire up the still."

"I think I'll start laying out plans to add on to the Three-Stop," I said.

"What?" Jack asked.

Preacher and I looked at each other and smiled.

"You heard the man," Preacher said. "It's coming and there's nothing we can do about it. Let's make the best of it. I'll sell more Potation this year than I've ever sold before, or probably ever will."

"And you'll sell more mules than you ever have," I said to Mother. "And Jack, if you don't turn this place into a real Three-Stop Café, well, I'd hate to see someone else do it right next door to you."

"And wagons too," Mother said, her eyes widening.

"I'll need more chickens," Jack said. "And more tables and chairs. You're right, Claude, we're gonna need more room."

The conversation turned from sour to sweet. Mother was talking so fast it was hard to tell her double chin from her bottom lip. Jack was pacing the floor, rattling off things he'd need faster than I could write 'em down.

In the following weeks we were busy making tables and chairs and gathering together whatever else we could dig up from the neighbors. Preacher and Jack decided to combine their efforts and sell Dan's Potation out of the Three-Stop Café, in the back room of course. We'd add on another room, half as big as the cabin, and put a wall in the back, separating the dining room from the kitchen.

Mother put on a hired hand to help with the wagon building and mule breeding. Fearing the mares wouldn't get the hint about the urgency of the situation, she bought up as many as she could find.

Word spread fast about the coming road and the jobs it would bring, and as in all economies prices rose to meet the demand. That irritated Mother and she'd taken to traveling half a day to hit the neighbors that hadn't heard of the coming boon. It was beyond her to believe that she'd become exactly what she was irritated about, but there was no explaining it to her. She even offered to make pies and cakes for Jack, but wouldn't sell 'em as a whole, wanting a price per slice, with Jack having to buy what was left over. She would do the slicing.

Jack worked on his menu every night around the fire, with the rest of us offering suggestions as he thought of every combination.

"How's this sound?" he asked. "Fried rabbit with fried potatoes."

"That sounds good," we said.

"What about this—fried chicken with mashed potatoes?"

"That sounds good."

"How about fried squirrel and fried frog legs and fried fish. How about fried ham, and fried quail?"

"You know how to do anything but fry?" Mother asked.

"I said mashed potatoes," Jack said.

"What about bread?" Mother asked. "Do you know how to bake bread?"

"I can bake biscuits."

"Bread?"

Jack's eyes went to the floor.

"Gravy?"

They stayed on the floor, the toe of his boot swishing a board.

"What about baked ham instead of fried?" Mother asked.

Silence.

"You're gonna need to hire a cook," she said. "Take no offense, Jack, but you can't fry everything."

"I like beans and cornbread," Elmer said. "Most people do. I say cut that menu down to beans and let it be."

"And stews," Preacher said.

Jack stepped over to the fire and sat down. "There's more to this than meets the eye," he said.

"It's what meets the stomach that counts," Mother said. "I'm not saying you can't fry, because I know you can, but there's got to be something besides grease on the menu. What about the rest of you? You know how to do anything but get lard hot?"

Mother knew we didn't. We could all throw something in a pot and let it boil, but when it came to cooking for real, well, we didn't know baked chicken from boiled beans.

"Just as I thought," she said.

"That's why I never opened the Three-Stop for eating," Jack said. "It was my wife's idea, and when she passed on it wasn't something I could keep up with."

"You best partner up with me on the Three-Stop," Mother said. "We'll split it fifty-fifty. You do the buying and the butchering and I'll do the cooking."

"What about the mules?" I asked.

"I can't breed mules fast enough. I've bought up every one I could lay my hands on and that'll have to do. It don't take much to write up a bill of sale, and my hired hand can do the rest."

"It's a deal," Jack said.

"Good. Now, we'll need two cook stoves, and you better hustle up more plates, cups, and utensils. You ain't got near enough pots and pans either. Put a counter across the floor from wall to wall. You can seat 'em closer there than at the tables."

I was writing down Mother's instructions as fast as I could. Jack was back on his feet pacing again.

"You'll need a waitress too. I'll see if Ginny Carson wants to help. She's getting old enough to work."

Ginny Carson lived back behind Mother's cabin several miles with her parents and two brothers and two sisters. She was a pretty girl of thirteen, with dark brown hair, brown eyes, and an infectious smile. Her mother was wrestling with stomach problems most of the time, so the kids had to do most of the chores. Ginny was the oldest of the brood and the opportunity to work at the Three-Stop would fit in well with her family's needs.

We worked hard on Mother's list and at the same time fixed up the inside of the Three-Stop to her specifications. Adding on the other room would have to wait until March, when the weather cleared.

Preacher kept his still going twenty-four hours a day. I'd always known he was proud of his hooch, but the energy he showed in this latest endeavor was unsurpassed. I'd sit with him late at night and listen to his stories.

"I was in the Boot heel of Missouri one time when Benjamin Harrison came through campaigning for the presidency," Preacher said, the sampling of his libation having loosened his tongue.

"It was around 1888. I was the featured speaker at a summer Bible school, or so I was led to believe. I noticed that the members of the class looked somewhat older than the children I was used to, but the teachings of the good Book draw many of different ages. I did notice their clothes were ill-fitted and I felt humbled that I could teach the humility of the Lord. The young girls' dresses were stretched so tight that some were bulging at the seams. The boys' shorts were so tight that several had split the seat. The other strange thing I noticed was the girls' hairy arms and legs, lending me to believe that the women in that part of the country tended to lean to the masculine side. A few of the girls looked as if they had a five o'clock shadow, and it broke my heart to think of the torture they must have endured from their other classmates. But I was not to be deterred. The Lord put all of us on this earth, and it's below me to pass judgment on the underprivileged, or the unsightly.

"My class was situated some fifty feet behind the Republican grandstand, and I was having trouble keeping the attention of my audience, the noise of the crowd behind me diverting their young minds. Mr. Harrison's speech was rambling on, and at the end of every sentence the loud hoorah's from his constituents reached a deafening roar. As he droned on it was getting more difficult to keep the youngsters seated. They had not yet learned the evils of politics, nor could they understand the virtues of the good word. After a short while I noticed that four of my students were behind me tying ropes to the uprights on the grandstand. Before I knew what was happening they were mounted on horses with the ropes wrapped around their saddle horns.

"'Here, here,' I yelled. *'What's going on!'*

"'You best get out of the way, Preacher,' one of them said. 'You've played your part, now it's up to us.'

"'Part. What part?' I asked. 'Come down from there immediately and be seated!'

"You can understand my astonishment. I was so startled all I could do was stare in horror. I turned around to warn the remaining pupils and was shocked to see them coming my way with clubs raised over their heads, the girls ripping their wigs off, yelling obscenities at the top of their lungs. Men—they were all grown men. I turned to face the horsemen just in time to see them kick their mounts and pull the grandstand's supports out from under it. It came down with a crash, and from that point on it was pandemonium.

"*'It's the Democrats!'* I heard someone yell. *'Let's get 'em!'*

"Apparently, I had in my innocence been duped into staging a fraudulent Bible class. The Republicans and Democrats were at war with each other and I was in the middle.

"'Get that tall preacher! He's one of 'em.'

"'No I'm not!' I yelled. 'My allegiance is to the Lord!'

"'He's lying!'

"I grabbed one of the blond wigs from the ground and quickly slapped it on my head. Sadly, in all the confusion I'd put it on backwards. The angry Republicans were chasing me and I was having difficulty seeing, trying to run, and spreading the curls at the same time. Finally, I crawled to one of the outhouses they'd put out for the crowd and locked myself inside. I sat there catching my breath in the stale air; they'd not dug a hole but only put a chamber pot under the seat. I was thinking how lucky I'd been to escape the hostilities, when much to my horror I noticed my blond curls hanging halfway out of the doorjamb. I reached for the handle to retrieve my golden locks, but I was too late.

"'He's in the outhouse! I see his hair!'

"In a matter of seconds I was surrounded. The crowd was attempting to overturn my safe haven, but after a few moments the rocking stopped. I could only believe the hideous horde had come to their senses, but the scraping noises I heard were a mystery, and I was still in a state of nervous agitation. Then I heard the sounds that would strike fear into any man's heart, any man hiding in a privy with a thunder mug that is. The villains were nailing the door shut. The scraping sound I heard was a rope being tied around the outside.

"*Let 'em go, boys!*" I heard them cry.

"I heard the stomping of horse hooves, and within seconds my small abode was jerked from the ground and was flying through the air. They drug me from one end of town to the other. They didn't stop until my closet was completely destroyed. All that was left was shards of lumber. The only thing that saved my life was my foul odor; no one would come near me. I was forced to bathe in a river. Not a single Christian would open their doors. I left town that evening with both Parties scouring the town for me."

I sat with Preacher many late nights that month, listening to his stories and watching him make his shine. They were good times and ones I would never forget. His adventures took me to places I'd never been and would probably never go, and in those late evenings I followed him back in his wanderings and became his silent partner, watching from the shadows as he once again stepped through time with the memories of his travels.

It didn't matter if they were true or not. I never doubted they weren't. What good would it do? The events of our lives are embellished by our own emotions, and without those feelings there are no stories. I sat by the firelight and listened to a man who had been many places, and not once did I hear him say he wished it were different. He'd settled in Dogleg, but that was not the end of his road and Preacher knew it, as I did.

I looked forward to those nights and couldn't wait until the sun went down and had walked Elmer back to the cabin. Making my trek through the woods by the light of the moon I wondered where we might go that night. What town would we be in and who would be the people we met? I didn't have the wandering feet Dan had, nor did I have the inclination to travel far from my home, but hearing his travels put me with him on those journeys, and in my mind I was there, and in my memory I shared the times of days long past.

If Preacher Dan regretted living in one place he never mentioned it. I thought from time to time I could see a gleam in his eye as he told his stories, and wondered to myself if he wished he were on the road again, but I don't believe he did. To Preacher, he hadn't stopped, but was only resting, and that gleam I saw was not the memories of the past, but the beckoning of tomorrow.

Chapter Twelve

"Weren't you glad about the chance to make more money than you ever had?" Pete asked.

"Money has a way about it," Claude said. "It changes people, and at the time it changed us. We knew it was short-lived 'cause the work would only last through the late spring, but when folks get to counting unseen dollars their imaginations tend to bolt like a runaway mule.

"The real truth was we were less interested than it seems. People aren't drawn to the mountains with the ambition of getting rich. It's like you said when we first met, there's nothing here to get rich on. We lived in the hills 'cause we wanted seclusion, nothing more. We weren't taking advantage of the opportunity, we were making sure others wouldn't. Once someone else took up residence it was likely they wouldn't leave. That would have given all of us competition, something we weren't interested in. Up until that point our moneymaking security lay in the isolation of our surroundings. We had our share of carpetbaggers and we also got more trouble than we'd ever had."

As we entered March our thoughts were trained on the work we had in front of us. The ground was still frozen but the weather was getting warmer and there were hints of spring. Dry creek beds were starting to run with cold, clear water, and the first shoots of grass were peeking through. Elmer had been right about the burn—it's a cleaning process and it gives new life to the fields and forest.

As the ground softened we began digging the ditch for the Three-Stop's new addition. I was building a stone foundation for the walls while Jack and Preacher cut the logs. We were only adding ten feet because Mother decided she didn't want any more room than was already there, saying the smaller the space the faster she could move the customers in and out. Jack decided the new room would be the perfect place to sell his dry goods.

Mother and Ginny worked on the inside, and before long it took the shape of a real eating place. Now when we met in the morning for coffee, we sat at a table in the corner where Jack's old counter was. Mother had put some new curtains up on the door and windows, and cleaned the floors and walls.

Jack took his ownership responsibilities serious, making us knock the mud off our boots before we came in. It didn't bother me much, but Elmer took it personal when Jack told him there would be no special talents permitted during business hours. Mother quickly agreed. It didn't do much to deter Elmer though.

It didn't take long to finish the room, and by mid-March we only had the roof left and one evening we were sitting in the Three-Stop looking at what was a real restaurant and supply store. Jack poured us a finger of Potation and we sipped on it, talking about the business and hoping for the best. Elmer was starting to nod off and Mother had already left, saying she'd be back in the morning, bright and early.

"Wake up, old man," I said, shaking Elmer's leg. "Time for us to go."

He sat there, his head leaning to one side, not snoring, but breathing quietly. "Come on, Elmer. Let's go."

He just sat there. The three of us looked at each other and then back at Elmer. You could feel something wasn't right.

I stood up and shook him by his shoulders. "Elmer—wake up."

He finally opened his eyes but didn't move his body.

"I can't," he said.

"Can't what?" I asked.

"I can't move."

"What do you mean you can't move?" Jack asked.

"My arms won't move, nor my legs."

I took his arm in my hand and lifted it, then let it go. It dropped in his lap like it had no life in it.

"Go get Mother, Jack," I said.

Elmer was awake but he was too weak to move. It seemed impossible that just a few hours ago he was up walking around. We'd never experienced a thing like that and could only stay beside him and wait. We talked with him and he wasn't in pain, but he was having trouble breathing.

Mother hurried through the door. "What's happened with him?"

"He can talk but he can't move his arms and legs," I said.

"Preacher, you go get a doctor," Mother said. "We'll not be able to take him."

The closest doctor would be in Harrison, and it would take Preacher the rest of the night before he'd get back. Jack and I hitched a mule to the wagon and laid Elmer in the bed with some quilts over him and took him to my cabin. We carried him inside and put him in his bed. The whole time he was talking to us and it seemed there was nothing wrong with him, except he couldn't move.

The three of us stayed with him that night, waiting on Preacher, keeping Elmer warm and wondering what could take him down so fast. As the soft glow of daylight spread through the forest I could hear Mother milling around the kitchen, fixing more coffee. Jack was lying on my bed and I was sleepily sitting in a chair next to Elmer.

As I stared out the window at the coming dawn, a great horned owl landed on the porch railing. He hopped along the rail in front of the window, trying, it seemed, to look inside. His head jerking from side to side reminded me of my own stiff neck. Something nagged at my thoughts but I was unable to pull 'em together. His presence meant something to me even though I didn't understand.

I walked to the window and watched as he twisted his head. He made no noise as he should have when confronted so closely. Mother stepped beside me and watched as I did. The owl didn't move. Then we saw Preacher and the doctor coming up behind him. The bird flew away.

"This is Doc Millstone," Preacher said, as they entered the cabin. "Took some time to run him down but I finally found him."

"Which one is it?" The doctor asked, seeing Jack in one bed and Elmer in the other.

"Over here," I said.

He pulled the chair closer to the bed and checked Elmer's chest and vitals. "Who's the next of kin?"

"No one," I said. "All he has is us."

Elmer was sleeping quietly and didn't seem to wake during the doctor's routine.

Doc Millstone stood up and took a moment to look at Elmer as he closed his black bag. He walked away from the bed to the far side of the cabin and we walked with him.

"How old is he?"

"Late sixties," I said. It struck me that I had never asked when Elmer was born. It never seemed important until now.

"I don't have much to give him or you hope," he said. "He's worn out."

"That's it?" I asked. "That's all?"

"He's got some fluid on his lungs and his pulse is slow. There's not much I can do about either one. You can bring him to Harrison and we'll put him in the hospital, but I can't say it'll do much good. The trip will probably do him in faster than just leaving him be."

"There's got to be something we can do," I said.

"You can keep him warm and try to get some food down him, but I doubt he's hungry. He's just worn down, son. He's lived longer than most. Keep him comfortable and listen to his ramblings. You might get something out of it."

"You need some coffee?" Mother asked.

"That would be fine," the doctor said. "Put it in a jar and I'll take it with me. I need to be heading back."

He handed Mother a bottle of medicine.

"Two spoonfuls twice a day. It'll help break up the phlegm, maybe help him breathe a little easier."

The sun was shining through the trees as we watched him step into the buggy and slap the reins. That was all the doctoring there was. Now it was like Mother had said—nursing was all that was left.

"Let's move him up to my place," Mother said. "I can take care of him."

"I'd rather not," I said. "We talked about it and Elmer said when the time came it didn't make any difference to him, but I'd just a soon he stayed here. We can take turns watching him can't we?"

"Sure we can," she said.

"We'll all take turns," Preacher said.

"Yeah," Jack said. "We'll all take turns."

"Preacher, you need some sleep," Mother said. "Go on and get some."

"I'm not tired."

"Mother, you've got mules to look after," I said. "I'd like to stay with him this morning. Someone come down after noon and I'll get out for a while."

"When he wakes up give him two spoons of this," Mother said, handing me the bottle. I'll make some broth and bring it down."

They left and I poured myself a cup of coffee and sat in the chair next to Elmer. He was laying quietly, his breathing normal as far as I knew.

"Is he gone?"

I was surprised to hear his voice. "Is who gone?"

"That ol' bone breaker."

"Yeah, he's gone."

"Good," Elmer said. "I felt him poking me. I heard what he said. I could have told you as much."

"Take some of this medicine," I said.

"You can give it to me, but it won't do no good. I can feel I'm slipping away."

"He said it would help you breathe easier."

"He said it might," Elmer said.

I lifted his head forward and watched as he swallowed the medicine. His eyelids were halfway open.

"Tastes like turpentine."

"I don't think it's supposed to taste good," I said.

I got his water and helped him take a few sips, and laid his head back on the pillow. He drifted back into silence. I stared out the window and watched the bright sunlight as it fell through the trees. I could hear the birds singing from time to time, faintly through the cabin walls. I walked out on the porch. The breeze was cool but comforting. Spring was coming again and Elmer would not live to see its colors.

I stepped off the porch and lifted my face to the sunlight, feeling its warmth. I breathed deeply, taking in the fresh air. I walked back to the porch and then heard the hooting of a great horned owl. Turning, I saw him standing on the limb of an oak. His head was turned and I could feel his black eyes watching me. Stepping off the porch I picked up a rock and threw it at him. The stone went over his head, through the limbs, close enough to scare him I thought, but he didn't move. Then, lightly, he lifted off, his great wings spread wide, and disappeared in the forest.

Mother came back with chicken broth in early afternoon. Elmer ate a few spoonfuls and drifted back to sleep. I met Preacher and Jack at the Three-Stop and helped the rest of the day. That night we all stayed with Elmer until early evening, when everyone went home. After they were gone, Elmer woke up. I tried to get him to eat more broth, but he wasn't hungry.

"My ma told me the worst part about dying was leaving the living," he said. "And the worst part about living was the dying leaving. Do you think that's so, Claude?"

"I think that's so, Elmer."

"I saw her today. I thought she died, but I saw her. I hate to go knowing she's still alive. I used to pick her flowers when I was a small child. In the winter I'd pick her flowers from her garden 'cause she'd tell me she missed me bringing 'em to her. She'd put the dead sticks in a can and sit it on the shelf. I said, 'Ma, they ain't nothing but dead sticks,' and she'd say, 'No they ain't. They's flowers 'cause you picked 'em, you just wait and see.'

"She watered them dead sticks all winter and then one day in the spring, there'd be new flowers where the sticks was. So every winter I'd pick her dead sticks and she'd water 'em all winter and come spring they'd be flowers. She had a way with flowers. I saw her today, Claude. She was walking in flowers."

He fell asleep with a smile on his face and I stayed in the chair a few more hours beside him. Then I went to bed myself, wondering if he'd still be with me in the morning.

"Help me up, Claude, I got to pee."

It was dawn. I'd slept through the night without waking up. Elmer's voice startled me.

"You're awful loud this morning," I said, hoping he was much better.

"You'd be loud too, if you had to pee as bad as me."

"Can you get up?" I asked, hopefully.

"Maybe, with your help."

He tried to push himself up before I got to his bed, but couldn't do it. I put my arm around his back and pulled his legs to the edge of the bed.

"I can't carry you outside, Elmer. Are you sure you can get up?"

"Just help me up. I can make it."

I pulled him up on his feet but it was no use, he couldn't stand on his own.

"Damnation," he said. "One day I'm walking and the next I can't stand. There ain't no use in it."

"Don't get all riled up," I said. "Use this chamber pot. You need to rest, Elmer. You don't need to be wandering around the cabin."

He sat on the edge of the bed and went in the pot, but I could see it was all he could do. I helped him back down but his labored breathing told me he wouldn't sit up again.

As the days went by, all of us shared in the caring of Elmer. He was bedridden and couldn't turn himself over on his side. His slim body was down to bones, his skin tough and flat. I stayed at the cabin through the nights, getting up every hour to make sure he was comfortable. He didn't need much tending by that time. He could still talk and had many clear thoughts.

"Do you think I've got a chance of getting out of this?" he asked one night.

"Getting out of what?"

"Getting well again. Do you think I'll ever walk the woods again?"

I struggled with my own thoughts. It would be a miracle if he ever had the energy to walk again, and I'd never seen a miracle. I was much younger than Elmer and didn't have the experience to answer the hope of a dying man.

"You're weak, Elmer. You're not eating and a body can't get stronger without eating."

"I ain't got no taste left."

In the following days, Elmer did his best to eat as much as he could, and I couldn't help but believe that the words I'd spoken were wrong. Perhaps I had given him hope when there was none, and I couldn't say in my own mind if it was the right thing to do. I knew he was trying, I could tell by his efforts to eat the puddings and mashed potatoes Mother would fix. But his bowels wouldn't move and the paleness of his skin remained.

"I ain't afraid of dying," he said, his bony arm stretched over the side of the bed. "I seen men die in the war and some screamed until they were gone. I watched men tear at their shirts to see if they was gut shot, 'cause if they were, they knew they was dead. And when they seen their own guts fall out of their torn shirts their eyes showed fear. I got no fear of dying. I'm with my family; the only family I got. That's what they was a feared of, not that they was gut shot, not that they was dying in the dirt and mud and blood, but they was dying alone. Thousands of 'em dying at the same time, side by side, and every one of 'em dying alone."

"It won't be long now," Mother said one evening. Elmer was sleeping and she and I were drinking coffee at the table.

"How do you know?"

"I been smelling it for the last few days. It's the death smell."

"It's just stale air," I said. "I need to open the window and let some fresh air in."

Mother shook her head. "It won't be long now. Jack and Preacher will be along shortly. Tell them to say their goodbyes."

"You don't know," I said too loud. "You can't know that."

She left me at the table and sat next to Elmer on the bed. She combed his hair and whispered to him, and with a cool damp cloth wiped his face and chest. She talked so low I couldn't hear her and I couldn't hold my tears back either. I didn't want to believe her but I did. Mother stayed by Elmer, quietly talking to him for quite some time. As far as I could tell he was still sleeping, but it didn't matter. Soon, she stood up and walked to the door. I could see the tears welled up in her eyes.

"You'll tell Jack and Preacher?"

I nodded.

That evening Jack and Preacher Dan each spent some time alone with Elmer. Preacher read a few passages from the Bible and then set it aside. He held Elmer's hand for the longest time and then walked out the door and set on the step without another word.

"I don't know what to say to him," Jack said. "He's been a friend so long. It ain't like my wife dying—I could talk to her. But Elmer... I..."

"Just tell him you're there," I said. "Tell him you can't wait till the river's up and you're sitting on the bank with him."

I walked outside and sat on the steps next to Preacher and looked at the full moon. Right then I couldn't believe that the sun would ever shine as bright again or that the moon would ever be as full. Pretty soon Jack appeared beside me, wiping his cheeks with his arm.

"I don't know if I said the right things. I don't know if I said the best I could've."

"Did he say anything?" I asked.

"No. He didn't say anything."

"Then you said the right things. Elmer would've cussed you if he didn't like it."

Jack chuckled slightly and wiped his eyes with the heels of his hands.

"You want me to stay tonight? I don't mind. Maybe I could do some good."

"Why don't you," I said. "I could use the company."

"I'm sticking around too," Preacher said.

"I'll make some coffee then," Jack said, walking back into the cabin. Preacher followed him.

I stayed on the steps a while longer, looking at the stars and moon, watching as a few clouds drifted by. Even by the light of the moon the night held no comfort for me.

Around midnight Elmer's breathing became more labored. His chest was heaving as he tried to get air. I kept a cool cloth to his forehead and tried to think of other things. I held his hand but could get no response from him. Then his gasping stopped and a thin smile appeared on his lips.

"Is she there, Elmer?"

A faint squeeze to my hand let me know he was still alive.

"It's okay, Elmer. It's okay to go. Go on, go walk in the flowers with your mother."

And then he was gone.

That morning I walked to the river and sat on the bank, trying to remember the past. I needed to bring his memories back, one by one. And then I realized I couldn't think of all the times we had together. They were buried in my mind and would come back at odd times, perhaps in my sleep or in the feel of a summer breeze, or standing by a fire on an autumn night. I couldn't bring 'em back all at once. I'd have to wait and catch 'em as they drifted through my thoughts.

I was pulled from my trance by the voice of a great horned owl, following the river downstream. As I watched him fly away my eyes fixed on the bend in the river, and there, standing in the water, was Tubbs. I stood and yelled his name, started to run and then stopped. He'd made no effort to come my way and I somehow knew he wouldn't. We stared at each other and a soft smile came across his face. He raised his arm and walked around the bend. I could've sworn I saw Elmer walking beside him.

I only saw Tubbs two more times after that, and I was beginning to understand what his presence meant. The changes he'd talked about were happening, and Elmer was a part of it. From that point on I didn't want to see Tubbs anymore, but somehow I felt I would.

We built Elmer a coffin and buried him in the small cemetery high on a hill overlooking the river. The ceremony was simple, Preacher saying some words from the Bible and leading us in the hymn, "Shall We Gather at the River." It was a fine day. The sun was bright, as bright as I'd ever seen in March and I knew that I'd been wrong about not seeing another day so good. Elmer must have been looking down on us and wishing us well. Everyone in Dogleg was there, and it was a fitting burial for such a fine man.

Afterwards we met at the Three-Stop Café where Mother and the other women had cooked a meal. She'd made a big pot of beans with cornbread, knowing it was Elmer's favorite, and we ate every last bean. We stayed up late that night beside a small fire in front of the Three-Stop. As the people drifted away, back to their homes and back to their lives, I thought about what Elmer had said, that the worst part about dying was leaving the living, 'cause the living must carry on, no matter the burden. The next day we went back to work as usual.

"We'll have this finished by the end of the week," Preacher said. He was nailing the boards on the roof as he spoke, shucking along on his hands and knees.

"You should have put a pitch on it," Preacher said. "It won't drain worth squat."

"I don't know nothing about pitch," Jack said, standing on the ground looking up. "Besides, if you wanted a slant to it, you was here. Should've said something. I'll put tarpaper on it. That'll keep the rain out."

"Do as you please, I don't have to stand in the rain. It's you that'll be setting out the pots."

"Quit bellyaching," Mother said from the porch. "None of you got sense enough to get in out of the rain anyway."

Mother was proud of her new business and had taken to coming to the Three-Stop at five in the morning. By five-thirty coffee was on and hot, just like it was when Jack made it, except now it tasted much the same every day, unlike the variations Jack contributed to.

The surveyors had been back during Elmer's illness, and the work on the ramp would start in a few days, weather permitting. Preacher and Jack decided they should move in with me for the duration. It was fine with me. The loss of Elmer's company in the evenings was difficult, and I wished for the conversations of my friends.

We were busy during those days and it helped take our minds from our loss. Jack had rounded up as many chickens as he could and was digging up worms for Reddy the Rooster in hopes his carnal appetite would increase with the same vigor as his eating habits. He had forty laying hens, but Mother was sure that wouldn't be enough and was making deals with the neighbors to buy eggs. She was sure we'd have to make a weekly trip to Harrison to buy supplies.

"Look yonder," Mother said, pointing up the road.

Two wagons were coming toward us filled with men and supplies. Out front was a man riding a horse. He was tall, with a heavy build, square-shouldered with a thick black beard, graying at the sides. He was riding straight in the saddle. They came to a halt in front of the Three-Stop Café.

"I'm Tory Brown," he said. "We're going to be building a ramp here at the river. I'm the foreman."

We introduced ourselves as he dismounted from his horse.

"Take those wagons down to the river," he said to the teamsters. "I'll catch up in a minute."

"You got coffee on?" he asked.

"Sure do," Mother said.

"I'll just have a cup then."

All of us went inside hoping to catch some news. Tory acted like a no-nonsense kind of a man. He stepped inside the Three-Stop and looked around, nodded his head, and took a seat at one of the tables.

"Who owns this place?"

"We do," Mother and Jack said in unison.

"Family?"

"Partners," Mother said. "No kin."

"If there's any men looking for work around here, I'm the man to see. If you don't have objections I'll set up hiring at one of these tables. I hate doing paperwork outdoors."

"That suits us just fine," Mother said, winking at Jack.

"I figure we'll be here three to four weeks finishing the job. Some of the men wondered if there was a place to board."

"Right you are, sir," Preacher spoke up. "We have a nice establishment just up the hill. All the amenities of home."

I looked at Preacher with one eyebrow raised, hoping he wouldn't take his description of the old cabin too far.

"How many rooms you got?" Tory asked.

"Sometimes it's not the privacy one affords but the companionship that benefits man the most," Preacher said.

"In other words, it's a cabin," Tory said, taking the cup of coffee Mother had just sat down.

"We don't have a boarding house," I said. "It's an old cabin we put some cots in. It's got a cook stove and fireplace and a freshwater spring close by. Twenty-five cents a day."

"That'll do," Tory said. "I'll need a place myself. Know of any?"

"I've got a back room at my place," Mother said. "If you're an honorable man."

"No problem there, ma'am. My intentions are to build this ramp and I have no other."

Mother nodded. She liked the cut of the man and we could tell she was impressed with his manner.

Tory emptied his cup and stood.

"Get the word around I'm hiring. Tell 'em eight o'clock tomorrow morning's sign-up time. Wear their working clothes. After tomorrow work starts at sunup. Ten hours a day, five days a week, six for those that want to work. Some of the men want to go home on the weekend. I'll be here until we're done."

"What about meals?" Mother asked.

"They get fifteen minutes for lunch, no more, no less. Most of 'em don't eat. Breakfast and dinner's up to them."

Tory laid five cents on the table for the coffee, tipped his hat to Mother and walked out the door.

"What a nice man," Mother said.

"You best keep your mind on business," Jack said.

"Don't go telling me what to keep my mind on, Peaches. You heard the man. Work starts at sunup. That means you start at four. Now finish up that roof and butcher me a hog. Those men'll be wanting ham and bacon in the mornings.

When you get done with that, butcher a steer. I've got a feeling beef's on the table at dinner."

That night we sat in the cabin sipping Potation and talking about our good fortune. Preacher was a cup ahead of Jack and me, and we could tell the wheels in his head were turning.

"All this activity reminds me of the time I was ministering the teachings of Christianity to a clan of Indians on a reservation in Oklahoma. I found myself the focus of admiration by the whole tribe, especially the squaws. The male Indians were a rowdy assemblage, and it became my personal obligation to teach them the customs of peaceful demonstration. They were not a happy lot, being confined to such a small area, and the Army was especially dependent on my services as a mediator between them and the hostiles.

"I studied the situation for weeks on end, finally coming to the conclusion that the first order of business was to eliminate their immoral sexual practices. I separated the men from the women by forming two lines of tepees, directly across from each other, a hundred feet apart. I positioned them so the openings were opposite each other. That way they couldn't sneak a peek at the comings and goings of the opposite sex. The Army consented to set up a huge tent in the middle of the corridor. This tent I used as a congregating area where I held my sermons.

"At night I allowed fires to be built in the center of the alleyway so they might gather together and discuss my latest lecture. I established a curfew of eleven o'clock and made it my duty to check every tent, making sure that all the occupants were safely inside. To my dismay it was impossible for me to check all the tents, so the Army lent me a man. He checked the male tepees and I alone took the responsibility of making sure the young women were appropriately situated in their small nests.

"It was a difficult task I had, turning heathens into Christian brothers and sisters, and there were many rivers to cross on their road to salvation. One particular habit unnerved me. It was summer and hotter than Hades. The Indians had a disturbing custom of sleeping completely naked. They had not yet learned the cultured ways of civilization, and try as I might I couldn't get enough bedclothes to suffice for all. I pleaded with the commanding officer to commission nightgowns for the exposed tribe, but unfortunately he could only come up with enough for the men. At my own expense I traveled to the nearest settlement and begged for more nightclothes. My efforts were rewarding but not to the fullest. There were not enough garments to cover all the women.

"I prayed for the answer and it came to me in a flash. My duty was clear. I had no choice but to care for the oldest members and so was forced to give the coverings to the elder squaws. My heart ached for the young girls and it was all I could do to keep the tears from my eyes as I swung back the flap on their wigwams and peered inside at their young bodies exposed to the elements. I obligated myself to check on them several times a night, not only ensuring their safety but comforting them with the knowledge that I would protect them, no matter what nature might throw their way.

"My efforts were not always received with the same gratitude they were given, though. At one point I was forced to defend my actions with the commanding officer.

"'Some of the Indian men say someone's been slipping into the young squaws' tepees in the middle of the night with a candle. You wouldn't know anything about that would you, Preacher?'

"'Of course not,' I said. 'I charge myself with the task of finding the villain though, and to set your mind at ease, I'll personally stand guard over the young women's sanctuaries. It's a monstrous miscreant that's among us and I won't sleep until he's apprehended.'

"'What about all those candle stubs out back of your cabin? There must be more than a hundred.'

"'Well…huh…I can explain those,' I said. 'I use many candles in my ceremonies, plus, I stay up quite late reading the Bible. It's part of the baggage I must carry in pursuit of salvation.'

"'Why don't you use a lantern?'

"'A lantern? My good man, it's out of the question. The spirit of the Lord is such that the trappings of wealth are nothing but a road to the devil's den. I could not do justice to the Lord by displaying the symbols of affluence.'

"'What?'

"'Never mind. Go with the knowledge that I shall apprehend this scurrilous scoundrel and all will be safe. Good day to you, sir.'

"I had no choice but to camp out among the tepees from then on. I kept a lantern lit at all times and stood on guard from dark till dawn. Any noises coming from within were quickly identified, this time by the bright light of a lantern instead of the dim glow of a candle. I never did capture the culprit but my presence vindicated the commander's suspicions of me.

"As time went on the Indians became more and more confident of me and my teachings. Before long I held more authority than the Army. I had two names given me by the Indians, and I'm quite sure they have gone down in the history of their folklore. The first was given to me by the males of the tribe—Sneaks

Like a Polecat In the Night; no doubt in reference to my tracking abilities, which were much respected among the Native Americans. The squaws gave me the second name and the one I am most proud of—Wandering Light, because of the light of Christianity I shed on their dark souls, I'm sure.

"The weeks passed and I was hoping for more response from my new friends, but they seemed depressed with their current conditions. I took it upon myself to visit with their leader, Chief Purple Splotch, named that because of the birthmark covering his face from chin to forehead.

"'Why won't your people live the Christian way?' I asked.

"He simply rubbed his thumb and forefinger together. I looked at him and shrugged my shoulders letting him know I didn't understand.

"'No money,' he finally said.

"'You don't need money,'" I told him. 'You have everything here you need. The government will take care of you.'

"He spit a very large stream of tobacco at my feet and threw his arms in the air.

"'No good. Warriors no happy.'

"'I see,' I said. 'The Lord does not wish that you covet material things.'

"'He no live on reservation,' the chief said.

"'I'll teach you how to make money,' I told him. 'And you'll see it won't make you happy.'

"'Try me,' was all he said. He'd apparently learned bits and pieces of the language from my sermons.

"I went to the commander and explained my problem, and asked if there were some way I could show the Indians they were better off living freely on the reservation. He had no ideas and told me that if I could think of something he would listen. The thought struck me that if they had to work for money they would see they were much better off just letting the government take care of 'em.

"'I think I know of a way,' I said to the commander. 'We'll let 'em do the laundry and pay 'em for their services and they'll surely see the disagreeable outcome of the American economic process. Hard work, long hours, and low pay; not even an Indian would jump into that pond.'

"'The U.S. Government won't pay savages to take money from the pockets of citizens,' he said.

"'By the time a month is up they won't want any money,' I said. 'They'll just want to go back to the way it was.'

"'If they do expect to get paid, it's coming out of your pocket,' he snarled.

"I was so sure of my plan I agreed on the spot. I spoke with Chief Purple Splotch and told him the conditions. He gathered his warriors around him. They stood in a circle and I watched as they talked it over in hushed voices, now and then one of 'em sticking his head up from the loop, smiling at me, and then dipping his head back into the crowd. I knew at that point my plan was a stroke of genius. Shortly, Chief Purple Splotch walked over to me.

"'Good,' he said, turned and walked away.

"I started immediately on the arrangement, gathering the soldiers' uniforms and delivering 'em to the Indians. There were still a few things Chief Purple Splotch didn't understand, one of them being that all the Indians had to work, not just the women. I never could get that across to him, even though I studied their language quite extensively. As the weeks went by, the soldiers were so happy with the way their uniforms were turning out, they all decided to let the Indians wash 'em. They even brought their boots along so they could shine them too.

"I could tell my plan was working. Only one thing disturbed me: as the chief and I walked along the riverbank where the women were working in the hot sun, the squaws always threw stones at us.

"'Doesn't that bother you?' I asked one day. 'Shouldn't they have more respect for their chief?'

"'Not throw at me.'

"I thought for a moment and then it came to me. The squaws were throwing the small stones out of their way so they could scrub with the larger ones.

"'Smart women,' I said to the chief.

"'Smart,' he said, eyebrows raised in wonderment.

"I'd never seen such activity out of Indians as I had in those few weeks. I couldn't have been prouder to be involved in such a learning experience for such uneducated people.

"Going into the fourth week I got a knock on my cabin door. It was four in the morning and I'd just gotten in from my last security check. It was the commander of the fort."

"'Where's all the Indians?' he asked.

"'I'm sure I don't know,' I said. 'The women were in their tepees a few hours ago.'

"'I'm sure you'd know that. I've got a hundred and twenty men out here with nothing on but underwear. The horses are gone and so are the Indians.'

"'You think the Indians took the horses?'

"'They've dressed up in the uniforms, you idiot. They tied up the guards, stole the horses, and walked out of here like U.S. Cavalry.'

"'You're surely jumping to conclusions. I've taught 'em not to steal.'

"'They didn't have to steal. They had the uniforms in their tepees, all nice and clean. They even had my men's boots.'

"'There's been some error made,' I said.

"'You made the error, Preacher, and now you're gonna pay for it. I'll have you strung up and quartered for this.'

"'Don't go to extremes. I'm sure they're just trying the uniforms on. They'll be returning shortly.'

"The commander's eyes got big, his face turned red, and he was spitting as he yelled. I couldn't understand a thing he was saying. Just then a garrison of guards walked up behind him and patted him on the shoulder.

"'I've got orders to put you under arrest, Commander,' the ranking sergeant said.

"The guards grabbed him by the arms, the commander still sputtering incoherently, and led him away.

"'You wouldn't know where I could find a Preacher Dan Deveneaux, would you?' the sergeant asked.

"'Me? Why, no I wouldn't. That's just what the commander was asking. Is he in some kind of trouble?'

"'He's in more than trouble. He may be wanted for treason. That's a hanging offense.'

"'Haven't seen him. Don't even know him.'

"'Keep your ear to the ground. If you hear of him, you'll tell us?'

"'It would be my pleasure. Anything to help the government.'

"The Indians went west that night and I went east that morning. I heard the commander lost his epaulets and spent several years in an asylum. The Army rounded up the Indians and brought 'em back to the reservation. The chief absolved me of any wrongdoing by explaining to the court that the commander was in charge of the laundry. I'll never forget ol' Chief Purple Splotch; he never went down in history, but he sure was colorful."

After Preacher's story we sat for a spell without talking. Even though our spirits were high from the opportunities laid before us, I felt somewhat melancholy, and believed I saw the same in Jack and Preacher. The Three-Stop Café was no longer the simple cabin we met at every morning. Now it would be packed with strangers, those who cared less about our lives. I would no longer have the solitude I'd been blessed with on my morning walks to meet my friends. There would no longer be those quiet evenings at the end of the road where we once sat and listened to the peaceful sounds of night on the riverbank. Our days would be filled with commerce—the one thing we had all hidden from.

The next morning we sat at the Three-Stop and watched as Tory signed up the workers while Mother hung over him like a hen.

"More coffee, Tory?"

"Just one more cup, thanks, Mabel."

"What about us?" Jack asked.

"Just hold your horses. Ginny's right behind me."

Ginny was kind enough to fill our cups. She was a sweet girl and turned out to be a hard worker, meeting Mother at four in the morning to get things started. Her thick auburn hair was pulled tight on her scalp and braided in a ponytail hanging to the middle of her back. Her skin was blemish free and darker than most, as if she had a tan all year. Even at thirteen you could tell she'd be a looker one day.

"What about you men?" Tory asked, looking at us.

"We have positions," Preacher said.

"Looks to me like they're sitting positions," Mother said.

"Our normal routines won't be disrupted by the machinations of the state," Preacher came back.

"I'll disrupt your routine," Mother yelled from the counter. "Peaches, you get up and move them dry goods into that new room. I'll not do all the work while you sit on your butt and drink coffee."

"Quit calling me that," Jack said.

"Peaches," Tory grinned. "Is that your nickname?"

"No, it ain't."

"It is when I say it is," Mother said, picking up our cups, which weren't all empty.

"How'd you come by that?" Tory asked.

"It's a swollen story with a short end," Mother said. "Now you three get going—you're taking up space. Tory said them surveyors would be coming back today and I've got things for Ginny to do, and it don't involve waiting on you. Tory, you can stay as long as you like."

"I've got to get down to the men. I'll be back later."

"Have a nice day, Tory," Mother said with a smile as he closed the door behind him.

"You're mooning over him like a newborn calf," Jack said.

"Never you mind about the moon, just get busy."

Mother's face was blushing as she wiped her hands on her apron.

We helped Jack move his goods to the new room and get it organized and then walked down to the river and watched as the progress unfolded. It was a mild morning, but the sky was turning gray, clouds moving in from the northwest. The wind was picking up and the temperature dropping.

"Little late for a snow," Tory said, as he walked toward us.

All of us looked at the sky, thinking the same thing. It doesn't happen very often, but it has before; a late storm in March has dumped many a foot of snow in the mountains.

"I hope it blows on by," Tory said. "I got a deadline to meet."

By noon the clouds were boiling and slate gray. A light mist was coming down and the workers were putting their coats back on. The surveyors that were supposed to show had never made it.

"They must have backed out," Tory said. "It probably looked like this in Harrison long before we saw it."

"It's stalled," Preacher said. "We're gonna get something."

"It's Friday," Tory said. "Some of the men wanted to go home tomorrow." He looked at the sky again. "We'll see."

By late afternoon the drizzle had turned to snow, big flakes, wet and sticky. Tory worked the men until he could work them no longer. It was close to five o'clock. He had his payroll with him and set up in the Three-Stop to hand out the wages. Some of the men decided to go home, but the rest stayed, and with their pockets full of money, sat at the tables and ordered dinner.

Mother had steaks with potatoes and gravy, apple pie with fresh cream, and hot coffee. Jack and I helped serve while Ginny helped Mother cook. Preacher had seen the snow as an opportunity to make some money himself and was setting up station back at the men's cabin. He knew they'd want a swig of brew, knowing they probably wouldn't be working tomorrow, and he was ready with his libation.

Jack was as happy as a mouse in cornbread, running here and there, delivering plates and picking them up. He only broke three and Mother said she was taking it out of his cut, but she was too happy to be ornery, serving Tory his dinner by herself.

It was eight o'clock before the place emptied and another hour before we had it cleaned up. Ginny left to stay at Mother's because of the weather, and Jack and I sat down at the table with Tory to do some jawing. It wasn't long before Mother came out of the kitchen with a pot of coffee and a cup. She filled Tory's cup and poured herself one, setting the pot on the table.

Mother was quiet and so was Tory. Jack reached for the pot and I grabbed his arm.

"I'm kind of tired, aren't you, Jack?" I asked.

"No. I'm all worked up. I ain't made this much money in my whole life. I'm enjoying myself."

I squeezed his arm and made a quick nod toward Mother.

Jack looked at me and then at Mother. "You know, now that you mention it, I am worn down a little. You want me to lock up, Mother?"

"No, you two go on. I'll lock up in a minute. Go find Preacher and don't let him get into trouble."

We said our goodnights and left.

"Well," Mother said to Tory, "I guess you're worn out yourself. Don't mind me, I'm just resting for a spell."

"I'm not as tired as I could be. If you don't mind, I'll just sit here for a while."

"Oh, I don't mind. I'd favor some company."

"How long have you been running this place?" Tory asked.

"Just started. I breed mules on my own. But, when it came down to building the road, well, we decided to make the best of it."

"Sounds like you're a good businesswoman."

"I knew Jack couldn't handle it, even though he'd a tried. He's a good man, but he don't know nothing about running a restaurant, not that I know that much."

"It takes a woman to make a place like this run right," Tory said, sipping his coffee.

"You probably miss your wife, don't you? Having to stay out for so long at a time."

"I don't have a wife, Mabel. It seemed I never had the time. I went from job to job, mostly, finally settling with the state some ten years ago. By then I guess I was too grizzled for a woman to pay much attention."

"Why, you don't look wore down at all. I guess you get tired of being gone from home all the time."

"Not really. I got nothing at home but space. It's nice to get out and see new things and meet new people."

Mother straightened her apron and brushed her hair back from the side of her head.

"What about you?" Tory asked.

"I had a husband once. A mule kicked him and killed him. That was a long time ago, when I was young."

"The best part of being young is living through it," Tory said.

187

"I suppose you'll be leaving when the ramp's done?"

"I'll be heading up the road crews. I'll still need a place to stay, until it gets too far away."

"Will you be staying here?"

"I think I'd like to, that is, if there's a place."

"Oh, I don't see any reason to close up shop, just because the ramp's done. Maybe I could fix up that back room a little, make it more comfortable."

"Don't go to any trouble, Mabel. I'm not used to a woman's touch."

Mother blushed and smiled. "More coffee?"

"I've had enough. Could I walk you home?"

"Yes, oh yes, that would be nice. Just let me turn the lights down and we'll lock up. It is getting late, isn't it?"

Mother took her apron off as she hurried back to the kitchen. She stopped in front of the mirror hanging over the washbasin in the back and straightened her hair before coming back out. Tory was standing by the door with her coat in his hands.

"Mind if I help you with this?"

Mother stopped where she was. She smoothed out her dress as she tried to hide the biggest part of her smile. She walked to the door and Tory held the coat open as she slid into it. Mother buttoned the front as he fixed her collar. His hands rested on her shoulders for a moment.

"It is nice talking with you," he said.

He opened the door for her and Mother locked it and they walked through the snow, side by side, talking the whole way.

Jack and I had walked up to meet with Preacher.

"Line 'em up, boys," Preacher hollered. "No pushing, there's plenty for all. Ten cents a pull."

"Ten cents?" one of the men said. "Beer's a nickel where I come from."

"This ain't beer, my good man. It's the finest libation that ever slid down your gullet. Take it from me, you'll not find better shine west of the Mississippi."

Preacher was standing behind a makeshift bar, a board nailed across two chairs, and was pouring a finger in each cup. They'd been at it for an hour before Jack and I got there, and Preacher had been keeping up with 'em, his pockets jingling with coin. There was a card game going on in the corner, and two men were arm wrestling on another table, with money laid down for bets.

"Come in, come in," Preacher said, as we entered. "There's plenty of room for more. Let me set you up with a snort. These men won't mind if I pour you one first, will you boys?"

"Snow's getting deep," Jack said.

"Good," Preacher said. "The more snow, the longer they'll keep drinking."

"You might be here all night," I said.

"That's fine. Makes no difference to me."

While Preacher took care of his customers Jack and I stood by and watched the crowd. There were fifteen men in the room, more than enough to pack the small cabin. The fire was roaring in the fireplace and the room was getting uncomfortably hot. We took our coats off and threw 'em in the corner behind Preacher. The men playing poker were serious about the game, and with the amount of greenbacks on the table I could see why. As the night wore on, so did the drinking.

The argument started at the poker table, which was no surprise. Out of the six men there, four had already lost their wages. They tried to borrow from the others, but none would have it. Now the charges of cheating went up, as normal when drink and cards meet each other. When the conversation grew louder, Preacher and Jack tried to calm the players, but the grog had taken its toll. There would be no stopping the threats.

One man pulled a pistol and fired into the air. The room went quiet. In that moment of silence a soft fluttering could be heard. Even the arguing men surrounding the table listened to the new sound. It was not the storm outside, nor was it the roaring flames of the fire.

Above the table was a large storage area, long forgotten, a place to store those things one would never use again, but refused to throw away. The entry was on the outside, accessible only by ladder. The bullet had splintered the boards and the heavy dust falling through smelled different than aged dirt. Then the squeaking began, which none of us could identify at the time.

In puzzled stare all eyes were directed upward to the sounds. Then the board began to crack and bend downward, with more grunge falling through the openings. Jack, Preacher, and several other men were standing beneath the compartment, necks bent backward, peering up at the ceiling. Then the slat fell, followed by several others, the filth landing in bucketfuls on the men below. Following that were the birds.

One by one they came, the darkness above making it difficult to recognize the type, but the flapping of their wings unmistakingly identifying them. Then the whole floor of the compartment tumbled down and out came masses of the flying animals, along with gobs of their droppings. Preacher and Jack were covered with the peculiar-smelling stuff.

Men scattered and in a matter of seconds the creatures were identified—

bats, hundreds of them. The room was filled in seconds with the flying frightened mammals. Everyone was scrambling, the bats smashing into 'em, tangling themselves in their hair, landing on heads and faces, and clinging to their clothes. Men and bats alike were hitting Jack and Preacher. They were stumbling over chairs and cots, and men were crawling on the floor, trying to wipe the bat guano from their eyes so they could see.

Jack stumbled backward, tripped over a body lying in the floor and landed in the fireplace. He jumped up fast, but not quick enough, his pants flaming as his feet hit the floor. He was screaming louder than the rest of the men now, slapping his butt with both hands, running into walls and men, still blinded by bat droppings.

I opened the front door and someone threw a chair through a window. I fought my way through the crowd, barely able to see myself what with the bats flying, and now the smoke from Jack's pants filling the cabin. I fought my way through the chaos, trailing Jack by the flames coming from his burning behind. I finally reached him and grabbed him by the arm, pulled him to the front door and threw him off the porch into the snow, him yelling as he flew through the air. The last vision I saw was Jack scooting through the snow on his butt, pushing with his hands and pulling with his feet.

I went back inside to find Preacher, who was still feeling his way around the room. He'd made it to a corner, but was confused about whether to turn left or right. Now that the door was opened the men were crowding in that direction, making it impossible to get through in a timely manner. I took Preacher by the back of the pants and the collar of his jacket, turned him around, ran him across the floor and pitched him out the broken window.

It didn't take long for the cabin to empty. Men were scattered all over outside, some still searching their bodies for signs of crawling creatures. As they calmed down we stood in the snow and peered inside, watching bats flying everywhere. Soon they found their way out by the broken windows and opened doors. There was no going back that night, though. The stench of warm guano was enough to turn our stomachs, and the place was a mess the likes I've never seen. It would take all day to straighten it out. We decided to bed the men down in the Three-Stop for the night, gathering as many blankets as we could from Mother's and my cabin.

Chapter Thirteen

"Elmer was one of the coffins they moved?" Pete asked.

Claude nodded. It seemed such a long time ago, but he could see Elmer's face like he was there with them. He'd seen it many nights here by the river.

Pete began pitching rocks into the water again and Claude thought he could see some sorrow on his face.

But it wasn't so much sorrow as it was guilt. Pete's own grandfather was ill and he made few attempts to see him. Hearing Claude tell of how Elmer's friends stayed by his side, even when he was only feeble, still getting around, made him feel uncomfortable. He didn't know his grandfather that well, and he thought how good it might feel to sit with him on a riverbank sometime, just like he was now, and hear the stories about his past. Pete looked at the gravel between his feet and closed his eyes. He thought how lonely his grandfather must feel. His wife was gone, most of his friends were dead, and his own family had little time to share with him. It was like Elmer had said, "thousands lying side by side, and all of 'em dying alone."

"Your family still intact?" Claude asked.

"Yeah, they're all still alive. My grandfather's sick, though, and I don't see him near enough. I just live maybe ten miles from him but I don't get over there very often. Usually at Thanksgiving and Christmas, sometimes at Easter. I've got a notion he's been through quite a bit too. I bet he's got some stories to tell, if a man would sit and listen."

"I'm sure he does. This coffee's about done, how 'bout a cup?"

"Sure, why not. It must be hard waiting for people to die. I've never had to do it."

"Friends don't die, Pete, you just can't touch 'em."

Claude handed him a cup of coffee and Pete held it with both hands, the steam was rising in front of his face.

"It must be nice down here when spring comes around."

"Spring's the best," Claude said. "But autumn's got its pleasures too, that is, when the woods aren't burnt. I can't say waiting for winter's one of my favorite pastimes, though. You're right, after March the forest and hills come alive."

The month of March had turned and April was on us. The snow had lasted two days and I could smell fresh air blowing through the mountains. The rains of April would cleanse the forest, and the warm breezes would tempt new growth. Trees were budding, flowers were growing, and the river was rising.

I took long walks along the banks then with only a jacket to keep me warm. We could fish late into the evening, sitting beside a small fire. I watched as the redbuds and dogwoods bloomed. It was my favorite time of the year, April, and I walked through the woods and wondered why I would live anywhere else.

The Three-Stop Café was busy then and Jack was always there, along with Mother and Ginny. The work on the ramp was almost done and preparations were being made to continue on with the road. Preacher was busy with sales of Passionate Potation and I was happily left to myself much of the day, wandering the woods and enjoying the mountains.

I spent much of my time repairing the wounds of winter, my trade as a mason in much demand. There were people moving closer to Dogleg, the beckoning road dampening apprehensions of distance. We still met for morning coffee, earlier than we used to, though. Mother always beat Jack to the café, so the coffee was always hot when we got there.

Mother's romance with Tory was keeping her spirits high, and she hummed songs most of the day; no amount of work seemed to dampen her mood. She'd sold half her mules to the state by then, with a little help from Tory, and had never been in better financial shape. The Three-Stop Café was doing great too, and both her and Jack were making enough money to set their minds at ease.

Preacher's moonshine sales were steady, what with his captive customers staying at the cabin for the duration of the ramp. Tory'd already signed up quite a few of the men to stay while the road was being built, and he estimated they'd be in the area for at least two more months.

I built a picket fence around Elmer's grave and Mother planted spring flowers in it. It looked as if someone actually cared then, and I was proud of it and sure Elmer would have liked it.

Jack and I made a trip to Harrison every Monday for supplies for the Three-

Stop. We'd start out before daylight and come back the next morning. Preacher stayed back, helping Mother and Ginny.

The building of the new road had changed our lives. The hustle of making money had taken the place of the calm times we'd been used to. No one seemed to realize it but me, and I often wondered if I'd lost my place in the scheme of things. It was more than I was interested in, though I enjoyed the happiness it brought the others, but also knew that it would end.

The road would bring more people to Dogleg, but only those looking for the river. I was sure the others knew as much, but I never mentioned my thoughts, letting them live in their prosperity for as long as they wished. I would find that they felt much the same as I did, and were tiring of the new and hoping the old was not far off.

I found myself fishing alone in the afternoons, not by the road anymore but farther downstream. The activity by the ramp was annoying to me and I needed the calm and quiet of the forest. Very seldom did my friends join me then; they were too busy making money, but I wasn't concerned. I liked the solitude it afforded me and took advantage as I could. Jack and Mother offered me a third of the Three-Stop, but I turned 'em down. Preacher offered me half of his business, but there was no concern from me. I knew my interests didn't lie in commerce; they were in the mountains and river and the money had no place there. I'd chosen many years before to leave the trappings of excess behind and would not pretend to second-guess my own judgment.

One night late at the Three-Stop my friends and I were the last ones there. I watched as Jack and Mother counted their daily earnings. Jack sat with one hand under his chin while Mother counted. Preacher was stretched back on two legs of his chair, whistling a tune. A knock on the door surprised us. The closed sign was already hanging.

"Hello, can I come in?" said the man. He wore a suit and hat and carried a leather case.

"We're closed," Jack said. "But we've still got some coffee."

"Oh, I don't need any coffee," he said. "My name's Sam Stevens. I'm down from Harrison looking for Jack Stepp."

"That'd be me," Jack said.

"I'm from the Harrison Investment Group, Mr. Stepp."

"The what?"

"We invest in new businesses. May I sit down?"

Mother stopped counting her money and pulled her hands down to her lap.

"Looks like you've had a profitable day, Mr. Stepp," the man said, opening his leather case. "Now let's see here, can you tell me how much income you're actually pulling in on a daily basis?"

"Why would I do that?"

"Well, we'd like to buy you out. You see, it takes a lot of money to keep a concern like this profitable, and it takes experience to keep it running. We'd like to help."

"But you didn't help me get started," Jack said. "I done it all myself."

"I'm not asking for any money, Mr. Stepp. I want to give you money. We'd like to buy you out."

"But I don't want to sell."

"Mr. Stepp, I can see that you're a talented businessman. You've built an impressive business here. But unfortunately, even though your instincts are correct, your business acumen leaves much to be desired."

"I sell breakfast, lunch, and dinner, and a few dry goods. That's all. I don't sell no acumen."

Mother kicked him under the table.

"Very funny. Would it be possible to see your daily receipts, starting from, let's say, January the first?"

"Mother keeps all the recipes, I don't know how to cook nothing."

"Receipts, Mr. Stepp. Those pesky pieces of paper which show how much money you've received on a daily basis."

Jack looked at Mother and she kept her eyes straight ahead, trying not to get involved. Preacher was stretching his arms and yawning, acting like he was leaving.

"I take it you are unfamiliar with the practices of keeping records of your finances. That's just what I'm talking about. We can keep it from going under due to poor accounting practices, such as keeping accurate records."

"You're a carpetbagger," Jack said. "A man starts making a little money and you thieves want to move in and take it away."

"There's no need to get upset, Mr. Stepp. Were merely trying to do you a favor. You obviously don't have the experience or the knowledge to keep this place in the black. Your best decision would be to sell it to us and take that burden off your shoulders."

"Are you saying I'm not smart enough to run this place?"

"Mr. Stepp, we will buy this operation from you one way or the other. It's just business. If you won't sell, then we'll run you out of business by building our own diner directly across from you. You might as well accept the fact that you're incapable of doing business the way it should be done. I have the authority to offer you three-hundred dollars on the spot, for the whole place, inventory, building, and land."

"I live here," Jack shouted. "You ain't been here fifteen minutes and you think you can walk in here and offer me something that wouldn't last a year?"

"I see you have the daily returns laying in front of us as we speak. How much is there? We'll take that number and multiply it by the previous number of days, back to January the first, and calculate the amount of income you've had."

"That ain't right," Jack yelled. "I didn't make no money in January."

"Mr. Stepp, that is exactly my point. You've been losing money most of the time. You have no business trying to operate something you have no expertise at. You've been buying supplies from an establishment in Harrison called the Grainger Food and Supply House. They have filed their quarterly returns and your name has come up referring to a substantial amount of purchases. Much more than you could ingest yourself, if I do say so. We want this business and we will have it, one way or the other."

"Mr. Stepp simply runs this operation for me," Preacher broke in.

We were all surprised to hear Preacher speak up, thinking the whole time he was ready to bolt. He held on to the lapels of his coat with both hands and tilted back in his chair like he owned the place.

"And you would be?"

"Preacher Dan Deveneaux. I'm in charge, even though Jack owns the building. He's been a blessing in these hard times, and there's many a man and child that would have wasted away if he hadn't put his own needs aside and worked for the charities of mankind."

"Come again?" Stevens said, eyeing Preacher.

"This small concern feeds the destitute and downtrodden. That money you see before you are the contributions of the community. Charity, my good man, charity. We were simply counting it to ascertain how little we had. We're running out of food and must make another trip to Harrison to accommodate the needy. They're sleeping down the road in another cabin, given to the church by Mr. Ghetter sitting beside you there."

I smiled weakly and nodded my head.

"You're telling me this restaurant is a charity? It's used to feed the homeless?"

"Right you are, sir. If you have time I'll direct you myself to the common house, where the poor undesirables are sleeping on cots in a cabin with boarded-up windows. We have not the money to fix it the way it should be. By the way, we are taking contributions."

"What about that sign outside, the Three-Stop Café? That doesn't sound to me like it's a free lunch."

"It's only there because it gives the poor wretches a sense of pride. You wouldn't have me put up a sign saying, 'Welcome Dregs of Society,' would you? Come on, Mr. Stevens, even the lowliest of God's creatures deserve to be uplifted."

"I want to see these people."

"Come with me, sir." Preacher said, as he stood. "Walk with me to the halls of horror where the depressed and diseased live their lives in neglected chaos."

"Diseased?" Stevens's eyebrows rose. "What did you say about disease?"

Preacher shook his head from side to side. "Nothing to worry about. A small case of the pox has erupted as of late, but there's only been three deaths in the last two weeks. A peek inside will do you no harm. Do you have a place to stay this evening? There are several beds available. As a matter of fact I could possibly use your help. There's one man in my opinion that is probably quite dead by now. I gave him three hours this morning and much to my surprise he's lasted all day. I'm sure he's passed by now, though, and you could help me carry him outside. There's a large trench in the back. You wouldn't mind carrying a bag of lime as we made our trek would you?"

Stevens pulled his watch from his pocket. "Look at this, would you? I should be on my way. I've a very busy day tomorrow. Perhaps I could visit some other time. I'm always interested in seeing those less fortunate being taken care of in such a fine way." He closed his leather case and stood hurriedly.

"I apologize, Mr. Stepp, for any inconvenience. Had I known your circumstances you can be sure this whole business would not have occurred. Good night to all of you."

Stevens couldn't make tracks fast enough. He stumbled over a chair and couldn't get the door opened. Preacher walked over and twisted the knob for him.

"About that contribution?" Preacher asked.

Stevens reached in his pocket and handed Dan three dollars in gold pieces.

"Thank you so much," Preacher said. "I'm sure this will be an uplifting experience for you, and be sure to tell the others in your group that their contributions are welcome."

"Of course I will," Stevens said, leaping over the steps to the ground. He jumped in his buggy and slapped the reins and off he went at a run.

"We won't see him again." Preacher smiled.

"Don't be so sure," Mother said. "Men like that are looking for something for nothing. They'll try anything to get what they want without working for it."

It hadn't taken long for the new to wear off. We'd never been bothered by the weight of money. The chains that drag behind it leave a trail that anyone can follow.

"It's all work," Jack said. "All the money's good for is to buy more supplies. There ain't enough left over to do no good. Just one day I'd like to pocket what we made without having to buy more stuff."

"We make some," Mother said. "It's not much, I know, but it's something. What would you be doing anyway?"

"I'd be fishing," he said. "Fishing don't cost nothing and you get something back. It ain't like work."

"It'll be over soon enough," Mother said. "After the road's built there won't be half as much business. You can get back to your old ways then."

"That's good enough for me. It can't happen too soon—if there's any fish left in the river by then."

It was late and we went our separate ways, still wondering how money had become the one thing in our lives disrupting the solitude we held most important. The excitement it afforded was short-lived and to us there was no success to measure by. Most of our needs were met by bartering and it had kept us well. We measured our achievements by how good we lived, not by how much money we had.

Jack was right; there was just enough money left to buy new supplies, and the pittance left over had no glory in it to celebrate. The flow of cash needed to keep the Three-Stop Café operating turned out to be the chains dragging behind the profits. On that trail were the signs of hard labor, and those tracks showed little comfort.

Dan, on the other hand, was as happy as a spring chicken. His profit margins were swelling and so were his pockets. His daily vigil keeping the fires going on his still were paying off handsomely, but it was taking its toll on him too. "My cup runneth over," he said, "but I'm too weak to swim over the brim with it."

One stormy day the rains had stopped the work on the ramp. It was another opportunity for Preacher to increase his sales, the men bored in their cabin with nothing to do. Dan had set up his bar as usual and whiskey started flowing early that morning.

"Women. We need women," some of the men said. "What kind of place is this ain't got no women."

"I don't trade in carnal pleasures," Preacher said. "You'll have to go elsewhere to meet those needs."

"And where would that be?" one asked.

"Not around here," Dan said. "Back to Harrison. That's where those times must be found."

The men were rowdy on that day. The work had been going on for weeks and most had stayed in Dogleg the whole time. It was a long way to Harrison and they knew there was no way to get there and back in time for the next day's work. The quiet conversations in the corners bothered Dan, and he tried his best to hear but could only make out bits and pieces. What he did hear he didn't like.

"I know where there's women," one said.

"So do I, " another said. "And money too."

The morning wore on and so did the whiskey and things got worse. Preacher Dan had been around enough to know when men's attitudes went from good to bad. A sober man could sense it. He was counting heads trying to keep track and he didn't like the way things were adding up.

Four men left the cabin by the back door, and Preacher thought they might be relieving themselves, but when they stayed gone too long he started worrying.

Things were slow at the Three-Stop and only Mother and Ginny were there. Jack was helping me mend some fences at my place in between the showers.

Preacher had one jug of Potation left sitting on the floor behind him. He uncorked it and kicked it over, letting it spill through the cracks. The men had had enough.

"That's it, men. I'm all out. I'll have to go get some more."

"Make it quick," they said. "We'll say when we're through."

"Right you are," Preacher said.

Dan had no intentions of going back. That day was ugly and so was the mood. Jack and I saw him coming through the field, in too big of a hurry for our thinking.

"Get your rifles," he shouted. "There's trouble, I can feel it."

"All them drunks getting rowdy are they?" Jack asked.

"More than that," Preacher said. "What they're after I can't provide. But I think I know where they're headed. Mother and Ginny still at the Three-Stop?"

Jack and I knew then, by the question and by the worried look on Dan's face.

"How many?" I asked.

"I've lost four, maybe more. It's hard to be sure."

We ran to the cabin and got our guns. All three of us jumped on the mule and kicked him hard. We rode up to the steps of the Three-Stop and scrambled down. Inside, all was quiet, not a person there.

"*Mother,*" Jack yelled.

No answer.

"*Ginny*," I yelled.

Still no answer.

We walked through the dining area and Jack checked in the dry goods room—nothing. We looked behind the counter and found the same. In the kitchen things were different; there'd been a scuffle.

We stood for a moment, thinking. Then we heard Jack's mule bellowing.

"The barn!" Jack said, already at a run.

"They may have guns," Preacher said. "I didn't see any but they may still have one."

We slowed as we reached the barn door, Jack rubbing the mule's snout to calm him. We could hear Ginny sobbing, and Mother's shouts.

"*Leave her alone!*" she yelled. "*She's just a child!*"

"She's woman enough. You keep quiet. An old woman like you will have to be second. We'll take the young 'un first."

Preacher pointed to the door of the barn. There was blood on the handle. Jack waved us to come with him. He stopped at a split in the lumber and looked inside, then nodded for me to do the same.

Two of the men were standing over Ginny in the corner and one man was holding a chunk of limb threatening Mother with it. The other was holding a shotgun on Tory. He was lying on the ground, his head bleeding from where they'd clubbed him. It looked as if they only had the one shotgun.

There was only two ways into the barn, the side door with the blood on it and the big access door we were standing in front of. There was no way to sneak up on 'em. The three of us looked at each other, shaking our heads. It would be dangerous to barge through the doors. The one might shoot Tory before we could stop him.

The next thing that happened took Jack and I by surprise. It was a simple movement, a calm, deliberate action; one that had to be done, but one which I'm not sure I could have mustered, at least not that quick.

Preacher shouldered me aside from the split in the door, raised his rifle and shot the man standing over Tory. He opened the door, Jack and I still standing in place for the second it took. Then we came to our senses and followed Dan inside. He went straight to the man he'd shot, Jack and I holding our guns on the other three. Mother had barreled into the man hovering over her and Ginny when he turned his head at the shot, and was fighting with him over the club. Jack stepped in and stopped the scuffle. It was all over in seconds.

Mother held Ginny while Preacher cared for Tory. Jack and I made the three men lie down on the ground while Jack held his shotgun on them. I took a look at the other man. He was shot through the shoulder and would live. We never knew if Dan had tried to place the shot or if it was just luck. We really didn't care.

We tied the men's hands behind their backs, feet all strung together. Tory had a good split on his head but Mother patched him up. Ginny was scared but they hadn't gotten to her. We worked on the man that was shot, cleaning the wound as best we could, loaded all of 'em on a wagon, and took them to Harrison. The sheriff came the next day to talk with Mother, Ginny, and Tory.

Mother had closed the Three-Stop, and after the sheriff had left, all of us were alone, drinking coffee at the corner table.

"Preacher…" Mother started.

"Say no more," he said. "The bar's closed. There'll be no more liquor sold on the spot, only when they're leaving town."

Mother nodded. "Thanks."

"I don't need the money that bad."

"That's not what the thanks is for," she said.

We'd all learned a good lesson that day. We weren't cut out for the fast pace of commerce and all of us knew it. The trouble it brought was more than the money was worth. The Three-Stop would remain open, but Preacher wouldn't sell any more liquor to the men, not unless they were leaving. All of us would be glad when the ramp was done and things were back to normal, the pace we were used to—slow and easy.

And slow and easy was how we liked it. We were getting things back to normal in our own way. Jack and mother still got to the Three-Stop at four in the morning and it was still eight or nine in the evening before they went home, but the worry had somehow disappeared. Mother didn't push as hard and Jack didn't run as hard. Ginny had stayed with 'em, even though the scare she had was difficult to forget. They let her keep all the tips even when they helped with the serving. They were starting to have fun and there was more laughter in the Three-Stop than ever before.

Preacher worked half as hard on his Potation as he did before, and joined me more often in the late afternoons on the riverbank. He'd made more money in four weeks than he'd made in nine months of the year before.

We'd build a fire close to the river and stretch out with our heads on a log and let the spring sun fall on our faces. Every now and then we'd check our bait but it wasn't a priority. We watched the opposite bank come alive with the new growth of a new year, and marked the river's rise with a stick in the mud.

We still met Jack in the morning for coffee before we went our separate ways,

Dan to his still, me to whatever work I had lined up, but around two in the afternoon we made sure we were done with the day's labor. Once in a while Mother would let Jack off early to go with us, on the slow days, when she'd catch him staring out the window watching Preacher and me walking to the river. It was on one of those days when the three of us ran into something we'd never forget.

We'd decided to take the flat-bottom boat that afternoon and do some floating and fishing, hit some of the holes that we hadn't thrown a line in yet. We drifted on the lazy water, passing the great limestone bluffs, listening to the water talk and hearing the chatter of birds and squirrels warning their neighbors of our intrusion.

It was almost dark and we were poling our way back upstream when the fish started hitting. A slow rising river will make the fish bite like no other time and that day they must have just woke up, 'cause they were striking on spit.

Preacher had brought a lantern just in case, and it was a good thing, 'cause it was dusk when we tied up to a stub under a bluff. It'd been a warm afternoon with very little breeze, and we'd taken our jackets off earlier to feel the hot rays of the sun. We were using crickets and worms for bait and the fish were damn near climbing in the boat. After we tied up they started hitting even harder and none of us wanted to leave.

Jack was in the front of the boat, I was in the middle, and Preacher was taking up the rear.

"It's getting too dark to see," Jack said. "Light up that lantern. I could stay out here all night."

"It's times like this I wish I'd brought two poles," Preacher said. "One to fish with and one to cold cock 'em as they jump out of the water."

I lit the lantern and turned it up high. The sun was going down behind the bluff, hiding the last remnants of light.

"Looky here," Jack shouted. "Two at once. That perch ate my worm and a bass ate him. I ain't had this much fun since I rode Pork Chop through the wall at the Fin and Feather."

"I heard they rebuilt," Preacher said.

"A new eating place?" Jack asked. "What'd they name it?"

"The Ham Hock. Nobody's seen the pig. I guess when you lose everything you got to start with whatever you got—family included."

I was unhooking a nice bass when I noticed a few flying insects collecting around the light. I swatted at 'em but it didn't make any difference.

"Hand me them worms, Preacher," I said, turning to look.

When I turned back I saw that what had been several insects had now turned into several hundred.

"These bugs are getting annoying," I said.

"They're attracted to the light," Jack said. "They won't bother us for long."

I baited my hook and threw back in, now having to swat continuously with one hand while holding the pole with the other. I noticed Jack was doing the same thing. Then it got worse. There were thousands of them, so many we could hardly see. One second they were just a nuisance and the next they were swarming.

"God a mighty," Jack said. "I'm choking."

"Me too," Preacher coughed. "What is it?"

"They're so tiny I can't make 'em out," I said. "It's too early for skeeters and they're too small for flies."

They were so thick it was like a black cloud had come over us. We could barely make out the end of our poles.

"*Pecker gnats!*" Jack shouted. "That's what they are, pecker gnats. *I can't breathe!* Every time I take a breath I swallow fifty thousand."

Jack was coughing and swatting like Preacher and I were.

"They're in my eyes," Preacher said.

"*Turn the light off,*" Jack yelled.

All three of us were standing in the boat, swinging our arms and batting at the tiny flying specs. I reached down and turned the light off, but it did no good. Now it was just dark, but it made no difference to the gnats.

"*Untie us!*" Preacher yelled.

"*I can't see!*" Jack shouted back.

"Turn the light back on, Claude," Jack said. "I can't see to get the rope."

"I can't—I can't find my matches." I turned around but couldn't see Dan. Then I located him, in the bottom of the boat with his jacket over his head.

"*Preacher,*" I yelled. "*You got to pole us out of here.*"

"Can't," his muffled shout came back. "I done ate a gallon of 'em and I think I'm gonna puke."

"Jack," I said. "Untie us."

"There's too many," came the answer. "I'm bailing."

"NO! Don't leave us here tied up."

That's when I heard the splash. Jack had jumped in the water to escape, leaving me standing with Dan hiding under his coat. I felt like warning Preacher, but then again I thought, what the hell, he dug in first. I dove in headfirst and headed for the opposite bank, right on Jack's heels.

We walked out of the water side by side, spitting and scraping our tongues, flinging off black specs with every slap. They were in our hair, ears, and nostrils, inside our shirts, and down our pants.

"What about Preacher?" I asked Jack.

"Only one thing to do. One of us has got to swim back over there and cut the boat loose. *Preacher, can you hear me?*"

We could hear nothing but silence.

"I'll go," I said.

"Good. I'm peckered out."

I walked back into the water and swam over to the boat. Once I got close enough and could see the front end, I dove under and cut the line and pulled the boat with me as I headed for the bank.

"*Help!*" I heard Preacher yell. "*They've stole the boat and took me prisoner!*"

"I've got the boat," I said. I was on the bank with Jack now, Preacher still curled up in a fetal position under his jacket.

The gnats were gone as fast as they appeared. We built a fire and stood back, waiting to see if they'd re-group, but they didn't. We stripped down and bathed in the cold water and warmed ourselves by the fire. We shook out our clothes as best we could, gathered our things and went back home. Jack said he was still coughing 'em up two weeks later and Preacher refused to use pepper for a month, fearing the tiny flecks might come to life.

It was soon after that when Preacher got a visitor. She was a large woman— plump would be the word. She had a round, red face, with an even redder nose, which sat on neckless shoulders, and her whole body turned when she faced a person. Her nun's habit covered her like a tent, and she kept her hands shoved inside the sleeves most of the time. Her toes pointed toward each other while walking and she took small careful steps. Her big behind was as wide as a wagon and shook her habit as she walked. Sister Caroline was her name, and she was blind and hard of hearing.

She had a tall, skinny woman with her, who was flat-chested, shorthaired, bony-fingered, hollow-cheeked, long-nosed, thin-lipped, and had a scratchy, irritating voice. She took an immediate dislike to Preacher Dan the second she saw him. The feeling was mutual, and Preacher took to calling her Lizard behind her back, though just loud enough for her to hear.

We were eating dinner, Preacher and I, when they walked through the door at the Three-Stop. Preacher immediately introduced himself, thinking he'd encountered two traveling nuns. Traveling they were, their destination had been Dogleg, and their mission was Preacher Dan.

"I'm Sister Caroline and this is Lizzie. We're from Little Rock, the Sisters of Mercy Diocese." Sister Caroline was staring past Preacher into the unknown. Lizzie turned her so she was facing him.

"Very glad to meet you," Preacher said. "Would you like to sit down and rest? I'm sure the trip has made you weary."

"We are not weary," Lizzie said.

"I am a little tired," Sister Caroline said.

Preacher pulled a chair out for her. "You may sit right here, Sister." He looked at Lizzie with a smirk.

"Why thank you," Sister Caroline said, and plopped down, missing the chair and landing on the floor.

"Now see what you've done," Lizzie said. "You've made her miss the chair."

"I thought you were helping her," Dan said.

"You don't do much thinking, do you?"

"There's no reason to get snippy," Dan came back.

"Well, help her up!" Lizzie said. "It's the least you can do."

I jumped up and with Dan's help we pulled Sister Caroline to her feet, which took quite an effort, and helped her into the chair. Lizzie stood by and watched.

"My goodness," Sister Caroline said. "That was quite a low chair. I say, is that chicken frying? Is this the kitchen that feeds the homeless?"

"The homeless?" Dan asked.

"Oh, yes indeed," Sister Caroline said. "We've heard all about it. Mr. Stevens told us."

"Mister Stevens?"

"Why, Mr. Stevens in Harrison. He told us about the charity work you've been doing here and we had to come and see. He even made a donation he said. I'm sure you haven't forgotten."

I looked at Preacher and he looked at me, his eyes widening. His lie had come back to haunt him.

Dan turned back to the two nuns. "Yes, yes it is. The work is tiresome but it's fulfilling."

Lizzie huffed. "This doesn't look like a kitchen for the homeless to me."

"What does it look like, dear?" Sister Caroline said, her head jerking up and down, left and right.

"Looks like a restaurant to me. I don't see any homeless people here."

"You're mistaken," Dan said. "Why, this poor wretch right here is destitute." Dan grabbed my arm and pulled me in front of him.

"And who might you be?" Lizzie asked.

"The poor soul can't speak," Dan said. "His tongue was frozen in a blizzard last January."

"What!" Lizzie said. "I've never heard of such a thing."

"Odd, isn't it," Dan said. "But, that's what I do here. I give shelter to the strange and deformed with no bias. They too have a place in God's world."

"You're full of—"

"Now, now, Lizzie," Sister Caroline scolded. "There's no need for dark talk. You'll have to excuse Lizzie, she's new to the diocese. She's had a difficult beginning in life, but we've taken her into our fold. It's her first year. She's just learning to take the faith to heart."

"I know crap when I step in it," Lizzie said.

"Now," Sister Caroline said. "I'm sure the good pastor doesn't understand that kind of talk. Lizzie has come to us from a broken home. She still has a touch of, should I say, coarseness, left in her attitude, but we're working on that, aren't we Lizzie?"

Lizzie curled her thin lip. "I've lived in the streets all my life and I can smell a turd in a barrel of dead fish."

"Your talents are impressive," Dan said. "If we have the time, perhaps we can use your endowments to our benefit. We have some small shacks in back of the cabins that you could clean for us."

"Why, you—"

"Lizzie had some problems with the authorities," Sister Caroline broke in. "We're trying to help her on her path to salvation. She has come with me on this trip as my helper. As you have noticed, I am blind and need some direction at times. She's been a big help too."

"May I ask what your visit is about?" Preacher asked.

"What did he say?" Sister Caroline asked.

"He wants to know what in the hell you're doing here."

"There's a well where?"

"Why...are...you...here?" Lizzie said, slow and loud.

"Oh, yes. It's about your work for the homeless. You see, we at the diocese are very involved with the homeless ourselves. When Mr. Stevens told us of your work, we just had to come and see. Not many servants of the Lord would put their well-being in the path of the oppressed. It's so good to finally meet someone of your caliber and commitment to the demoralized. Mr. Stevens said you were quite low on funds and we wanted to see if we could help. We have some resources available for charities such as yours."

"I see," Preacher said.

"You don't see nothing," Lizzie said. "You smell money. This ain't no homeless shelter and that fella there didn't have his tongue froze off either."

"You're such a sweet child," Preacher said. "You could be of some assistance to us. There's a rattlesnake in the chicken house. Wait until dark and see if you can find it."

"Sister Caroline," Preacher said loudly, "I am honored that you have taken the time to visit our poor but adequate facility. Would you like to sample some of our simple fare before we tour the shelter?"

"You're so kind."

"I'll just go tell the cook. I believe we have some chicken left for you, Sister Caroline, and maybe some grits for Lizzie."

Lizzie stared at Preacher.

"What did he say?" Sister Caroline said.

"He's gonna get some food, if that's what he calls it."

"Wonderful," Sister Caroline said. "We must sample what the destitute have consumed."

Preacher took me by the arm and we went back to the kitchen. Mother, Jack, and Ginny were busy cleaning up.

"What are you gonna do now?" I asked. "Your story to Stevens has pushed you in a corner."

"I don't want their money," Preacher said. "But if we don't play this thing out she's liable to tell him the truth. I know that Lizzie will, and Stevens'll make his way back."

Dan told the story to Mother and Jack. Mother just shook her head. Jack thought it was funny. He always liked to see Preacher in a pickle.

"Jack," Preacher said, "you'll have to play along. If you don't, Stevens might come back."

"What've I got to do? You should have made up a better story in the first place."

"It was on the spur. How was I supposed to know he'd tell the first sister he came across? Besides, I did it for you."

"Just tell her the truth and be done with it," Mother said.

"Can't," Preacher said. "It's against the rules."

"What rules?" I asked.

"The rules of storytelling. There's laws to be considered when stories is told. One can't back down just because a spoke broke. You got to keep on rolling."

"What's your plan?" Jack asked.

"First thing is to feed them two. That'll give me time to think."

"You'll need more time than that," Mother said. "I'll fry some more chicken. Ginny, mash some tators."

"The way I figure it, we can't take 'em back to the cabin. Them men in there won't play along, especially since I quit selling 'em whiskey. We'll have to use your cabin, Claude. You and Jack head that way and act like you're both at the bottom of the trough. I'll walk 'em up there when dinner's over. It's that Lizard that'll give me trouble. She's got a suspicious mind."

Jack and I went out the back and Preacher made his way back to the table.

"A sample of our honest fare will soon appear," he said. "It's not much, but not all sustenance comes from food."

"Some of it comes from bullsh—"

"Lizzie!" Sister Caroline interrupted. "That language won't do. Preacher has offered his simple repast and we should be thankful."

"Your last name wouldn't be Borden, would it?" Preacher asked Lizzie.

"What are you saying?" Lizzie asked, her eyes narrowing.

"Nothing, nothing, just trying to make conversation. Now, Sister Caroline, are you sure you'd like to see the shelter tonight. Perhaps tomorrow might be better. I'm sure your trip has tired you."

Sister Caroline sat motionless. Lizzie nudged her.

"Yes, dear?"

"He wants to know when you're leaving."

"Oh, we must visit the poor and helpless at the soonest possible moment. Will we be able to sleep in the same shelter? Are there accommodations available? We'll need some privacy, but very little."

"There are few beds available," Preacher said. "But I can assure you we can find ample space. Miss Lizzie, there's a tree right outside the shelter you can hang from."

"What did he say, dear?"

"He's a lying, rotten snot!"

"Oh, yes. That would be fine. We can sleep on a cot. Make no special efforts for us. Our bedding must be the same as the unfortunate."

"I'll tell you what's unfortunate—"

"Might I interrupt for a moment," Preacher said. "Sister Caroline, would you allow me the privilege of sitting with you as you dine? Perhaps Miss Lizzie would like to freshen up. There's a water bucket and a tack brush out back. Feel free to discard them when you're done."

"What?" Sister Caroline asked.

"He's about as close to a preacher as I am to a priest," Lizzie said.

"Oh, my goodness. Preacher Deveneaux, you aspire to be a priest? Your ambition will inspire us all. Please sit beside me so we can talk."

Ginny brought out two plates of dinner and set 'em in front of Lizzie and Sister Caroline.

"It smells delicious," Sister Caroline said. "You'll have to help me, Preacher Deveneaux. Once I get my bearings I'll be fine."

Preacher was smiling at Lizzie as he helped. She could see Dan was whittling his way into the sister's confidence, and Lizzy wasn't happy with the way things were going.

"Well, Preacher," Lizzie said. "Are there many more snakes in the pit, or are you the only poison?"

"I've wrestled many a demon in my day, many as impudent as you. I'm not afraid to say I've paid my dues."

"What'd you pay 'em with, tithes?"

"It's regrettable that our paths did not cross sooner," Dan said. "I could have saved the poor Sisters of Mercy some time by taking you fishing and using you for bait."

"What?" Sister Caroline said.

Dan bent close to the Sister's ear. "I said, what a wonderful young lady Miss Lizzie is."

"Oh, she's a beautiful child, isn't she?"

"Beauty is not a strong enough word. It almost hurts to look upon her."

"Just where are these homeless people you've been taking care of?" Lizzie asked.

"The shelter is just over the hill. It won't take but a minute to get there. You may start ahead of us if you wish. When you get to the river, jump in."

"I'm sticking close," Lizzie said. "You're not worth much, but you're worth keeping track of."

"Are you ready, Sister?" Preacher asked.

"What?"

"Are you through with your dinner?"

"It was very good, thank you. Shall we go now? I'd like to meet some of the people you've helped."

Sister Caroline laid her napkin down on the table and felt for the edge of the chair.

"Help me up, would you, dear?" she asked Lizzie. "I don't want to tumble over that low chair again."

"Hold on to my arm, Sister," Lizzie said. "I don't know why you're going on this visit. You're just as well blind, 'cause you're not going to see anything."

"What, dear?"

"Nothing. Come on, let's get it over with."

"You go get the buggy, Lizzie," Preacher said, taking hold of the sister's arm. "I'll just help Sister Caroline myself."

"You keep your hands off her, you buzzard. I know what you're thinking. You'll push her down the steps so she can't make it to the shelter, or whatever you call it."

"What?" Sister Caroline asked.

"Pay no mind, Sister," Preacher said. "Miss Lizzie was just jabbering. She's so excited about being in my company she can't contain her tongue."

"I can see how a man of your standing would impress a young girl," Sister said. "But don't get any ideas, Preacher Deveneaux, she's going back with me."

"Have no fear, Sister. I wouldn't let her stay if both of her legs were broke."

"What?"

"He threatened to break my legs," Lizzie said.

"She's so star-struck her mind's leaving her," Preacher said. "Maybe we should leave her here, let her calm down."

"That might be a good idea," Sister Caroline said. "Lizzie, you stay here and calm yourself."

"I'm not staying. There's no telling what he's up to."

"Very well, dear. Well, you see Preacher Deveneaux, Lizzie's turning into an upstanding young woman right before our eyes."

"It's my eyes I'm worried about," Preacher said, turning his head.

"What?"

"It's okay, let her come. She probably wants to get as much experience as she can while she's here with me."

"The only experience I need is getting out of here. Let's get this over with so Sister Caroline can get back to Little Rock and tell 'em what a big crook you are."

"What?" Sister asked.

"She said she's got a crook in her neck," Preacher said. "If she would only let me I could cure it for her."

"Dear," Sister said, "let the good preacher fix your neck. It's no surprise to me that he'd have some healing ability the way the good Lord has seen fit to empower him."

"He ain't touching me!"

"What?"

"She said she's cured."

"Oh, Preacher, I'm so glad I brought Lizzie with me. I can already tell you've made such an impression on her."

"It's a gift, Sister"

"This is making me sick," Lizzie said.

"What?"

"She said she's sick," Preacher said. "Now, watch your step." Dan had her by the arm and helped her into the buggy, pulling himself up in the seat next to her.

"Where am I gonna sit?" Lizzie asked.

"I think it's best you walk," Preacher smiled. "Behind the buggy, if you don't mind. I don't want the horse to spook."

"I'm gonna paint a white stripe down your back."

"What she'd say?" Sister Caroline asked.

"She said she needs a bath. She smells like a skunk."

"Now Lizzie," Sister Caroline said. "That's no way for a lady to talk. If you need some time alone, I'm sure the Preacher can direct you to the proper place."

"I can tell her where to go," Dan said.

Dan slapped the reins, leaving Lizzie standing in front of the steps.

"It's right around the bend," Preacher said. "It won't take a minute."

At they pulled up to the cabin Dan could see Jack peering out the window. Preacher waved at him, motioning him to get in bed.

"Watch your step, Sister," Dan said, as he helped her off the buggy. "I don't want you to take another fall like before."

"That was so embarrassing. I can't believe I did that."

"I wish I'd been closer," Dan said, "so I could've helped."

"That's so nice of you, Preacher Deveneaux. Where's Lizzy?"

"Oh, she's walking behind us."

"Are we here? I'm so proud of you. I do so want to know the mercy you have shown. Now, you'll have to explain everything to me."

"I will. Don't you worry about a thing."

Dan knocked on the cabin door.

"Oh, you have to knock?"

"I only do it as a sign of respect. I want 'em to know that this is their home and I'm not here to impose my will on 'em."

"You've a heart of gold, Preacher. I'll tell the other sisters how wonderful you treat these poor souls."

"Stand back just a little," Dan said, pulling on her arm. "I'm swinging this screen door our way. "There you go. Step up just a little."

The two of them stood inside the cabin door and Preacher was looking at Jack and me, both of us in our beds, our clothes still on. He walked Sister Caroline over to the beds.

"Now," Preacher said. "This unfortunate here is Jack. His belly's swollen from starvation. He's lost most of his hair and somehow all of his height."

"Oh, my Lord," Sister Caroline said. "Is he in much pain?"

"He looks as if he's been through quite a bit. Here, you can touch him."

Dan pulled her hand over Jack's head and laid it on top. She patted him like a puppy.

"You poor soul, you have lost your hair. Pay no mind. The Lord will see fit to give it back. If not, then you don't need hair anyway."

"Here," Preacher said, taking her hand. "Feel his stomach."

Jack wasn't happy at the way Preacher was describing his body.

With Dan's guidance Sister Caroline laid her hand on Jack's stomach.

"Lord have mercy, he's so swollen. Preacher Deveneaux, you must keep me informed about the outcome of this poor wretch's life. We'll be praying for his soul."

"As I do, Sister, as I do."

"I ain't sick," Jack said.

"What'd he say?" Sister Caroline asked.

Dan was waving his hands at Jack to shut up. "He's out of his mind with misery. He must be having dreams."

"I ain't gonna be a part of this," Jack said, throwing back the covers. "You ought to be ashamed of yourself, Preacher."

"I'm lost for words, Sister," Preacher said. "The malnourishment has driven him insane. Pay no heed to his madness."

"I'm with Jack," I said, jumping out of bed. "This isn't right."

"Who's that," Sister Caroline asked, swiveling her head my way.

"That's the one done had his tongue froze," Lizzie said, as she walked through the doorway. "I told you he was a skunk, Sister."

"Preacher Deveneaux," Sister Caroline said. "What is this? What have you done?"

"Nothing, Sister, nothing at all, insanity has taken over. We must leave at once, I'm fearful for your safety."

"You just hold on there," Lizzie said. "Your egg's been broke. It's time for the law to step in, you trying to steal money from the Sisters of Mercy."

"You misunderstand," Preacher said. "Tell 'em, Jack. You tell 'em, Claude. It's all a big mistake."

"Don't be pulling me into your shenanigans," Jack said.

"Preacher Deveneaux," Sister Caroline said, "I don't know what to say. My faith has been shattered. What you have done will no doubt haunt you."

"I hope it does," Lizzie said. "He looks like a scarecrow anyway."

"I wasn't going to take any money. I only wanted to help. Stevens was trying to buy him out. I made up the story to steer him away. Right, Jack?"

"Don't drag me into it. You've lied your way into jail, looks to me like."

"Claude," Preacher said, his hands stretched out. "Claude, you've got to tell 'em."

"Sorry, Preacher. It's a low thing you've done, trying to bilk the sister."

"Sister Caroline, all I was trying to do was help my friends."

"I'm afraid I'll have to report back to the diocese that you've squandered your ministry. You'll be stripped of your doctrine. Pray with me, Preacher Deveneaux, pray that God will forgive your wanton ways."

Preacher got down on his knees with Sister Caroline and they both bowed their heads.

"I'm going for the law," Lizzie said. "I've never done nothing this bad. Stealing from the Church—it's the worst I've ever heard."

"No, don't go," Preacher said. "Kneel down beside me. We'll both go to the house of the Lord, repentant sinners."

"Pray with me, Preacher Deveneaux," Sister Caroline said. "Say these words after me: Lord, I have sinned. Throw not my soul from your side, for I repent."

Preacher said the words, his hands clasped together, eyes closed, head bent.

"Please, Lord," Sister went on, "even though I've lied, even though I've shamed myself and my friends, even though I'm as low as a snake's belly, even though I've lusted after women, even though I've swam in the fiery waters of libation, I pray to you to forgive my sins."

I saw Preacher's eye lift open ever so slightly, looking at Sister Caroline as she went on and on, but he continued repeating the prayer.

"And Lord," Sister continued, "trust in me, I will never drink whiskey again."

Dan was having trouble saying the words. She'd hit home with her prayer and Dan hated having to say something in front of the sister that he knew he couldn't live up to. Lizzie stepped up and shoved her foot at Preacher's butt.

"Say it, you skunk, or I'll get the sheriff now!"

Dan didn't like being kicked in the rear end by nobody, especially Lizzie, but he didn't want the law down on him either. He gritted his teeth and repeated the words.

"And Lord, I will never tell another lie," Sister said. "Come on, Preacher

Deveneaux, repeat after me. Lord, I will never lust after women. From now on I'm taking a vow of chastity."

"Uh, can we talk about that one?" Preacher said. "This here didn't actually have anything to do with women. I'd just a soon leave them out of it."

"What do you think, boys?" Sister Caroline asked. "Has he had enough?"

Preacher jerked his head straight. He knew then he'd been had. Sister Caroline pulled herself from the floor, reached in her pocket and pulled out a plug of tobacco, biting off a mouthful.

Mother Mabel stepped through the door, from her hiding spot by the window.

"You can get off your knees now, Preacher," Mother said. "This is Caroline all right, but there ain't no Sister in front of it. She's my cousin. And this is Lizzie, true enough. She's Caroline's daughter. I got a letter saying they were coming to visit and I got with Jack and Claude and thought it might be fun to see you squirm for a while."

Preacher Dan got up from the floor, brushed off his knees, and straightened his shirt and jacket.

"I was merely playing along. I knew the whole time that something was amiss."

"You're lying again," Lizzie said, smiling. "What about all them vows you took?"

"I had my fingers crossed," Preacher said, finally seeing the humor in it. "It's an old trick I learned in El Paso, Texas. I was the headmaster of an all girls' school. I found myself in a disturbing situation, being trapped in a stall in the gymnasium dressing room. In only minutes the bell would ring, dismissing the girls from their workout, and I…"

"Oh, shut up, Preacher," Lizzie said.

"I've heard enough, myself," Caroline said. "What's this I hear about Passionate Potation? Let's have a sample. I'm about to sweat myself thin in this outfit."

"Come on, let's go back to the Three-Stop," Mother said. "All this lying's got my thirst up too."

213

Chapter Fourteen

"It sounds to me like you had a lot of good times," Pete said.

"We did have," Claude said. "That's one thing about living in the mountains, folks kept their humor about 'em. They had to. Life was hard; sometimes all it was was hard. People were scratchin' out a living and it was a meager living at best. I believe that's part of the bond that mountain people have, 'cause it was so difficult to get from year to year. You had to have others there to help in times of need, and that trust and pride is what held 'em together."

Claude looked at the sky and saw the full moon was in line with the river, making the water shine with a white glow down its length. Traces of haze were forming on its surface, and he knew that soon the mystery of the water would unfold its treasures. Pete wouldn't be able to see it, but Claude would.

Over the years more of his friends and family had found their way to the river's haven, and now he was waiting one last time to see them as they rose from the mist. He wondered if they knew he was leaving and wondered still if he would ever see them again. Would he be a part of that sanctuary if he no longer lived in these hills, or would he be alone, trapped by himself with strangers?

Claude poured another cup of coffee for him and Pete settled back on his seat.

"Why do you think folks drifted away from here over the years?" Pete asked.

"Times changed," Claude said. "They wanted more for their families, or at least they thought that more was somewhere else. I believe you'll find that those generations that stayed in the mountains have fuller lives than those that left, but opinions are free and worth the same. Commerce has a way of tickling the ego as well as the pocket, but most folks don't understand that the value of life isn't printed on paper. My friends and I wanted our lives back the way they were, but sometimes there's a toll for coming out of the storm."

The ramp was done and the new road was stretching farther from us. The sun-filled mornings of May greeted us with the sweet scent of springtime and awakened our ambition to float the river. The Three-Stop's business was slowing down and Jack was anxious to do something besides stay inside. Mother and Ginny could take care of everything, and Mother said Jack was underfoot most of the time anyway.

That time we took a canoe big enough for the three of us, and stayed on the river for just two nights. We packed some lard, flour, bacon, a frying pan, a few utensils, and a jug of Potation.

We let the river push us along, rarely sticking our paddles in the water. Our boat passed by towering bluffs, and at times we just sat in the alcoves at the base, leaning back, fishing, and listening to the river slapping at the boat.

The calm day was a blessing for us and we accepted it without reservation. The sun was straight up and we could feel its heat on our shirtless bodies, the first real heat we'd felt in a long time.

My thoughts kept going back to Elmer and the fine times we'd all had together on our float trips. Those memories were on the raft floating in front of me and Elmer was looking back, waving his walking stick. I started to wave but caught myself, realizing it was only a vision, but for a moment I was with him, and I wished I could put my arm around his shoulders and ask some nonsense question just to hear him talk. I could see him in my mind but I couldn't hear his voice. I listened carefully, struggling to shape the sentences he would say, but still I couldn't hear the sounds. I'd already lost part of him and thought how easily it had happened. If I closed my eyes I could see Elmer perfectly, could see his lips moving. It hurt to be able to bring him so close and not be able to talk to him.

"Let's pull up across from that next bluff," Jack said. "We'll set out a trotline and do some catfishing."

"It's the middle of the afternoon," Preacher said.

"So what? You got somewhere to be?"

"Guess not," Preacher replied. "I think I might take a bath."

"Good," Jack said. "I can't think of a better stink bait than you sitting naked in the water."

The gravel crunched under the boat as we hit the bank. We were under a large birch tree leaning out over the water. Jack unrolled the trotline while Preacher stripped down for his bath, and I unpacked the boat and gathered firewood.

Jack kicked up the gravel at the edge of the water to form a pool and we started looking for crawdads to bait the trotline.

"We may be eating these for dinner if we don't catch some fish," I said.

"Nothing wrong with crayfish," Preacher said. He was sitting waist deep in the river soaping down his arms and chest. "I remember the time I was scouting for the cavalry in Kansas."

"Scouting!" Jack said. "You can't sniff your way to an outhouse."

"I beg to differ," Preacher said. "There are descriptions of my exploits in the annals of military history. Sometime in the near future I'll send for the particular heroic events that have positioned my name at the top of the list of Honored Scouts and Trackers."

"Never heard of it," Jack said.

"Nevertheless," Preacher continued. "The truth is in the print. Now, as I was saying, we were looking for a small band of renegade Indians who'd stolen some horses from a local rancher. I remember it like it was yesterday.

"We were in the middle of a drought that left the earth scorched to a point where not even a wagon loaded with cannonballs would leave a trail. That's when the Army post called for my services. They'd heard of my reputation and knocked on my door early that morning. I tried to explain that I no longer dealt in the art of tracking, that I'd given myself to the service of the Lord. They pleaded with me to lead 'em to the troublemakers, and I couldn't find it in my heart to let 'em down. It was the last time, I said, that I would offer my services to do the Army's job. I saw tears come to some of the men's eyes when I agreed to save the day. They didn't want to make their way into unchartered territory without the leadership of an experienced frontiersman."

"That frontiersman was you?" Jack snorted, as he pulled the pinchers off a large crawdad.

"Please don't interrupt," Preacher said. "Now, where was I? Oh, yes. I led the men from the fort amidst the cheering of all the troops. 'Dan's the man,' they were yelling and screaming. 'He'll find those Injuns.' I told the men to hold ranks and be quiet, as I needed all my faculties to track the brazen heathens.

"We rode west for half a day, but as I said before, the earth was scorched and tracks were hard to find. Then I saw the first signs of our culprits—horse droppings. The other men were amazed at my abilities and cheered as I waved for 'em to follow. Then, the horses having dropped all the droppings they could drop, the trail ended. The troops were devastated. They had no idea how I was going to keep tracking when there were no signs of the marauding maniacs.

"I could see they were distraught and depressed. The searing sun bearing down on us was taking its toll, and I knew at that point I would have to proceed on my own, without the help of the distressed cavalry. I told the sergeant to let the men rest, and I would go forth alone to identify the hiding place of the rebels. He begged me not to leave, for fear his men would revolt without my leadership, but I told him there was no other option. I ordered the men to maintain their position no matter how long I was gone, and I'd come back for 'em. Some men wept as I rode away, and others merely yelled my name in their attempt to honor me.

"I rode into the sun, my horse's head hanging in front of me, tired and thirsty. I stopped to give him some water; half of my canteen, knowing full well it might be my life he was drinking. As I lifted my hat of water to the horse's mouth the sounds of a frightened rattlesnake broke the silence. My horse bolted, spilling the water and leaving me stranded in the sweltering heat. I'd hung my canteen on the saddle horn and now had no sustenance whatsoever. The only weapon I had on me was a bowie knife, so I threw it at the snake, killing it instantly. I skinned him and threw him over my shoulder, knowing he might be my only nourishment for some time.

"I walked for hours, still tracking the thieves, even though I could barely continue in the stifling heat. At sundown I cut the snake into pieces and ate what I could. I knew I'd need the nourishment to continue on. During the night I could see to the west what appeared to be a dim light on the horizon. There was no need for me to wait till morning, as my strength was waning. I gathered myself together and stumbled in the direction of the light.

"During the night my condition worsened. At times I was crawling on hands and knees, sometimes clawing my way forward. I began hallucinating, seeing visions in front of me, lovely rivers of cool water, dinner tables filled with potatoes and steak. I must admit it was only my inner strength and determination that kept me going.

"At first light I found myself on a small ridge, barely able to see or move my limbs. I pulled my body forward to peer over the top, and to my astonishment, there were the Indians and horses. Somehow, during the night, my acute senses had taken over and my ability to track became instinctive.

"The Indians had slaughtered a horse and cooked him over a large fire. That was the light I'd been following. They'd decided they were free from the cavalry, not knowing I'd been enlisted to track 'em. I knew I couldn't just walk down among 'em the way I was, so I stripped off my clothes, making a loincloth of my shirt, and twisted my long hair together on both sides of my head, tying them with strips of my pants. I cut my hat in half, tying the pieces on my feet with the sleeves of my shirt, constructing a crude form of moccasins. I put a small stone in my mouth, gathering as much saliva as possible, then, spitting in the dry dirt, I muddied my face, arms, and chest. They wouldn't be able to tell the difference between their own brothers and me.

"I mustered my remaining strength and stood on the ridge, shouting and waving my knife in the air. The ruse worked; they believed I was a warrior and humbled themselves below me. I wandered through the crowd of renegades like a chief. They fed me and gave me water, all the time shouting in their native tongue their admiration and respect.

"Days turned into weeks as we traveled through the barren, parched land. My prowess as a hunter and guide made me the most respected man among them. Ultimately I became their leader.

"I quickly mastered their language and was able to speak fluently in a matter of days. They are a complex people but their speech is attractively simple. Sign language was something they understood easily, and so I used it as much as possible, at times merely pointing in a direction and saying 'Ugh.' Later I was posthumously given the Masters Award in Language from the Native American Institute of Higher Learning for my astute grasp of the Indian tongue.

"My charade was working. Slowly I turned the renegades around, heading 'em back in the direction of the fort without their knowledge. You may wonder with amazement how I did this, but it was quite simple. They didn't have the same capacity as I did when it came to scouting and tracking. I easily kept 'em going in circles until they were so disoriented that they followed my instructions without question. On the fifteenth day I pointed to a high ridge and led 'em over the top. Much to their surprise, the fort was before us.

"The cavalry, which had taken me for dead, rode out to intercept us. It took the commander some time to recognize me, as my person was now almost imperceptibly the same as my prisoners. Once he understood who I was and what I'd done, his congratulations were so bountiful that I was forced to parade throughout the fort, men and women showering praises on me like a hero."

"I've seen you get lost trying to find your bed," Jack said.

"I was merely practicing my art," Preacher said. "One must continuously hone the edges of talent to keep it sharp."

Finished with his bathing, Dan walked to the fire to dry off.

"You sure have a lot of talents," Jack said.

"I understand how you may be baffled by my skills, but it's only your good fortune to have me in your presence, as you'll never know when you may need to use my innate abilities."

218

"Help me tie these hooks on the trotline," I said to Preacher. "We've got enough crayfish to bait two times over."

Dan got dressed while Jack and I strung out the line on the bank, tying hooks on and baiting 'em as we went.

"It's a good night for a trotline," Jack said, looking at the sky. "It'll be a full moon tonight and it looks as if there's a storm coming in. The thunder'll make them big cats start stirring."

Jack jumped in the boat with one end of the line, heading across the river to a large hole. Once he'd tied it to the bluff he wrapped some line around a large rock and tied it in the middle of the trotline, letting it sink to the bottom. I tied my end around a large rock on the bank while Preacher fixed up his fishing pole. We would run the line at ten o'clock, midnight, and four in the morning, then again at daybreak.

We caught three catfish with our poles while we were sitting on the bank. Preacher cleaned 'em and I got the frying pan ready to cook. I salted down the slabs of white meat, dipped 'em in some cornmeal, and laid 'em in the hot grease. We listened to the frying fish and watched as the thunderheads moved in. Jack and Dan fixed up a lean-to with a small tarp we'd brought so we could get out of the rain, and we were ready for a nice evening.

All of us heard the commotion upriver at the same time. Then we saw a man riding a mule, walking down the river. We'd never seen that before, not that we hadn't seen mules in the water, but we hadn't seen anybody riding one downstream.

"Hold up there, Fishbait," the man said, pulling back on the reigns. He looked to be fifty or so, and had on overalls without a shirt, riding the mule bareback. There were two large potato sacks roped together hanging behind him on either side of the mule. His short, gray hair stuck out in spikes, and his arms were so thin they were mostly just bones. He stayed on the mule while he talked.

"Howdy," he said. "Smells like you've got dinner cooking."

There was a pause for a moment while we sized up each other.

"This here's Fishbait, my mule," he said. "Best swimmer in four states."

"Why are you riding him downriver?" Preacher asked.

"I always ride him when I'm going downriver, and upriver. Beats wrestling with them boats you got there."

"And you would be…" Preacher asked.

"Stu Peaker's my name. Just passing through."

"Do you always pass through by the river?" Jack asked.

"Most often, when it ain't too cold."

"Running from something?" Jack asked.

"Probably, but not the law. I ain't done nothing wrong, if that's what you mean."

"I didn't mean to say you did," Jack said. "It just seems a little odd."

"This mule can walk the rivers better than you can float 'em."

"Seems smart enough," Jack said. "Where you from?"

"Not from around here. I come from Missouri and I'm headed wherever this river ends."

We introduced ourselves and asked him to step down if he wished.

"Don't mind if I do," Stu said with a smile. "Old Fishbait needs a rest. Time was when he and I could walk the rivers from sunup to sundown, but we're both getting a little old now."

He let the reins fall in the water and Fishbait began drinking from the river.

"Smells good."

"There's plenty if you want to eat," I said.

"Don't mind if I do, but I'll add something to the spit if you don't mind."

Stu walked over to the mule and opened one of the sacks. He reached in and pulled out three large potatoes.

"Fried fish and fried tators go together real well," he said. "I'll just cut these up and add 'em to the pot."

"Why do you travel by the river?" I asked. "Don't it take longer than the roads?"

"Sure it does." Stu was washing the potatoes in the water. "But I ain't in no hurry. Never was and don't intend to be. Yeah, it takes longer, but most of the time I have the river to myself. It's quiet and peaceful and Fishbait likes it better. He gets antsy on the roads and I don't like the dust."

"Don't the snakes bother him?" Jack asked.

"He likes to kill 'em and eat 'em," Stu said. "Darndest thing you've ever seen. One time we were riding a swollen river and the cottonmouths were swarming and we rode right through 'em. Fishbait got bit so many times I couldn't count 'em. I was standing on his back to keep my legs out the water and he just walked right through 'em. He foamed at the mouth for a few hours but that was it."

Stu walked back over to the mule and pulled a frying pan from the sack.

"I'll just borrow some of that grease you got there and get these chips to heating."

Preacher took a snort of Potation and passed the jug. When it came around to Stu, he declined.

"I don't drink no more."

"Those potato sacks make good carriers, don't they?" I asked. "I knew a man once before that used 'em."

"They sure do. They're cheap too. You say you knew a man once before that used 'em? What became of him?"

"Don't know for sure," I said. "Woke up one morning and he was gone."

Stu smiled and stirred the potatoes. He wiped the sweat from his brow and stayed squatted low to the fire.

"Sometimes a man's got to pick up and go, no matter if he wants to or not."

Something seemed familiar about Stu, but I couldn't understand what it was. His mannerisms caught my eye and the potato sack reminded me of Tubbs, but I knew I'd never met this man before. I turned my attention back to the bluff across from us and saw an owl sitting on a limb jutting out from the rocks. I looked back at Stu and he was still tending the frying pan, paying no attention to the owl or me. When I turned my head back to the owl, he was gone.

"What brings you down this way?" Preacher asked.

"Just traveling through," Stu said. "I pick up work where I can, enough to get me by. I've no family and no property and I like it that way."

"You just sleep in the woods all the time?" Jack asked.

Stu laughed. "I'm not afraid to sleep in a bed, if that's what you mean, but I don't mind bedding down on a sand bar either. Many's the night I'd prefer the song of a whippoorwill to the noise of a town. These chips are done whenever you're ready."

We each took a pan and scraped out some tators and fish, Stu waiting until the last.

"I just passed a place upriver," he said. "Dogleg, I think is what she said. That'd be where you come from, if I don't miss my guess."

"You'd be right," Preacher said. "You must have talked to Mother Mabel at the Three-Stop."

"That I did. Fine woman she was too. No work though. She said things had been slowing down since the road work had finished."

"Don't bother me none," Jack said, pulling a fishbone from his mouth. "I'll be glad when it stops altogether."

"It won't stop for a while," Stu said. "I see it everywhere I go. People are moving; they're restless; they believe one more length of road's going to be their salvation. For some it will, for others it won't. It's always been that way. The railroads caused most of it, but there's other things too. I've heard there's a buggy that pulls itself along without a horse or mule. Things are changing fast."

"I don't want things to change," Jack said. "I like 'em just the way they are."

"It'll do no good to hide," Stu said. "Some will live to meet the change and some won't, but the changes will come, and wishing they don't won't stop them."

"Have you been this way before?" Preacher asked. "Your talk reminds me of someone."

"Maybe I have; I lose track anymore. Storm's a coming. I'd best tie up Fishbait before it hits; he gets skittish when the thunder rolls."

Stu stood and went to the river and walked the mule back to camp while we cleaned up the dinner and pitched our bedrolls under the tarp.

"There's room for you under here too," I said to Stu.

"I'll take you up on that," he said. "In my old age I'm not as interested in sleeping in the rain as I used to be."

As darkness fell the winds blew in. The roar in the trees grew as the storm picked up speed. Sparks from the fire blew sideways just before the rain came down.

"It won't last long," Stu said. "It came in too fast. Let's pick up some of those hot coals and I'll get some coffee boiling. I'll be interested in seeing what comes out of that hole tonight. A good storm riles up them big mudcats."

We sat under the tarp and drank coffee until the storm died down. Preacher, Jack, and I sipped some shine and we talked until ten o'clock. Then it was time to run the trotline. Jack and I got in the boat and started from the bank. Jack was in front raising the line and pulling us forward while I picked up the rear holding it out of the water, all the while trying to keep the lantern from tipping over.

"Got one ahead," Jack said. "It's a channel cat."

Jack unhooked him and threw him in the boat, moving on to the next hook. We were in the middle of the hole then, about where he'd tied the rock on. We struggled to keep the canoe from turning over as Jack pulled the rock toward the surface, but he was having trouble.

"Must be something besides the rock I'm pulling up," he said.

As he gathered in the line I saw him lean far over the edge of the boat and in that instant he flipped over and out, splashing in the water, tangled in the line. I still had my hold on the line and tried to keep it while I balanced myself inside the boat. I couldn't see in the water but I could feel the pull.

"I've lost him," I yelled.

"Let go," Preacher yelled. "Cut the line at the bluff and we'll pull him in from here."

I grabbed for the paddle and pushed my way to the bluff. I pulled out my knife and cut the line, watching as it disappeared in the river. There was no sign of Jack. I paddled back to the other bank to help and could see Preacher and Stu struggling with the line, trying to pull him in. I jumped from the boat and grabbed the line in front of Stu to help pull. There was still no sign of Jack.

"Something hanging up," I said. "We're not making headway."

Then Stu let go and dove into the river. He went under while Dan and I kept pulling as hard as we could. Then the line went limp; it snapped somewhere before Jack.

Dan and I stood on the bank looking at the quiet water. No sounds, no splashing, nothing. The light from the lantern still sitting in the bottom of the boat made a yellow glow over the water. I could hear the soft breeze from the dying storm sweep through the trees and felt the soft droplets of rain as they sprinkled around us.

"Let's go in," I said.

"*Let's go*," Preacher shouted.

Both of us dropped to the ground to take our boots off. I had one boot off and Dan had both of his off when we heard the noise downriver—something struggling in the water.

"I've got him," Stu shouted.

I grabbed the lantern and we raced to the noise, still not clear where they were. As the lantern lighted our path we quickly saw 'em. Stu's arms were cradled under Jack's armpits, a giant flathead between his legs, his mouth clamped halfway up his forearm.

Jack was spitting river water while Stu was pumping his gut, trying to push their way out of the water at the same time. By the time Dan and I reached 'em they were half in and half out, the flathead snaking its huge tail, trying to fight its way back into the river. We pulled 'em up on the bank, Preacher grabbing the catfish by the tail and swinging it across Jack's lap.

"He's a monster, ain't he?" Jack coughed.

"He sure is," Stu said, trying to catch his breath.

I pulled apart the flathead's mouth with both of my hands. Jack pulled his arm out, scraping some skin as it came.

"Noodled him," Jack smiled.

"What'd you do a thing like that for?" Preacher asked. "He must weigh eighty pounds."

"I didn't know that when I did it," Jack said. "I just saw his face and seen him jerk his tail. I knew he was big and I wasn't about to let him go, but he spit the hook out just as I was about to grab him. Wasn't nothing left to do but jam my hand in his mouth and grab some guts. Hell of a ride, it was. He took me straight to the bottom, fighting all the way. I couldn't get my feet to catch and I was just going with the fish, holding on to the trotline. Then I had to let go of the line. If Stu hadn't grabbed me that old mudcat would've took me home."

Preacher and I lifted the fish and carried him back to the camp. Stu was stirring the fire trying to get it started again, and Jack was stumbling behind us, still trying to catch his breath.

"Biggest one I've seen in years," Stu said.

"That was an awful brave thing you did, jumping in the river after someone you just met," Preacher said. "He could have died in that hole."

"Didn't seem so brave at the time," Stu said. "Besides, I think Jack's right— can't let a fish like that get away."

We sat by the fire watching the fish gulp for air.

"He'll still be alive in the morning," Jack said. "Fish that big can live for a long time."

"Let's tie him up in the shallows," Dan said. "We'll clean him in the morning and head back. Looks like we'll be having a big fish fry come tomorrow night."

"You'd be more than welcome to come with us," Jack said to Stu. "I can't thank you enough for jumping in after me."

"I might just do that," Stu said.

We stayed up late that night and even Stu took a sip of Potation, breaking his rules, but saying it was worth it. The next morning at daybreak he was gone. We could see Fishbait's tracks heading downriver.

"I thought he was going back with us," Jack said.

"I think he had other places to be," Preacher said. "He was here for a purpose and I believe he did what he came to do."

As we loaded the boat and prepared to go I saw the owl again, flying along the river in front of us. He swung toward the bluff and landed on the same limb as the day before.

"Look at that would you," Jack said. "Owls don't usually come out in the open in daylight. And another thing, don't you think it's sort of odd, a man riding a mule down the river?"

It didn't make sense to any of us, but the owl made sense to me. I was beginning to understand what Tubbs had meant on that winter night, about the omen. The owl was the sign—a predator. It was my sign on the day I met Tubbs, and it was there the night Elmer died. It was there yesterday when Stu, or whoever he was, showed up, and when Jack almost drowned. I had a feeling he wasn't through with us.

"Let's go," I said. "It's getting late."

When we got back to the Three-Stop, Ginny was the only one there.

"Where's Mother?" Jack asked.

"She went back home. Said she had things to do."

"What kind of things?" Jack asked. "There's things to do here."

"It's not that busy. Tory came by this morning and they sat in the corner for a long time and then he left. After that, Mother left too."

"I'll go check on her," I said.

When I got to Mother's cabin she was standing at her sink looking out the window. I stood at the door knowing she'd heard footsteps on the porch, but not acknowledging someone there.

"Mother, it's me."

"Go away. Can't you see I'm busy?"

I stood at the door for a moment and Mother never moved, just staring out the window.

"What's wrong, Mother?"

"It don't concern you, Claude. Can't a woman have a little time to herself?"

"Sure you can, but something's wrong. I can listen as well as talk, you know."

"Oh, come on in."

She kept her back to me, but I saw her wipe her eyes with a handkerchief before she poured two cups of coffee.

"You're back early," she said. "I thought you'd be gone another day."

"Jack caught a big flathead. We didn't want him to spoil."

"You make sure he gets that mudline out of him. It'll ruin the taste."

Mother set the cups on the table and I knew she'd been crying for quite some time. She sat down across from me and we were silent for a few minutes.

"I heard Tory was here today," I said.

"Yes, he was here, but he won't be back."

She wiped her eyes again and crumpled the hanky in her hand.

"He said he wanted more than to be just friends. He said he never expected to run into a woman he wanted to be with all the time, and now that he had, he needed more than just a visit every now and again. Well, I never thought I'd meet a man like him either. I guess I'm too set in my ways. I never loved my first husband—it was a marriage of convenience, like most are when the choices are slim. I've lived a long time without a man and I didn't think it'd come back to haunt me, but it has. But I just can't do it; I can't see myself depending on a man.

"I've got a heart, Claude. I swear I do. I know it's been coarse and hard for a long time, but it had to be. When I felt the edges chip away I did what I've always done—picked up the pieces and made a whole stone again. When I met

Tory I felt that same stone breaking apart and I felt something soft and it didn't fit. When I lost my children I knew in my heart I couldn't stand the pain of loss again; I made sure I wouldn't have to. I sealed that stone so nothing could pass through. I sealed it too good, didn't I?"

"Calluses turn soft when you quit using 'em, Mother. It serves no purpose to hurt forever. There's others that need your heart. You've always taken care of us, always taken care of those who needed you."

"That's what it was, Claude—their need."

"Don't confuse the two, Mother—their needs and your needs."

"I don't know that I need to love a man. I don't know that I'm missing what I never knew."

"I'd say you're right about the first part, but you're wrong about not missing what you never knew. Love's an opportunity; it's a chance to give. It's about holding something close and keeping it safe. Sometimes you can't hold it close enough; sometimes you can't keep it safe. It's what makes us human, that chance to make someone else's life meaningful."

"Maybe I have been missing something," Mother said. She wiped her eyes again.

"I think you misunderstood me, Mother."

"What?"

"I said, you may be right, you don't have to love one man, but you're not missing anything. You give to everyone around you. Not many can say the same thing. If love is giving, then you have more than most. I'd say Tory or any other man that thinks he can have you all to their selves has misjudged you're intentions. He'd have to fight us all if he wants to keep you for himself. I doubt he could stand the competition."

"You all feel like that?" she asked, a small smile finally showing.

"We could call you Mabel," I said. "But it wouldn't be the same, would it?"

She stood from the table and straightened her dress. She wiped her eyes one more time and picked up the coffee cups and put 'em in the sink.

"Well," she said, "we best be getting back to the Three-Stop. You know that Jack, he can't walk forward two steps without turning around to see where he's been. And that Preacher, he's probably stopped all the work with one of his nonsense stories. And you, what do think you're doing? Jack'll have that catfish butchered up so bad we'll think we're eating chitlins."

Mother walked us both out the front door, still talking, straightening her bonnet as we left.

"Now there's lots I still need to do. I haven't finished the garden yet and I'm gonna have a talk with Jack. He's got to stick around a little more until I can get things…"

Mother's life had been hard. The road she'd chosen was a lonely one, but she'd filled it with other people's troubles and that's how she got by. She deserved more but it wasn't meant to be. She was wrong about her heart, though—it was no stone.

"I don't know how I got hooked into putting this garden in," Jack said, wiping the sweat from his forehead. "This thing's three times as big as the one I usually put in."

"Quit your belly-aching," Mother said. "These vegetables will make us money. It's just that much less we'll have to buy to keep food in the diner."

"Might be 'cause you're so short," Preacher said. "You're closer to the ground. The rest of us have to bend over to plant, while you're already down there."

"Keep them lines straight," Mother yelled. "I won't have a crooked garden. Looks tacky, like a person don't care."

"Well, I don't care," Jack said. "These beans don't know they ain't in a straight line. They'll grow just as tall zigzagging as they will in a line."

"Them's pole beans," Mother said. "They have to be in a straight line. What are you gonna tie 'em to—a bird?"

"The birds'll get most of 'em anyway."

"I don't want to argue about it," Mother said. "You're just like a child when it comes to work. The quickest way out of it, the better you like it."

"Jack don't know a bean from a pea anyway," Preacher said.

"How come Preacher gets the easy part?" Jack asked. "Anybody can stake a tomato."

"That's not all I'm doing. I'm praying for a good harvest. Without my connections this garden might as well be deer food. I've not only got to pray for good growing, but I've got keep the varmints out too."

"Well, run one of those stakes down the back of your shirt and we won't have to make a scarecrow."

"Quit being belligerent, Jack," Mother said. "And hurry up. Claude should be back anytime."

"That's another thing, why does he get to do all the fishing?"

"It's not his garden," Mother said. "Besides, I need those fish for the corn."

"If you bury fish under those corn stalks you'll have every coon in two counties over here."

"That'll be your job," Mother said. "Keeping the coons out, and rabbits too. You'd best be figuring out how you're gonna do it."

"I've already got an idea. Dan would work. But we'd be a laughingstock with a drunken preacher in our garden. All we need is a scarecrow, but the thing is, a scarecrow's got to move. Movement is the only thing that'll keep a pest scared. I'll hang him from the limb of that tree, right there in the corner. All I have to do is figure out how to make him jump around. It'll be so real we'll have to put on blindfolds 'cause we'll be too scared to pick. Coveralls, an old shirt, some straw, a rag for a head, and a hat—that's all I'll need."

"What's gonna make him move around?" Mother asked.

"I'm thinking," Jack said.

"This'll be a short visit to the brain barn," Preacher said.

"I've got it," Jack said. "I'll stake my mule twenty or thirty feet out, run a rope from him over the limb to the scarecrow, and as he walks around he'll pull him up and down."

Mother looked at Preacher with surprise.

"That just might work, Jack," she said. "How'd you come up with that?"

"He must have seen it somewhere else," Preacher said. "That makes too much sense to come from him."

"You can take notes, if you want to," Jack smiled, happy with himself that he'd come up with something that Mother and Preacher thought was halfway smart.

"You might as well get started on it," Mother said. "The rabbits have been eating on my lettuce already. And them carrot tops have been gnawed to the dirt. I'm going back to the cabin to do some chores."

"Come on, Preacher," Jack said. "Let's gather the stuff we need."

They tied knots in the legs of the pants and stuffed 'em with straw. The shirt was easy enough and so was the head, Preacher adding some eyes and a mouth with charcoal. Jack stuck an old straw hat on him and the scarecrow was ready. They staked the mule and gave him twenty feet of lead, putting some hay at the far end and a bucket of water at the other. Making a loop on the rope, they hung it from the scarecrow's neck.

"That ought to signal all kinds of varmints," Jack said.

Everything went fine until they saw the mule was too close to the tree, ending up eating what he could reach from the scarecrow's dangling parts. The closer the mule got the higher the scarecrow went until he was left folded over the limb.

"You'll have to get him down," Preacher said.

"I don't like getting up that high," Jack said.

"It's your idea," Preacher said.

Jack stood on the mule's back to reach the limb, climbing up and sitting on it with the scarecrow. He pulled the rope off, letting it swing in the air while Preacher handed him some extra straw to fill the voids.

"I'll stake the mule farther out," Dan said. "You yell when you're ready."

As Preacher led the mule, Ginny called at him from the Three-Stop. "Preacher, come help me move this stove. I've spilled grease down the back and it's smoking something terrible."

"I'll be right there," he said. "Jack, I'm staking the mule and then helping Ginny."

"Go ahead. I'll just swing down when I'm ready."

Preacher wasn't paying attention to the fact that as he walked the mule away from Jack the rope came with him, the noose slipping up over Jack's boot. Dan left and went to help Ginny.

Everything was fine until a six-foot black snake decided he was hungry and made a trail to the hen house, heading across the mule's territory.

The mule started bucking and snorting, running in circles to get away. Jack turned to see what was happening, but it was too late—the noose tightened around his foot, jerking him off the limb. As the mule ran to the far end, Jack's legs straddled the limb, his crotch stopping the mule's progress, then turning around, the mule ran as fast he could the other way, dropping Jack like a rock, thumping his head on the ground.

The mule, stopped by the rope again, turned around and headed back. Up and down Jack went, yelling for help, clutching the scarecrow, straw flinging out every time he hit. Shortly, his agonizing shrieks went silent as the tether snapped, dropping Jack to the ground. The snake slithered out of sight and the mule calmed down, making his way over to Jack, helping himself to the straw surrounding his helpless body.

I was making my way up the hill with a stringer full of sunfish when I saw Jack lying on the ground, his hands white knuckled holding his crotch, eyes watering, his knees drawn up to his chest. Preacher came out of the Three-Stop about then and Mother was walking down the road. We met at the garden about the same time, standing over Jack, looking at him squirming around in the dirt and straw, and by then, quite a bit of mule manure.

"Can't leave him alone for a second," Preacher said. He was eating a chicken leg as he talked. "I told him not to get confused on where to put that noose."

"What he's doing?" Mother asked. "I told him to get finished with that scarecrow, and here he is lying in the straw, dreaming like a baby. And look at that, he's got manure all over him."

All we could hear from Jack was a few moans and groans, nothing we could understand.

"Leave him lay," Mother said. "At least he's spreading fertilizer."

I hung the fish on the tree, Preacher put the mule back in the corral, and we went in for some coffee.

May would be a turning point for the Three-Stop, most of the business from the new road having moved far enough away that the State found a new landing to deliver supplies. All in all, none of us were thrilled about the changes that were coming, no matter the riches that trailed behind it.

There's something about living in the Ozark Mountains that binds the people together—it's not about wealth or the trappings that come with it, it's about holding on to the past and keeping things the way they were. It's not about how hard it is to make a living—that's understood. The mountains offer a way of life all its own, and the people who live here do so because they want to, not because they're forced to.

The people take care of each other because that's the way the culture is. All of us know the rules by which we must live, and there's very little taking involved, it's mostly giving. No one moves to the mountains looking for wealth; only the richest parts of life are to be found: the help of a neighbor, the sharing of work, the Saturday night gatherings, and the Sunday picnics after building a barn. The roots of the mountain people grow deep and hold tight.

It's a way of life most people wouldn't think of enduring, but to us, we couldn't think of ever leaving it. A lazy man won't last long in the mountains— there are no handouts. Daylight to dark is the rule of work, and in one form or another every task is one of survival. Progress is unavoidable, and it'll force its way deep into the culture no matter how formidable the walls, but the traditions of mountain life are written in stone, and it would take many years to smooth it.

We did work hard that spring, and it took its toll on Mother. Her hired hand left and joined the road crew and she felt no need to employ another, taking on the chores of the farm and the Three-Stop by herself. I could see the exhaustion in her face, and at the end of the day her stooped shoulders told of her weariness. Jack's decision to shut down the Three-Stop at the end of May was a welcome one, not only for Mother but for Ginny too. Her mother's illness had taken a turn for the worse and her family needed her at home. Things were getting back to what we considered normal, and once again we were able to live the lives we had intended.

We'd decided to go ahead and build Preacher's cabin, things slowing down the way they were, and cutting the logs was first on the list. We started at daybreak, Mother bringing us lunch at noon, and would stop at dusk, just in time to get home before dark. One day we were headed back, all three of us riding the seat on the wagon, sipping on Potation, taking in the nice sunset.

As we rounded a bend on our trail we saw a little man walking toward us. He had a pack and a small bedroll on one shoulder and a shotgun strapped across the other. He was a man of slight build with a long brown beard and was about the same height as Jack. His straw hat was set back on his head with dark brown hair hanging past his shoulders and he was whistling, "Oh! Susanna." His busy eyebrows shadowed big, bright, hazel eyes and a missing front tooth didn't detract from his happy smile.

"Howdy," he said. "I've been looking for somebody on this trail."

"Trail is what it is," Preacher said. "The only reason it's here is we been hauling logs."

"I see that," he said. "Big ones too. Building something, are you?"

"A cabin," Preacher said.

"A man's got to have a place to hang his hat. My name's Skip, or that's what folks call me. "Wagner's my Christian name."

Preacher held out his hand. "I'm Preacher Dan, and this is Jack, and he's Claude."

"Pleasure," he said.

"What brings you this way?" Dan asked. "Are you lost?"

"You might say that, but then again you might not. I'm headed south out of Missouri, looking for my wife."

"What happened to her?"

"Good question. She either run off or was tempted to do so."

"We haven't seen any women we don't know," Dan said.

"Don't surprise me," Skip said, taking his hat off and running his hand across a pearly white scalp. The only hair he had was in the back and on the sides, pulled tight behind his ears.

"It's a long shot I'll find her, but I thought I'd give it a try. She's got my dog with her. I sure do miss that dog."

"You don't have any idea where she took off to, I guess?" Jack asked.

"South, that's all I know. She's a scrapper. I doubt I'll find her. I would like to find the dog, though."

"Wouldn't you like to find your wife just as much?" Preacher asked.

"Don't know what good it'll do. If she run off on her own, she most likely won't come back, and if she was tempted to run off, well, then I'm right sure she won't come back."

"We're headed back to Dogleg," Preacher said. "You're welcome to ride along."

"Thank you kindly," Skip said. He picked up his pack and hopped up on the rear of the wagon.

By the time we got to the Three-Stop, Skip was laid out on the logs, fast asleep.

"The wagon'll keep until morning," Jack said. "I'll put the mule up."

Preacher woke up Skip and we went inside to get some coffee.

"Nice place you got here."

"It's Jack's," I said.

"It's got to be somebody's, don't it? I sure appreciate you letting me tag along. My feet were about to wear out."

"Don't you have a mule or horse?" Preacher asked.

"Sold my horse and my cabin. Weren't nothing left for me there anyway."

"What if you find your wife?" I asked.

"To tell the truth, I ain't looking that hard for her. She had a barb for a heart. The dog's the thing. He's been with me longer than she has. We were only married for six months—the hardest six months I've ever had. She took to lying in bed till noon, then sitting in a rocker till dark. I told her I didn't need no full-time flatbacker. I said she'd have to pull her own weight. After six months and another hundred pounds I was wondering whether she could do that."

"So, where you going from here?" Preacher asked.

"Keep heading south, I guess. I got two hundred for the cabin and land, and another ten for the horse. I'll settle in somewhere, sooner or later."

Jack came through the back door and yelled from the kitchen, "Anyone wants some beans and cornbread, come and get it. Mother's left us some."

We went into the kitchen and filled our bowls. Skip emptied his first bowl while the rest of us were still filling ours. When we made our way back to the table, he filled up a second time and came out of the kitchen with a mouthful of cornbread, most of it crumbling down on his scraggly beard.

"This is best beans I've ever tasted," he said. "Can't beat a woman that can cook. That last wife of mine couldn't fry spit."

"There was lots of women wanting me too. I got some kind of animal attraction that women can't pass up."

"You say you been married for six months?" Preacher asked.

"Almost to the day," Skip said, forcing another spoonful of beans into his full mouth.

"Marriage seems to be difficult for you," Preacher said. "A man that's gone through that many wives might think about staying single."

"I wish it was that easy. Are you through with that?" Skip asked, reaching for Preacher's half-full bowl.

"Help yourself," Dan said.

"It's been a while since I've eaten," Skip said.

"You sure have had your share of problems," Preacher said

"They ought to put all the women in a corral and just let 'em out at night. That'd solve a lot of problems. I think it's got something to do with daylight. They start stirring around and cooking up trouble."

"Could have something to do with daylight," Jack said. "I never thought of it like that."

"Could have something to do with sleeping all night too," Preacher said.

Jack looked surprised at that statement, but Skip, he just kept eating.

"You gonna eat that cornbread?" Skip asked Jack.

"You can have it," Jack said. "If you combed your beard you'd get a plate full."

"What would the fleas eat? It's the only way to keep 'em from biting. That's another thing, what's all this stuff about bathing? Women take more baths than a frog. They keep a man busy just hauling water. Women got to take more baths than men, you know why? They don't sweat. It all builds up inside of 'em. Next thing you now, they explode.

"Most of the time it comes out in angry talk. You ever just be sitting on the front porch with your feet up, taking in the day, when all of sudden the front door flies open and out comes a tornado with hair on it."

"I think they're kind of nice," Preacher said. "They're soft and sentimental."

"On the outside maybe," Skip said. "On the inside you can't crack 'em with a sledge."

"That's him." Mother was standing at the front door with a woman about the same size as Skip. She had delicate features and long, blond, curly hair. She was fair-skinned with a slender build. Her blue eyes set behind a thin nose and her high cheekbones lay atop a curved jaw. She was a fine-looking woman, more woman than we expected to see looking for Skip.

Skip stopped talking and eating. His eyes popped wide and his jaw dropped, crumbs of cornbread falling on his lap.

"Come on," she said. "Let's go home."

"Boys," Mother said, "this is Maggie Wagner. She's looking for her husband.

Looks like she's found him."

"Never seen her before in my life," Skip said. "See what I mean, men? It's a curse."

"Get up, Skippy," Maggie said. "It's time to go."

"But I just got here."

"I hope Skippy hasn't caused too much trouble. He gets carried away sometimes."

"No trouble," Preacher said. "It's a pleasure to make your acquaintance."

"Me, too," Jack said.

"Mine, too," I said.

We were all quite taken with the young woman and wondered to ourselves why Skip would want to leave her.

"Skip was just telling us," Preacher started, "how you've just recently been married, six months, I believe."

"Thirteen years, come June," Maggie said. "I suppose he's told you about the three other wives he's never had?"

"Well, we've heard quite a bit."

"That's the way it usually goes," she said. "His name isn't Skip, either. It's Arnold. The family just calls him Skippy. He skips out on me every spring, about this time. I have to find him and take him back home."

"I can see how that might be troublesome," Preacher said.

"It's not that bad. At least he's entertaining. I love him for what he is. The rest of the year he does just fine. In the spring he gets a squirrel up his butt and takes off."

"Maggie," Skippy said, like he'd just noticed his wife. "What are you doing here? I was just getting ready to head home."

"I know, Skippy. Let's go."

"Well, men, it was nice talking to you, and thanks for the food. Sometime I'll return the favor."

"Skippy can't boil water," Maggie said. "From the looks of your beard you can't eat any better."

She walked up to Skippy and brushed the crumbs from his beard and gave him a peck on the cheek.

"Are you ready to come home now?"

"I always was," he said. "I've stayed longer than I should, I know, but we've been having such a good talk I guess I lost track of time."

"Well, thanks to you men for keeping an eye on my Skippy."

"You're more than welcome to spend the night," Mother said. "We can find plenty of room."

"Thanks, but no. He's been gone for five days and I've been gone for four. There's kids at home that need taken care of."

"You certainly have an understanding nature," Preacher said.

"The only wandering Skippy does is with his feet and in his mind. I can't hold too much against him."

Maggie led him out the door and they stepped into their buggy and off they rode up the hill.

"Quite a woman," Preacher said. "How does a man like that end up with a woman like her?"

"It's good intentions and bad intentions," Mother said. "He lets her take care of him—most men let their pride do it."

We became good friends with Skippy and Maggie, and every spring he'd come to Dogleg and visit, and it got to where Maggie would just come with him and not have to travel alone.

In a way he reminded me of Jack, being a little crazy at times, and in another way it was Preacher I thought of, his far-reaching stories a test of truth. As the years went on I looked forward to Skip and Maggie's visits.

Chapter Fifteen

We would finish Preacher's cabin in the month of June. He wanted it small and that's what he got. A place to sleep was all he was interested in. I thought it was too small, but he said it was fine. Life's too short to spend it inside, he said. Besides, we sleep in the cabins, but we live in the mountains.

Our evenings were spent at the river, fishing, a small fire lighting our lines. Mother would meet us about sundown with a pot of gumbo to heat over the coals, at times just frying the fish we'd caught. The days were getting longer and the stars in the sky were brighter and we would lie back on the bank, hands cradling our heads, legs stretched out with our feet crossed, eyes to the heavens, listening to the fish jumping, the frogs croaking, the crickets calling, and the whippoorwills sighing. The air was full of lightning bugs, their silent, yellow glow sprinkling the night with dots of fire, signaling for a mate; their short lives adding to the urgency.

Preacher's stories kept us entertained, along with sips of Potation, and Jack's bad luck was always there to talk about. On those nights we were much like kids, our worries left back at the cabins, far up on the hill, hidden from us in the woods. With only the river in front of us, flowing steadily away from us, yet always permanent, our lives were intertwined, our souls blending together like water.

It was on one of those nights that Preacher's thoughts turned weighty. He was never one to dwell on the future or the hereafter, but I could tell that after the incident with Jack almost drowning, sometimes he'd get a notion to get melancholy.

"How long do you think you're going to live?" Preacher asked Jack one night.

"What kind of question is that?" Mother demanded. "No one knows that answer."

"I think I'm gonna live as long as I'm alive," Jack said. "Nobody's ever told me different."

"How long do you want to live?" Preacher came back.

"As long as I'm alive," Jack said. "Where you going with this, anyway?"

"I don't know. I was just looking at them lightning bugs and thinking they've got such a short life, the only thing they get done is mating. It's like they've only got one thing to do in life; seems so simple."

"You better stay off the hooch," Mother said. "You're getting breezy-brained."

"Don't it make you wonder how much you got left to do?" Preacher asked.

"You think there's an agenda?" I asked.

"I knew a girl named Glenda, once," Jack said. "Pretty girl, too. I tried to get her to like me, but she wouldn't have it."

"Why not?" Mother asked.

"I sat on her one day and she said I liked to squashed her. After that she wouldn't have nothing to do with me. We were just kids and I never had a chance to say I was sorry. She died a month later with pneumonia. I always hated that."

"It didn't have nothing to do with you sitting on her," Mother said.

"I suppose not, but I never sat on anybody again."

"There's got to be a list," Preacher said. "That's why some people live longer than others—they get their list done and the Lord takes 'em home."

"I think we make our own list," Mother said. "Some people make a list every day and some just take things as they come."

"I believe there's a plan, but I don't know that He's the one that makes it," I said.

"I think all the water's in the bucket when you're born," Preacher said. "You pour it out as the years go by and when it's empty, that's all there is. It don't fill up again."

"How do you know how big the bucket is?" Jack asked. "Elmer must have had a rain barrel and Glenda must have had a cup."

"That's the mystery—how big's the bucket?"

"Let's talk about something else," Mother said. "Some just live longer than others and that's all there is to it. There's lots of luck involved, too."

"That don't set well with me," Jack said. "I don't have good luck."

"Some say they make their own luck," Preacher said.

"It's arrogance what makes 'em say that," Mother said.

"Who's that?" Jack asked.

"It's not a who, it's a what. Means you think you're better than others."

"Well, I'm a better fisherman than Preacher. He couldn't catch a rock if he was sitting on it."

Just then a black dog came trotting down the bank of the river and stopped fifty feet away, staring at us. He was a mutt, we could tell, but none of us had seen him before. We watched him as he watched us. Then he took off at a dead run, coming straight for us. As soon as reached the campfire he growled and bit Jack on the ankle. Jack jumped up, yelling and kicking, trying to shake the dog loose, but the mutt held tight. Preacher tried to pull him off but the dog would have none of it.

"Throw 'em in the river," Mother yelled.

I hopped up. Preacher and I grabbed Jack and the dog, ran 'em to the river, and tossed 'em in. The dog let go, swam to the other side and ran off into the woods.

"See what I mean," Jack said. "I ain't got no luck at all. How come he didn't bite Preacher? He's got more leg than I have."

"It's not the leg he was after," Preacher said. "It's all that meat you got on it. Are you hurt?"

"Naw. He got a mouthful of boot was about all."

"You ain't seen Rustler, have you?" came a voice from behind.

We turned to see who it was.

"How come you're standing in the river?" the man asked.

"I been dog bit," Jack said.

"Was he about knee-high, black, of questionable breeding?"

"That's him," Mother said.

"He's mine. Hope he didn't bite too hard. I don't know what gets into him sometimes. He's a quick learner, but a faster biter."

"You can say that again," Jack said, walking out of the river.

"I'm Brad Moore. I was just walking down this road. Didn't know it was a dead end."

"Kind of late to be walking around, ain't it?" Preacher asked.

"Not if you don't know where you're going. I was just following Rustler."

"Where are you going?" Jack asked.

"Nowhere in particular," Brad said. "Lost my job on the road crew a few days ago and I just been following the dog ever since. He's got a better nose for grub than I do." He was eyeing the pot of gumbo.

"There's some left," Mother said. "Help yourself."

Mother took a bowl and washed it in the river for him.

"Guess there'll be more men wandering around looking for work," I said.

"I wasn't the only one let go," Brad said. "'Bout ten of us today. Good gumbo, by the way."

"You'll be needing a place to stay, I guess," Mother said.

"I left my bedroll up at that café. I tried to raise somebody, but I guess the place is closed. Rustler was making his way down here and I just followed."

"You're welcome to sleep in the barn," Jack said.

"No need. The river bank's good enough for me."

Rustler came out of the woods on the other side and stopped at the water's edge and stared.

"Come on, boy," Brad said.

Rustler jumped in the water and swam across. When he reached our side he stopped and growled at Jack.

"Come on now, Rustler. These folks won't hurt you."

The dog walked up to Brad. He poured some gumbo on the ground and Rustler ate it.

"He sure does know good grub when he smells it," Brad said.

"He must know good grub when he sees it too," Jack said, rubbing his ankle.

"It's getting late," Mother said. "I'm heading back to the cabin."

"Me too," Jack said.

We started up the hill, Brad and Rustler bringing up the rear. Just before we reached the Three-Stop, we noticed there was lantern on inside the store.

"Did you leave a light on, Jack?" I asked.

"You know I never leave a light on."

"You folks just keep on walking," Brad said.

We looked back and saw that he had a pistol drawn.

"Just do what I say and no one's gonna get hurt. All we're looking for is a little money and some food to carry us over."

"You're not from the road crew at all, are you?" Mother said.

"Not likely," he said. "There's easier ways to make a dollar than working in the hot sun all day. Now, go on inside and do what I tell you. My friend in there don't have the same calm I do. His finger's got a twitch in it."

"You know this will come to no good," Mother said.

"You're so far down in the hills that by the time one of you gets to a sheriff we'll be miles away. Now, show me where the money is."

"What makes you think we got any money," Jack said. "Does this look like a thriving business?"

"Any business at all looks like more than what we got," Brad said. "You're lying if you're telling me there ain't none."

Brad waved his pistol at Jack, motioning him to move. Jack walked to the counter and opened the drawer, pulling out what little money was in it.

"Six dollars is all you got?" Brad asked.

"We shut the diner down after the road crews left," Jack said. "All I got is a little bit of trade from the neighbors."

The other man was searching through the Three-Stop, ransacking the place.

"He don't have to tear the place apart," Mother said.

"Shut up," Brad said. "You found anything yet?" he said to his partner.

"Nothing. This place is poorer than we are."

"Take what you can carry then," Brad said. "We'll be taking that mule out back too. Men like us need to ride, not walk. Go get that mule and meet me out front."

"You men won't make it to the next county," Preacher said.

"You'll be wise if you don't try to follow," Brad said. "I don't take kindly to being bothered. Just hold your places until we're out of sight. If you try to follow, I'll shoot you."

"We won't follow," Preacher said. "We won't need to, everyone around here knows Jack's mule."

"You stay put," Brad said. "I'm backing out of here, closing the door behind me. If I see anyone move, I'll shoot."

Brad backed out of the Three-Stop and jumped on the mule, behind his partner. There was barely enough room for the both of them, with two bags of dry goods hanging on either side of the mule. They took off at a trot up the hill, the black mutt following.

Jack grabbed his rifle from the kitchen while we stepped to the front porch. When Jack got there we could see the men topping the hill. Jack whistled and his mule's ears perked and it was all the two men could do to stay on him. He was bucking and snorting, trying to turn himself around, thinking Jack had thrown some food out for him. The dog was barking, following the mule in circles, nipping at his hooves, making things worse for the two men. We watched as the mule fought his way around, struggling to head back home. It wasn't long before the two thieves hit the ground running up over the hill.

"Should I shoot 'em?" Jack asked.

"No," Mother said. "It's not worth it. Six dollars won't get 'em very far. You boys should warn the neighbors, though. Those men'll be looking for better pickens."

"Don't know who to trust anymore," Preacher said.

"Country's going to hell," Mother said. "That's what progress brings you."

We each got our mules and rifles and went in different directions to warn the neighbors while Mother started cleaning up the mess in the Three-Stop.

Things were changing and it didn't seem for the better. Mother was right— the more people, the more problems. We'd used our guns more often against others in those last six months than we had in the last six years. The prosperity after the war, the railroads, people moving around the country, all the good that was supposed to be coming the nation's way, was also bringing its fair share of hatred and crime. Not even those of us who had chosen to stay in the mountains, far distant from the crowds, could hide from the wave of change.

Our lives were changing in ways we'd never thought of, and the improvements that were supposed to make our existence easier, was the dead weight that hung from the neck of progress. We were not improving, nor did we want that kind of change. But we were a small group of people that had chosen not to lend our voices to the growing concerns of the country. We wanted to be left alone, but our small community would be affected, no matter our wishes.

I thought about the changes to come and knew they were not what I wanted. We couldn't move much deeper into the mountains. We were surrounded by towns, small and large, all growing faster than we could imagine, all being connected by new roads and the railroad. Our way of life was slowly eroding, and the transformation would be complete in our lifetimes.

But our lives went on and we did the best we could to accept the changes. One of the best things about the folks living in the hills was getting together for the celebrations. You got to visit with others you hadn't seen in months, and they were always fine times. Preacher and Jack always made those times special too.

"It's a wedding and we're all going," Mother said. "Bessie Calder's getting married this Saturday and her ma and pa want us all there."

"She's the youngest, ain't she?" Jack asked. "Seems to me there was three of them girls."

"That's right, there still is three of 'em. The other two are a bit on the homely side, but they're all good girls. You might want to take a peek at the other two yourself, Jack. Wouldn't hurt you to take a wife."

"I had a wife," Jack said.

"You either, Claude, wouldn't hurt you, or Preacher."

"I'm not ready to settle down," I said.

"What do you call what you're doing? You look about as settled as any man

I've seen. And you, Preacher—I think your wandering days are over. The good Book don't say nothing about not getting married. You ain't a priest, you know."

"My taste in women run to the slimmer side. If I remember correctly, the Calder girls have a tendency to be hefty."

"Hereford comes to my mind," Jack said.

"A plump woman will keep a man warm at night better than bones," Mother said. "Besides, it ain't looks that count."

"The count runs pretty low in that family," Jack said.

"Never mind about that. They've invited us and we're going. There's not enough weddings in these hills as it is."

"Who's she marrying?" Preacher asked.

"Darrell Portman. He's a hog farmer over by Pocahontas. She'll be leaving soon as the wedding's over."

"Seems fitting in a way," Jack said.

It was a two-hour wagon ride to the Calders' place. We left around ten o'clock Saturday morning and pulled in after noon. Everybody we knew was there and some we didn't. It was the biggest wedding we'd seen in a long while.

"This is quite a send-off," Preacher said as we pulled up. "Jacob Calder must be in a good mood."

"Must have got a hog or two in the trade," Jack said. "Ordinarily it takes a crowbar to get the wallet out of his pocket."

"That's enough out of you two," Mother said. "This is a happy occasion and I don't want you three doing something to upset little Bessie."

"It'll take more than a little something," Jack said.

"Let me out here," Mother said. "Claude, you help me with this fried chicken and these pies. You other two park the wagon."

Jacob did have a fine spread laid out. Two long tables were set side by side down the hill from the house. They were filled with roast and ham, mashed potatoes and gravy, greens, and every vegetable you could think of; pies and cakes, salads, soups, biscuits, and bread. At the end of one table was a three-layer wedding cake Mrs. Calder had spent two days preparing. Under a large hickory tree was four ice cream makers covered with blankets. Jacob had hauled the ice, packed in sawdust to keep it frozen. Some had brought their fiddles and banjos, others their juice harps, harmonicas, and guitars. It was bound to be a grand wedding. The weather was perfect, a nice breeze was blowing and the sun was shining and it was a wonderful warm day. It looked as if nothing could spoil the afternoon for Bessie and her beau.

"Well, who is this fine-looking young man?" Mrs. Calder asked.

"You remember Claude, don't you, Martha?" Mother said.

"Why, Claude, you sure have grown into a fine young man. It's been so long since I've seen you; I'd almost forgot what you looked like. You don't come around near enough."

"I know," I said. "It seems things just keep me busy."

"When was the last time you saw my Cassie? She's all grown up now. Cassie!" she yelled. "Come over here." Martha was bigger than Mother and her voice was larger than both of 'em.

Mother nudged me in the side. "You could do worse, Claude. All these girls know how to cook and sew. They're mountain bred and stout as a mule—take note."

"And Sissy," Martha said. "You haven't seen my Sissy lately either, have you? She's the oldest but she's the best with the animals. Sissy! Put that goat down and get over here. You'll get your dress dirty. That girl, she just loves animals. She's a fine cook, too."

I saw Cassie lumbering down the hill from the house, almost at a dead run, her dress held up to her knees, her legs making wide swings, like she had a barrel between them, the ground shaking as she stomped toward us. Sissy came running too, still carrying the goat, held tight against her large chest.

"I told you to put that goat down," her mother scolded. "Ladies don't carry a goat with a dress on. Now girls, straighten up. This here is Claude. He lives over at Dogleg, close to Mother Mabel. Ain't that right, Mabel?"

"That's true enough," Mother said. "And a fine upstanding man he is."

"Well, say hello, girls," Martha said.

"Hello, Mr. Claude," they said in unison.

"Hello," I said back. "Just call me Claude. That'll do fine."

"Oh, my," Martha said. "A man with manners. Those are few and far between around here."

"Oh, looky there, Ma," Sissy said. "Who's that?"

"My word," Martha said. "That looks like Jack Stepp and Preacher Deveneaux. Am I right, Mabel? Is that them?"

"That's them."

"There's so many eligible bachelors here today," Martha said. "My girls are so shy, though. Now girls, don't run and hide just because there's unhitched men around."

"We won't, Ma," they both said in unison, again.

"That thort one," Cassie said. "He lookth like heth about my thize."

For the first time Mother and I noticed that Cassie was missing a front tooth.

Martha must have seen us looking at each other because she quickly gave us an explanation.

"Cassie had an accident just the other day. Her tooth was kicked out while shoeing a horse. Jacob's getting her a wooden one made in Harrison. She's so pretty when her mouth's full of teeth."

"Accidents will happen," Mother said. "That must have hurt something terrible, Cassie."

"Hurt like thit," Cassie said.

Martha slapped her on the arm. "I told you not to say that. I swear I don't know where you get that tongue. Must be from your pa."

"But, Ma, you thaid to tell the touth."

"You can just pick your words more carefully. Men don't like to hear such words coming out of a young girl's mouth."

"You remember Cassie and Sissy don't you, Jack?" Mother asked. "I'm sure Preacher does."

"It's been a long time," Preacher said, "but I do remember."

"Mother," Martha said, "you do have the most well-mannered men over there at Dogleg. How in the world do you think they landed on your doorstep like that?"

"They weren't sent from heaven, I can tell you that."

"Well, you could have fooled me. Jack, don't you own the Three-Stop Café?" Martha said, nodding at Sissy.

"Yes, I do."

"It must be wonderful to own your own business. I bet you can't count the money with both hands."

"I just makes ends meet, that's all."

"Don't be so humble, Jack Stepp," Martha said. "I can see from here you're a man to be reckoned with. Can't you see that, girls?"

"I thure can," Cassie said.

"And Preacher," Martha said, nudging Sissy. "It's so good to see you. Wouldn't it be nice to have a man of the cloth in the family? Don't you think so, Sissy?"

"He's such a gentleman," Sissy said, a quaint smile on her lips.

"Now girls, you show these men where the punch is. You men can nibble on some food, but don't fill yourselves up. We're going to have a feast just as soon as we get Bessie married. Go on now, don't be shy."

I was obviously not the pick of the crop, as Sissy sidled up to Preacher, taking his arm in hers and leading him off. Cassie did the same with Jack. I followed behind.

"What kind ob thuff do you thell?" Cassie asked Jack as they walked.

"What?"

"Thuff. You know, thuff in your thore?"

Jack looked at Cassie real close. "I guess you know you got a tooth missing?"

"Oh, yeth," Cassie said. "I thure do. It hurt like thit. Don't tell Ma I thaid that. Thee gets mad when I thay thit."

"I won't, " Jack said.

"Your tho nithe. Do you know how to wide a bithickle?

Jack turned around and looked at Preacher and me.

"A bicycle, Jack," Preacher said. "You've seen 'em before."

"Oh, sure, sure," Jack said. "Anybody can ride a bike."

"Thath tho wonderful. Will you take me for a wide? Pa bought uth eath one, thince Betthie wath getting married."

"Oh, yes," Sissy said, pulling on Preacher's arm. "Please take us for a ride. We've only just begun to learn. You could teach us."

"No problem," Preacher said, regaining his balance. "I've ridden many times."

"It'th tho esthighting," Cassie said.

"We'll go right after the wedding," Sissy said.

The men stood around the punch bowl while the girls and other ladies helped with the arrangements. Soon, Preacher waved Jack and me to follow him and a few others back behind the barn for a few swallows of Potation he had in a flask. As a matter of fact, he had three pockets with flasks in 'em and a jug in the wagon.

The women were getting more and more excited as the wedding got closer and the men got more and more drunker at the thought of it being over. Soon we were ready for the ceremonies to begin. We wandered out from behind the barn, some stumbling more than wandering, and made our way to the chairs by the tables.

The ceremony only lasted thirty minutes, which was a good thing, considering the condition of most of the men. A lot of the wives were unhappy with their husbands for starting the reception before the wedding, and showed their displeasure with a few stern looks. Not that it mattered much, as the men couldn't make out their wives' faces anyway.

With the wedding over it was time to celebrate. Once again the men headed for the back of the barn while the women prepared the tables for the feast. Cassie and Sissy were up at the cabin rolling out their bicycles, looking for

Preacher and Jack.

"Looks like you two are being scouted out," I said. "The girls must be ready for their ride."

"I don't know how to ride a bicycle," Jack slurred.

"There's nothing to it," Preacher said. "It's like riding in a wagon, only you got something to hold on to."

"It don't look that simple to me," Jack said.

"The trick is to keep moving," Preacher said. "We'll start on top of the hill and ride down. That way we won't have to pedal. Just set the girls on the handlebars and tell 'em to hang on."

"Come on, Mr. Thepp," Cassie yelled. "Ith time to wide the bithickle."

"Let's go, Jack," Preacher said, taking one last snort. "Let's get it over with."

Jack and Preacher met the girls and walked the bikes up the hill not far from the barn. The rest of us stayed behind, still sipping on shine and watching the show. It was a good hundred yards from the top of the hill, past the barn, down to the tables and chairs, where the folks were milling about, getting ready to eat dinner and cut the cake. Jack and Preacher pointed the bikes in that direction and Cassie and Sissy sat themselves on the handlebars, legs straddling the front wheel.

We could hear Preacher instructing Jack and the girls.

"Now, Jack, when we get to rolling just keep the front wheel straight and hang on, we'll coast to a stop down at the bottom."

"These bars hurt my butt," Sissy said.

"Push off, Jack," Preacher said.

They shoved the bikes forward and started down the hill. Both bikes were a little wobbly at first, until they got their balance, but once they got straightened out things seemed to be going fine. The field was rough and both girls looked as if they were having it tough hanging on, but they were laughing and giggling and having a good time. Jack and Preacher, on the other hand, were having trouble seeing past the girls, their large masses obstructing the view. Jack was swinging his head from side to side, trying to catch a glimpse of what was ahead of him, and Preacher was doing the same, although his extra height gave him some vision as he stretched his long neck over the top of Sissy's head.

As they reached the barn we could tell they were picking up speed, and I could see a worried look on Jack's face. The pedals were spinning faster then and both men's legs were pumping so hard they were just a blur. There was a small dip just below the barn, and they were going so fast that when they topped it, the bikes almost came off the ground, flipping the girls backward with their dresses flopped back over all four of their heads with the girls' legs spread as wide as the ol' Mississippi. The giggles had turned to screams and the people down below turned and stared, astonished at the sight.

"Oooh thit!" Cassie screamed.

"Stop!" Sissy cried.

"I can't see," Jack yelled.

Both bikes were neck and neck, four blind people controlling their own fate. The girls' legs were stuck out front, their pantaloons shining in the sun, Preacher and Jack hidden under a vast layer of white cotton. It didn't take long for the folks at the bottom of the hill to see that things were out of control. They started scattering, running and bumping into each other, kids screaming, women grabbing their skirts up and high-stepping for safety. Preacher and Jack were yelling, the girls were screaming, the people were running, and the bikes were just a blur.

They hit the end of the two tables at the same time, flipping all four riders up and over the handlebars, the girls on the bottom, Jack and Preacher laid out on top, sliding from one end to the other, fried chicken flying in one direction, mashed potatoes in another, cakes and pies flopping through the air. When it was over, Jack and Cassie were more inside the wedding cake than splayed on top of it. Preacher was face down in the punch bowl and Sissy was laid out on the ground with a dollop of potatoes on her forehead and a chicken leg on her chest. Bessie was crying, Darrell was comforting her, Martha had fainted, and Mother was mad. Jacob's dogs were in a feeding frenzy. Cassie was licking cake icing off her fingers and Sissy had decided that the chicken leg shouldn't go to waste.

"Can't take you two anywhere," Mother said. "Now get up. Preacher, you get some of that shine so I can get Martha to stirring again. You girls quit eating and go get cleaned up. Jack—" Mother just shook her head.

Everybody pitched in and cleaned the place up as best we could, even saving some of the wedding cake so the newlyweds could have a taste. The fiddlers starting playing and since there wasn't much left to eat or drink, the moonshine started flowing. All in all, it turned into a good time and Bessie forgave her sisters. Jack had trouble with the dogs the rest of the day, them smelling the gravy on his pant legs, and Preacher stayed busy swatting the flies swarming his head, the sweet punch making his hair stick out like weeds in a fence row.

We danced and laughed and drank until late in the evening, finally getting home about midnight; Mother berating Jack and Preacher the whole time.

Three days after the wedding we got the news that James Parsons had died.

He was only thirty-eight and strong as an ox the last time we'd seen him. He left behind a small farm, two young kids and a wife. We didn't see him very often but he did buy some dry goods from time to time. We heard he had a bad heart. His kids found him in the barn, laid out with a shovel in his hand. His wife, Kristen, had only been with him for seven years. Holly, their youngest daughter, was only five, and Sean was six; they were fifteen months apart. It would be a rough time for the three of 'em, but Kristen said she was staying. She'd lived in the mountains all her life and was only twenty-three.

Kristen was a small woman with long auburn hair and petite features. The hard years in the mountains hadn't taken its toll on her body yet—she looked younger than her age. She would need a man to help her run the farm, though, but with her looks and determination we were sure she'd fare well. She had one older brother, Lewis, that would help, but it wouldn't be enough. He had a place and family of his own.

Kristen wanted James buried in the same cemetery as Elmer. We held graveside services with Preacher doing the eulogy. Life in the mountains was tenuous at best. Doctors were few and far between, and usually when a person went down they went down for good. Kristen would need help with the kids too, and Mother volunteered whenever Kristen needed her. The kids took a liking to Jack, 'cause he wasn't that much taller than they were, and his general outlook on life being somewhat less mature than theirs. As it turned out, Jack did well with the kids, teaching them how to fish and stock the Three-Stop's shelves with dry goods.

They started following him everywhere and all of us were surprised at the attention he was willing to give 'em. His attitude changed a little and he refused to drink liquor in front of 'em, and even held back on his cussing slightly, although he always complained that he was having a problem with his sentences, having trouble finding the correct descriptive words to fill in.

Preacher helped out too. He taught the kids about the Bible, or as much as he knew. He even did some studying on his own, it being quite a while since he'd visited some of the verses.

As it turned out, I started helping Kristen with her farm, in between my own chores and jobs. I liked her a lot and she seemed to return the feeling, although it was something I hadn't thought of for a long time. I knew she must be lonely, even though she had the kids, but being in the mountains can be a lonely place at times. The nights can be long for a woman without a man. It was good it was turning into summer though, 'cause if it'd been winter, it would've been even tougher on her.

We kept busy that early summer, finishing up Preacher's cabin and taking in what the mountains had to offer. As the seasons turned we took advantage of the game it brought forth and there was a never-ending supply. One of the things Jack liked best was fried frog legs.

"Let's go frogging," Jack said one day.

"I'll get the gigs," Preacher said.

"Let's walk the bank upriver first," Jack said. "Then we'll turn around and come down the other side."

"I must take a sip of libation first," Preacher said. "I really don't like the slimy creatures, although their meat is especially delicious."

"Let's just try for the big bullfrogs," Jack said. "They'll make a bigger target and we won't need half as many."

We waded the banks, me holding the light, Jack and Preacher on either side of me, listening for the croaking to lead us in the right direction.

"You got to be quiet," Jack said. "Else you'll scare 'em off."

"How can you be quiet wading in the water?" Preacher asked.

"Frogs don't know you're out to stick 'em," Jack said. "We might just be another frog jumping around."

"Frogs ain't six feet tall," Preacher said. "Now, you might pass for one of 'em, what with your body being the same, and your face has certain similarities, too."

"Let's stop and listen," Jack said. "Pass the Potation."

We sat on the bank, listening to the night and spotting the frogs in our memory.

"It's a good night for frogging," Preacher said. "I'll miss these nights."

"Where you going?" I asked.

"Nowhere, that I know of," he said. "But a man don't live forever."

"Don't go off on another spell like before," Jack said.

"Well, when you see a man like James Parsons dying so young, it puts a man to thinking."

"It don't put me to thinking," Jack said.

"Why don't that surprise me." Preacher passed the shine my way. "That Kristen, she sure is good-looking woman. Whatd' you think of her, Claude?"

"I think she's a good woman. I don't know that she'd be interested in a man anytime soon."

"Women are always interested in a man," Preacher said. "It's too hard living in the hills without one. You ought to pay more attention to her, Claude. You don't want to end up like Jack and me."

"What's wrong with ending up like us?" Jack asked.

"We got nothing but the hills," Preacher said. "You and me, we're not leaving anything behind."

"You're getting on my nerves," Jack said. "You've caused me to urge. Hand me that lantern, I'll be back in a minute."

"I've never seen a man that can urge that many times in one day," Preacher said.

He and I sat in silence. It seemed as if his mind was somewhere else.

"What's wrong, Dan? You don't seem yourself tonight."

"It's nothing I can put my finger on. I feel a loss, somehow. I didn't know James that well, so I know it ain't that. It just seems that things are changing so fast and I'm not keeping up with 'em."

"Maybe you need to get out of the mountains for a while."

"I've never been anywhere I'd rather be. It's not the mountains, it's something else—a feeling, you know, something in my gut."

"I've heard of people getting hit by lightning and they say they can see the future," Preacher said.

"I wouldn't want to see the future," I said. "Good or bad, I don't want to know. Besides, we can all say one thing about the future—we know we're leaving sooner or later. That's as much as I want to know."

Just then we heard Jack yelling and a splash in the river. We ran to where he was and saw him thrashing in the water, swirling in circles, going under and coming back up, spitting water and gulping air, then diving in again.

"Could be a snake," I said.

"Unlikely," Preacher said. "If it was a snake, he'd be running through the woods."

"Got him," Jack said, as he came up again.

He was holding a big bullfrog in one hand, his overalls in the other. He came walking out of the water, stumbling as he came, water draining out of his pants as he held 'em in the air.

"What've you got there?" Preacher asked.

"Biggest bullfrog I've seen in years. I thought I might have been too close to the bank, but it was the closest log I could find. I guess he thought I was calling him. Next thing I knew, when I stood to pull up my pants, he jumped right in the middle of 'em. At first I thought I'd made a big mistake, maybe not hanging over the log far enough, but then he started squirming and struggling; probably seen he was out of his element, and then I knew—wet and clammy and all, it had to be a frog. He took me by surprise so much I fell backwards over the log and into the river. Then the fight was on. Wasn't nothing I could do but show him who was the best swimmer. He got down in one of the pant legs and I couldn't grab him, what with my leg in there and all, so I had to take 'em off. He's a dandy, ain't he? There's enough meat on them legs for two of us."

"You can have both of 'em," Preacher said. "Knowing where they've been has tainted my taste buds. Your seasoning techniques are primitive."

Jack was standing ankle-deep in the river, the frog croaking in one hand, his pants dripping in the other, the full moon shining down, making his round white body glow in the dark.

"Put your pants on," Preacher said. "You'll confuse the critters—they'll think there's two moons."

Jack clubbed the frog, passing him to me to hold while he climbed back in his pants.

"I may have found a new way to catch 'em," he said. "I wish Elmer had a been here—he'd be proud."

We spent four more hours walking the river, up one side and down the other, the full moon shining on the water, showing us the way. We'd gig for a while, stop and sip some shine, talking and laughing the night away. We ended up with forty frogs, enough to feed us all and quite a few more. Jack tried his calling method several more times but it never had the same result, although he did have to get back in the river and do some cleanup.

"I guess it wasn't such a good idea after all," he said. "Takes too much out of you."

June was fast coming to a close. The days were getting hotter and the heat was holding late through the evening. The small finger springs that fed the river were drying up, leaving only the rains to supplement what little growth was left. There wouldn't be enough. The banks of the river were widening, leaving pools that would fester and die, trapping minnows and crawdads, stagnating long enough to support the mosquitoes.

It was in those days that we did our hardest work, knowing the stifling heat of July would have us searching for shade and the cooling waters of the river.

Preacher was busy putting the final touches on his new cabin, while Jack entertained Holly and Sean, the kids hanging on to him like he'd been around forever. I helped Kristen as much as I could. Her brother Lewis didn't have much time to help and didn't really seem to care one way or the other. Mother was still selling mules to the state, one by one, when she could. The hot weather was hard on her and she spent more time in the shade, fanning herself, resting, waiting for the garden to produce its bounty. She would spend many hours over a hot stove canning and putting up vegetables for the coming winter.

I took long walks in the evenings that time of the year. I knew that soon it would be too hot to make the treks up the mountainsides, the air so thick it seemed to hang motionless. The forest and the pastures were glazed over every morning with dew, the white, glistening blanket covering the ground; a final effort of nature to give what water it had left. Soon, even that would disappear as the heat stayed through the night, and only the moisture deep below the dust would be left.

Kristen walked with me on some evenings, when her work was done and the kids were quiet. I'd grown more attached to her than I wanted, and couldn't pull myself away, as much as I thought I should. My silences on those walks were not intended to be rude. She walked beside me, calmly, quietly, a woman that had hard times thrust on her through no fault of her own, a woman with hardships facing her every morning she lifted herself from bed.

She never mentioned the difficult life ahead, only the beauty that surrounded her. She'd pull the flowers as we passed and smell the sweet fragrances and look into the sky and sometimes take my arm to steady her as we walked along the rough edges of the forest. She too was quiet, much like me. I enjoyed my friends and the times we had together. I loved the mountains just as much, and Kristen seemed to have the same thoughts.

"Life might be easier closer to a town," I said to her one day.

"Will you be leaving then?"

"No, not me. I meant for you. There's more opportunities in a town. Better schools for the kids, for one. And people—lots more people."

"Too many people make me nervous. Besides, I've never thought about leaving. I've been to a town too many times. It's never quiet there; it's always busy. Not busy with work, just busy with things that don't mean much. People running from here to there, saying they don't have time to do this or that. My kids will learn how to take care of themselves, but the kids in town will need someone to take care of them for a long time to come."

"You think you'll stay in the mountains forever, then?"

"Until I die, or something forces me out. Why would someone leave here? I think our biggest problem will be too many people moving to the mountains. You've seen the changes; you've seen the troubles that come with growth. I'd rather walk through the woods than walk on dirt paths. I'd rather listen to the wind at night than the sounds of a thousand voices."

"You think you'll ever marry again?" I asked, the question startling myself.

"Are you asking?"

"No—I mean, yes…I mean, I'm asking you about you."

"Oh, well, I suppose I might, if the right man asked. You've gotten too much sun, your face is red."

I turned my face away.

"You married young," I said.

"Doesn't every girl in the mountains. A man needs a woman to help just like she needs a man. I wasn't going to stay with my folks forever. I tell you this much, I won't marry a man fifteen years older than I am again. How old are you?"

"Well, I'm a lot older than my years. That's the same thing."

"Sure you are. We're about the same age, aren't we?"

"I'll be twenty-three in August," I said.

"I'll be twenty-four in September. I was sixteen when I married James. Seems a long time ago now, but it really wasn't. He was a good man, better than Lewis, anyway. But, God bless him, we didn't laugh much. He was always working and never took the time to just sit and talk."

"But you'd do it all over again?"

"You mean get married again?"

"Yeah."

"Sure I would. I don't really want to live in these mountains alone. I will if I have to, but I need someone to share it with. Have you ever thought about marriage?"

"One time I did, but I haven't in a long time. I'm not sure I see the need."

"Oh," Kristen said, dropping her eyes to the ground. "You must like living alone."

"I don't mind it. Of course, I had Elmer with me for a while, but I don't think that counts. He just needed a place to stay."

We walked for a while without talking and soon turned around, heading back toward her cabin. I wasn't quite sure how the talk had turned to marriage. Somehow in the back of my mind I think I initiated it, but I hadn't meant to, at least I don't think I did.

I hadn't felt that way about a woman in so long I'd forgotten how good it was, but I was still torn about the reason why. It wasn't something I was looking for, nor was it something I had wanted.

So far my life had gone according to my plan and no one else's, and I took pride in knowing that I was capable of handling my own direction. The thought of having someone else to think of confused me for some reason. It was something I couldn't shake off, and the more I thought about it the more I thought of her, and the more bewildered I became. In one way I wanted to leave her standing there, and in another I could already feel the pain of having to part with her.

We came to a small creek, the mud on both sides wallowed out by the cattle and mules. I looked for a better place to cross but there was none.

"You'll have to jump across," I said. "You'll get muddy if you don't."

She looked at the mud and then at me and I could see in her eyes the need for something, something I didn't understand.

"We could walk on down a ways," she said. "It might be easier."

I looked up at the sky and saw the sun setting behind the mountains, a bright orange glow, like a halo crowning the hilltops, ever so slowly fading from view. And when I looked back at Kristen the radiance of light was full on her face, was streaming through her hair, the golden glow cascading over her body, her blue eyes fixed on mine, a thin smile pursed on her lips. She was waiting, waiting for me. I picked her up and held her in my arms, walked through the mud, crossing the water, her arms around my neck, her cheek pressed against mine, her soft, sweet hair dancing across my face. I set her feet on the dry ground, but found myself still holding on and could feel the pressure of her hand on my back, staying there, her eyes still looking in mine.

"I don't know anything about marriage," I blurted out.

"There's not much to know. It's just harder than being alone."

"How long will you be grieving the loss of your husband?"

"There's no time to grieve in these mountains. You might lose the day if you close your eyes too long."

I held her hand for most of the way back, letting go as we got closer to the cabin. Mother was sitting on the porch, Sean and Holly playing in the front. I said goodnight and told her I would try and come by the next day to help with the chores. She only smiled and said thank you. As Mother and I walked along the path away from her I couldn't make the smile on my face disappear, wanting to see Kristen one last time.

"Quit your fidgeting," Mother said. "She's still there."

"What?" I said, trying to act unconcerned.

"I said, she's still there watching."

"Well, what would she be watching?"

"You men are dumber than stumps."

I turned to see if I could catch one more glimpse of her and sure enough, Mother was right. She was still there, watching as I walked away. I could only stand and look, knowing that something had happened that evening, something that would change my life forever.

"Come on, Claude, you're young. She'll still be there tomorrow. You saw that sky didn't you? That orange means it's up to no good."

"It didn't look that bad to me."

"Something tells me you weren't looking at it all that much. Look at it now."

It was almost dark, but I could see what Mother was talking about. Big black boomers were following the sunset, coming out of the west. We could feel the breeze picking up as we walked along.

"Better pick up the pace," Mother said. "There's a storm behind those clouds and if I don't miss my guess, storm's putting it lightly."

"You're not thinking it's a twister are you?"

"I think it's best to be prepared. When we get back you better make sure your livestock's tied up. Tell Preacher and Jack too. I've seen 'em before and I wouldn't wish 'em on the dead. Go on ahead and warn the others. If the winds come up, get in the root cellars."

I started running but hadn't gone far when I stopped.

"I've got to warn Kristen," I yelled as I turned back and passed by Mother.

"Hurry up," she yelled. "The wind's rising."

When I got to the cabin Kristin was cooking supper for the kids.

"I didn't expect to see you back so soon." She smiled.

"I didn't either. Mother thinks there might be a twister in the storm that's coming. If the wind gets up, take the kids to the cellar. I'll go tie up your cow and mule, then I've got to take care of my own."

"I've seen twisters before. We'll be all right. Just take care of yourself."

"You can come with me if you want, but we've got to hurry."

"No, you go ahead. We'll be fine."

I ran to the corral and pulled her mule to the barn, stopping long enough to grab the milk cow on the way. I put 'em in the barn and barred the doors and then started running toward the Three-Stop. I caught up with Mother when she was turning toward her place. I yelled and she waved me on.

When I reached Jack's place he and Preacher had already seen the warnings and had taken measures. All three of us raced to my place and shoved the livestock in the barn. We went in the cabin and put a pot of coffee on. By then the air had cooled down and it was starting to rain, not hard, just sprinkling, but we could see, even in the dark, the clouds building on top of each other.

We went to the porch and waited. What wind there was had died down and a calm had set in. The rain had stopped but the air was still cooler than it had been. Within minutes the lightning started and the thunder rolled.

"It's coming," Preacher said. "Why is there always cold air in a twister?"

"Beats me," Jack said. "But it always happens that way. Maybe we'll get lucky."

"Maybe," Preacher said, looking at the sky.

I couldn't keep my mind off Kristen. Even though she said she'd seen one before, some people take 'em too lightly, waiting until the last minute to run for cover.

Just then the thunder boomed, shaking the cabin, and the lightning followed, cracking so hard it hurt our ears. The wind picked up, but this time it kept building. The dust was boiling and we could hear the limbs breaking in the trees.

"I've got to go make sure Kristen's all right," I yelled.

"Don't be a damned fool," Jack yelled back.

I could hardly hear his voice, even though I was still on the porch with him.

"She knows what to do," Preacher shouted. *"She's lived here long enough."*

"I don't care," I yelled. *"She's got the kids to help."*

I jumped off the porch and started running, Preacher and Jack on my heels. The wind was blowing so hard against us we had to bury our heads in our arms, and the grit was so thick we could barely see. The rain was blowing sideways and it was all we could do to make headway. Then came the noise, so loud, so constant, we couldn't even hear each other. Jack grabbed my arm and I looked his way. He wanted me to stop at the Three-Stop. I shook my head no. Preacher took my other arm and they dragged me to Jack's root cellar, my feet hardly scraping the ground. They shoved me inside, followed me, and slammed the door shut.

"What do you think you're doing?" Preacher yelled. *"You want to get us all killed?"*

"I've got to help Kristen!"

"You got to do nothing but stay put," Jack yelled. *"She'll be all right. We've got to wait this out."*

The roar was still out there, howling around us. The rain was pounding against the cellar door and the wind was shaking it. The noise was so terrible we put our hands over our ears.

And then it was over. That fast. We listened and looked at each other in the darkness. It was still raining hard but the wind was dying down.

"I'm going," I said.

"There could more behind it," Preacher said.

"I'm going now."

"Let's go then," Jack said.

We opened the cellar door and started running. Debris was scattered over the road. The Three-Stop looked fine but Jack's barn was missing its roof. We kept running. We reached the turn-off to Mother's.

"*I'll go check on Mother,*" Preacher yelled.

Jack and I kept running. I thought my heart was bursting and my legs felt like sacks of rocks, but I kept going, Jack pulling up the rear. I looked back once to see where he was and saw him stopped, bent over, puking.

Finally I made it to the path leading up to Kristen's. I ran faster. And then I saw it. I stopped for a moment, not believing what I was seeing. There was nothing left—the house was gone, the barn was missing three sides and the roof, one side standing up as straight as the day it was built. Only the fireplace was left where the house used to be.

"*Kristen! Kristen!*" I yelled. I kept yelling her name. As many times as I'd been there, I'd never noticed the root cellar.

Jack had caught up with me by then.

"God almighty!" he said. "Where's the cellar?"

"*I don't know, I don't know!*" Tears were welling up in my eyes. I was wiping 'em with my forearms, the dirt off my shirt making it harder to see.

"*Circle the house,*" Jack yelled.

He started off one way and I started off the other. We were kicking up boards and jumping over chairs. I saw the milk cow bent around a tree, dead. I kept running.

"*Kristen, it's me. Where are you?!*"

And then I heard a voice.

"*Here, Claude, over here.*"

I ran to the voice, on the north side of the rubble, meeting Jack there at the same time.

"Where's it at?" Jack asked. "I heard her voice."

"*Kristen, where are you?*"

"*Here, Claude. Can you hear me?*"

We were standing right on top of the cellar. It was hidden under the trash. We started throwing boards and limbs and rubbish, a dead chicken, a wagon wheel, the gate to the corral. Finally we saw the cellar. We pulled out more trash and opened the door. They were all right. The kids were crying, but okay. Kristen was holding both of them in her arms. I grabbed Sean and handed him to Jack and did the same with Holly. I took Kristen's hand and helped her out of the cellar. She was pale and shaking but she'd saved herself and her kids. When she saw that her home was gone, tears came to her eyes, but she refused to let 'em fall. She wiped her eyes with her hands and turned to the kids, taking each by the hand.

"What about the cow?" she asked.

I shook my head slowly.

"The mule?"

"Haven't seen him yet."

"I have," Jack said. "He's in the field. Looks like he's okay."

"Can things get any worse?" Kristen was trying to be strong for the kids but I saw her lower lip trembling.

"Yes," I said. "It could have been a lot worse."

"You can stay at Mother's," Jack said. "And the kids can stay with me if they want to."

"We'll come back in the morning and salvage what we can," I said. "And then we'll start rebuilding. There's nothing we can do tonight."

Jack picked up Holly and I took Sean. I put my arm around Kristen and we started off to Mother's.

There was very little damage at Mother's place. The twister had jumped around enough to miss most of the cabins. Kristen's home and Jack's barn had taken the brunt of the storm. Mother was glad to take her in, and in the following weeks the kids stayed at one place or another, sometimes with me, sometimes with Jack. They liked staying with Jack better. For some reason he just had a way with those two kids.

Chapter Sixteen

By now it was four in the morning and Claude thought he could see a tired look in Pete's eyes. The first hint of daylight would be breaking over the mountains and through the trees in another hour or so, and Claude, for the first time in his life, wished it would hold off. He knew it meant little to the young man sitting beside him, but for him it meant the end of what he held the closest.

Claude got up and stepped to the water's edge, bent down and cupped his hands full of cool river water and splashed his face, then took another handful and drank it. Pete knelt beside him and did the same.

Pete didn't want the night to end either. Somehow he could feel their presence—Mother, Jack, Elmer and Preacher. He wished he could speak to them all, touch them, know them, be a part of them. Right then they were closer than his own family, but that would change, he would make sure of it.

"It was Holly and Sean, wasn't it?" Pete asked. "They were the kids that were drowning."

"Yeah, it was them. They were so little I hardly I knew I had 'em in my arms."

"Where exactly was that tree?"

Claude stood and starting walking downstream and Pete followed. It was just some thirty feet.

"There's the stump where it broke during the storm," Claude said. "And that rock there, that's where the base of the tree was sitting. When the limbs broke it just rolled over like a wagon wheel. Just bad luck."

"Their father died and they made it through the twister, and then the tree rolled over on them," Pete said. "I'd say bad luck was sticking close to them."

Claude sat on the rock and Pete sat beside him. The fire was burning down but it spread a thin light in their direction. Claude saw no reason to throw more limbs on it; it would be daylight soon and he didn't want to tarnish the morning with a false light.

"The Three-Stop," Pete said. "It was the one place where you knew to meet, wasn't it?"

"It started our day," Claude said. "And many times it ended there. Without it I don't know if there would have been a Dogleg or not. I think it was the one thing that drew us in, kept us together somehow through that year.

"After the storm we picked up the pieces and thought the worst was surely over, but Tubbs would visit again, and I knew it wasn't."

The warm days of June were past and the July sun poured on us as if it were falling from the sky. Soon the heat would destroy the green grasses, turning 'em a dull lifeless brown. The leaves would wilt, flowers would die, gardens would starve for water, and all that survived were weeds and brush.

The river slowed its roll, as if waiting for replenishment, but there would be very little and not enough to fill its dwindling banks. Grasshoppers were thriving in the heat, locusts were tormenting what was left of the living, and flies were devouring 'em both. The burning nights were keeping the tired from sleeping, while the hot, humid days turned simple movements into exhausting torture. The stifling heat filled the valleys; ponds became mud holes, then dust bowls; wells dried up; springs refused to flow; and life began to drain from what was once alive and thriving.

That was the bad part. The good part was we spent most of our time in the river, swimming, fishing, and floating, and sometimes just sitting in it. Jack was particularly adept at wallowing out a trough, spending hours skipping stones and squirting water through his hands. We seined for minnows and let our fishing lines float with the slow flow of the water, laying back half-submerged with our heads on a log, hoping a fish might take the bait, but not really caring. Even they thought it was too hot and laid up in the deep pools, refusing to eat.

It was slow going rebuilding Kristen's cabin, the heat taking its toll on all of us. We'd start early, before daylight, and work till noon, but by that time we were wore down. Kristen worked right along beside us, though, and we admired her determination.

Mother watched the kids most of the time while we worked, staying at the Three-Stop during the day, watching the store for Jack. She'd make lunch for us and we'd meet there after noon. All of us had our own chores to do and right after lunch we'd finish those and meet at the river. Preacher taught Sean and Holly how to swim, while Jack instructed 'em on the finer points of floating, his white, round belly looking like a dead carp.

It took three days to fix Jack's barn roof, which wasn't bad considering his fear of heights kept him on the ground and Preacher and me in the air.

We wrapped a rope around an old saddle and hung it from a limb over the river. It had a good long swing to it and you could get high in the air before jumping off. All of us took turns, but Jack was the most daring. He'd swing back and forth and get it going as fast as he could. The height didn't seem to bother him if he thought he'd land in the water.

"I'm going again," Jack said. "It reminds me of my bronc-busting days."

"You can barely stay on a mule," Preacher said.

"A mule ain't no bronc; I can stay on them."

Jack pulled the saddle into the bank with a long pole he'd rigged up, and Preacher held it while Jack got on. Dan gave him a shove and Jack flew out over the water, yelling like a cowboy.

"When I swing back in, give me another shove," he shouted. "I want to get all the air time I can."

When he swung back to the bank Preacher was waiting. He gave him a running shove that took Jack as high as we'd ever seen it.

"One more time," Jack yelled.

As he flew back toward the bank, yelling and waving one arm, he was gaining so much height we were afraid he was gonna catch on a limb, but he didn't.

Just as he swung back the rope broke. Jack flew through the air still waving his arm but now he was screaming. He went over the top of Preacher, Dan's eyes following him all the way, and hit about fifteen feet behind him in a large patch of wild blackberries. He rolled through those stickers like a rabbit and ended up in the middle of the patch, the saddle on top of him.

"That's gotta hurt," Preacher said.

Jack's screams had dropped to a moaning whimper. We could barely see him through the tall mass of thorns, but we did locate him by the sounds of his sobs.

"Those stickers are bad," Mother said. "I won't pick berries without gloves on. It's a bloody mess, anyway."

"How you doing in there?" Preacher asked.

No sound came out, just some moaning mixed with whines.

"I've never seen anything like that," Kristen said. "Kids, you turn your heads."

Then we heard Jack. "Help." His voice was so weak we could hardly hear it.

"You'll have to speak up, Jack," Mother said. "We can't hear you."

"Can't move," he said.

"I bet he can't move," Mother said. "He's nothing but a pin cushion."

"Just lay still, Jack," Preacher said.

"We'll have to cut him out," Mother said. "It's the only way. If we try to go in there we'll be cut up like him. It's too bad he didn't have nothing on but shorts."

"I'll go get a brush cutter," I said.

"Put some clothes on," Mother warned. "And gloves. Preacher, you better do the same. I'll stay here and comfort him. Them berries are ripe; he'll be stained when we get him out. Jack, you're dumber than a board. Kristen, run up to the cabin and get them tweezers out of my sewing kit and bring a good-sized needle too. We'll have to dig some out. Jack, don't you worry none, we'll have you out of there in no time."

It took about an hour before we finally got a path cut to him. That was the easy part. Lifting him out was the worst, the thorns stuck to him so hard it was all we could do to gently pull him up on his bare feet. Preacher let him climb up on his back and walked him out.

His body was covered from head to toe with purple stains mixed with blood. It was hard to tell where to start picking, there were so many. Mother decided it was best to start with the bottom of his feet. That way he could at least stand while she worked on him.

"One of you men will have to pick 'em out of his rear end," Mother said. "That's ground I ain't digging in."

Preacher did the honors and when he got done Jack's butt looked pretty strange, but not as odd as the rest of him. The purple splotches took weeks to disappear, and he had one dot on his forehead that never did go away. I guess the puncture filled with berry juice and stayed like a tattoo. We put the swing back up but Jack never did get back on it again. Preacher surmised that Jack's bronc-riding days were over.

At night we'd build a small fire on the bank, no matter how hot it was. We liked looking at it; the sparks flying and spitting, the hot coals blazing like a morning sun, and the sounds of the hissing and popping of burning wood.

Those evenings were the best. Most of the time we'd eat dinner at the river, Mother cooking up a pot of beans and frying fresh-caught catfish right over the fire. She'd bring some cornbread with her and every now and again she'd bring a fresh-baked cobbler. We paid little attention to the fishing, listening to the sounds of the night, watching the stars and telling stories. It was on those nights that I hoped I would never have to leave these mountains.

It was on one of those lazy nights that we had a visitor. We were doing what we always did, just laying back, fishing lines in the water, hands behind our heads, a coffee pot simmering on the fire, stretched out like we owned the world. We heard someone behind us but thought it was probably Mother, coming down for one last visit. It wasn't.

"How's everybody doing?"

"Tubbs," we shouted.

"I thought I'd find you three here. Don't you do nothing but fish?"

"I can't say as we do," I said, standing to meet him. "What brings you back?"

"Just passing through. Couldn't come this close and not stop and say something."

"It sure is good to see you," Preacher said.

"Yeah," Jack broke in. "You sure stay gone a long time."

"It's been a busy spring," Tubbs said. "I see that twister came through. Anybody hurt?"

"No," I said. "It did some damage but nothing we couldn't fix. Sit down and have some coffee."

"That'd be fine. I can't stay long, though. I've got business elsewhere."

"What kind of business would that be?" Preacher asked.

"I've got a message to deliver."

"Do we know who it is?"

"I don't believe you do. How's life been treating you?"

"Jack had a run-in with a blackberry patch," Preacher said, laughing. "Other than that it's been fairly quiet."

"How's the Potation?" Tubbs asked. "I ran into a fellow over in Tate County that mentioned your name, Preacher. He went on and on about your special brew. I didn't think he was ever gonna stop. He gave me a taste and sure enough, it was yours."

"Got some right here. Want a sip?"

"Don't mind if I do. Spring's a long time gone, isn't it? I heard about Elmer passing. I was sorry to hear it."

Tubbs gave me a sideways glance, as if knowing I hadn't mentioned seeing him in the river after Elmer died. I don't know why I hadn't said anything, just a feeling inside I guess, something telling me not to. In a way I was not as happy to see Tubbs as an old friend should've been. There was something between us, something I couldn't figure out, but it'd nagged at me ever since we'd met and for some reason I believed that him being there was not the best thing. I could see it in his eyes; they had a look to 'em, and they drifted away from mine too quickly.

"How long can you stay?" Jack asked. "The fishing ain't so good, what with the hot weather and all, but Mother's cooking's still good."

"I'll be leaving tonight," he said. "But I'll be back again."

His eyes met mine this time and I felt a chill run up my back.

"Tell us where you've been," Jack said.

"I've been up and down this river so many times I can't count 'em. I've just been helping out folks as best I can. I stayed here longer than I've ever stayed anywhere. Just can't seem to plant my feet. How's Mother?"

"The same," Preacher said. "She had a special friend for a while, but it didn't turn into anything. She's just as sassy as she always was."

"She's a good woman," Tubbs said. "How about that girl that's living with her?"

"How'd you know about her?" I asked.

"I heard she lost her husband and then the twister took her home. News like that travels fast. She must have plenty of gumption to stick it out like she done."

"She does at that," I said. "She's stubborn and works hard."

"Sounds like you know her pretty well."

"Oh, he knows her all right," Jack said. "He's sweet on her. She's got an eye for him, too."

"I don't blame him. A woman like that's hard to find. I met her husband one time."

This took me by surprise. We'd spoken of Tubbs before in front of Kristen, but she had never said anything about knowing him.

"I never met the wife, though," Tubbs said, as if he knew what I was thinking.

"How'd you happen to run into him?" I asked.

"I was just passing through, kind of an accident, really. He was working the fields when I spotted him. He was sitting on a stump resting, trying to catch his breath, having a hard time, too. I gave him a drink of water and sat with him for a spell. After a while he seemed to get better and I moved on."

We sat and talked for the better part of the night, catching up on things, good and bad. Tubbs acted like he didn't want to leave, but he said he had to. It must have been two in the morning when he stood and said his goodbyes.

"Don't stay away for so long the next time," Preacher said.

Tubbs looked straight at me and said, "I'll be back soon."

"Good," Jack said. "The fishing might be better."

"The fishing will be better, Jack." Then he turned to me. "Claude, remember the sign?"

I nodded and he nodded back, then he took off walking downriver.

"What'd he mean by that?" Jack asked.

"Nothing," I said. "It didn't mean nothing."

"It sure was good to see him again," Preacher said. "I wonder where he goes, just wandering around like he does."

"Don't make much sense to me," Jack said. "You'd think he'd take roots somewhere."

Then we heard an owl call from upriver. I could hear his wings flapping as he passed in front of us. He landed on a dead tree lying halfway in the water. The twister had blown it down. We could just make him out by the firelight. He was staring our way.

"That's the same owl we saw in the daylight the other day," Jack said. "Well, at least he got his days and nights straightened out."

We packed up our poles and the coffee pot and headed to our cabins. I couldn't stop thinking about Tubbs and so I got no sleep that night. Something kept gnawing at my gut and wouldn't go away. Sometime, just before daylight, I walked over to Mother's place and woke up Kristen. I held her for the longest time, not saying a word, just holding on.

We were making good progress on Kristen's cabin. She wanted it bigger than the last one for some reason; she wanted her own bedroom this time. The other cabin was just one big room. I built her a large fireplace out of fieldstone and cut her a big oak slab for a mantel. She was proud of that and it made me feel good to be able to do something that she was proud of.

Mother helped her make some curtains and even traded a mule for another milk cow. Things were coming together for her and the kids. Even the neighbors pitched in and helped. The men built another barn while the women helped sew clothes for Kristen and the kids. They gave her pots and pans and plates and even some furniture. By mid-July we were ready to put the roof on.

As the days went by we were all together more than we'd ever been. From daylight to dark we spent our time together building the cabin for Kristen, going for supplies, back to the sawmill for boards, fishing, swimming, and floating. They were the happiest days that I remember.

Jack and Preacher were always in to it about something, Mother getting in the middle of it to make the call on who was right or wrong, not that it made any difference. Mother was happy too; you could see it on her face. It must have been having Sean and Holly around so much, reminding her of the two children she'd lost. She played games with 'em and fixed 'em special things to eat like cookies and candy.

Kristen helped Mother with her chores, along with her own, spending most of her afternoons working in the gardens, both hers and Mother's. They enjoyed each other's company, and the hours they spent together putting up vegetables for the winter rewarded 'em both. That was hot work, standing over the stove all day, the heat in the nineties anyway. Mother was especially grateful to have the help, the heat hurting more and more as she got older.

"We need more windows," Kristen said one day. "I want to have some light in the cabin."

"Windows cost money," I said.

"What about Elmer's old cabin," Preacher said. "It's just rotting away up there."

"That place gives me the jitters," I said. "You know what happened the last time I was up there. That's when I brought Elmer down to live with me. Something's not right with that place."

"Come on now," Mother said. "Surely you don't believe in spooks."

"I don't think I do, but there was something going on, something that scared Elmer and me. He didn't want to go back either."

"You're getting addled," Jack said. "I been up there many times with never a spot of trouble."

"Me too," Preacher said. "Let's go, we need a break anyway."

"I'll go," I said. "But I still say something's not right."

"I'll pack some food to take," Mother said. "Now go on and hitch up the wagon."

Jack and Preacher were having a good old time on the way, having the day off as it were, but I still had my doubts. We were sipping on Potation through the day, Jack and Preacher just having fun. Myself, I was using it to bolster my confidence.

We reached the cabin around eight o'clock, leaving the wagon a good quarter of a mile back in the woods. We unhitched the mule and led him with us as we walked the rest of the way. The sun was just beginning to drop behind the hills. The winter had taken its toll on the place. The front door was open, some of Elmer's things still scattered on the porch along with the leaves and dirt. The front steps had broken down in the last year and the roof was caving in.

A dead tree had fallen on one side of the cabin, knocking a hole in the side of the wall. There were three windows that were worth saving. We walked through the cabin while there was still some light and found that there was some old furniture that Kristen might be able to use.

"Place don't look scary to me," Jack said.

"Don't bother me none," Preacher said. "Remember that time we were out in the woods and we ran into the Howler. Maybe this is where he lives." Preacher laughed along with Jack, but I didn't join in.

"Come on, Claude, it's not that bad," Jack said. "There's no such thing as ghosts."

"What about the Howler, then?"

"Probably just somebody out to scare us."

I remembered that night and it occurred to me that none of us at the time thought it was someone out to scare us.

"Place is run-down, ain't it?" Preacher said, kicking an old broken chair out of his way. "But it ain't much worse off than when Elmer lived here. He didn't take much to house chores."

"Where we gonna sleep tonight?" Jack asked.

"I think I'll roll out my blanket outdoors," I said. "One of you can sleep in Elmer's bed."

"I'll sleep outside," Preacher said. "It's kind of stuffy in here, anyway."

"Suits me fine," Jack said. "I'll sleep in Elmer's bed, in here with the spooks."

I built a small fire outside, beneath the same tree that Elmer and I had stayed under. Mother had packed a small pot of beans and cornbread for dinner and some bacon and bread for breakfast. We sat the pot of beans on the fire to let it warm, while Jack fixed up his bed in the cabin, wiping off the mattress and throwing his bedroll on top. Then he came out to join us.

"Nothing going on in there," he said, grinning. He was still having fun with the ghost story.

"I don't know nothing about ghosts," Preacher said. "But I do know something about the devil. One time I was in Kansas City visiting an old friend from seminary school. I'd just sold some horses I'd come by in payment for a funeral service and needed a place a stay. He offered me a bed at his place and I gladly accepted.

"We stayed up late talking about the old days and he said he'd been having nightmares about Satan. I asked what kind of nightmares he was having and he said he'd been waking up about midnight with the cold sweats. The room, he said, was as cold as a winter storm, even though it was August. And the windows he'd kept open would all be closed. He'd get up and open 'em, but they'd fall right back down again, just like somebody was pushing 'em. So he'd go back to bed and pull the sheet up over his body to keep warm and just as he was slipping back to sleep, whoosh, the sheet would go flying off of him, landing in the floor.

"When he'd finally get to sleep he'd have nightmares about the devil, riding a big wild-eyed pig, a giant of a man with flaming horns coming out of his head and breathing fire. The pig was as big as a horse and could fly. He said the devil would come and get him, put him on the pig and take him down to Hades, showing him off to all the poor wretches he'd already brought down. They were screaming all the time, as if in pain, and the devil would make him eat maggots and drink blood.

"We went to bed late that night. I was sleeping on a couch in the outer room. Sometime during the night I woke up, hearing noise coming from the bedroom. I lit a lantern and made my way across the room to his door. Opening it slow I peered inside. There was my friend, opening and closing the windows, one after the other. He'd go to his bed and tear the sheets off, throwing 'em on the floor, and then let out a wail that would wake the dead.

"I went into the room with my lantern and as soon as he saw me he came a running. He knocked me down to the floor and stood over me, screaming gibberish I'd never heard before. He startled me so much that my protective instincts went into action, my foot coming up and kicking him in the crotch and doubling him over. Sounded like a wagon wheel rolling over walnuts. Well, that woke him up.

"I helped him back to bed but couldn't get him to talk, his face contorted in pain like them demons he'd seen. He was turning blue because he was having trouble catching his breath, and so I was looking around for something to help him with. I grabbed the first thing I thought would do the best and threw the water from the washbasin on his face. That helped him get his breath back.

"I opened the drawer on his bed stand, looking for a rag, and lo and behold, you'll never guess what I found. Seems he'd been having headaches and the doctor had been giving him laudanum. He liked it so much he'd been drinking near a bottle a day. It just made things worse for him. Of course it helped with his headaches, but it took his mind on a tour through hell. I poured the bottle out and the next morning explained what he'd been drinking.

"After that he didn't have any more trouble with Satan, although I did hear later that he ended up running an opium parlor, catering to the tormented souls that walk in the depths of despair."

"What's laudanum?" Jack asked.

"It's a painkiller," Preacher said. "Tainted with opium. It makes your mind see things it ought not to, and it makes a person do things they shouldn't."

"Like what?"

"Like the things *you* do every day except you don't need opium to do 'em."

We ate our beans and cornbread while the sun drifted out of sight. Then, with the darkness settling in, we could hear the silence of the forest, broken only by the sounds of crickets and tree frogs.

"Not much stirring up here is there?" Preacher said. "Seems like there should be some night sounds, like an owl hooting or a coyote howling."

"Not much of a moon tonight either," I said. "We should have brought a lantern."

"I think there might be one inside," Jack said. "I'll go take a look."

Jack walked up the broken steps, through the door and into the blackness. Preacher and I watched as he disappeared from sight.

"Sure is dark in there," Preacher said. "He ought to strike a match."

Jack must have had the same idea, we thought, 'cause we saw a sharp light as he moved around the cabin. It went from one end to the other, slowly, effortlessly, swinging up and down, from side to side. Then we heard something. It was Jack. We turned around and saw him walking in behind us.

"Couldn't find one," he said. "I went out the back door, thinking there might be one out there, but there wasn't."

We looked back at the cabin and the light was gone.

"Has anybody got matches?" Jack asked. "I forgot to bring some."

"You didn't strike a match in there?" Preacher asked.

"I told you I didn't have any."

Preacher and I stared at the cabin again. It was silent and dark. He looked at me and I stared back at him, and we both looked at Jack.

"Maybe you should sleep out here with us," I told Jack.

"Why?"

"Just a thought."

I didn't want to say anything and I could tell Preacher didn't either. It must have been a reflection of the moon, even though it was just a sliver, or maybe a shooting star. Preacher wasn't saying much, just looking into the fire. It was only about nine o'clock and none of us were tired, not that I was likely to get much sleep that night, anyway.

Jack was in high spirits. He hadn't had that much to drink lately because Sean and Holly were hanging around him all the time, and so he was making up for lost time. Preacher had been hitting the jug right along with Jack, but seemed to have lost most of his interest. I'd quit drinking when the sun went down. What courage I thought I'd consumed seemed to be leaving as fast as it came. Jack said he had to relieve himself and walked a few steps away from us.

"Did you see what I saw?" I asked.

"I thought I saw a light, but I guess I didn't. It must have been a reflection, maybe from the fire."

"It's not reflecting now."

"I know it's not, but that don't mean it wasn't then. Something could have made it happen. Strange things happen in the mountains, especially when you're this deep in 'em. Why did Elmer live this far back?"

"It was the only place he had."

"Well, it's too far back in the hills for me. I've got to be around some folks, even if I don't like 'em."

"I feel a lot better now," Jack said, picking up the jug again. "Let's go into the cabin and talk to the goblins."

"You go right ahead," Preacher said. "I'll just stay out here by the fire."

"You don't believe in spooks, do you, Preacher?"

"No, I can't say as I do, but I've no intention of inviting 'em to dinner."

"Chances are they don't eat beans, anyway," Jack said, giggling.

It wouldn't be long before Jack went down, the way he was guzzling the liquor. I hoped he would just pass out by the fire, but instead, around midnight he stumbled toward the cabin.

"It's time for me to hit the sack," he said. "You two ain't much fun tonight. A spook must have spooked you. See you in the morning."

We watched as he staggered to the cabin, barely able to climb the steps, swaggering into the open door and finally finding his way through the opening. We heard him clomp to his bed and fall on it.

"He could sleep through a catfight tonight," Preacher said. "Maybe it's for the best. I think I'll turn in too."

"I'm right behind you. Let's get up early and get what we want and head back home. I'm not that interested in staying up here for another night."

"I'm with you there," Preacher said. He was staring at the cabin. "Sure does look like a lonely place, don't it?"

"I'm not sure lonely's the word."

I threw another log on the fire, not wanting it to go out. I laid on my bedroll but was unable to close my eyes. I could tell Preacher was having trouble getting to sleep, tossing and turning the way he was. It was just too quiet; nothing was stirring, not even a breeze. All we could hear was the fire and Jack's snoring and after a while, even that quit.

I stayed awake for at least another hour. I could hear the soft breathing of Preacher, and then I dozed off myself.

Wham! The door slammed shut on the cabin. I woke up, not really knowing what the noise was, and as I turned over I could see Preacher was leaning on his arm looking toward the cabin.

"What was it?" I asked.

"The door on the cabin. You think Jack got up and shut it?"

"I don't think Jack could've found it."

"Whoever shut it don't know their own strength," Preacher said. "You think we should take a look?"

Then we heard the noise. It sounded like something heavy being pulled across the floor, a bed maybe. It went from one end of the cabin to the other. The thump, thump, of the legs hitting the uneven boards as it kept moving, back and forth.

"Come on," I said. "We've got to go in."

Preacher jumped up at the same time I did. "I sure wish I would've brought my shotgun," he said.

"I don't think a shotgun would do you any good."

We ran up to the porch and stood in front of the cabin. The noise had quit. It was dead silent then.

"Jack!" Preacher yelled. "Jack, are you awake?"

Nothing. We stepped forward, placing our feet on the first step of the porch. It creaked with our weight, the only sound we could hear. We stepped over the second one and stood in front of the door.

"Let's light a match," I said, handing Preacher one.

Just as we started to light it, the door flung open so hard we could feel the wind hit our faces. It slammed against the wall and out through the opening came a chair, the one Preacher had kicked earlier. It hit both of us, making us stumble backwards, falling over the steps and onto the ground. Then all kinds of things started happening inside, pots and pans slamming against the wall, furniture being thrown around and breaking up and crashing to the floor, and then came the wailing. It sounded like a maimed animal, one that was near death, high pitched and howling so long it hurt our ears.

"*We got to get Jack!*" Preacher yelled.

We both hit the porch with one leap, through the door and into the darkness. I got hit first, with what I don't know, but I could feel the blood flowing down the side of my nose. I was holding onto Preacher's shirt when we went in, but let go when I got hit. I was still standing but couldn't see. I took a match from my pocket and lit it—the bright flash letting me see for just an instant. The first thing I noticed was Preacher lying in the floor in front of me, and then I saw the air filled with everything from plates to pieces of wood. I bent forward and grabbed Preacher by the shirt.

"Get up, Dan!" He moved but didn't get to his feet.

"Over here," I yelled, pulling him to my left. "The bed's over here." I could barely make it out and the light was burning down to my fingers. I shoved Dan toward the bed and threw the match to the floor. I lit another one, standing right behind Preacher.

"Is he there?" I shouted.

Preacher seemed dazed. I shoved him aside and looked at the bed. Jack was lying on his back, a sheet wrapped all the way around the bed, from underneath, across his throat. I could barely make out his wide-opened eyes filled with fright. There was another sheet halfway down holding his arms tight against the mattress. I threw the match down and tore at Preacher's arm.

"Here, take this," I yelled, handing him a match. *"Light it!"*

Preacher swiped the match against his pant leg. It didn't strike.

"Come on, Preacher, light it!"

This time it took. As it flashed I opened my pocketknife and cut the two sheets. I grabbed Jack by the shirt with both hands and jerked him off the bed. When his feet hit the floor he barreled into Preacher, shoving him backward through the door and I followed right behind. Jack and Preacher flew off the porch and rolled on the ground. I jumped and landed on my feet. I helped 'em get up and we stumbled to the fire.

Preacher had a knot on his head the size of a walnut. Neither he nor I knew what had hit him. I had a cut at the hairline on the front of my forehead that needed stitching up, but it would have to wait. Jack had a burn mark on his throat where the sheet had been pulled tight across it. Other than being scared to death, we were all okay—out of breath, but still alive.

"What in God's name—" Preacher started.

I reached in the fire and brought out a flaming log.

"What are you doing?" Jack asked, still choking.

"I'm burning the place down."

"Good for you."

"What about the windows?" Preacher asked.

"You want to get 'em?"

"Might be all right in the morning."

"You really want to get 'em?" I asked again.

"Commence burning," he said.

"I'll buy Kristen new ones," I said. "This place needs to be burnt."

I walked up to the porch and threw the burning log through the front door.

272

In just a few minutes it caught and the place started burning. We watched as the flames engulfed the cabin, spreading over the floor and up the walls. Soon the flames were shooting out of the roof.

It took the rest of the night before the cabin was completely destroyed, nothing left but charred wood and the rock fireplace. We waited until noon before leaving, making sure what was left of the fire wouldn't spread.

Two days later we went to Harrison to buy windows and Jack picked up a few supplies he needed. Kristen went with us and Preacher and Mother stayed behind. We didn't tell the story of that night—there was no reason. It was something we didn't understand and something no one really needed to know. I never wanted to go back up there anyway, but in a way I needed to, just to satisfy in my own mind that what had happened when I saw Elmer that night wasn't just my imagination. We talked among the three of us, though, but never came to any conclusions. None of us believed in ghosts or the supernatural, but we did believe that something happened that night that only the good Lord could understand. Later I came to believe that it was unfinished business.

We finished Kristen's cabin in the fourth week of July. She and the kids moved in, which saddened Mother. Not that she didn't know it was going to happen, just that she would miss the company.

Jack missed the kids also, not having 'em around much during the days anymore. Kristen stayed busy keeping the farm up and the kids stayed with her most of the time. I helped as much as I could, but she was having a hard time of it. She took in sewing and quilting to help make ends meet, but it wasn't enough. She needed a good corn crop. That's what James had always counted on, but that was not the year for it. She would have to make do with the little she had that year, but with the help of the neighbors and us, she would live through it.

Her garden was producing well and she was putting up everything she could for the winter. Preacher, Jack, and I would provide plenty of deer meat, along with some hog and beef we'd butcher. If she was willing to stick it out, then everyone was willing to help.

We were sitting in the shade of the Three-Stop's porch one day when Mother and Kristen showed up with the kids.

"We've got green beans to put up," Mother said. "These kids want to go swimming."

"We were just thinking the same thing," Jack lied.

"We'll come down to meet you when we're done," Kristen said.

"Let's not waste any more time then," Preacher said. "Hop on and we'll race to the river." He bent down and let Holly hop on his back and Jack did the same for Sean.

The state's ramp prevented us from enjoying our old sitting spot—the river having undercut the edge leaving nothing but mud and debris. We picked a spot over by the tree that had fallen during the twister. It was half on the bank and half in the water. The trunk had landed on a boulder, so there was enough room for the kids to play between the base and the gravel. The rest of the tree was in the water, maybe twenty feet of it, getting deeper as it extended out. The limbs were holding it up the farther out it went. The tree was a good place for the kids to play, jumping off the trunk and landing in the river. We swam for a while and sat in the water and then we'd toss the kids from one to the other, sometimes letting 'em fall in the river. They were screaming with laughter and having the time of their lives.

It was late afternoon when Jack and Preacher went back up to the Three-Stop. They'd bought some candy and soda pop for the kids on their last trip to Harrison and wanted to get it for 'em. I stayed with Sean and Holly. They were sitting on the tree close to the bank, kicking their feet in the shallow water, and I was sitting on the bank skimming stones. It was a lazy afternoon and the river was as pleasant as I'd ever seen it.

I skimmed a rock across the river, watching to see how many times it skipped before hitting the other bank, when I noticed the owl sitting on a limb on the other side. It looked like the same one I'd seen so many other times. I watched it for a while and it seemed to stare back at me. I threw a rock at it, but it didn't scare him. He just sat on that limb, watching.

Then I heard the kids screaming. I turned to see what was happening and I saw the trunk of the tree roll off the boulder and twist in a half circle. A limb in the water had broken, forcing the heavy trunk off the rock. Sean and Holly, too young to realize what was going on, stayed on the trunk and rolled with it. It only took a second and the kids were flat on their stomachs in the water, their legs trapped under the trunk of the tree.

The water wasn't deep, but it was deep enough that their faces were in it, and their arms were too short to hold their heads up—they were drowning. I jumped to the tree and tried to roll it back, but it was too heavy. I tried lifting it but couldn't. I knelt in front of the kids and pulled up on their heads, trying to keep their mouths out of the water. They were screaming and coughing, spitting out water and straining to get free, but the tree had 'em pinned.

I yelled for help. I screamed for help. I knew I was hurting their necks, pulling on 'em like I was, but it was the only answer. I couldn't leave or they'd die. I talked to 'em, telling them to hang on. They were scared, gasping for air, flailing their arms, twisting their little heads and making it even harder for me to keep their faces out of the water.

Neither one had a shirt on so I had to straddle both of 'em with each arm over their shoulders and under their chests, pulling their heads up. But I could only get their mouths up to water level and they were still pulling it in, choking and screaming and drowning. I kept yelling for help as loud as I could and kept telling the kids to be calm, knowing it was only a matter of minutes before it would end.

Then I saw Jack and Preacher running toward us.

"Hold on, Claude," Preacher yelled, *"We're coming."*

Jack and Preacher went straight to the tree trunk beside me and tried to lift it, but it was too heavy, even for the both of them. I couldn't let go of the kids to help or the three of us might have done some good.

"We've got to get some leverage, Jack," Preacher yelled. *"We've got to go to the far end and lift."*

They jumped to the end of the tree and lifted but it still did no good. They ran back to me and started digging around the kid's legs, dragging out handfuls of gravel and sand.

"You're taking too long," I yelled. *"They're drowning. I can't keep their heads out of the water long enough."*

"Over here, Preacher," Jack yelled.

He'd moved down about five feet from me and had started digging.

"There's some clearance under here," he yelled. *"Dig under here and we'll crawl under and lift it with our backs."*

Preacher jumped around the kids and started digging with Jack. The kids were getting weaker. It was all I could do to hold on; my arms were straining so much they were starting to cramp.

"Come on kids," I said as calmly as I could. "Just hang on, hang on. We'll have you out in a second."

They were barely moving. When I'd give an extra pull on their chests they weren't helping at all.

"Hurry," I said. *"I'm losing 'em."*

"Let's try to crawl under," Preacher said.

They both went underwater and struggled to get under the tree, but could only get as far as their shoulders. They tried to raise the tree and I could feel it rise a little. I pulled on the kids but their legs wouldn't move. Jack and Preacher came back up.

"It's not enough," I yelled.

I saw their hands were bleeding from the digging, but they went back under and started clawing again. The kids weren't moving anymore and I knew they had little time left.

Jack and Preacher came up for air.

"I think we can get under it now," Preacher yelled. "Take a deep breath, Jack. Claude, when you feel it come up, jerk 'em out with all you got—it might be the last chance."

They each took a breath of air and went back under. I could see their feet kicking against the gravel, trying to force themselves under the tree far enough to get some leverage on the middle of their backs. They made it; I could see they'd made it.

Then the tree started rising. I pulled with all my might and could feel the kids' bodies moving. I turned around so I could grab their arms and pulled harder. The trunk rose a little more and I pulled again. God, they were coming. Just one more inch, Lord, just one more inch. The tree rose again and I pulled as hard as I could. Free. They were free.

I was dragging 'em out of the water and up on the bank. I laid 'em with their heads pointing downhill and got in between them and pushed on their backs. I wasn't sure I knew what to do. They were lifeless, just lying in the hot sun. I turned 'em over and started pushing on their stomachs. And then I saw signs of life.

Holly started coughing up water and then Sean did the same. They were spitting water and dirt and sand, coughing and puking at the same time. I rolled 'em over on their sides and held each one while they coughed up the mucous and finally started to take in big gasps of air.

They were gonna make it, I could tell. I turned 'em loose, and with my knees on the gravel, my head hanging to my chest, I thanked God He let 'em live. And then I jolted up—Jack and Preacher—where were they?

"Jack," I yelled. "Preacher!"

I ran to the tree and saw their legs still under the water, their bodies still under the tree. I grabbed Preacher's legs and pulled, but he wouldn't move. I grabbed Jack's legs and jerked as hard as I could, but it did no good. I gripped the tree and tried to raise it, but couldn't. I jumped over it to try and pull them out from the other side, but when I reached into the water and took Jack's hands, I knew— he was gone. I took Preacher's hands in mine, but there was no life in them. He too was gone.

I stumbled back to Sean and Holly and sat on the gravel. Then I heard talking and saw that Mother and Kristen were walking down the bank. They waved, but

I was too weak to wave back and they noticed something was wrong and started running toward us.

The kids were crying and Kristen picked up Holly and Mother picked up Sean and I sat there, too shocked to speak or move.

"What's happened?" Mother asked.

"The kids were sitting on the tree and a limb snapped in the water. It rolled over and pinned 'em. I held their heads above the water while Jack and Preacher raised the tree up high enough so I could pull 'em out.

"Thank God," Kristen said.

Mother put her hand on my shoulder. "Are you all right?"

I could only nod my head.

"Well, where are those two?" Mother asked. "They turned out to be good for something, didn't they."

"They're dead," I said.

"What?!"

"They had to dig under the tree to lift it with their backs. They must have used all their strength. They couldn't get out from under it."

Mother set Sean on the ground and walked over to the edge of the water by the tree, and from there she could see the legs of our good friends. She steadied herself and then sat down on the gravel, close to the water. Holding her face in her hands, she cried out loud.

Kristen put Holly down and knelt beside me, holding me in her arms. I could hold back no longer and began crying myself. And then we were all crying and the sun was drifting behind the mountains, and the quiet evening was falling over the forest.

Shadows were stretching across the river. A breeze was moving through the trees and the soft sound of running waters surrounded us—never knowing or understanding the grief that consumed us.

Downriver, at the bend, stood Tubbs. I knew he would be there. I could see on his face the same sadness I was enduring. There would be no more signs for me, and I would never see Tubbs again. Somehow I knew it.

He was a messenger, but he was also the hand that led to the gates of heaven. I knew my friends were with him. He lifted his sack over his shoulder, turned, and walked downstream.

I pulled myself together and asked Kristen to get help. Leaving Mother at the river I walked to the cabin and harnessed a team of mules. Tying a rope to the fallen tree, I pulled it off my friends and carried 'em to the bank.

Kristen had come back with some neighbors and a wagon. We lifted

Preacher and Jack and laid 'em side by side in the bed of the wagon. Mother and I took 'em to Harrison that night. There was no reason to wait until morning; sleep would not invade our grief. Two days later we brought 'em back to Dogleg and buried 'em next to Elmer, on the hill overlooking the river.

With the help of the neighbors we finished Kristen's cabin. It was a confusing time for me, getting up in the morning and passing the Three-Stop, its door locked shut. I swore I could smell coffee simmering.

I spent my evenings alone for the next few weeks, walking in the forest or sitting by the river. I wasn't feeling sorry for myself, only sifting through the memories. I knew that as time went by and my life took on new meaning, my friends' memories would quietly rest in the depths of my mind, surfacing only with a spark of recognition. I wanted to spend as much time as I could with 'em before the trials of living hid 'em silently away.

Every evening I went to the river and cut up the fallen tree, piece by piece, and burned it on the bank until it was gone. Some nights Kristen and Mother would sit with me and we'd fish with the kids. Mother would cook our catch over the fire and we talked of days gone by and the times that were coming. We laughed a lot on those nights about Jack's bad luck and Preacher's far-reaching stories, but always at the end came the tears, until one night the tears did not come, and we knew that it was time to move on.

Of course my life changed after Jack and Preacher died, not for the better and not for the worse, just changed. Those days were always with me, though, and not even the course of time could replace them.

July had turned to August and the hot weather remained, scorching the earth and turning the forest brown and crisp with the ever-dwindling source of water. The rains were few, but it was still a sign of progress, autumn patiently waiting to begin the process once again.

On those quiet mornings in that late summer I walked the banks of the river alone. I watched the leaves, caught on a warm breeze, as they drifted over the water and gently lowered beneath the river's mist. My friends are in these waters.

It was early dawn and the day's light was just beginning. Pete and Claude were both looking out over the river, watching as the smoky haze lifted to the heat. Pete began his walk back to his dozer and left Claude by the water.

Claude stayed by the riverbank for some time before he walked back to the cold coals of the fire. He saw the frying pan and coffee pot, but made no attempt to gather his belongings. He picked up his fishing pole and looked back over his shoulder at the slow drift of the water. He had not been able to see his friends on this morning, and he knew it was time to leave. Today, he wouldn't join them, but he knew they were there, waiting.

When he got to the Three-Stop Café he climbed the steps and sat in the rocker. He heard the dozer fire up but paid no attention. He closed his eyes and felt the breeze pass his face and smelled the summer air. Then he heard the footsteps and opened his eyes.

"I'm getting ready to leave," Pete said. "Do you need a lift?"

"No. Someone's coming to get me. I thought you weren't through. I thought you had one more job to do."

Pete looked behind Claude at the run-down Three-Stop Café and smiled.

"I'm through," he said. "This building will be underwater in a few days, and no one will care, just you and me. So long, Claude."

"Here," Claude said. "You can have my fishing pole. I won't need it anymore. There's nothing better than sitting by a river, fishing."

Pete took the pole and walked to his pickup and got in. He sat there before starting it, staring down the path toward the river. As he watched through the windshield something caught his eye, a shadow moving above the mist. Then he saw the owl, silently gliding over the water, following the river's course around the bend.

Pete opened the door and swung around on the seat to face Claude.

"Hey, old man," he said. "It's been nice talkin' with you." He hesitated for a moment, looked back at the river, and then at Claude again. "You're not leaving, are you?"

Claude just smiled, the old chair creaking on the back rock.

The End

Epilogue

I married Kristen in the fall of that year and stayed in the mountains and raised Sean and Holly. I took over Jack's Three-Stop Café and sold a few dry goods but we never did reopen the diner.

Sean was killed in World War I at the Battle of Argonne in 1918. Holly left the mountains when she was sixteen and moved to Kansas City, Missouri, and lived with Kristen's sister. She became an English teacher and raised two kids of her own. Kristen passed away in 1945; she was seventy-two. I have never stopped missing her.

Mother Mabel lived a good long life, dying at the age of eighty, in 1931. She continued to breed mules for the rest of her life and still had a half a dozen when she passed. After Jack and Preacher died I became much closer to Mother and she lived with Kristen and me for the last three years of her life.

I ran into Fiddlin' Phil one time when I was in Harrison. He no longer had his wagon train of female musicians and had gotten rich in real estate. He remembered Preacher and Jack with humor, and offered his condolences.

Annie Eldridge, the young mother who had lost her husband in the flood and had come close to death herself, came through Dogleg with her new husband in the late spring of 1902. She was headed back to Iowa to see her family. Carmen, Annie's sister, and Frank Jr. were still in Batesville with Jake's aunt at the boarding house. Things had worked out well for them and Carmen was seeing a man and thinking about getting married. Frank Jr. had grown a foot, she said, and was doing well in school. She seemed deeply saddened by the passing of Elmer, Jack and Preacher and promised to relay the message. She stayed with us at the cabin for two nights and I was sorry to see her go. They'd been lucky that day on the river, and I was glad to see 'em doing so well.

I continued our float trips, sometimes with Kristen and the kids, sometimes by myself. I saw Jake, of Jake's Landing, several times a year until he passed away at the age of fifty-six. Jasmine's love affair with the horse trader had only lasted ten days and she showed up back at Jake's place ready to take up where she'd left off, but Jake had other ideas. He took off for a month, just running the river, but it did no good. He figured Jasmine would leave again, but much to his dismay she was home to stay. His only salvation happened when he got back home. Jasmine met him at the cabin door, oak stick in hand, and made a running swing at him; he ducked and she rolled down the hill, hit the dock and flopped into the river. When he pulled her out she had a broken hip and her right shoulder was dislocated. She was never the same after that and tended to stay close to the cabin, leaving Jake pretty much on his own, which suited him fine. She did outlive him, though, and ran Jake's Landing until it got to be too much for her and then moved up North somewhere. I lost track of her after that.

Mother or I never did see Cliff again, Jack's brother. We did hear that he was killed in a bank robbery in Jacksonville, Mississippi. We always figured he'd end up in a bad way. Those two sure were different, but like Preacher said, you can't pick your kin.

Mother had sent a telegram to Bonnie Caldwell when we took Preacher to Harrison, but she hadn't gotten the message in time to come to the funeral. She showed up three days after we buried him and it was difficult at best to see her under those circumstances. She was a strong woman, though, and was making a living in St. Louis, teaching music and playing in an orchestra. She came to Dogleg three more times in the following years, but after that we never saw her again. But she did write to Mother and I every year in the month of July. She married well and had a good life with three children—Dan, Danny, and Danielle.

Pearl, Jack's soulmate, or so she thought, came back through the following year, still wearing her buckskins, and needing more mules. She was heading up North, having found nothing in New Orleans to suit her tastes. She figured her future lay in the rougher environments, where fewer people lived and there was less competition, and the odds of trapping a man were more in her favor. We never saw her again after that.

Whenever we went to Horseshoe Bend we always ate at the Ham n Hock. Pappy remembered me and always sat and talked through our dinner. His father, Pappy, died in the summer of 1904. The city was growing and business was doing well but he never did replace Pork Chop, nor did he say what became of him. He did mention that after the fire at the Fin & Feather the start up of the new restaurant was difficult and he was forced to rely on all of his assets, giving me the impression that Pork Chop had pitched in what assets he had to get the place up and running. It was fitting, seeing as how he was just like family.

Tory Brown remained a bachelor for the rest of his life. He visited Mother from time to time when he was in the area, but they made no attempt at romance. He retired at the age of sixty-seven and died three days later of a heart attack.

Ginny Carson, the young girl who helped Jack and Mother with the Three-Stop Café during its busier days, had a good life. Her mother passed away not five months after Jack and Preacher. They said her insides were just no good. We now know she had cancer of the stomach and there was nothing anyone could do.

Ginny left the mountains and moved to Texas. She married a man that struck it rich in the oil fields and in her later years was able to help take care of her brothers and sisters.

Skip Wagner, or Skippy, as his wife Maggie liked to call him, made it a yearly ritual to run away from home every spring and come to Dogleg. He'd stay at our cabin and visit until Maggie would come and get him. It worked out well for her, knowing exactly where he'd be, and it got to where she'd bring an overnight bag and spend a couple of days with us.

Cassie Calder did get her front tooth and lost a hundred pounds. She won a beauty contest in Harrison and got a job modeling clothes for the Sears and Roebuck catalog in Chicago.

Sissy Calder never did lose her weight, but she did marry a newspaperman who ended up owning his own publishing house in Sacramento.

Mother's cousin Caroline enjoyed dressing up and acting like a nun so much she joined a theatrical company in Kansas City and became a fine stage actress. Lizzie, her daughter, followed her to Missouri and worked in the costume department and in time started designing her own clothes, eventually moving to New York City.

Printed in the United States
28567LVS00004B/58